"All laws banning homosexual activity will be revoked. All churches who condemn us will be closed. Our only gods are handsome young men."

A Gay Activist, 1987

THE LAMBDA
CONSPIRACY

THE LAMBDA CONSPIRACY

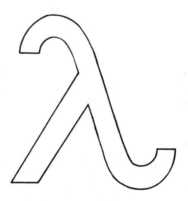

SPENSER HUGHES

MOODY PRESS

CHICAGO

Scripture quotations, unless noted otherwise, are taken from the *Holy Bible: New International Version®*. NIV®. Copyright © 1973, 1978, 1984, International Bible Society. Used by permission of Zondervan Bible Publishers. All rights reserved.

The Lambda Conspiracy is a work of fiction. Except for occasional general references to nationally recognized figures, the characters are the product of the author's imagination and are not intended to represent actual persons.

ISBN: 0-8024-4738-4

1 3 5 7 9 10 8 6 4 2

Printed in the United States of America

Dedicated with gratitude
to the family members and Christian friends
without whose generous support and counsel
this work would not have been possible

I dare not speak your names, but you know who you are.
You are everywhere.

1

Chase McKenzie was jammed shoulder to shoulder in an impatient, buzzing mass of humanity. The crowd carried him along with it into the Hart Senate Office Building and surged up to the second floor. There, two thick streams of spectators converged in the wide foyer of the central hearing room and shuffled up the sloping entrance. These were the fortunate or well-connected. They had tickets for reserved seats at Washington's prime political theater—a Senate confirmation hearing à la 1998.

Why did the crowd remind him of ancient Romans jamming the amphitheater, thirsting for the blood of gladiators or hapless Christians?

Bread and circuses, he muttered to himself. *All we lack is the bread.*

Contested confirmation hearings for high federal office had acquired all the trappings of the Roman arena except spilled blood. *No blood,* thought Chase, *but public disgrace, tarnished reputations, and ruined livelihoods—that was the modern equivalent.*

He flashed his press pass to the Capitol Hill police detail struggling to regulate the flow. Then he pushed toward the table on the left reserved for the media. Up front was a vacant seat that had a good view of the dais and witness chair. He moved toward it.

"McKenzie, I thought you'd gone into show business. What are you doing here with us *journalists?*" The voice was female, the words mocking and sharp.

He turned and confronted the speaker, his old antagonist, May Berg, of New York City. May styled herself "Convener" of Global Sisters, reported to be the world's largest feminist organization. Global Sisters claimed to represent women in every corner of the globe and in every circumstance, but especially the downtrodden and deprived—hungry Third World women and their children, women victimized by traditional, patriarchal cultures; and of course, those women Global Sisters regarded as the most oppressed of all—lesbians.

Even apart from the difference in gender, no two people could have been more unlike, and the antagonism between Chase and the woman was instantly palpable.

May Berg was short, middle-aged, dark-haired. She once might have been considered attractive, but her face wore a thinly disguised smile that carried no hint of warmth. Despite the warm season, she wore a shapeless black garment, matching her demeanor.

Chase McKenzie was a vigorous and youthful thirty-five, a little over six feet, hair light brown and cut short. His fine-boned but durable features were accented by a well-shaped nose and dark, restless eyes—probing eyes that held an expression of slightly amused good will. He managed a stylish but casual look—lightweight blue blazer, khaki cotton trousers, white shirt, plaid tie. He carried himself confidently, a trait not born in him at the Virginia Military Institute but certainly reinforced by four years of weekly drill and dress parades.

May Berg eyed him. "And I hear it's 'Doctor' McKenzie now." Her smirk was condescending.

"Well, May, you know it's only honorary." He smiled beatifically. He knew what annoyed her. "From my alma mater. But you can call me 'Doctor' if you like."

"Oh, yes. That place. VMI."

Chase's politeness faded to bare civility. "That's right, VMI. What're you people going to do now that you don't have VMI to kick around anymore?"

"What do you mean, 'kick around'?" Her voice rose a notch. "All we did was correct an injustice. And it was long overdue."

The Virginia Military Institute had been one of the nation's most illustrious military colleges. With an all-male corps of cadets, VMI had been one of the last public institutions in the nation to cling to its single-sex status. But that had made it a prime target. Feminists and their allies in the Justice Department pursued the college relentlessly for nearly a decade.

Finally, after a gallant and prolonged legal battle, VMI had been ordered to admit women in a celebrated case that had gone all the way to the Supreme Court. The high court unexpectedly issued a ruling that obliterated the school's traditional status.

The cadets decided VMI's proud traditions and record of service were incompatible with the feminist ethos. At the last graduation ceremony—the one at which Chase had received his honorary doctorate—the remaining cadets passed in review across the parade ground one final time, retired the colors, and left the post, vowing not to return.

The State of Virginia was trying unsuccessfully to reconstitute a viable civilian institution at the spartan, austere campus. Thus far the stately old crenelated buildings stood vacant.

The Institute won't be heard from ever again, Chase had said to himself, with the deep bitterness only an alumnus and a Virginian could feel.

"So what's the next target of the Thought Police?" he asked May Berg.

She did not rise to the bait. "I should think that's obvious. We're going to stop *this* outrage. If the president thinks he's going to put a pig like Hastings Whitmore on the Court, then he's in for the fight of his life. We thought we were through with people like him, and we'll fight to the death to keep what we've won."

Chase could think of nothing polite to say and turned to glance around the austerely wood-paneled hearing room. The place was much larger than the Judiciary Committee's chamber in the Dirksen Building and had been designed especially for major events such as this one. Spectators continued to swarm and jostle their way in, jockeying for the best seats. He could feel the building tension. In his imagination he saw the Coliseum again—and May Berg, a harridan in Roman dress, pointing her thumb down and screaming for the kill.

Confirmations for the Supreme Court, for many decades the unacknowledged legislature of the land, had attracted special public interest since the historic Clarence Thomas hearings in 1991. The Court was in fact far less liberal and activist than in the past. Now that social revolutionaries could no longer rely on the Court to enact their agenda, the Kulturkampf had shifted primarily to the Congress and to state legislatures and local governments.

But liberals were determined to preserve their recently attained one-vote majority. Every vacant seat was critical to maintaining that foothold. Panicked at the thought of losing a seat to a conservative, they were making the political demolition of Judge Whitmore top priority. As the controversy heated up, the Senate sergeant-at-arms decided to issue tightly controlled tickets for reserved seating as soon as the Judiciary Committee scheduled the hearing.

It was day one.

People without reserved seats had queued up hours ahead of time, waiting in lines that stretched all the way outside the Hart Building and into the already sweltering morning of a typical Washington summer. Under the watchful supervision of Capitol Hill police, the two dozen National Service Corps volunteers assigned to the Senate shepherded in the first group of visitors. Each contingent could sit and watch in open seating for a half-hour stretch, then would have to vacate their places for the next group.

Outside, several hundred chanting demonstrators paced the sidewalk across Constitution Avenue. Not allowed to picket next to the Senate office buildings, they pushed, shoved, brandished signs, and shouted invective at the few bold passers-by who dared express support for the nominee.

And inside all three Senate office buildings, hundreds of lobbyists from every imaginable public interest group and issue-oriented organization roamed the halls, seeking out the offices of senators to press their case for or against. It appeared the cons far outnumbered the pros.

"McKenzie, even *you* have to admit that this nomination is dead on arrival." May Berg seated herself. "But since the president's determined to go through with the charade—well, we're going to teach him a lesson he won't ever forget. *And anybody that sides with him.*" She scowled, and the ominous edge in her voice told him her threat was more than rhetorical.

"You know, May, I believe you probably will. And more's the pity." He had learned long ago that a rational discussion with this woman was futile. Yet his journalistic instincts made him persist, as if he might gain some glimpse into the inner working of her mind. But everything about her, except her sanctimoniousness, was opaque. Even her threats.

Chase left her to find a seat. In addition to leading Global Sisters, May Berg was editor-in-chief of *The New Feminist* and had a choice seat at the press table, where she had saved additional chairs for her female colleagues from the major dailies. He slid around to the opposite end, as far away from May Berg as he could get.

A table was allocated to the national news magazines and journals—next to television reporters the highest caste among journalists—and another for the newspaper reporters. Along the left side of the chamber in an elevated glass-fronted gallery were the cameras and equipment of the TV networks.

Chase noted with interest that SIS, the Satellite Information Service, had prime vantage points both in the rear of the witness table and also in the raised media gallery, traditionally the private preserve of the major networks. Evidently Wynn Pritchett, SIS's controversial and flamboyant president, had acquired considerable influence with the Senate leadership that controlled media access.

Chase no longer had to cover congressional hearings in person. As the host of the highly successful "Pulse of the Nation" program on the Direct Broadcast Network, he had plenty of research assistants to cover events and bring back the important details. But old habits die hard, and he did not want to lose touch completely with live, day-to-day journalism. Covering events, meeting people, asking questions, above all just getting out of the studio and into the world, was his way of taking the nation's pulse. His was now the third most popular public-affairs talk show in the nation, closing in fast on "Front Lines," and in the process making him somewhat of a national celebrity.

He could usually smell a big story before it broke. That kept his show from becoming stale like so many other public affairs programs. He called it his "Fingerspitzengefuehl," a sixth sense, an intuition residing as it were in his fingertips. That sixth sense told him the spectacle that was about to unfold in the Hart Building would be the most controversial confirmation battle since that of Clarence Thomas.

A few minutes before 10:00 a sudden but momentary hush fell over the buzzing hearing room. Hastings Whitmore, a Federal Appeals Court judge from Florida, slipped through the crowd filling the entrance and made his way to the witness table, while his wife sat in the front-row seat reserved for her. The judge was slight, portly, in his early sixties, bespectacled, gray haired, and garbed in funeral blue. Wearing a fixed smile, he chatted for a few moments of forced gaiety with his few supporters in the audience.

Clearly the man knew his nomination was in deep trouble.

Judge Whitmore was a lifelong Republican, a successful attorney, a devout Roman Catholic, and a strict constructionist— moderately strict, not fanatical. He had a creditable record on minority issues, which the White House staff believed would make him acceptable to the traditional civil rights lobby, from whom they expected the most opposition.

At the same time, and somewhat paradoxically, the judge had acquired a reputation for being tough on criminals and drug traffickers, reflecting the hardening attitudes of a public beset on all sides by violence. That made him popular with the average voter.

In the bitterly contested 1996 presidential campaign, in which conservatives played a decisive role, President Darby had pledged that his first Supreme Court appointment would uphold conservative, traditional values. Nominating the principled but seemingly innocuous Hastings Whitmore came as close to fulfilling this promise as one could expect and still have reasonable hope of confirmation.

But the White House had focused almost exclusively on the imagined reaction of civil rights activists, overlooking the increased political power of other special interests, most notably the feminist-homosexual alliance.

Nowadays high-stakes confirmations were decided in advance—in the media, in public opinion polls, and especially in the late night caucuses among Senate staffers and lobbyists. Insiders knew that unless a nominee for high appointive office passed this sub-rosa confirmation, his official confirmation hearings would be a mere show, designed to ratify a foreordained decision, yet allay public disquiet by observing the outward forms of democracy.

Judge Whitmore had presumably heard rumors of the backroom veto of his nomination. He acted like a condemned man putting his best face on the final ride to the gallows.

Precisely at 10:00 A.M. the solemn looking senators of the Judiciary Committee began to trickle in one by one through the rear entrances behind the dais. These were followed by even more solemn looking staff members, full of their own importance, most bearing armloads of files and papers.

Senator Norman Lockwood, chairman of the Judiciary Committee, gaveled the hearing to order. He welcomed Judge and Mrs. Whitmore and then began to dismember the judge verbally in an opening statement, criticizing his lack of compassion, sensitivity, and progressive ideas about the law.

From that point the drama did not unfold entirely as Chase had expected. The Committee was clearly stacked against the judge. The majority Democrats were all opposed, and most of the Republicans were intimidated and lukewarm in their support. But Judge Whitmore proved to be a game opponent, playing his part with as much grace and skill as anyone could muster under the circumstances.

He avoided sweeping or doctrinaire statements that would antagonize the Committee. He shrewdly avoided the worst traps laid for him. And when he could not escape a direct confrontation over a fundamental principle, he put up a spirited and convincing defense that seemed to win him grudging admiration, if not agreement, from the audience.

It was good political theater, Chase mused. The judge's performance had unexpectedly lowered the boredom quotient. Now a detectable groundswell of sympathy for the man injected a new factor into the equation, raising the possibility, however slight, that the proceedings might not yield the planned outcome after all.

He watched the judge's opponents. They appeared to sense the shifting tide and redoubled their efforts to tarnish his judicial standing, his reputation—anything that would make him appear unfit to sit on the high court. They could make nothing stick, however, and they had to proceed carefully to avoid a backlash of sympathy for an embattled underdog.

By late morning the senators had put a few rhetorical shots into his hull, but, though battered, the judge's chances for confirmation were still afloat. Even if the Judiciary Committee voted against him, Judge Whitmore still might win a majority of the full Senate unless the Committee could make a more damaging case.

Senator Lockwood seemed to realize that. He paused at the end of the second round of questioning to confer for a few moments with his senior counsel and another senator, Arthur Peel.

Chase suspected that the next round of questions would reveal the heavy artillery.

Senator Lockwood opened without any preamble to give warning. "Now, Judge Whitmore, I'd like to turn the Committee's attention to another matter and ask your views on the proposed Human Rights Amendment to the Constitution."

The judge tried to evade the issue. "Senator, amending the Constitution is so far outside the prerogatives of the federal bench that I really haven't considered it very deeply. As you well know, it's up to the people and the Congress to enact amendments to the Constitution. My job is simply to adjudicate disputes when questions or uncertainties about the law arise."

"I realize that, Judge. That's not my point at all. I'm asking you what you think of the amendment itself."

"I'm not sure I understand."

"It's quite simple," said Lockwood, annoyed. "Are you in favor of the amendment or not?"

"Senator, if by some chance this amendment were to become part of the Constitution, I very well might have to rule on an appeal stemming from its application in the future. For that reason, I don't think it would be responsible of me to make such an all-embracing, categorical statement."

"I see. But what about the basic principle involved? That's really what I'm after. I'm simply trying to get you to illuminate for the Committee your basic views of jurisprudence and fairness under the law. After all, the HRA's a simple text. Let me just read the primary clause:

'Equality of rights under the law shall not be denied or abridged by the United States or by any state on account of sex, sexual orientation, or sexual preference.'

"Now, do you agree with the principle enshrined in this text or not?"

Chase tried to guess what was going on in the judge's mind. Whitmore stood poised on the edge of an abyss and could only doggedly take refuge in his earlier evasions. He could not in good conscience endorse the amendment or the thinking that lay behind it—it was far worse than the old Equal Rights Amendment defeated back in the 1980s. He knew it was an unequivocal endorsement of homosexuality and the gay political agenda, a Pandora's box that would spawn endless litigation.

But he also knew the power of the national gay lobby. He would have to tread with the utmost caution, especially since none of the Republicans on the Committee had rallied to his defense —and since the White House, intimidated by the virulence of the media attack on him, was doing very little to support him either.

"Senator, with all due respect," the judge said in his most conciliatory tone, "I just don't feel it would be proper or professional of me to offer characterizations of the amendment while it's still under consideration by the people, before it becomes law—if indeed it ever does become law. And of course if it passes, the court would have to take legislative intent into account in any future opinion. Legislative intent, as you know, is determined primarily from the context of an amendment's history and the congressional debates that lead to passage. As of yet that context does not exist."

"But I don't care about possible future opinions, Judge. I want to know what you think of it now. I want to know whether you think it's all right to discriminate against the gay community."

"All I can say, Senator, is that I'm sworn to uphold the Constitution of the United States."

Exasperated, Senator Lockwood threw up his hands. "My time is up. But I must say to the Committee, I've never seen such a disgraceful spectacle of evasion and equivocation from a sitting federal judge, much less one who aspires to the highest court in the land. I hope my colleagues can do better than I have in getting some straight answers in the next round of questions."

He glared at the judge. "I can tell you right now, Judge Whitmore, unless you can find some way to be more forthcoming, this senator is going to have a very difficult time voting for confirmation."

Chase admired the man's composure. Whitmore sat immobile and stone-faced under the withering verbal fire.

Every Washington insider knew the Committee chairman would vote against confirmation no matter what the nominee said or did. Lockwood was simply frustrated by his failure to trick the judge into a fatal tactical blunder. He still needed some damaging admission or statement to justify a predetermined negative vote and conceal from the public the fraudulent nature of the hearing.

The feinting and sparring went on for another hour. Other senators fired off their questions, and still the judge continued to duck and dodge, avoiding a direct hit. It became increasingly apparent, however, that he must take a dim view of the Human Rights Amendment, since he could not be induced to say a single favorable thing about it.

Obviously, the sheer relentlessness of the attack was finally beginning to beat him down. Toward noon, Senator Peel of California succeeded in breaching Whitmore's defenses. When the judge tried to dodge again, saying merely he would uphold the law of the land, Senator Peel began to tongue-lash him. He accused him of deceiving the Committee, of lack of good faith, of deliberate obfuscation of the issues and his views.

Chase could not remember such a vitriolic personal attack on a Supreme Court nominee. The judge looked helplessly toward the Republican senators, expecting them to interrupt this slashing assault. But only one Republican objected, and his objection was feeble at best.

Worn down and dispirited, the judge finally offered an opinion. "Senator Peel," he said with resignation, "if the primary purpose of the proposed amendment is to extend the full protection of the law to homosexual citizens, then it may be redundant. I feel these citizens now enjoy full civil rights. And where there are specific problems, there are ample laws at every level—county, state, and federal—to protect homosexuals from discrimination. As a jurist, I can't help but think that under these circumstances such a sweeping amendment to the Constitution is hardly necessary."

Instantly cries of outrage burst from the audience. A dozen spectators stood up as if on cue and screamed, "Homophobe! Bigot!"

Chase noticed the TV cameras pan immediately to the disrupters and follow the disturbance as Capitol police hustled two apparent ringleaders out of the chamber, still yelling and shaking their fists.

"I see," said Senator Peel, when order was restored. "Then you believe that some Americans do not deserve equal protection

16

of the law, just because they don't happen to share your particular sexual orientation or your views of morality? Tell me, Judge, are you really so arrogant that you think you can impose your narrow, outmoded morality on others?"

The triumph in his voice competed with his attitude of contempt for the Judge. Peel had shrewdly avoided a direct mention of Judge Whitmore's religious affiliation, yet in code had called attention to his theological conservatism.

"Senator, that's an extremely facile characterization of my position. With all due respect, I would even say it is an unfair mischaracterization," the judge replied wearily.

Again boos and catcalls from the audience. To Chase's practiced, cynical eye, Senator Lockwood appeared intentionally to let the demonstration go on for a few moments, allowing the TV cameras to record it all, before pounding his gavel and demanding order.

"I understand how many of you feel," Lockwood said magisterially. "Many of you no doubt share the concerns of this Committee. But there is a proper way to register your concerns about the nominee's fitness to fairly represent all Americans on the Supreme Court, and interrupting this hearing is not the proper way.

"These proceedings must remain orderly, and the nominee, no matter how repugnant his views, has a right to be heard," he pontificated unconvincingly.

It was now noon, and since Senator Peel's interrogation had finally drawn some blood, Chairman Lockwood obviously felt it was safe to break for lunch before the judge could recover. He declared the session ended, to resume at 2:00 P.M.

2

When the hearing reconvened, Chase could feel the rising undercurrent of anticipation in the chamber, far more electric than in the morning. Both participants and spectators knew the quarry had been wounded, and suspense was high as they waited for the pack to close in for the kill.

But a new witness appeared. Chase recognized the senator from Tennessee, Branch Trumbull, who entered the room with the Whitmores. Senator Trumbull, a slim, interesting looking if not attractive man in his early fifties, confidently strode up to the dais to speak briefly with Senator Lockwood. He smiled engagingly and greeted members of the Committee, then took a seat next to the judge at the witness table.

An audible murmur rippled through the crowd at this new development. It was not unusual for the home state senator to introduce a nominee and offer an endorsement. But Trumbull was from Tennessee, not Florida.

Chase did not know the senator personally. He did know some of his history. Trumbull had a reputation as an effective Senate in-fighter and had emerged as a champion of the dwindling conservatives in the Senate. Intensely curious, Chase leaned forward to hear what the man would say.

Lockwood pounded his gavel. "The Committee will come to order and resume its examination of Judge Hastings Whitmore's nomination to become an associate justice of the Supreme Court.

"We are departing somewhat from the planned procedure. My colleague from Tennessee, Senator Trumbull, has asked to be allowed to testify on behalf of Judge Hastings. Quite frankly, some members of the Committee objected. This request came to us during the lunch break, and we've only had a short time to consider it. Furthermore, we hadn't planned for other witnesses to appear until after the judge's testimony was complete. But Senator Trumbull advises me his duties on the Armed Services Committee will not permit him to appear later in the week and has invoked senatorial courtesy in asking to testify this afternoon. I had the Committee polled during the recess, and a majority has agreed to hear from Senator Trumbull. So welcome, Senator, and please proceed."

Trumbull pulled the microphone closer and began to speak.

"Mr. Chairman and members of the Judiciary Committee, thank you very much for the opportunity to appear today on behalf of Judge Whitmore." His face clouded briefly. Then he brushed back his thinning brown hair, pushed his tortoise-shell glasses back to the bridge of his nose, and continued.

Chase found his voice interesting—Southern certainly, but not the grating twang of Appalachia. A strong but cultivated voice.

"Mr. Chairman, I hate to repay the graciousness of the Committee by addin' fuel to the flames of controversy. But this morning, the Committee in effect took the position that Judge Whitmore is unfit to serve on the Supreme Court unless he endorses the political agenda of militant homosexuals. He's a man of principle and a jurist of distinction. And he's understandably reluctant to engage in debate on this issue or to be drawn into committing himself as to how he might rule on a future case before the Court if he were confirmed.

"So I'm here to speak—but not just on his behalf, although it's quite obvious to me and most Americans that he's eminently qualified to sit on the high court. I also want to address the issue you raised as well, the Human Rights Amendment—falsely so-called. If the Committee persists in this despicable and reprehensible attempt—"

Senator Lockwood hammered the gavel block. "I caution the witness!" he spluttered, suddenly red in the face. "As the senator well knows—or should know—this body has a strong tradition of decorum. It's more than a tradition—it's a rule. If you can't refrain from immoderate language and inflammatory attacks on this Committee, than I'll have no choice but to rule you out of order, and you'll forfeit your opportunity to testify."

Trumbull was not in the least chastened. It was mostly an empty threat. Lockwood could not afford to appear too high-handed before a national audience.

"I thank the chairman for his timely warnin'," he replied with good humor. "I'll try to restrain myself and observe the rules of the Committee. In my defense I can only say that in seeking the acceptable threshold of 'immoderate language and inflammatory attacks,' I was just taking my cue from the Committee's treatment of the nominee in this morning's session."

Laughter and scattered applause erupted from the audience. Trumbull had shrewdly tapped the sentiment of the crowd, mixed though it might be. Lockwood banged the gavel vainly but did not speak. As the mirth subsided, Trumbull went on.

"Mr. Chairman, in the United States today there is an unprecedented climate of tolerance and acceptance of homosexuals. There is more tolerance for them today than at any time in our history, and perhaps more than any other nation in the world. In fact, many Americans are convinced that there is too much tolerance for the destructive behavior that is all too common among homosexual men in particular."

Angry mutters and hisses arose from the audience.

Trumbull ignored them. His tone was calm and reasonable, and Chase realized the senator was reaching out to a wider audience —the nationwide television viewers—not just those in this room.

"I'd like to ask the Committee—and all Americans: Which of the basic constitutional rights guaranteed to every citizen in the Bill of Rights is denied to homosexuals? The right to worship, speak, and assemble freely? No, certainly not. Freedom from excessive bail and cruel and unusual punishment? No. The right to bear arms, to due process and a proper trial, to vote and hold public office? The answer is clearly no. Are they denied the right to own property, to operate a business, to emigrate or travel freely? No, obviously not.

"In other words, homosexuals already have full human rights, exactly as Judge Whitmore said. To the limited extent that homosexuals are identifiable as a discrete class of citizens, they suffer no group proscription. And even the social stigma and ostracism that used to attach to them individually is largely a thing of the past."

Shrill whistles and catcalls.

Lockwood called out perfunctorily, "Order! Order!"

"What is it then that they want? And why might Judge

Whitmore object to this amendment, along with the many millions of Americans who do object strenuously to it?" asked Trumbull.

Lockwood interrupted him again. "Senator, we're not here to provide you a forum to speak on the Human Rights Amendment. We're here to consider the qualifications of Judge Whitmore for the Supreme Court."

"Mr. Chairman, this morning the Committee made the Judge's endorsement of the Amendment a litmus test for his confirmation. You and the Committee turned this hearing into a debate on the HRA, not me."

"I'm going to have to insist that you speak to the issue of the judge's qualifications."

A hard edge came into Trumbull's voice. "I promise you this, Mr. Chairman. Since you made the judge's lack of endorsement of the HRA an issue, I'll either be allowed to address the matter now, or I'll address it later on the Senate floor, when I'll have a number of senators at my side, and where you will not control the proceedings. And if it comes to that, I think you'll like what I intend to say then a lot less than what I have to say now."

Senator Lockwood blinked and stared hard at Trumbull for several seconds.

Senator Peel put a hand over the microphone and whispered something in the chairman's ear.

Lockwood shook his head and cleared his throat. "Senator Trumbull, in the interest of fairness I'm going to allow you to continue. But I remind you again to confine yourself to the issues before this Committee and to avoid personal attacks."

"I thank you, Senator. Let me reiterate, homosexuals already enjoy all the constitutional rights that everyone else enjoys. No one on the Committee—no one in this room—can deny that fact. Nevertheless, organized homosexuals have succeeded in portraying themselves as victims."

"We *are* victims! Victims of bigots like you!" screamed a man, leaping up in the rear of the chamber.

When he refused to sit down and be quiet, two policemen led him out.

Judge Whitmore, at the witness table next to Senator Trumbull, was beginning to look decidedly uncomfortable, as if unsure whether Trumbull was going to help or hurt his chances for confirmation.

Senator Lockwood again admonished the spectators. "Ladies and gentlemen, I'm well aware of how offensive the witness's views may be to some of you. But I must warn you—unless these outbursts stop, I'm going to have to clear the room of everyone except representatives of the news media. And Senator Trumbull, I would encourage you as well to make your case succinctly and avoid language that would unnecessarily provoke the audience."

"Well, I'm not tryin' to provoke anyone, Mr. Chairman. But I do have a case to make, and I'm sorry if some people don't like it. It's regrettable that those who insist on their right to be heard won't grant the same right to me."

"All right. Please continue. But be brief."

"I'll be brief. As I was saying, Senator Lockwood, many years ago the homosexual movement embarked upon the most fantastically successful public relations campaign in history and succeeded in portraying themselves as victims. Using their considerable political power, they've managed to get this idea adopted in the nation's public policy and much of its domestic law—that they are an oppressed, disadvantaged minority, like blacks or Hispanics, and that they are therefore entitled to special legal status and protection."

"Excuse me, Senator Trumbull, but how can you suggest they aren't an oppressed minority? I can hardly think of any segment of our society that has suffered worse discrimination."

"Well, Senator, there are millions of blacks and Hispanics who would disagree with you—and who deeply resent their cause being associated with the homosexual agenda. But let's just look at the record. In the past forty years of civil rights legislation and litigation in this country, the courts and the Congress have historically used three criteria to determine who is a disadvantaged minority needing a special protected status in federal or state law."

Trumbull turned to Judge Whitmore. "You'll correct me if I'm wrong, won't you, Judge?"

"Yes, of course."

"And I'm sure you're familiar with these criteria, Mr. Chairman."

"Well," said Lockwood, after a long pause. "I suppose I could come up with them. But in the interest of time, why don't you tell us."

Chase was amused to see Lockwood shift uncomfortably in his seat. The Committee chairman was taking a new tack, trying to debate and perhaps embarrass Trumbull rather than trying to silence him. But the gambit seemed to be failing. The senator from Tennessee had seized the moral and tactical high ground, at least for the moment.

Chase was curious to see if he could hold onto his commanding position. The whole affair had suddenly assumed the character of high drama, and Chase, cynical and suspicious of all members of Congress, began to wonder if he had not found a new hero.

"Thanks, I will," said Trumbull, "though for brevity's sake I won't go into all the case law. But here are the basic criteria:

"First, a true minority group has to show evidence of an inability to obtain adequate education, job opportunity, or economic income as a result of discrimination.

"Homosexuals simply don't qualify. They are among the most affluent, well-educated, and privileged people in the country. They are prominent in almost every business or profession. Their average annual income is far above the national average and about four times that of disadvantaged African-American households. More than three times as many homosexuals as average Americans have college degrees, and about six times more than African-Americans and Hispanics.

"Market research shows that seventy percent of homosexuals travel overseas—more than four times the percentage of average Americans. Homosexuals travel on airlines and ships more than fifteen times the percentage of average Americans. Homosexuals have 150 newspapers and magazines—even more if you count the sado-masochism and pedophile publications. And they have their own cable TV channels, radio network, and programming on SIS. Now that is simply not a picture of a deprived class of people."

"What about the military?" Lockwood rejoined. "Gays are still treated like second class citizens in the military. And largely thanks to you and your Armed Services Subcommittee on Force Requirements and Personnel, so I'm told, there's been no legislation to correct inequities in promotions and assignments."

"Well, Senator, the prohibition against homosexuals in the military has been removed by executive order, but that doesn't mean the vast majority of servicemen and women accept the policy. The majority still feel that homosexuality is a moral and social evil and that open toleration of homosexuals in the military is seriously undermining morale, discipline, and combat effectiveness.

"And the American people seem to agree. That's why the Congress has refused to make changes in the Uniform Code of Military Justice. I think the government's already done more than enough in coercin' the military on these social issues. We don't need any more legislation that would punish the good men and women in uniform who think this policy is wrong.

"Of course, the HRA would make all this moot. Under the HRA, a homosexual could actually sue his commanding officer for failing to promote him. Think what that will do to what's left of discipline in the services!

"But in any case," he continued, "even before the Defense Department's official policy on homosexuals was reversed, the Pentagon had already bowed to homosexual pressure and intimidation. Yet homosexuals weren't the only group excluded from the military on grounds of national security. Physically handicapped people, for example, are protected by all kinds of federal and state laws, but no one tried to put them to drivin' tanks and flyin' F-22s.

"So I ask you, Mr. Chairman, if openly practicing homosexuals are suitable for military service, why exclude anyone at all? Why not recruit necrophiliacs, or people who prefer sex with animals, or people who commit incest—"

"Enough, senator! Please make your point, or I'll rule you out of order!"

"All right, back to the main point, then. The second criterion is that 'protected classes' should clearly demonstrate political powerlessness that can only be redressed by special protection in law. Now I don't need to tell you of all people, Senator Lockwood, that homosexuals have immense political power, out of all proportion to their very small numbers in the population."

There was another burst of laughter in the chamber, longer

and louder than before, and Lockwood scowled angrily at his colleague at the witness table.

"Their political power is evident not only in this hearing but in their many representatives in Congress, perhaps many we don't even know about—"

Another wave of laughter interrupted him.

"And organized homosexuals have succeeded, once again despite their small percentage of the population, in gaining passage of laws and ordinances conferring all sorts of special privileges and benefits. In many states and localities, they enjoy rights that go far beyond those enumerated in the Constitution."

"Well, gays have been forced to migrate in large numbers," Lockwood shot back, "mainly to avoid persecution in more benighted areas of the country." He stared pointedly at the senator from Tennessee. "And I don't have to tell you of all people, Senator, where those areas are." He waited for the laughs, but there were only a few sniggers. "And in certain 'safe' localities they have the votes to pass local ordinances protecting themselves. We live in a democracy. I see nothing wrong in that."

"Yes, Mr. Chairman, but now they want the HRA in order to impose the values of San Francisco and New York—or lack of values—on all the rest of us."

This time boos and catcalls drowned out the guffaws, and Lockwood did not attempt to restore order.

Chase sensed that Trumbull was just getting worked up. The senator still kept absolute control of himself, but a persuasive passion had entered his voice.

"But the worst thing of all, Senator Lockwood, is that homosexuals have used their disproportionate political power to pressure medical officials all across the land into discarding public health measures that would control the spread of AIDS, which has killed hundreds of thousands of Americans. Now there's political power, Mr. Chairman. That power has gained homosexuals virtually full legal sanction to commit acts that have caused the exponential spread of a 100 percent fatal disease for which we still have no cure.

"So in short, Mr. Chairman, you can't argue that homosexuals are politically powerless. Their power has produced the first politically protected plague in human history."

By now the angry heckling that began when he mentioned AIDS had intensified into a full-blown uproar. Dozens of homosexual activists were in the chamber, some sitting in groups, others scattered singly throughout the audience. Now they were standing and screaming epithets at Trumbull. But the majority of the spectators, seeming to sympathize with Trumbull and Judge Whitmore, yelled at the demonstrators to sit down and shut up.

Lockwood had to shout over the din. "Are you quite finished, Senator?"

"Almost, Senator. I would have been by now if the audience would let me." He waited patiently, and in a few minutes the noise tapered off.

"Now to the final benchmark. A disadvantaged or specially protected class must exhibit obvious and unalterable distinguishing characteristics—for example, race, color, gender, national origin. Something that defines them as a group and is the reason for discrimination against them.

"Now the homosexual movement claims that homosexuality is simply a biological condition, like being left-handed or blue-eyed. And since they're born that way, the argument goes, their sexual preference can't be condemned as immoral. It can't be made illegal, and it can't even be seen as abnormal."

Lockwood opened his mouth, but Trumbull cut him off.

"I know what you're going to say, Mr. Chairman. You're goin' to tell me all about the recent 'scientific' discoveries that prove homosexuality is a biological condition. The problem is, Senator, the studies you'd like to cite are seriously flawed.

"The much touted Waterman-Lemon study of last year is a good example. It was commissioned by a leading homosexual activist, paid for by several homosexual rights lobbies, conducted by two homosexual researchers, and was so flawed in its methodology and results that reputable sex research organizations with no ax to grind have called it an embarrassment.

"The Simon LeVay study of 1994 was also severely flawed, and it was conducted by a man who left science to become a full-time homosexual activist. Of course the news media have suppressed this information, but the facts are there for anyone who cares to look for them.

"Since homosexual behavior is connected with the most powerful of all human impulses, certainly their compulsions must seem inborn—especially when they also have social and political motivations to rationalize it. But if time and circumstances permitted, I could cite you hundreds of cases where homosexual men and women have admitted that their condition is a matter of choice or at least a compulsive habit, a form of sexual addiction that can be broken with the right kind of counseling and nurturing.

"But just like alcoholics or drug addicts, they have to recognize they have a problem, take responsibility for themselves, and seek the right kind of help. The politically correct but bogus science that plagues us these days makes it easier for them to avoid facing reality and taking personal responsibility. It's the worst possible thing we could do to them."

Cries of rage again rent the air. "Homophobe! Bigot! Fascist!" The demonstrators screamed, punching the air with their fists. Wadded balls of paper flew toward the front of the room, and a cordon of Capitol Hill police quickly moved up and took position in a line between the audience and the witness table.

Trumbull continued, as unflappable as ever. "No, despite the gnashin' of teeth we see here today, homosexuals are not victims, any more than a drug addict or compulsive heterosexual rapist is a victim. Homosexuals fail to meet the third criterion as well as the others. They are defined not by what they are, but by what they do. And what many if not most of them do is acts that are not only unnatural and immoral but insane and destructive from a medical point of view."

Now pandemonium reigned. Several activists, shouting and gesticulating, struggled to get to the front but were impeded by the closely packed spectators—many of whom were enjoying the spectacle—and the thin line of policemen.

Lockwood banged his gavel. "Order! We will have order!"

Senator Trumbull leaned close to his microphone and spoke loudly to project his summation over the din. "Mr. Chairman, the HRA is a declaration of war, an unprecedented act of cultural and social aggression against the majority of Americans who vehemently disapprove of homosexual behavior.

"Senator Peel, you complained this morning that the judge

would impose his morality on you. Well, this amendment would impose *im*morality on us. Homosexuals know that only the coercive power of the law can compel America to condone their lifestyle. But coercin' millions of people of traditional values and religious faith will fracture the social compact and destroy what legitimacy the federal government has left."

Trumbull's voice rose above the din. "And yet you are seriously considerin' an amendment to the US Constitution that would give sodomy and pederasty the same constitutional stature as our sacred freedoms in the Bill of Rights. And you want to hold a good man's confirmation hostage to such a measure? It's outrageous."

Lockwood, Peel, and other members of the Committee were trying to be heard. "Your *testimony* is outrageous, as the people here today are telling us! Ladies and gentleman, I apologize for the irresponsible and inflammatory behavior of my colleague!" shouted the chairman.

By now there was bedlam in the chamber. Those expelled earlier had gone out to the streets for reinforcements. Scores of activists poured into the hallway and foyer leading to the hearing room, stomping their feet, pounding on the walls, and chanting, "Bigots! Bigots! Bigots gotta go!" They pushed their way into the entrance, forcing back the outnumbered police detail.

But the tumult gave Lockwood a means, however feeble, to recover from his embarrassment and put the blame for the riot on his antagonist all at the same time. "Well, Senator Trumbull, I hope you're satisfied!" He banged his gavel furiously and made himself heard only by means of the PA system. "This hearing is adjourned until tomorrow at 10:00 A.M."

The Committee members slipped quickly out the rear entrance behind the dais. Chase watched Trumbull take Judge and Mrs. Whitmore by the arm and, with a police escort, exit the same way to keep the Whitmores away from the demonstrators.

He gathered up his notebook and tape recorder and noticed May Berg scowling at him across the press table. He could not resist a parting shot.

"Well, May, quite a day, wasn't it? I don't think I've ever seen that pompous airbag Lockwood deflated so neatly. Too bad. Looks like Judge Whitmore is still in the game."

She was seething and almost speechless. "Why did you come here anyway?" she demanded.

"Well, May, I'm a working journalist, here to report the news just like you."

"Journalist!" she scoffed. "You're just here to help your friend Trumbull."

Chase was surprised. He had never met the Tennessee senator, but evidently May Berg assumed that all conservatives were in league. But he did not want to give her any satisfaction in denying he knew the man. *Let her think what she wants.*

"Yeah, May, wasn't he disgraceful?" he said. "When he was attacked, he had the gall to defend himself."

At last, somebody in the Congress worth knowing, Chase added to himself with satisfaction.

She looked at him with undisguised venom. "I'm warning you. You make a hero out of that fascist bigot Trumbull, and I'll personally see you regret it."

3

As a high priest of the "safe sex" movement, Percival Garden Monnoye practiced what he preached, at least partially. He never used condoms. But then, the attractive young men he hired by the score as interns and research assistants served as the vessels of his desire, never the reverse. Nor was he promiscuous, at least by his own definition. He preferred the term *serial monogamy*. As long as he maintained this strict regimen and screened the newcomers carefully, he believed the risks to himself were minimal. This was *his* definition of safe sex. He was confident of his power to protect himself from the AIDS virus.

Monnoye was president of the Paragon Foundation, the leading voice of the New Age Movement. A fabulously wealthy tax-free foundation, Paragon lavished millions on the arts, cultural events, medicine and health care research, environmental studies—anything to promote universal peace, justice, and unity through "a higher collective consciousness," the watchword of the New Age.

Young Adonises came to his employ eagerly. He paid handsome wages. His wealth, power, and intelligence combined with their energy and hard work had been highly successful in advancing the homosexual agenda and in making gay rights the cutting edge of the New Age campaign for universal peace, justice, and unity.

An entire department at Paragon was in effect a tax-free lobby for the Human Rights Amendment and similar initiatives, though Monnoye was careful to designate it as research, education, and advocacy to avoid an open violation of the tax laws.

Wealth and power were not the only things that drew young men to him. He was a man of immense charm and physical attractiveness. Tall, taut, tan, well-muscled but imperially slim, he wore his light brown hair slightly longer than the fashion. An unruly forelock was constantly falling across his forehead, and he would habitually thrust it back with a studied insouciance, an affectation that only added to his boyish appeal. His face was all planes and angles, Nordic in its severity but softened by a wide, winning smile that made his countenance seem all teeth—very white, dazzling, perfect teeth.

The Foundation had its own medical staff and laboratory, and all the young men on the staff were tested once a month for HIV. Furthermore, Monnoye's security team maintained an informal surveillance to make sure they were not frequenting gay bars and bathhouses. If they wanted to bask in the reflected glory of Percival Garden Monnoye, they had to agree to remain as part of a "closed system," as Monnoye so delicately put it upon hiring them.

Monnoye had worked hard to acquire his reputation as a humanitarian. He gave generously. He lobbied diligently for more money—tax money, other people's money, not just his own—in research for a cure for AIDS. He had convinced many Americans that the federal research effort was not focused sufficiently on a cure.

Many medical researchers believed a cure for AIDS was in sight—a virus-killing vaccine could be developed before the end of the century. Paragon's advocacy of more funds for vaccine research seemed appropriate in light of the continuing ravages of the disease. Many citizens, not only gays, took up Monnoye's battle cry, "A cure for the sick, not just care for the sick."

To be sure, he and his allies were genuinely concerned about the dead and dying, whose numbers continued to rise geometrically after more than fifteen years into the epidemic.

It was also true that they had another, stronger motivation for their single-minded pursuit of the magic bullet that would kill the HIV. Only a cure for the disease would allow them to return to the old uninhibited lifestyle, the way it was before AIDS put such a deadly damper on their sexual adventuring.

Monnoye and the Foundation owned property all over the world. As he became more active politically and more powerful, however, he had found it necessary to spend more time in Washington. He had a large apartment in the Watergate complex and also luxurious living space on the top floor of his main headquarters, the Paragon Building. Strategically located on Maryland Avenue on Capitol Hill, near the Supreme Court and the Senate office buildings, the Paragon Building was the ideal setting for Monnoye's weekly staff luncheons, where congressional staffers and Supreme Court law clerks came to consume the finest in food, drink, and gay rights propaganda.

As his operations began to focus increasingly on the nation's capital and its social and political elite, he had needed a more suitable location for entertainment than the Paragon Building. Seeking a place large enough for a festive crowd, yet private and secluded, he finally bought an elegant estate in northern Virginia's horse country near Upperville, three hundred acres of well-tended pasture and woods graced with a hundred-fifty-year-old brick mansion.

The house crowned a grassy, tree-clad eminence overlooking a picturesque creek and valley. Monnoye enhanced the view with elegant landscaping and renovated the dwelling with every modern amenity, sparing no expense. The result was an imposing yet tasteful blend of the traditional and the contemporary.

Here at Waverly Ford Farm he threw opulent dinners for the Washington elite. His "Garden Parties" became legendary, and anybody who considered himself somebody in Washington schemed and maneuvered to get invited. Monnoye seldom discussed business or politics at his parties but quickly developed personal relationships with influential luminaries in government, politics, and the media. The lavish hospitality purchased goodwill that he could later cash in for direct access and influence when it was needed.

He had quickly grasped the rudiments of Washington psychology. According to the town's protocol, it was simply impossible for a congressman or senator to refuse access to a man who just a few nights before had entertained him like royalty, maybe even slipped him a thousand bucks for the campaign if he was facing a tough reelection battle.

Early in the evening after the first day's hearing on Judge Whitmore, Monnoye took the elevator to the top floor office in the Paragon Building and headed straight for his desk. Close on his heels followed Tristram Kramer, executive director of the Foundation, and four young Ganymedes who served as staff writers.

32

"One of you please bring me and Tris a Scotch and soda," he said to the courtiers. "And stand by the fax machines. It's going to be a long night."

He picked up the phone and began to dial. His initial calls were to those who were already in his camp and had opposed Warren in the hearing. And as he expected, he had no trouble getting through.

"'Lo, Norm, this is Garden Monnoye. I want to thank you for your efforts today. But I'm very disappointed that you weren't able to put the judge away."

Senator Lockwood appeared to squirm a little on the other end of the line. "Garden, I don't know what to say. I thought we *had* put him away until Branch Trumbull showed up. None of us had any idea he was going to come at us hammer and tongs like that."

"Yes, Trumbull set us back rather badly, Norm. I'm afraid we're going to have to start exposing your colleague's bigotry and homophobia in our friendly media, like SIS. So be prepared—we'll do what we have to. In the meanwhile, you've got to undo the damage in tomorrow's hearing. Just tell me how I can help."

Monnoye's tone of authority was understated but unmistakable. With Lockwood he had to be forceful yet courteous, with just the right touch of deference. There was no point in recriminating over the chairman's dismal performance. Now was the time to salvage the situation.

Lockwood replied in frustration, "Garden, I feel we did all the damage we could do. We've got to preserve our credibility. We just can't afford to look like pit bulls. That'll only win the man sympathy."

"I understand that. Nevertheless, the judge has got to be stopped, whatever the cost. It won't do you any good to keep your public credibility and lose it with your most reliable supporters, now will it?"

"No, I guess not." Monnoye had contributed heavily to Lockwood's last reelection campaign. "But Garden, this guy's not as easy a target as you may think—"

"He's a homophobe and a bigot," Monnoye shot back. "He proved it in his opinion in the Leslie case. That's where he's vulnerable on this issue, and maybe that's where you need to bore in.

When I hang up I'm going to call our other friends on the Committee and ask them to back you up by going over the Leslie case tomorrow. We'll send out questions and talking points to everybody. But you've got to take the lead. This is just too important for us to leave it to chance. So Norm, tomorrow, please, take no prisoners, OK?"

It took hours of calls to reach all his targets on the Committee and shore them up for the next day. Then he laid out the attack themes on Branch Trumbull with friendly journalists.

While he was engaged in that process, Kramer called the leaders of Monnoye's gay rights coalition, asking them to weigh in with the Committee as well. The four interns were kept busy writing and faxing talking points and draft statements, attacking the Fifth Circuit opinion on the Leslie case and Branch Trumbull's testimony.

Before shutting down, Monnoye placed a final call, this time not to the Hill, but to the White House, where he had contacts inside the Office of Legislative Liaison and access to the president's counsel, William Kerrigan. Two short conversations convinced Kerrigan and the president's key legislative affairs staffer handling the Whitmore confirmation that the White House would only lose more of its diminishing store of credibility and influence by putting up a fight for a lost cause.

Late that night, after all the calls had been made, Monnoye leaned back in his leather chair, rested his feet on the desk, and closed his eyes wearily. The waves were rippling out from the center, and he was confident his damage control operation would prove successful in the morning.

"Well, Tris, it's been a long night, but I think we've got him. Some of our friends needed the old strong-arm tactics, but most went along with the voice of reason."

"Perce, they'll end up hating you. Not to mention the White House. They'll hate you . . . ."

"Let 'em hate—as long as they fear."

★ ★ ★

On the second day of Judge Whitmore's confirmation hearings, Chase McKenzie was back at the press table. He had been deeply impressed by the counterattack from the judge's lone ally. He half believed that the Tennessee senator's intervention, risky as it seemed at the time, had turned the tide in the judge's favor. He was not prepared for the violence of the counterattack.

Senator Lockwood and his cohorts wasted no time. They proceeded to demolish the nominee quickly, before any more Branch Trumbulls could surface. Fortunately for Lockwood there had been a steady barrage against both Trumbull and the judge in the previous night's major television coverage. The media artillery had softened up the target.

Now it was time for the final bayonet charge. Each Committee Democrat, and three Republicans with large, politically active gay populations, issued furious denunciations of Trumbull's arguments of the previous day. They savaged the judge with classic guilt-by-association charges, painting him as a homophobe and a bigot.

This time the concerted, bipartisan character assassination did not produce the backlash of sympathy Chase expected. Instead, the constant repetition of accusations, and the vehemence with which they were expressed, began to have a cumulative effect. It was such a dramatic reversal from the day before that he could not help but wonder what had happened overnight.

His political instincts told him something more was at work than the spontaneous indignation of the Judiciary Committee or simply a matter of a weak, vacillating White House.

Although the president's support was notable only by its absence, that in itself was not unusual. Two years into his term, President Darby had shown no stomach for tough political battles. He chose more often to compromise and conciliate rather than stand and fight.

With sinking heart Chase listened to the Committee exhaust its condemnation of Judge Whitmore for his failure to endorse the HRA. And when all members had gotten their statements on the record to satisfy their homosexual voters back home, Senator Lockwood struck hard from a new direction.

Now he raised *Leslie* v. *South Florida Presbytery,* a human tragedy that had become a landmark case in the ever-increasing tension between gay rights and religious freedom.

In 1995 a prominent Boca Raton area church had dismissed its music director after he confessed to being a practicing homosexual. Leslie was married and a long-time church member who had ostensibly met all the requirements for his position. But for years he had also led a clandestine double life, frequenting south Florida's gay bars and vacationing secretly in Key West, a favorite gay vacation spot.

The church was theologically conservative, and its doctrine and historic stand on homosexuality had left the congregation no choice but to terminate the man's employment. In doing so, the pastor and elders diligently attempted to counsel the man, hoping to restore him to fellowship, if not his job, and to preserve his family. But Leslie was unrepentant. He refused to submit to church discipline. Once again, the congregation was left with no choice under their by-laws and Scripture but to separate him from the assembly.

The embittered Leslie went to the Center for Law and Human Dignity and its legal arm, the Lambda Legal Defense Guild.

Lambda Legal was a national public interest law firm specializing in gay rights issues. It had been looking for a test case —the right plaintiff, the most favorable circumstances, and the best venue—and had litigation already prepared for just such an eventuality. The fired choirmaster and his battery of lawyers promptly hauled the church into a Florida court in the gay hot spot, Miami.

Before the dazed church elders realized what was happening, they were up to their necks in depositions and discovery actions that exposed them and the entire congregation to a steady torrent of legal harassment.

To the alarm and astonishment of conservative congregations everywhere, Leslie carried the day in the Florida district court. He won reinstatement, back pay, and punitive damages. As if that outcome were not shocking enough, the pastor and elders were ordered to attend "sensitivity enhancement sessions." These were under the auspices of the county Human Rights Commission but were actually conducted by homosexual activists. The church leaders were required to submit to probation and monitoring by the Commission for a year to ensure that their attitudes had changed.

They of course refused to yield. With their own legal representation and the American Council for Law and Justice, the embattled church appealed. The case had gone all the way to the Fifth Federal Circuit. There Hastings Whitmore, along with a majority of his colleagues, reversed the lower courts. They held that the First Amendment and freedom of religion took precedence over the gay choirmaster's employment rights or the relevant county Human Rights Ordinance.

Senator Lockwood's summary of the case and Whitmore's pivotal role was a masterly distortion of the First Amendment issue. He deplored the fact that homosexual litigants could never obtain a fair judgment from a Supreme Court with such an obvious homophobe on the bench.

"He divides Americans," Lockwood intoned. "He puts his own narrow prejudices above fundamental fairness and human rights—and above the clear thrust of enlightened jurisprudence in America today. For the millions of Americans who are gay and lesbian, appointing Judge Whitmore to the Supreme Court would be tantamount to denying them justice.

"At a time when we need to make full use of the contributions of all Americans so that we can remain competitive in today's world, he builds walls that keep us separated. When we need unity, he turns the law into a weapon that discriminates against millions of our most energetic and talented people."

Lockwood paused, brow furrowed as if the responsibility for safeguarding justice, decency, and tolerance weighed heavily on him. "Men and women don't become brothers and sisters just by saying so. Shared experiences, working toward a common goal, building decency and tolerance in our public life—these are the great begetters of brotherhood and unity. In my opinion, we need men and women on the Supreme Court who understand this.

"You concern me deeply, Judge Whitmore. The nation's high court must be a venue of fairness to all Americans, not a bastion of bigotry and intolerance."

Lockwood now lapsed into poetry:

> "Away with outworn nations, faiths, and creeds,
> With swelling voice the whole of mankind sings.
> Break down the walls behind which hatred feeds,
> And then embrace the Oneness of all things."

His gorge rising at the brutal attack on the judge, Chase was struck by the verse. It was familiar. He knew he had heard it before. It was memorable because almost all contemporary poetry was blank verse. But this poem's trendy New Age message was clothed in traditional rhyme and meter, and that had struck him as odd when he first heard it. Yes, the more Chase thought, the more certain he was that he had heard it before.

The puzzle rattled around in his subconscious amid the closing arguments of the chairman, during the cab ride back to his office, and later that night as he prepared for bed. Then, as he lay there before dropping off it suddenly came to him.

He had heard the verse from Garden Monnoye, who had appeared on "Pulse of the Nation" some months ago to debate the New Age Movement. Chase recalled hearing later that Monnoye was a powerful, behind-the-scenes homosexual activist as well as New Age apostle. And Monnoye had invoked the exact same quatrain. How odd that a senator on the Committee would use the same obscure poem.

Chase got up and went into the den. He pulled the videotape of the broadcast with Monnoye from his personal archives. Yes, there it was, the identical verse.

Next morning Chase embarked on a little detective work, better known around town as "investigative journalism," something he was quite good at. First he ran a NEXUS computer search. Considerable time and effort finally produced the elusive quatrain. It was part of a longer piece by a contemporary woman poet named Pitney Smith.

This person had first published the poem in, of all places, *The New Feminist,* where, further search showed, most of her works were published and where she regularly got ecstatic reviews from editor-in-chief May Berg. A few telephone calls later, Chase discovered that Pitney Smith was the younger half-sister of Garden Monnoye.

A touch of foreboding came over him. May Berg's warning still echoed in his memory, and when he tried to dismiss it, another voice whispered, *Don't underestimate these people.* If they could dominate so many US senators and key sectors of the media, then their power was more extensive than he had imagined.

4

Chase logged off the NEXUS system and began to print the information he had downloaded from available data banks. Then he sketched a rough diagram of the interconnecting relationships he had uncovered.

This is like a wild blackberry patch.

His mind flashed back to an episode in his boyhood in Woodstock, Virginia. His father had assigned him to clear a piece of ground behind the house. The area was covered with brush, including a variety of wild blackberry, a hateful plant that put forth a thick profusion of thorny vines but little fruit.

Chase struggled the entire day, getting scratched and torn. He recalled how surprised he was the first time he grasped one of the vines in his gloved hands, gave a fierce tug, and ripped up a hidden network of roots and runners for a yard in every direction. It took hours of exhausting work to cut out the underground networks, and shoots still sprang up later from the runners he had overlooked. He had to come back a few weeks later and finish the job.

Now, holding his NEXUS notes and the diagram in his lap, Chase felt as he had that day in the wild blackberry patch. He had gotten hold of one exposed shoot of the gay rights movement and by pulling hard had revealed an interlocking underground network of political power and influence. He did not doubt that this particular vine could tear him bloody if he were not careful.

Chase had never harbored doubts about the growing power of the gay lobby. Yet the form and substance of gay influence had never been clear to him. It was clandestine and insidious. It made its presence felt by the pricks of its thorns but was always careful to conceal the full extent of its subterranean networks. But now he had a glimpse into the who, what, and how.

He had done something no other journalist had done, so far as he knew. He had traced the connection between members of the Senate Judiciary Committee, homosexual leaders Garden Monnoye and May Berg, and certain news media, especially the powerful Satellite Information System of Wynn Pritchett. What he lacked was confirmation.

On impulse, he picked up the telephone and placed a call to Norman Lockwood's Senate office.

"This is Garden Monnoye," he said, making an effort to mimic Monnoye's cultivated voice. "I need to speak with the senator, please. It's very important."

The receptionist rang him through to Lockwood's executive assistant.

"Oh, Mr. Monnoye," she said respectfully. "The senator's over on the floor. But you can reach him in the cloakroom."

"No, thank you. It's not something we can discuss while he's in the cloakroom."

"Well, if you really need him, I can call him off the floor and ask him to come back and give you a ring."

But Chase had learned what he wanted to know. It took some clout to pull a senator away from the floor debate to make a telephone call.

"No, that won't be necessary. Please don't trouble him. I'll call him later."

With mounting excitement—and still posing as Garden Monnoye—he dialed other members of the Judiciary Committee. In almost every case he was treated with deference, and the calls went through immediately. On three occasions the senators were present, and he hastily pretended to be cut off.

For the rest of the day, Chase read everything his personal files and the computer data banks could turn up on the Paragon Foundation. Until now he had always thought of it merely as the purveyor of New Age nonsense, and Garden Monnoye as a wealthy dilettante with more money than good sense. The whole New Age scene had always seemed frivolous to him, but now he began to wonder if there was not a more sinister purpose behind all the poppycock.

Paragon supported an astonishing array of educational, artistic, and cultural activities. Many seemed harmless enough. But then he found that the Foundation paid for the development and distribution of Project 2000, a sex education curriculum used in public school districts across the country. Ostensibly intended for use in conjunction with AIDS education, Project 2000, he knew, was little more than propaganda for the homosexual lifestyle, now subsidized by the taxpayer.

Paragon, he learned, also gave educational grants to dozens of other gay groups as well as to New Age organizations and publications. It appeared that Garden Monnoye was attempting to fuse the two movements under the rubric of oneness, tolerance, openness, and universal brotherhood.

He dug further. He discovered that Paragon was the primary source of funds for the Campaign for Human Rights. This was now the fifth largest political action committee (PAC) in the United States and the Goliath of all homosexual political organizations. In fact the Campaign was really an umbrella coalition under which all of the major gay groups pooled efforts and jointly conducted their non–tax-free political activities, including direct lobbying for passage of the Human Rights Amendment.

He checked out the Campaign's Washington headquarters address. It was located in the Paragon Building.

And then there was the Center for Law and Human Dignity, a public policy research organization, and its operational arm, the Lambda Legal Defense Fund. Garden Monnoye was a member of its board, as was Senator Arthur Peel. He was interested to learn that the Center, which had been the chief player in the landmark case of *Leslie* v. *South Florida Presbytery,* also enjoyed the largesse of several million dollars a year from the Paragon Foundation and kept Washington offices in the Paragon Building.

Chase leaned back and locked his fingers behind his head. From what he could gather so far, the Campaign for Human Rights was the prime mover of the gay movement. In effect it was little more than a subsidiary of the Paragon Foundation—the Foundation dressed in combat fatigues. But unlike the Campaign for Human Rights or the Center for Law and Human Dignity, the core Paragon entity was a tax-free "educational" organization and could not openly lobby without jeopardizing its tax status.

Yet Chase knew that its president, Garden Monnoye, did lobby in subtle ways. Paragon's self-proclaimed mission was to usher in the New Age with the arrival of the new millennium. Monnoye appeared to be focusing Paragon's efforts toward creating a cultural environment in which the gay agenda could flourish and triumph—in part by enlisting New Age arguments and rhetoric in the service of gay rights.

The approaching millennial year 2000 held an enormous psychological appeal, Chase mused. If Monnoye could harness some of that extraordinary psychological and emotional pulling power in behalf of the homosexual agenda, there was no limit to what he might achieve.

By this time evening had fallen. He grabbed a cold beer from the kitchen, went back to the den, and switched on the television in time to catch the nightly news—and Hastings Whitmore's political epitaph. Inside-the-White-House sources, viewers were told, revealed that the administration had done the usual quiet vote-count and decided not to pursue Judge Whitmore's confirmation.

Chase fumed. That was typical. Always invoke the vote count. He had heard it countless times: "We just don't have the votes!" It was the favorite excuse not to fight, not to lean on wavering Republicans, not to call in political favors, not to go out and *get* the miserable votes!

He had entertained a vague hope that all the information he had turned up on the judge's opposition might somehow be aired in time to stave off defeat. That had not happened. Now the challenge to him was how to use most effectively what he had learned. And since Hastings Whitmore was now history, the most timely opportunity for using the information had eluded him.

Maybe it's just as well. He switched off the TV. He considered himself fearless. He never shrank from puncturing the egos of the capital's most powerful figures. He never shied away from telling the truth—always humanely, he hoped, but always the truth as he saw it.

And yet there was something about this gay underground and its new generation of leaders that made him uneasy. Years ago, as a young reporter for Washington's alternative newspaper, the *Standard*, he had tangled with the emerging gay rights crowd. But today's homosexual movement appeared far more sinister—and far more powerful—than any other faction he had ever encountered.

His political principles, his sense of journalistic duty, and his pride would not let him back down from a fight if it came to that. But he sensed it could be very dangerous to tangle with these people and fail.

If I start shooting, I'd better not miss.

* * *

Branch Trumbull watched little television. In his opinion TV's vast wasteland of the 1950s had degenerated into a polluted garbage dump in the 1990s. With the advent of high definition TV, digital broadcasting linked to personal computers, and direct broadcasting via Prometheus satellites, the medium had become far more sophisticated. Hundreds of local cable companies, SIS and the Direct Broadcast Network with their plethora of satellite channels, and of course the traditional Big Four networks, offered a seemingly inexhaustible menu. Every special interest from astrology to zoology had its own program or channel. Yet the squalidness of programming seemed to have grown in direct proportion to the technical advances.

But lately he had begun following "Pulse of the Nation" on DBN, featuring that interesting fellow Chase McKenzie. An idea was slowly taking shape in the back of his mind. There was something about McKenzie that he found immensely appealing.

It was not just McKenzie's looks, although he was a good-looking young man, handsome in a way that was neither too rugged nor too refined. There was something else about him—an on-camera presence, an indefinable air of engagement. He possessed a restless, probing, intelligent curiosity. He always seemed intensely interested in everything his program guests had to say. And though he often disagreed with a guest, his gentle wit and wide store of knowledge always produced lively, illuminating discussions instead of the raucous free-for-alls typical of "Front Lines" or "Washington Spotlight."

Senator Trumbull had begun to realize how urgently he needed a national media forum. Chase McKenzie's show would be the perfect choice—if only he could come up with a way to get invited.

In addition to "Pulse of the Nation," Trumbull had begun watching the other special interests broadcasts. Tonight, in the den of his spacious, book-lined home in Potomac, he was watching a new channel with curiosity. He had just heard from his daughter, Libby, about the Dignity Channel on Satellite Information Service. Dignity offered eighteen hours of programming a day for homosexuals.

Dignity aired the standard entertainment fare, musical programs, movie reviews, news and information, and public affairs programs in which various gay groups promoted their particular causes or notable homosexuals gave interviews. The commentary on Dignity had been especially vitriolic during the Whitmore hearings, and the senator had gotten perverse delight in hearing himself vilified even more than the judge.

Now he was watching a convocation of the National Human Rights Appeal, the prime fund-raising arm of the national homosexual coalition, sort of a homosexual United Way.

There was certainly a celebratory mood over the defeat of Hastings Whitmore, and the movement was claiming full credit for keeping him off the Court. Yet he noted that the speakers and audience seemed to be taking great pains to appear calm, rational, reasonable, even good-humored, since the conference was being broadcast to the American public at large.

What a contrast, Trumbull thought, to the annual Washington March for Human Rights, where ACT-OUT, Queer and Present Danger, the National Man-Boy Love Association, Leather Necks, Lavender Lions, and assorted drag queens, sado-masochists, transvestites, and pederasts marched.

Or to their closed meetings and briefings. Jimmy Tolliver, his chief-of-staff, had given him videotapes of such meetings, where the movement gave voice unrestrainedly to its rage and frustration with the straight world—and its determination to change society at any price.

It was quite clear to Branch Trumbull, even apart from the issue of homosexual "rights," that homosexuals as a political force were fundamentally at odds with him and his thinking on other issues as well. As a group, they were among the most liberal and most active on behalf of every conceivable socialist, statist, and collectivist cause. Now that they were considered respectable and mainstream, they vociferously supported the most left-wing political candidates.

Yes, he knew, there was clearly a consistent homosexual ideology that went beyond sex, something antithetical to him in their fundamental worldview.

The Dignity Channel aired its restricted programming in the late evening and early morning hours. Despite himself, Branch had tuned in to assess it. He had to understand this subculture better.

Unaccustomed to staying up so late and a little groggy, he was suddenly galvanized by revulsion. A short five years ago it would have been beyond anyone's imagination to see such explicit sex acts except in some seedy porn theater off Times Square or Castro Street. Now homosexual skin flicks were on national television.

After a few minutes he had seen all he needed to see. Switching off the set, he sat and prayed in the early morning darkness. He asked God to cleanse his mind of the images he had just witnessed and was immediately refreshed by a sense of His presence.

God had blessed him beyond all measure, Branch reflected. He had good health and vigor. He could reasonably look forward to a long, productive life. He had wealth and property. He need never fear for a livelihood, even if he should leave the Senate. He was a respected member of the community. Above all, he had the love of an extraordinary woman, Clare, and his two fine children, Libby and Branch IV—"Banks."

More and more he had begun to feel that to whom much was given, much was required. The time had come for him to start giving something back to the One who had blessed him so abundantly.

Branch could sense Clare's nearness before he heard or saw her. Perhaps it was her perfume or perhaps something even more subtle. Clare Trumbull had a presence, a force of character to which he was still drawn after thirty years of blissful marriage. They were truly one.

Now he heard the swish of her nightgown, then felt her arms slide around his neck and the cool softness of her cheek against his.

"Hello, dear," she said in her throaty voice.

"Hi, sweetheart. Why're you up so late?"

"I just couldn't sleep. And I thought you might want to talk."

He smiled. She knew him heart and soul. She could tell he was troubled. She also knew when he would welcome company and when he wanted to be left alone. Now was one of those times when he needed her counsel.

"I was proud of you," she said. "No one could have done more than you did. In fact, you did far more than the White House. If the president won't stand by his own nominee . . ."

"Even so, maybe I should've waited till the next day. In retrospect I think it was a tactical error to testify so soon in the process. But the judge seemed so discouraged by the first mornin's attacks, and nobody was coming to his defense . . ."

She sat on the arm of his chair. "No, love, you had to jump in then. He might've lost on the first day if you hadn't. Don't criticize yourself. You made the best call you could at the time."

"I know. I'm not feelin' sorry for myself. Really."

"What then?"

"Well, there was a moment when I actually thought we had a chance. It wasn't just my testimony, though that certainly helped. But it was Whitmore himself. He's no great moral philosopher, but he's a fine judge and a good man, the best we might have hoped for. And you know, he really came across well. He was reasonable, and he showed judicial temperament. Yet he was firm when Lockwood and his jackals started ripping into him. He showed he had some principles and backbone too. More than I thought he had."

"Yes, he did, didn't he? I called the office tonight before you got home, and Jimmy told me there were hundreds of calls to the Hill and the White House in favor of confirmation. And your switchboard was inundated by callers thanking you for standing up the way you did. Of course, you also got a ton of hate calls and telegrams." She paused and stroked his cheek.

"Yes, victory was actually within sight, if only for a few hours."

"But then something happened, didn't it?"

"Uh-huh. It's obvious." Branch was still puzzling over the post mortem.

Clare got up and started for the kitchen. "I'll get some iced tea."

"The tide was running our way Tuesday afternoon," he called to her. "But then literally overnight we lost it. You could tell a change had set in with the Committee as soon as they resumed yesterday morning. I called Langdon Smith at eleven on Wednesday—he didn't want to talk to me. It was clear the White House had already thrown in the towel by then. Somebody got to them too, as well as to the Committee."

She brought a tray, set it down on the coffee table, and handed her husband a glass. For a while they both sipped without speaking.

Branch thought over the day's events. "I guess the opposition pulled out all stops."

"But did you honestly expect any different?"

"No, not really," he said slowly. "I figured he'd lose. But there's something strange here—what strikes me is how well orchestrated the opposition was. Like an invisible hand was stage-managing the whole debacle."

"We've had hotly contested Supreme Court nominations before, Branch. This was no worse than the controversy over Clarence Thomas's nomination—except that *he* won."

"No, sweetheart, this time it *was* different. Clarence Thomas was opposed by the traditional civil rights lobby—along with militant feminists, mainly because they feared he would help overturn *Roe* v. *Wade*. Of course, his bein' black took some of the starch out of the civil rights groups, so the feminists carried the brunt of the battle.

"But the main point is they had to find something other than a policy disagreement or philosophical difference to oppose him with, even if they had to make it up. So they focused on the sexual harassment issue, even though later it all turned out to be a lie.

"The Whitmore battle was different," Branch continued reflectively. "The opposition hardly even bothered to raise a character or qualifications issue. They defeated him strictly on the basis of his opposition to the homosexual agenda. His traditional beliefs automatically disqualified him. That's a dangerous but historic first."

In fact, Branch thought, *if opposition to the homosexual politi-*

cal agenda disqualifies somebody from serving on the Court, then we're in far worse shape than I realized.

"Clare, the next Leslie case is out there, just waiting. Though it's only three years since we won that one, the federal judiciary has changed so much that we can't rely on winnin' next time. I doubt we'd even get the same opinion from the Fifth Circuit if the case came before them today. Judge Whitmore would hold the same, but the composition of the court has changed."

"You know," she offered after a moment, "we're really living through a revolution. It's gradual, but in some ways it's the most sweeping and radical social revolution in modern history."

"You're right."

"In fact, it's a sort of a secular counter-Reformation," Clare observed. "It's undoing the social and cultural framework we inherited from men like Luther, and Calvin, and Knox."

"You could say that. The civil rights movement was a kind of social revolution. But it took place within that accepted cultural and moral framework. When civil rights activists demanded an end to injustice against blacks, they were appealing to commonly held moral assumptions. But today's revolution is far outside that framework. Yet few people see it. That's what's surprising."

Clare considered for a moment. "Well, the main reason is that it *has* been gradual. It's like the old folktale about the frog in the pot. You heat him up gradually so he won't jump out, and before he knows it he's cooked. And there's only one answer to it all—the Spirit of God, God's Word, God's grace. Those are the only things that'll redeem the culture."

Branch nodded. "Then the time has come to start fightin' back, hasn't it?" He pulled her off the arm of the chair and into his lap, where he hugged her close, breathing in her fragrance.

"It's way past time," she said.

"We've been resting too long on our laurels from the Reagan years. And even then we only won partial victories. Our people haven't been fightin' for a long time."

"No, they haven't." She stroked his face tenderly. "And one reason is they've had no leadership for a long time."

"Christian leaders are too easily pacified and misled. You know how it is. Whenever they get restive, Jim Darby invites them over to breakfast at the White House. They get their picture taken with the president of the United States. He tells them he's doing all he can, and they go away satisfied, and nothing ever changes. In the meanwhile, people like Garden Monnoye are winning victory after victory."

"Branch, you've said many times the Lord brought you to Washington for a reason, and I've always believed it too. Maybe now He's showing you what that purpose is. I believe you're His man to stand in the gap. My only question is this: have you prayed about it long and hard, so that you're sure the Lord wants you to do whatever it is you've decided to do?"

"Yes, I've prayed. Mostly I've prayed, 'Why me, Lord?' But try as I might, I can't shake the conviction that God has brought me to this place in my life—and for this purpose. Honestly, I'm so disgusted with politics and the Congress, I can't see any other point in being a US senator, except that it gives me standing and credibility for something else."

"Then you must follow His will, no matter what."

He shook his head ever so slightly. "I just hate to . . ."

"I know what you're thinking. But don't use us as an excuse. Libby's grown and on her own. Banks is nearly a man. And I want to do this with you—to stand alongside. You need a woman's advice. And besides—" she giggled "—I'm tired of Congressional Spouse teas."

"I do need you, sweetheart. More than you can imagine. I just know if I go through with what I have in mind, it's going to change all our lives. You're right—I can't do it unless you're with me. But you need to know it'll demand a lot more than we can possibly anticipate on this side of the decision."

"Now Branch, don't get scared off by the cost."

"Well, what I have in mind *will* cost. A lot. A lot of time. A lot of abuse. Maybe cost us our friends. It'll take total commitment. And of course, a lot of money."

"Our real friends will stand by us. Those who don't aren't true friends anyway. And as for money, we've got plenty. More than we need, anyway."

"Well, I hate to spend the children's inheritance."

"Branch, we've taught them to love the Lord. That's the best inheritance—in fact, it's the only inheritance that will last. That, a good name, and a free country is what we'll leave them. And if the things we both see happening do come to pass, you know they won't inherit a free country."

"You're right—as always."

"And besides, I've got the ranch in Wyoming. We don't really need it. Now that Mom and Pop are gone, nobody ranches anymore. It's just a vacation spot, and we can do without that. Les has always been willing to sell it, and lately I've been thinking about selling it too. Let me put that money into—into whatever it is."

"You really want to do that?"

"For what shall it profit a woman to keep her own ranch, but lose her whole country?" she teased.

"Do you want to hear what you're investing in?"

"Certainly."

"I'm going to launch a kind of campaign, an organization for a specific kind of spiritual warfare. We'll apply biblical truth intelligently—and aggressively—to the big questions of the day. We have to start redeeming the culture, God willing.

"And the first thing we're going to do is stop this so-called Human Rights Amendment in its tracks. Did you know that every important constituency in the country has a major think/action tank, except us?"

"Well, we have the church, of course," said Clare.

"Yes, we have the church. And we have the cause. But we need a vehicle geared expressly for this effort. And I'll give them the vehicle. I want to call it the Nehemiah Foundation, or something like that."

"That's good, Branch. Rebuilding the walls."

"And if this doesn't get our people involved once again in the life of the nation, then nothing will. In which case it's already too late."

5

The last few years of the twentieth century were not bolstering Chase's confidence in the future. Violent crime stalked the nation's cities and spilled out into the suburbs and rural villages. Massively destructive urban riots were common. Addiction to mind-destroying drugs continued to climb. AIDS and other sexually transmitted diseases were still rampant. And the economy, while beginning to stir under the Darby administration, was still mired deeply in a state of stagnation and decline.

Chase's father, now dead, had been a wise man, though in the eyes of his rebellious son entirely too consumed with religion. He had often told Chase that modern man worshiped no gods but Money, Lust, and Power.

Chase had stubbornly resisted the piety and religious devotion of his parents, but he had to agree that in 1998 money, lust, and power were still the chief temporal deities. These obviously did not fill the aching void of men, however, for people were turning in legions to the occult, earth mother worship, Eastern mystery religions, channeling and spiritism, witchcraft and Satanism.

He was not entirely a child of his times and felt slightly misplaced. He was not completely at home with the troubling present, yet—unlike some of his Southern kinfolk—was not living in the past either. Basically hopeful and optimistic, but realistic, even with a slight touch of cynicism—that was Chase. He *wanted* to believe in the future. Yet he saw the cracks in the foundation far better than most and was beginning to grasp what it meant for the edifice of a great nation to begin to disintegrate.

Of course, it had been crumbling for years, but gradually. Men had become accustomed to the small fissures. But the fissures grew wider, spreading into great gaps. Most people were too close to see the pattern of disintegration that was spreading throughout the structure. Nothing too serious, they said. It's to be expected. After all, the structure has stood for centuries. It will always stand and is sound enough to absorb a few shocks. The doomsayers, religious fanatics, and Bible thumpers have always been warning that the end is near. But nothing has happened yet, they said.

Chase had tried to dismiss the warnings. But one didn't have to be a theologian to see that current social policy, the media, and popular culture were powerful acids corroding society drip by drip.

No matter how resolutely he fought against the claims of his parents' religion, he could not help but notice that communities where faith was strong were largely free of the social pathologies he saw everywhere else. But he took refuge in detachment, telling himself his function was not to change the world but simply to explain it.

I'm a journalist, an observer, not a participant.

Unlike most of his contemporaries, he knew his own family history. He had deep roots and believed simply in remembering. And now he, Stuart Chase McKenzie, bore the family name and the responsibility that went with it. But nothing was as certain to him as it had been to his forebears. Their devout faith seemed a little quaint to him. He respected it, but at the same time it embarrassed him. He was determined to fight his battles where he could truly make a lasting difference.

Despite his skepticism and scant regard for the simple country faith of his ancestors, though, a vague knowledge resonated quietly in the recesses of his mind, giving him the ballast to keep him righted in the rough seas he was beginning to encounter.

Chase knew that involving himself again in the controversy over the homosexual movement would demand a price, perhaps a higher price than he was willing to pay. He understood vaguely that the struggle was religious at its root, one perhaps that he was not well-suited to wage. Still, all that prayer, all that teaching, the hours in church and Sunday school, the hours of Bible memory had given him a particular lens through which to view the world. And he owed something to his past and his forebears. He had to remember, and then he had to act. The time for reflection was over.

The most significant action he could take, Chase decided, would be to use the resources at his command. These were considerable resources—a nationwide TV platform, with tens of millions of eager, loyal viewers. The first thing to do was to get Senator Branch Trumbull on the air to talk about the Hastings Whitmore episode. Then he could use Trumbull's presentation to make public what he had learned about the Paragon Foundation and the homosexual lobby as well.

★ ★ ★

Chase burst into the small, cluttered office of his boss, Hugh Mahan, vice-president of DBN and head of programming.

Mahan was tall, slow, heavy, only a few years Chase's senior, but his appearance and worried manner made him seem older. His brown hair was thinning—he told Chase he pulled it out from anxiety—and he wore little granny glasses on the tip of his nose whenever he pored over Nielson ratings. He motioned Chase to a chair.

Chase did not sit down. "Hugh, come on. Let's go shooting."

"Where?" Hugh asked somberly.

"They've opened a new sporting clays range over near Warrenton."

"Why?"

"Oh, come on, don't be so grumpy. You need to get away and loosen up some. Shooting's the best therapy there is."

"I mean why *now?*"

Mahan had hired Chase to do his first politically oriented talk show. The two men had much in common. Chase considered him a good, if not close, friend.

"Well," Chase said hesitantly, "I need to talk to you about something . . ."

"Ah, there *is* an ulterior motive." Mahan laboriously stood up and with a practiced hand caught the granny glasses as they dropped off his nose. He laid them on top of the computer printout he had been reviewing. "OK, I'm game. Let's go."

Chase already had his gun and gear in the back of his Jeep. They swung by Mahan's elegant townhouse in Georgetown for Hugh's equipment. Then they headed west on I-66 toward Warrenton.

The two men paid the shooting fee and with guns and ammo bags proceeded to the first station of the course. The path was wooded, the June air humid. Presently Chase broached the subject that had been occupying his mind.

"Hugh, I've been thinking about the show . . ."

"Me too. 'Pulse of the Nation' is the best public affairs talk show on TV, Chase. But I hope you haven't brought me out here to hit me up for a raise. The network is still in bad shape financially—we've got to amortize the investment in all that fiber-optic equipment—"

"Oh no, it's not about a raise. But since you brought it up— what if I could increase the audience share? I mean by several points. Would that help our cash flow?"

"Sure. How would you do that?" Hugh was clearly interested, but wary.

They met the course attendant and went through the first round of targets. Chase hit all but one. Hugh was still warming up.

"It's the gay rights issue, Hugh," Chase continued as they walked to the next station. "The Whitmore confirmation hearing touched a raw nerve in a lot of people. I want to do a series of shows on the issue, and I want to start by putting Senator Trumbull on 'Pulse.'"

Mahan nodded thoughtfully. "Trumbull's impressive. He almost turned the Whitmore defeat around single-handed."

"He's articulate. He's well informed. He has a sense of humor. He doesn't come across as belligerent. But there could be a downside," Chase added.

"Sure could be."

The targets became increasingly difficult. Hugh remarked that Chase was a fine wing shot—his reflexes were quick.

Chase did not press him concerning "Pulse."

Finally Hugh asked, "Do you really think this would give 'Pulse' some added punch?"

"I do. People like controversy, they like intrigue, and they like sex. This issue has all three. And last but not least, these gay militants are going to ruin the country if somebody doesn't challenge them."

Hugh said finally, "We'd have to tread lightly though. And

be real careful. The law's full of all kinds of pitfalls, not to mention FCC regulations."

And Chase knew he had won.

"I'm willing to let you try to pull this off," Hugh said. "Maybe it'll be successful. But I have to tell you, my responsibility is to the network, and I have to answer to the CEO. If things go against you—if you get tagged as a religious fanatic—"

"Hugh, this isn't about religion. It's about politics."

"I know, but the liberals will try to paint you as a religious nut if you're not careful. And if they succeed . . ."

"You're saying I'm expendable."

"Chase, you're the network's chief talent. But there's a lot of risk here. How much risk I can't say. I will say that if there's a backlash to your exposing queers on 'Pulse,' I may have to ask you to cease and desist and go back to traditional topics. That's fair enough, isn't it?"

"Sure, that's fair, I suppose," Chase said amiably.

"OK, then. Go ahead and invite Trumbull."

6

Chase watched Senator Trumbull pick his way across the DBN studio, accompanied by a dark-haired, heavy-set man in his thirties. They carefully avoided the huge cables that snaked across the floor and the banks of lights and cameras the technicians were rolling into position. The senator had been properly made up in the back, and he wore a charcoal gray suit, a pale blue shirt, and burgundy tie.

Chase smiled. *Looks like he's used to being on TV*. Chase also was dressed in gray suit and pale blue shirt, but with his trademark Scottish tartan tie.

Trumbull glanced around the set. It was a small platform furnished with easy chairs, tables, and bookcases made to look like Everyman's den in the suburbs.

Chase came over and shook hands.

"Good evening, Senator. Welcome to DBN. I trust you got everything taken care of? Did you get some coffee?"

"Yes, I did, thank you. Chase, this is Jimmy Tolliver, my AA and chief-of-staff. He's fillin' in as press secretary tonight. Wants to make sure I keep out of trouble." He grinned amiably.

"Hi, Jimmy." Chase reached for his hand. "You've got a big job, keeping this man out of trouble."

Tolliver laughed. "Yeah. And if I guess right, your show's not going to be an exception."

"Well, fine. It ought to be a great show, then."

This *was* going to be a memorable show. The prebroadcast interview had been cut short because of Trumbull's demanding Senate schedule. But they had talked briefly about the Whitmore hearings and touched on the gay rights issue. Chase had suggested several lines along which the discussion might proceed.

Trumbull appeared easy-going, not at all fanatical or preachy.

Yet he was saying things no one else was willing to say. Just the right formula for a successful broadcast.

Tolliver disappeared into the visitors' viewing room, and the two men settled into the armchairs on the set while the sound man attached their microphones. Chase liked the senator's ease of manner. There was a clear strength about him, but a benign strength, not the arrogance that usually went with power and position.

In the few minutes before air time, Chase was overcome by curiosity and asked him point-blank, "Senator, I imagine you've been in great demand after the Whitmore debacle. Just why did you agree to do my show?"

Trumbull smiled. "I was just asking myself why you wanted me. As one of your counterparts on SIS said last week, surely I'm persona non grata among all right-thinking people everywhere." He gave a self-deprecating chuckle.

Chase laughed back, liking him still more.

"Well, this is not a politically correct program, Senator. But that creates a problem of its own—it's getting harder and harder to find anybody who isn't 'right-thinking' to appear. You're part of a vanishing breed. And what's more, the producer said that when he called last week to see if you might like to appear, Mrs. Trumbull told him you were actually watching tapes of the show at that very moment. So I guess we had no choice but to bring you on."

"I believe the Lord has a special purpose in mind by directing me to your program. Maybe He has a special purpose for you too."

Chase's comfort level dropped into a trough of near panic. *Oh, no,* he thought. *Not one of those Holy Rollers that God talks to all the time. Tells them where to find a missing sock in the morning. I better find out quick if this man is some kind of religious nut. We're on the air in three minutes.*

"You mean a voice from heaven told you to come on my show?" His sudden anxiety was audible.

Trumbull chuckled again. "No, nothing quite like that. But I have been watching your program lately, and I found myself drawn to your show. I can't answer for other people, but God directs me in much quieter ways than by an audible voice from above."

"Oh," said Chase, much relieved. "But I take it you're a very religious man."

"No, not really."

Chase looked at him quizzically.

"What I mean to say is that I don't do a lot of religious things in the sense that most people use the term. But I do love the Lord Jesus Christ, and I try to serve and obey Him in all things."

Chase struggled to conceal his embarrassment. He smiled faintly and gave a polite nod. He had heard all this God-talk before, throughout his childhood and youth, from his parents and grandparents, and had learned how to respond as if in agreement.

"I see. Well, are you going to talk about the Whitmore controversy in religious terms? I mean, just how theological should I anticipate our discussion becoming? I need to know, because as you remember from the preliminary interview, part of my technique, even with a fellow conservative, is to play the devil's advocate.

"I take a debating position that might seem to be at odds with my guest—even when I agree with him—just to bring out all the aspects of the issue. I even get very argumentative from time to time. Fortunately my audience understands that this actually does our cause more good than if I simply agree with everything a guest says."

"I understand." Trumbull nodded. "And that's why your show is so good. It's not just a string of superficial sound bites. You really do develop an issue. But don't worry. I'm not going to preach a sermon. Still, you need to understand that it's impossible to discuss the power—and the danger—of organized homosexuals in America today without ultimately considering what God's Word has to say about homosexuality."

"Sure, that's OK," agreed Chase, though he was still a little nervous. "The devil has enough advocates anyway. Maybe we need to be more concerned about balancing the odds."

Trumbull laughed, but then asked gently, almost in an off-hand manner, "Chase, do you know the Lord?"

He managed an embarrassed grin, then blurted, "Why, sure, I guess so. I was raised in a Christian home. My parents were very devout."

The senator gave him a slight smile and a nod. Chase doubted whether he had really fooled the man, but fortunately Trumbull was too courteous to press him.

The chief cameraman signaled the thirty-second warning, and he quickly turned his attention to the business at hand, making a show of looking over his notes again.

Then the ten-second countdown began, followed by the on-the-air signal. Now they were going live, and Chase gave the lead-in.

"Good evening, and welcome to 'Pulse of the Nation.' I'm your host, Chase McKenzie, and tonight we're privileged to have the Honorable Branch Trumbull, Republican senator from Tennessee, helping to take the pulse.

"Those of you who watched the recent confirmation battle over Judge Hastings Whitmore will recognize Senator Trumbull as the man whose controversial testimony nearly turned the tide for the embattled nominee on the first day of the hearings.

"Tonight our discussion will focus on the historic defeat of President Darby's first Supreme Court nominee—defeated, one has to concede, because of his opposition to the gay rights agenda. In the next hour we'll hear Senator Trumbull's version of the debacle from his unique vantage point as the only congressional witness to speak in favor of Judge Whitmore, and as one of the few national political figures to speak out against the proposed Human Rights Amendment to the Constitution."

They broke for the long commercial segment, and Chase busied himself again with his notes. Furtively he observed the senator and noticed that Trumbull was studying him as well. *I do like the man, but he makes me nervous. I'm a good Christian. Why can't these people just leave you alone?*

Back on the air, he began to lay out the basic facts of Trumbull's political and personal history.

"Senator Trumbull, you're now the senior senator from Tennessee. You're from Chattanooga and were in the newspaper business. In fact, you still own several prominent newspapers in the state. You fought in Vietnam and reached the rank of full colonel in the National Guard. You also fought in the Persian Gulf War in 1991, commanding a National Guard artillery battalion, and that helped you defeat Senator Mizell, who had opposed the war.

"First elected in 1992, you're at the end of your first term, and you became the senior member of your state delegation when Senator Waller retired in 1994. Amazingly, you have no serious opposition in the November election. You're married and have two children, a son and a daughter."

"That's right."

"And your committee assignments?"

"I'm on the Ethics Committee, Labor and Human Resources, and Armed Services."

"Senator, I recall it was your outspoken leadership on the Armed Services Committee that first brought you to the public's attention. A few years ago you were the most vocal and effective opponent of putting women in combat units. And then you fought hard to maintain the Pentagon's policy of prohibiting gays in the military."

"Well, Chase, that's correct up to a point. I found myself the ranking Republican on the Armed Services Personnel Subcommittee, and so I did have some influence on these issues for a while. But I can't claim to've been very effective in the long run. I lost— the nation lost, I should say—on both counts.

"We now have women serving in combat units of all the armed services. And then the president overturned the prohibition against homosexuals in the military. First we feminized the military, and now you might say we've sodomized it."

"That's strong language, Senator. Yet a lot of people, both gay and straight, feel just as strongly the other way on this issue. And since we're on the subject, why *shouldn't* homosexuals serve in the military? Don't they have the right—or even the obligation—to defend their country just like anyone else? For that matter, why should we discriminate against them at all, in any capacity?"

"Society *doesn't* discriminate against them as a class. It didn't even before the heyday of the organized homosexual movement. As long as they were discreet, there was little, if any, effort to seek them out and persecute them. Society does disapprove of homosexuality—or used to—as it's entitled to do. But laws against homosexual behavior discriminate only in the sense that laws against robbery discriminate against robbers. The law condemns *acts*, not classes of persons."

"That may be the case in criminal law, Senator Trumbull," Chase pursued, "but isn't it true that the military, for example, did discriminate against them as a class? You didn't have to be caught in a homosexual act to be kicked out of the military—you only had to admit you were homosexual."

"No, that's not quite correct. The military ban was based on behavior—homosexual *acts*, in other words. But the services held —logically and correctly in my view—that declaring you were a homosexual also meant you were likely to engage in the prohibited behavior. That's why they were separated—not simply for saying they were homosexual."

"Senator, I have to tell you, after all those years of controversy and public debate, that this is the first time I've ever heard the military ban clearly explained."

"Well, I tried. That's what the Armed Services Committee hearings attempted to do. But we never got much coverage."

"But why didn't the Pentagon make its own case better?" Chase's frustration was genuine. The habitual response of the Defense Department to criticism on the issue had usually been a resounding silence.

"Frankly," he said, "in all that time I never heard a good defense of the antigay policy from the Pentagon. The military always acted evasive and embarrassed when called on to testify about this on the Hill or explain it to the public. They just said, 'That's our policy,' or mumbled some platitude about 'good order and discipline,' as if that explained everything."

"I certainly have to agree with you there, Chase. When it comes to issues like this, the Defense Department has been its own worst enemy. Its defense of the basic moral factors so essential in a good fighting force has been dismal for as long as I can remember."

"And so the Pentagon's ambivalence on the issue has been exploited by certain members of Congress?"

"Absolutely. The most vocal congressional advocates of homosexuals in the military are not concerned about the military's combat effectiveness or—in my opinion—the nation's security.

You'll find they consistently oppose new weapons systems, research and development, and adequate defense budgets. They never show any interest in military issues except when it comes to using the armed services as the engine of social revolution."

"OK, I guess it would be hard to quarrel with that observation. But let's get back to the main point—your objection to gays serving in the military."

"My objection to their serving in the military is the same as my objection to them overall. It's just that homosexual characteristics are even more rapidly destructive to the armed forces than to society as a whole, given the peculiar nature of military organizations and the unique demands placed upon the military by its mission—"

"Which is?" Chase interjected.

"To preserve our freedom and safeguard our national interests by waging war if necessary, not to serve as a laboratory for radical social experiments."

"And just what are those homosexual characteristics?"

"Now we get to the heart of the matter." Trumbull appeared to collect his thoughts. "First, there's an anarchic impulse at the core of the homosexual character, whether they're discreet and monogamous or wildly promiscuous. I know this offends against the false pieties of the day, but you have to understand this— homosexuality is a profound act of rebellion against the natural moral order.

"Second, homosexuality is sociopathic. It's a psychological disorder. The homosexual is utterly self-absorbed and narcissistic, so much so that he simply can't understand how offensive his behavior is to millions of others."

"What exactly do you mean, 'self-absorbed?'"

"Well, unlike the heterosexual, the homosexual defines himself exclusively in sexual terms—I mean, his embrace of deviant sexual choices is literally what makes him what he is. His sexual impulses even determine his politics, ideology, and moral worldview.

"His whole existence is a form of sexual preoccupation. There's no way you can call that anything but a disordered personality, even if many of them appear normal on the surface."

"I'm not sure I understand. Aren't heterosexuals preoccupied with sex? Don't they have sexual hangups, too?"

"Sure, heterosexuals may have sexual problems. They may be rapists, sex addicts, adulterers, child abusers, exhibitionists. But heteros tend to define or identify themselves in other terms besides sexual identity—for example, their role as fathers or mothers, their profession, their nationality, or their religion. Don't you identify yourself in terms other than sexual behavior? You're an American, a journalist, a McKenzie.

"I identify myself through my family. I'm a husband and father. And I identify with my region, my history, my cultural heritage. I am proud to be a Southerner. Somewhere way down the list I may classify myself as a heterosexual. It's a fundamental part of my identity as a person, but it doesn't dominate every aspect of my being."

"So you're saying that homosexuality by its very nature tends to be all-consuming."

"Yes, tends to be. And that means there's an intellectual dimension to the problem. The homosexual represses the reality that his behavior is abnormal and undesirable.

"Now that can't occur without a massive impact on his understanding of the world, and so he engages in massive self-delusion and self-justification. It's a disorder of the intellect as well as the soul."

"I suppose you raised these points during the Armed Services Committee's hearings on gays in the military?"

"Yes, I did. Nobody liked it much, but since the Pentagon couldn't defend its own policy with any effectiveness, I felt obliged to do it. These are highly unpopular positions, but somebody had to talk about how these traits that exist in various degrees in the homosexual personality are simply antithetical to the demands of military service, especially combat."

"But only if you regard the military as unique."

Trumbull looked at his host patiently. "Chase, have you ever been in combat?"

"No, Senator, unless you count all the riots—like L.A. in 1992, the Great Detroit Fire in '95, and the riots in Washington last year."

"Well, that may seem like real warfare, especially if you're a policeman or National Guardsman. But that kind of violence, while it might be deadly, tends to be limited and random. Combat, on the other hand, is unique among all human endeavors. There's nothing in the civilian world that quite equals it. Waging war means killing other human beings in a planned, concerted, organized, deliberate fashion. It also means exposing yourself to being killed.

"Imminent death and organized violence place unique demands on soldiers and military units, and those demands are primarily moral in nature. In a bloody firefight, would you want a soldier on your right or left who was morally, psychologically, and intellectually disordered? Of course not.

"Furthermore, a combat-ready army is built on mutual trust between leaders and led. If I'm going to obey your command to attack that hill and maybe get shot in the process, then I have to be able to trust your character. I have to trust you're not sending in my squad to be killed because the other squad leader is your catamite. Such commands are moral transactions. Anything as profoundly wrong as homosexuality destroys the trust and moral order necessary for effective command and discipline."

"So you're saying that flying an F-22 in combat, or crewing a tank in a battle, are not just mechanical processes? They're not just a higher version of driving a bus in heavy traffic?"

"That's exactly right. Combat is more than mechanical and material. The decisive factor is spirit."

"Well, Senator—" Chase shook his head "—I can see why the gay community calls you Public Enemy Number One. And now, after your controversial testimony for Judge Whitmore, I hear they are really out to get you. They've declared you their number one national target in the upcoming elections, even though your opponent isn't given much of a chance. Does that worry you?"

"Not particularly. Everyone knows the nationwide homosexual movement has immense power and money. They've had me on their hit list from day one. But the people of Tennessee are still supporting me. We've always known this issue could make or break a candidate for office in states like New York and California. What does worry me is that now we're seeing how militant homosexuals can determine someone's confirmation for appointive offices as well.

"That means there's now a religious test applied to hold public office, despite Article Six of the US Constitution, which says that no religious test shall be required for public office in the United States. Is this what we want in America? To say to the Christian segment of the population, 'Forget the Constitution. No Christians need apply'?"

"Well, Senator, a lot of people do support gay rights. The latest polls show a majority of Americans in favor of the Human Rights Amendment."

"That may be true, or it may not be. These days I've come to regard all polling data as suspect. But it's also true that most Americans don't understand the full ramifications of the HRA or of the homosexual rights movement in general."

"Well, your testimony certainly got people thinking about the issue. But it seems to me, based on what both you and Judge Whitmore said in the hearing, that the HRA is almost superfluous. I mean, gays appear to have virtually everything they want."

"You're right," Trumbull said. "The homosexual agenda has advanced so far in this country that the HRA *is* almost superfluous. There isn't much in the way of so-called homosexual rights that hasn't been granted—except maybe formalizing homosexual marriages. And even that's hardly the case, since so many cities and states have domestic partners ordinances that confer many of the legal and economic benefits of marriage on homosexual couples."

"Then why are you making such an issue out of a piece of legislation that can't really accomplish a great deal?"

"It can accomplish far more than we can foresee at the moment. Passage of the HRA will enshrine the homosexual agenda in the fundamental law of the land. And what the law permits, the law encourages. So it will remove whatever few legal, cultural, and social barriers remain to the destructiveness of open, organized homosexuality.

"Furthermore," the senator added, "it will give homosexuals almost unlimited power to suppress those who disagree with their agenda. It will put the full power of the state behind their goal of disenfranchising the traditional moral community."

"Aren't you overreaching a bit, Senator?" This time Chase's question was sincere. He couldn't imagine things going this far. This was the United States of America, after all.

"I'm sorry if this is hard to swallow. But just look at the history of any constitutional amendment. And look at how liberal courts have interpreted and built on them. An amendment is a sweeping thing. And one like this, in the hands of a militant, organized special interest group, with allies in the courts, Congress, and the media, is a loaded gun aimed at our liberty.

"Furthermore," he insisted, "the HRA's significance isn't just legislative or political. It's also symbolic. Passing the HRA is saying loud and clear that the secular transformation of our culture is complete, that God and His laws are dethroned and exiled forever from our laws and our public life. And when that happens, it's a sentence of death.

"So you see, Chase, I have to do this. To me, stopping the HRA is like the final fire wall that stands between the self-immolation of our society and the possibility of survival and recovery."

Chase stopped the discussion at that point for another commercial break, and the show's producer rushed out of the control booth. He conferred with Chase, gesturing wildly. When the producer left the set, Chase came over to Branch.

"Senator, we seem to have a problem."

"What is it, Chase?"

"Well, it's what we call a 'phone blitz.' As you know, we usually stop about halfway through and go to the live telephone discussion. But it looks like the gays've got their people all calling in and jamming the lines. Whenever Jack picks up in the control room, they shout obscenities at him. We can't risk putting out that kind of stuff on the air."

He pointed to the telephone console on an end table by his chair. Every line was lit up.

"Then what'll we do?"

"The producer says to skip the calls and just keep on with the discussion—he says it was too good to stop anyway. Do you mind? Have you got enough material for a few more minutes?"

"You're kidding." Branch Trumbull grinned. "I could go on for hours."

"Great. And I'll jump in too with some things I've uncovered, if you don't mind. Remember, I *am* on your side."

Back on the air, Chase explained to the viewing audience that they were the target of a phone blitz, "from parties unknown, but you can guess," and that they would not be taking calls. Then he resumed.

"Senator, your colleague Senator Lockwood said yesterday on Capitol Hill that your appearance in the Whitmore hearing was 'extremely unfortunate,' and that, but for congressional immunity, you might otherwise have been charged under the Hate Crimes Act. How do you respond? Do you hate gays?"

"No, of course I don't hate them. I'm a follower of Jesus Christ, and His command is to love my fellow man. But I deplore what they do, both their immoral and unnatural sexual behavior and the political agenda that goes along with it. The homosexual movement itself is in fact built on hatred—hatred of God's law and hatred of the traditional moral order."

"Well, you've got a point there, Senator. I didn't see the Capitol Hill police arresting demonstrators for calling you and the judge fascists and homophobes. But if your position on this issue is theological, why don't more Christians take the same view?"

"That's the most important question of the evening, because ultimately this issue can only be resolved by theology."

The senator paused, appeared to think hard, took a sip of water, and proceeded. "We're all prone to do evil, and God condemns many of the things we do habitually. We lie, cheat, steal, commit adultery and murder, and God rightfully condemns these sins. But the sin of homosexuality He calls an abomination. This sin of unnatural sex is especially abhorrent to Him and has always brought down a sentence of death upon the societies that practice and tolerate it.

"This is an unequivocal teaching of the Scripture—and the position of the church for two thousand years. The greatest tragedy in all this controversy is the failure of the church to remain true to God's Word and its historical teachings. The mainline churches no longer base their theology on God's truth. They base it on man's version of truth—on humanistic sociology and psychology."

"Senator, for the purposes of our discussion, I've been playing the devil's advocate. Of course, I had some honest questions about your views. But now I want to shift focus a little."

Chase proceeded to tell what he had learned about the Paragon Foundation, Garden Monnoye, and the interlocking networks between the Congress, the media, and gay rights groups. He concluded by relating how on the previous day he had sent a research aide, posing as a congressional staff member, to crash one of the lavish lunches at the Paragon Building. The aide reported that an influential assemblage of Supreme Court clerks, Capitol Hill aides, media mavens, and staff from the special interests all attended.

"This issue is clearly a fundamental social and political issue," Chase pointed out, "yet conservatives have nothing to compare with the high-powered Paragon Foundation. How can you hope to succeed if your side's not even in the battle?"

"Your rebuke is more than justified," Trumbull said soberly. "In fact this has been weighing on me for some time. And so I finally decided to lead an effort just like you suggest."

"What do you plan to do?"

"The first thing is to call on everyone watching this program —everyone who loves the Lord—to pray. I'm asking them to intercede with God on behalf of the nation and ask Him to heal our land.

"And here's the second. Tonight, on this broadcast, I'm announcing the formation of a Christian campaign organization. It'll be called the Nehemiah Foundation, and it will combat the secular humanist revolution that's destroying our nation. It won't be as well funded as the Paragon Foundation, but we'll still be able to mount an effective effort. And I've already gotten commitments to serve from some of the best Christian minds in law, government, and public policy. D'you know who Nehemiah was, Chase?"

"I know he was in the Old Testament, Senator . . . "

"Yes, he was—"

Chase suddenly recalled a Bible story from his childhood. "I remember now. He was the Israelite who came back from captivity and rebuilt the walls of Jerusalem."

"Exactly. The Nehemiah Foundation's first effort will be to rebuild the walls of our Jerusalem—to defeat passage of the HRA."

7

On that note the broadcast ended. Chase was proud of the product, despite the senator's too frequent references to the Bible and religion. Trumbull had spoken with an unusual conviction, a kind of authority, and he lacked the sanctimoniousness Chase had come to expect of preachers.

He was about to thank the senator profusely and invite him back when the producer again rushed up to the set.

"Chase, security says there's a mob outside, and they're howling mad. You and the senator better wait for a while—or go out the back."

Alarmed, Chase demanded, "Who are they—gay militants?"

"I guess so." The producer shrugged. "I mean, who else?"

"Did security call the police?"

"Yeah, but Chase, you know how unlikely it is for the police to act against gays in this town. They practically run the place. Go out the underground garage exit. Please."

"I'm not going to skulk out the back way," Branch Trumbull said, to the obvious surprise of the worried DBN staff that had collected on the set.

"That's foolish," objected Chase.

"You can't go out there! They'll tear you apart," argued the producer.

"Listen, Chase, whatever danger you may think's out there, my life is not in the hands of those people." Trumbull seemed totally unperturbed.

"Senator, you're being foolhardy and—"

"I don't expect you to fully understand," Trumbull interrupted gently. "But I belong to the Lord of the universe. He covers His children with His wings. Christians are not to fear those who can kill the body."

Jimmy Tolliver, the aide, joined them.

Trumbull smiled at him and said, "Jimmy, why don't you go ahead now—I don't guess they'll recognize you or bother you—and get Charlie to bring the car round front. Will you do that for me?"

"Yes, Senator." Jimmy smiled back at him, a strange, confident smile.

This is weird, stupid, Chase said to himself. "Senator, I feel responsible for your safety. I'm the one who brought you on the show. I egged you on. I wanted controversy, and—well, I got it. So listen to me, please. Let's wait for a police escort if you won't go out the back."

"Chase, you have to understand what's happening here. The homosexuals are winning because they've used two weapons successfully: lies and intimidation. The only antidote to lies is truth. I've tried to tell the truth here tonight, truth as I see it.

"And the only antidote to intimidation is courage. We've got to start facing these people courageously. Do you think after making my big announcement tonight I can just turn and run out the back door like a coward?"

"OK." He drew a deep breath. "Then I'm going out with you."

"You don't have to do that," Trumbull said, surprised. "Now *you're* bein' foolhardy."

"I'm sorry, Senator. I'm responsible, and I'm going out with you."

"Chase, I'm a child of the Most High God. I can claim His promise of protection. But can you make the same claim?"

Almost choking on the words, he said, "No. But I claim your protection. Weren't there people living in Canaan who put themselves under Israel's protection when the Hebrews conquered the land?"

Branch put a firm hand on his shoulder. "Let's pray then." He bowed his head and prayed a short prayer not only for protection but also for an opportunity to show the glory and mercy of God to those who needed it the most. Then they took the elevator down to the lobby and went outside.

A seething, swaying, densely packed mass of humanity completely blocked the street. DBN used the studio and broadcast facilities in the US Chamber of Commerce Building on I Street, right off Lafayette Square, and a block away from the White House and Pennsylvania Avenue. The crowd filled the entire expanse of I Street. No police were yet in sight, though Chase could hear sirens.

He could not estimate the size of the crowd. It faded into the darkness, but there had to be five hundred or a thousand at least. Some were half-naked, many were in studded leather, some dressed in parodies of nuns. Some were in normal street clothes, but on the whole the crowd was garish, bizarre, and loud—until struck speechless by Trumbull's unexpected appearance on the high marble steps of the building.

Then all began to scream again, louder now that the enemy was there to hear. A deafening, relentless, rhythmic chant rose and fell in cadence. "TRUM-bull, BI-got, HOM-o-phobe! TRUM-bull, BI-got, HOM-o-phobe!"

Senator Trumbull looked calmly over the sea of contorted faces.

Chase, trembling inside, realized with amazement that the man was truly not afraid. There was a peace, a serenity about him. He did not fear the crowd, and, as he had said on the program, it was clear he did not hate them either.

Finally the chanting and defiant yells dropped slightly, then began to subside altogether, whether out of awe or simple surprised curiosity, Chase could not tell.

When he could be heard, Trumbull spoke in a quiet voice, yet one that carried. "You want to feed your spite on me. But it's not me you hate—it's God. And perhaps even yourselves. But you don't have to be the way you are. Call on Jesus Christ. He can deliver you from the bondage you're in, no matter how permanent you think it is. And now, in His name, I ask you to let us pass."

He began walking confidently down the steps.

An astonished and worried Chase stuck close beside him, looking neither to the right or left, but feeling the palpable menace around them.

The crowd parted like the waters of the Red Sea.

Trumbull casually crossed the street to where his dark sedan was waiting, held open the door for Chase, and unhurriedly got into the car. Only then did the shouting resume. But the demonstrators made no move to stop them, and they slowly drove off down I Street toward St. John's Episcopal Church, turned right on 15th, and were soon gone from the scene.

Trumbull said nothing but sat next to Chase, thoughtful.

Chase exhaled, slowly and audibly in relief, and muttered, "I would never have believed it."

"But you *did* believe, Chase, you *did* believe. And you see, God is faithful. Now, where can we drop you?"

★ ★ ★

It was shortly after the broadcast that the church burnings began. The first was Saint Mary and All Angels Catholic Church in Tallahassee, where Hastings Whitmore worshiped. At 3:00 A.M. on a Saturday morning the church's fire alarm began to flash in the control room of the local fire department. The department duly dispatched pump and ladder trucks, but the firefighters found the entire sanctuary engulfed in flames and impossible to save.

The telltale odor of kerosene or other inflammable liquid was not present, but investigators could not trace the fire back to one point of evident origin. Unlike an accidental fire, this one seemed to have started almost everywhere at once and then burned with unusual intensity. Furthermore, it had spread to the interior of the adjacent buildings, not the roof or walls, and without a clear means of transmission from the sanctuary. The fire department declared it arson.

At about the same time a fire broke out inside Branch Trumbull's church, Potomac Presbyterian. But this was a new building, with a good fire alarm and sprinkler system, and the blaze never got off to a good start.

Regardless of who torched the two churches, someone else obviously thought it a grand idea. A week later the Shiloh Baptist Church of Houston and the Sycamore Street Presbyterian Church in Atlanta were firebombed. Then, in states as widely separated as California, Illinois, and New York, a half dozen churches were either burned or damaged by deliberate fires. Law enforcement agencies began to take notice.

Chase McKenzie's former employer, the *Washington Standard*, covered the church fires extensively, and in a major editorial warned that more such "homosexual terrorism" could be expected.

72

"Senator Trumbull in effect has issued a declaration of war," the editorialist said, "one perhaps long overdue. But the enemy is skilled, determined, and experienced in decades of shadowy warfare on cultural and political battlefields and has been quick to counterattack. Let us hope that having thrown down the gauntlet, Senator Trumbull and his new organization, the Nehemiah Foundation, have the guts and the means to carry the fight into the camp of the militant homosexuals and their allies."

NEWS ITEM,
the *Los Angeles Record*

Rev. T. C. Moreland, pastor of Suburban Baptist Church, an independent congregation in Glendale, was convicted today in Los Angeles County Superior Court of involuntary manslaughter for the death of Michael Larkin, who died of a self-inflicted gunshot wound last February.

Larkin had been under "pastoral counseling" from Rev. Moreland for several months prior to his suicide. Notes and diaries found in Larkin's room, and testimony from his friends and family, revealed that Rev. Moreland had attempted unsuccessfully to change Larkin's homosexual orientation. According to Rienzi Page, L.A. County Assistant District Attorney, this counseling caused Mr. Larkin to fall into a deep depression and was the direct, material cause of his taking his own life.

Rev. Moreland, who has said he will appeal the conviction, will be sentenced in a separate court appearance next week. Larkin's family has also filed a civil suit against Suburban Baptist for wrongful death and has asked for $5 million in damages.

In a related development, state senator Hugo Montero has introduced a bill in the California state assembly to require all "pastoral counselors" to meet the same professional qualifications as licensed family or marriage counselors and clinical counseling practitioners.

Under the proposed legislation, church-based counselors would have to undergo a period of professional psychological training in accredited institutions, be licensed by the state, and obtain malpractice insurance before they would be legally allowed to counsel parishioners.

8

Neeley Durant was not what men would call a classic beauty, but she was striking and exuded such charm and sensuality that few noticed that her Roman nose was a little large and the planes of her cheekbones were a little flat. Tall, slender, exquisitely shaped, she moved with unconscious, sinuous grace.

And her hair. To say merely that it was light brown was an injustice. It was long, with golden tints that made it positively luminous in bright sunlight—fine, gossamer, but full and wavy.

There was something elusive, though, about her eyes. If the eyes are the windows of the soul, hers were shuttered, as if she would see out but let no one see in. At times she seemed distrustful, yet generally she concealed the wariness in a rollicking sense of fun.

Neeley was no great intellect, but she did have a sharp wit, confidence, and self-possession that appealed immediately to men of equal self-assurance—men such as Chase McKenzie.

"Well, Neeley, here you are. My favorite place in the entire world." Chase threw out his arms in a wide gesture, as if to embrace the entire Shenandoah Valley.

Here the thick growth that covered the mountain opened slightly where the roots had never been able take hold in the exposed rock. A lush meadow, punctuated with rocky outcroppings, extended behind them for a few dozen yards, an island of grass in the wooded slope. Parallel to the crest ran a well-worn footpath, passing above the soft grassy ledge on which they sat. Down the path a few hundred yards and back in the trees stood Chase's log cabin retreat.

They sat next to a bulging basket and several bottles of wine, where the ledge's overlook provided the perfect spot for a picnic.

"Well, it *is* grand." Neeley gazed out over the famous Valley of Virginia. Silvery loops of the Shenandoah glinted here and there among the trees. Verdant farms and fields and vivid green copses of hardwoods stretched out far below across the Valley floor to the west, climbing in the distance to merge with the heavily forested Alleghenies. "But the world's a big place."

"I know," Chase replied agreeably. "I've seen a bit of it. I've hiked all over Bavaria and in the Black Forest. Bummed around France and England. I've even seen a bit of South America. But to me, this is still the finest place in the world."

"And not least because it's yours," she teased.

"Yes, it's mine. My special private place. I don't just bring anybody up here, you know."

"Chase, how long have we been going together? Three months? Four? And it's taken you that long to share your hideout with me?" She gave a sigh of mock reproach. "Well, anyway, I guess I should be flattered that you brought me at all."

She peered into the middle distance, pointing to a toy town on the valley floor. "What's that place?"

"Woodstock. The county seat. If you look real close, you can see the spire of the courthouse sticking up. It's the oldest courthouse still in use west of the Blue Ridge. The old Lutheran church stood nearby, where one of my German ancestors was the minister. He was also a famous general in the Revolution."

"A minister and a soldier? Wasn't that a bit unusual?"

"Yeah, I suppose. But he was an unusual man. There's even a statue of him in the Capitol."

"And over there? What's that little town?"

"That's Edinburg. Many of the settlers who came here were Scots—or Scotch-Irish to be precise, like my ancestors. And they named their new homes after places in Scotland. That's where the first CCC camp was, back in the 1930s. D'you know what the CCC was?"

"No, I don't think so."

"The Civilian Conservation Corps. Way back in the Great Depression, the CCC put a lot of unemployed men to work on public lands and roads, paid them a small wage, and gave them room and board and something useful to do."

"Sounds sort of like the NSC," she said brightly.

"I guess that's a good comparison," he agreed. He didn't welcome her reminder of that latest assault on the traditional liberties of Americans, the National Service Corps. "Over there's my grandfather's old grist mill. It's a famous Valley landmark. You can't see the actual mill from here. It's on the other side of that little rise to the left of the town." He pointed.

"What's so famous about it?"

"Well, in 1865 the Yankees came up the Valley from Winchester—"

"Up the Valley? Don't you mean down the Valley? Winchester's north of here."

"Nope. In the Shenandoah, up is down, and down is up. If you're going southwest, toward Lexington and Roanoke, you're going up the Valley, even though it's down on the map."

"I see." She smiled. A city-bred girl, Neeley was amused at the quaint customs of these rural Virginians.

"Anyway, " Chase explained, "the Valley supplied much of the food for Lee's army. So the Yankees burned the crops and farms. But when they set the mill on fire, the women of Edinburg went to General Sheridan and begged him not to burn up their flour, or they and their children would starve. He relented—and then both the Yankee soldiers and the townsmen pitched in together, put out the fire, and saved the mill."

"What a wonderful story!"

"And finally, right down there—just below us—you can see my stretch of the river. That's the North Fork of the Shenandoah. And there's Burnshire Bridge. On the other side, between the River and Woodstock, is the family farm where I grew up."

"Oh, Chase, it's beautiful. It's dreamlike, like a painting almost. I can just see the house through the trees. Is that the one your grandfather built?"

"Yes, on the foundations of the house burned down in 1865. He also built the cabin up here on the mountain. I've been coming up here to Powell Mountain Overlook and picnicking on this ledge ever since I can remember."

"And what's that big, rocky cliff over there?" She pointed to the right of their grassy ledge, where the tree-clad face of the mountain had been sheared off, exposing a high vertical cliff with a vast jumble of boulders and rubble at its base.

"That's Draper's Leap. Five hundred feet straight down. That pile of limestone down below's a part of the mountain that just split apart and fell off, who knows how many thousand years ago. Some rock also split away from where we are now. That's how this ledge got here. But over there it left a gaping hole in the side of the mountain. It's a great vantage point. On a real clear day you can see all the way to Strasburg in the north and New Market to the south."

"Why's it called Draper's Leap?"

Chase was delighted at her genuine interest. "Well, in 1774 there was an Indian massacre. At that time the Shenandoah was prime hunting ground for the Indians. They say the grass used to grow five to six feet high in the Valley, and before the white man came there were huge herds of buffalo. Plus a lot of deer and other game.

"So the Indian tribes came from all over the region to hunt —and fought each other as well as the white men. Anyway, by the mid-1750s, the Valley had been pretty well settled. Then the Shawnees decided enough was enough. A big war party came over the Alleghenies from the Ohio River region and killed a number of settlers."

"And one of them was this Draper?"

"Yes, a husband and wife. The Drapers lived up here, right about where the cabin stands now. Anyway, the Shawnees chased them up to the edge of the cliff there. In fact, the path above us continues right on up to the Leap. Draper knew he would be tortured and killed and his wife would be raped and taken as a slave. And she couldn't bear the thought of leaving him and maybe ending her days as a Shawnee. So they both jumped."

"Did it kill them?"

"Oh, sure. I mean, look at that drop. You couldn't fall five hundred feet onto those rocks and survive."

Neeley lay on her stomach on the horse blanket and looked pensively down at the foot of the Leap, chin in hands, her long, tanned bare legs angled up behind her. The story seemed to have captured her imagination.

Chase wondered what she was thinking. She was so inscrutable at times.

★ ★ ★

He had met her quite by chance, thanks to her position as Director of Communications of the Republican National Committee. He had agreed to participate in a panel at Georgetown University to discuss the impact of the 1998 Campaign Reform Act on the First Amendment and the freedom of the press. He had arrived at the auditorium to find that Neeley was also a member of the panel.

Chase had known her only by reputation and caught only rare glimpses of her on nightly news clips. She was well-regarded by the working press and was said to be competent and tough. Yet she seemed to be without the hard-edged machismo that so many women in politics and communications felt they had to affect.

Oddly, the first thing he had noticed about her that night at Georgetown was not her face but her voice. She spoke in a rich contralto, without the annoying tinny sound of so many ingenues around town. And when she spoke, it was with poise and assurance.

She seemed almost too confident and self-contained. She would pause dramatically in the discussion and look at him pointedly, or at her other interlocutors on the panel, as if to say, "What foolishness." She intrigued him.

Later, when the panel discussion ended and she stood, his heart lurched. She possessed all the power and mystery of her kind, and she knew it. And when she turned her dazzling smile on Chase, he was totally captivated.

"Would you like to continue the—uh—discussion over a late dinner?" he had asked, approaching her as the other men, apparently intimidated, moved away.

"Oh, I don't know," she teased.

He knew he had not hidden his disappointment, and she may have liked that, for she added quickly, "I think I'd rather discuss something besides politics."

"In this town, what else is there?" He laughed, much relieved, and she laughed with him, a rippling but throaty laugh.

And then she looked at him, directly and unblinking, as if

appraising him inside as well as out. After a long moment, as if she liked what she saw, she flashed that smile again, and there it was—that deliciously exciting but mystifying force field that seemed to grip them both simultaneously.

Neeley suggested Chatelaine's. They walked there from the stately, paneled Gaston Hall auditorium at the university, enjoying the coolness of the night air and soaking up the rich ambiance of the campus and the old city.

That night they enjoyed a memorable dinner, two bottles of fine wine, and stimulating conversation. The spell did not fade. It only intensified as they talked and laughed and shared personal anecdotes.

Finally Chase could prolong the meal no longer. He pulled out his Electronic Debit Card, but Neeley objected at once—in the best of humor, of course. To maintain the fiction that it had been a business dinner, they held a delightful mock argument over who should pay, the RNC or "Pulse of the Nation."

Finally Chase acquiesced, forced to agree that the affluent RNC could better afford it and that Neeley had made the more significant contribution to the evening's panel discussion.

She laid down her EDC, giving Chase the opportunity to propose, "Next time I'll pay."

"Oh, and will there be a next time?"

"Yes," he said firmly, but with an infectious smile. "Lots of next times." And indeed there had been many "next times."

To Chase's delight Neeley proved to be adventurous. In addition to the usual dinner dates, movies, and lunches, she cheerfully accompanied him on canoe trips on the Potomac and the Rappahannock. She was an accomplished equestrienne. She kept her own horses and often took Chase riding where the mounts boarded at Mason's Neck.

Soon they were spending as much time together as their busy work schedules would allow.

"Chase," she was saying now, "I can see why you love this place. It's beautiful. It's peaceful—and has so much history. Sometimes I forget how little Fairfax County resembles the rest of the state." She paused, as if in doubt, but then plunged ahead. "But what are you escaping from when you come up here?"

"Escaping?"

"Yes, you're running from something. Is it me—us? Is that why you waited so long to bring me up here?"

"Of course not, Neeley." A hint of annoyance crept into his voice.

"Well . . . " She left the thought unfinished.

"Neeley, I don't come up here to escape. Just the opposite. I come here to . . . seek," he volunteered finally. When she did not respond he added, "I haven't been running away from something —I've been searching for something."

"For what?"

"Oh, I don't know. What everybody searches for. Peace. Contentment." He looked at her intently. "Love, maybe. And I can't explain why, but this place is so much a part of me, somehow I've always known I'd find whatever it was I was looking for up here."

"And have you finally found what you're looking for?" she asked, dropping her eyes coquettishly, as she refilled their glasses.

Chase gave her his most engaging smile. "Yes, I believe I have," he said emphatically, reading her expression. But in his heart he feared he lied. He wanted to be in love, yet he was still uncertain about her. Some unarticulated ambivalence gnawed at him vaguely. Did she really love him? Was *he* in love?

★ ★ ★

Chase drove several miles in silence as they wound down the mountain.

Neeley wondered what was on his mind. But she was used to his moods and rarely gratified her curiosity by pressing him for explanations. Some things were better left alone, she believed.

And intuitively she feared their relationship harbored fundamental incompatibilities. She knew she might not like what she uncovered in peeling back the layers of mystery. She was content to indulge his sulks and sudden inexplicable silences, telling herself this dark, brooding nature only added to his romantic appeal.

One thing did worry her, one thing that might be a threat to developing the perfect relationship, and that was his hyper-opinionated activism. Of course, she was glad he was politically sophisticated—they had to have that in common. But she feared he could prove to be what political people called a "loose cannon."

Paradoxically, it was also his commitment to something beyond himself that attracted Neeley. He really believed in things. There was a solid center in him, not the vapid emptiness of so many Hill staffers, campaign aides, and political groupies she had to deal with daily.

Undoubtedly she liked him, maybe even was in love with him. Certainly she enjoyed his company. She found him far more interesting and stimulating than anyone else she had ever dated. But his enthusiasms and dogmatic opinions on everything under the sun would have to be controlled—especially his evident preoccupation with gays.

Neeley thought back to their first meeting and the memorable dinner in Georgetown. She recalled how she had rushed in the next day to pore through old files in the RNC's newspaper morgue to research Chase's history.

His stellar career as a journalist had begun at the *Washington Standard* when he published a series of articles on the now infamous Greg Spitz and friends. Spitz had been a big-time Washington lobbyist, political fund-raiser, deal-maker, contact broker, name dropper, con man, and party-giver to the elites. Chase McKenzie's exposé had stunned the city.

Chase had uncovered the call boy ring that Spitz ran from his lavish Kalorama mansion, a homosexual prostitution service whose clientele extended into the top echelons of both executive branch and Congress. There were even indications, though no absolute proof, that the KGB had infiltrated Spitz's escort service and used it to entrap top government officials for blackmail.

Thanks to Chase's dogged reporting, several high level people in the Departments of State, Defense, Energy, and Justice had been forced to resign. The once popular Mr. Spitz become a discredited pariah. A year later he died of AIDS. It had been an extraordinary piece of investigative journalism, though it earned Chase few friends and little gratitude outside his newspaper. But he had righted a severe wrong and may have even protected vital national secrets at the very climax of the Cold War.

As fine as this achievement was, Neeley still found it vaguely distasteful. Chase had acquired overnight the reputation as Washington's number one gay basher.

Fortunately, after a foray or two into the homosexual demimonde, Chase had settled down to more normal journalistic fare. In fact, it had been nearly ten years since he had done any notable work on the gay issue.

She was glad to see he had matured. But the history was still there. In a perverse way, gays had catapulted him to stardom, and she worried that now he was reaching back for the old success formula to propel him forward again.

It wasn't that she particularly liked gays, she reasoned, or even approved of their agenda. It was just that she found the whole topic distasteful and not really relevant. The things people cared about were the economy, taxes, jobs. Gay rights got people stirred up unnecessarily.

And on the Republican side, she felt it brought out the worst in people. She despised ACT-OUT and Queer and Present Danger. But she despised the zealot gay bashers and homophobes in her own party almost as much. Gay rights had proved to be even more distasteful, divisive, and inflammatory than the abortion issue—and, frankly, as unnecessary.

Well, Neeley mused, she would just have to work with him. He was not a homophobe. He got just excited about a lot of things. He was an everything-phobe. She laughed silently at the thought.

I just need to be a moderating influence on him. Keep him from getting too involved with Senator Trumbull. She experienced a twinge of guilt at that thought. After all, she *was* a loyal Republican, and Trumbull was the senior Republican senator from Tennessee.

At length Chase, presumably seeking familiar conversational terrain, broke his silence and broached the subject of politics.

"I hear President Darby's got a nominee for the Court. Know anything about him?"

"What makes you think it's a him?"

Chase shrugged and grinned at her. "Well, him or her—do you know who?"

"I've heard, but it's not official, and I'm not supposed to talk—especially not to a working journalist."

"Oh, come on."

She wagged her index finger back and forth, then pressed it to her lips in the universal sign that she wasn't talking.

Chase appeared to decide that discretion was the better part of valor. Instead of pressing her directly, he took a different tack.

"Well, I may not know who the nominee'll be," he said, "but I have a good friend at Justice. He told me about a new development that could have a major impact on the confirmation. The next one could end up being as controversial as Whitmore's was."

"Oh, really," she said, instantly curious. "What's that?"

He took a hand off the wheel and duplicated her finger-on-lips gesture.

"Don't play games, Chase. Tell me."

"I propose an exchange of information," he intoned.

"Chase, I really can't. I've been given strict orders not to tell anyone until he's cleared all the hurdles and the White House makes the announcement. It could mean my job—"

"So it *is* a he!"

Flustered, Neeley insisted, "Listen, I'm just not going to talk about this anymore. I wish you hadn't brought it up. You know, we're really going to have to find a way to keep our personal lives and our professional lives separate."

"I'm sorry, Neeley. I don't mean to put you on the spot. And I promise, I won't try to use you as a source. You're right. We *will* have to separate our love life from our work life."

She nodded, but the frown was still in place, and tension still hovered between them.

Chase seemingly tried to go the second mile. "And you may as well know, since I brought it up. The word from the Justice Department is that the president is going to disbar the Bar Association."

"That doesn't make sense."

"I mean, he's going to tell the American Bar Association to take a running jump. After their treatment of Judge Whitmore, and then their vote endorsing the gay rights amendment, the president is going to announce that he will no longer submit his nominees for the federal bench to the ABA for evaluation. The ABA will no longer have any role in vetting federal judges."

So, Neeley thought, the administration was finally showing

some sign of life. But if Chase was assuming that she would share his pleasure, he was mistaken.

"Oh, Chase, that's *awful!*" There was a note of near panic in her voice. "I really can't believe the president would do something like that. I mean, why pick a fight with the whole legal profession over something so—so—stupid?"

Chase sent her a surprised look. "I'm sorry you feel that way. But can't you see the ABA has just become another special interest, just another political pressure group? It's not objective anymore."

"That may be. But they're also the most powerful professional group in the country. How can you expect to take *them* on and win? It's so unrealistic."

He negotiated a hairpin turn. "Well, look. Don't blame me. I think it's the right thing to do, but I didn't make the policy. The attorney general did. It's a done deal as far as Justice is concerned. The AG has made the case to the president, and Darby's signed off on it. They're just waiting for the right moment to implement. I guess that'll coincide with the announcement of the new nominee."

"Chase, you seem positively happy about this."

"Well, I am. It's about time."

"But don't you see how it will only embarrass us all? The news media will have a field day. I can just hear the commentators: 'The president has to be the president of all the people.' They'll attack him as a tool of the gay bashers. It's just going to make things a lot harder for all of us—harder to elect more Republicans to Congress."

Chase opened his mouth to reply, then stopped and began again. "I guess it *will* make your job harder. The RNC'll certainly be on the firing line. But look at the positive side. It'll give a good issue to a floundering administration. The legal profession may be powerful, but the vast majority of Americans don't like lawyers. Or militant homosexuals, for that matter."

She sat upright and waved her hands futilely. "Chase, I know the gay issue helped launch your career. And that's fine. You did some great work back then. But don't let it obsess you. Frankly, I think you've been listening to too many gay bashers." She didn't name Branch Trumbull, but she had him in mind.

"Not so, Neeley. I just listen to the news and watch what's going on around me," he replied severely. "Look at the church fires, for example. They're not just isolated events. They're part of an orchestrated campaign of intimidation. And it's not gay bashing to point that out."

Neeley did not disagree but looked down morosely.

"I'll tell you something else," he continued. "The whole sabotage job on Judge Whitmore was engineered by the gay lobby and their allies. P. Garden Monnoye in particular."

He told her then about his discovery of the Monnoye-Berg-Lockwood connection. "And there's more. I went over the FEC records of Monnoye's campaign contributions. He's the bag man for the gay lobby on the Hill. He gives tens of thousands to congressmen who then vote like he tells 'em.

"And his Paragon Foundation gives hundreds of thousands in soft money to other gay, lesbian, feminist, and radical organizations. The groups in the homosexual coalition use Monnoye's building as their Washington headquarters. And most of them pay one dollar a month for rent."

Neeley stared blankly as the mountain road entered the Valley. As an official of the RNC, she was quite familiar with election law, and she regarded possible violations of the Federal Election Commission's regulations as a serious matter. She had had no idea of the extensive, interlocking nature of the activist gay alliance—or of the huge sums involved—and was duly chastened.

"Well, that's pretty scary," she admitted. "But what can you do? Monnoye's entitled to contribute to the things he believes in, just like you or me. As long as he obeys the election laws, that is."

"Yeah, he's entitled. But speaking of election laws, there're some odd things going on. Monnoye only gives cash. Oh, he stays within the $1,000 personal limit. But he only gives cash.

"I'm as certain as I am sitting at this wheel that a vast amount of his money to Congress goes unreported. But he's such a big shot, and the gay lobby's so strong, the FEC won't look into it. Of course, if they do, he can just say the congressman forgot to report it—and then make sure the guy enters it on the next quarterly filing."

Neeley said nothing, but her thoughts churned.

"You see, it's not just the homosexual agenda that bothers me," Chase said. "It's the arrogance of these guys. They think they can do whatever they want. Monnoye and his gang are buying political influence on the Hill and in the media at an unprecedented level. And if somebody doesn't expose him—"

"But why does it have to be *you?* You can't take on the whole legal establishment, the entire news media, and the gay lobby without getting chewed up in the process."

Chase looked over at her soberly. "You may well be right." He turned his attention back to the road. "Chase McKenzie may get chewed up good if he's not careful."

After a moment he continued. "But I have to do it. Somebody has to. I'm lucky enough to have a platform and some insight into what's going on. I just can't stand idly by and watch these people pay the US Congress to enact their agenda. I'm going to keep investigating Monnoye and his connections. And when I have something solid I'm going to discuss it on the show. But it'll be done in a responsible way."

Neeley's mind was in a whirl. Why was everything so complicated? She was frightened—for him, and even more for what might happen to her if she became too closely associated with him. She was distressed at what his determination might do to their blossoming love affair. She was angry that he would put his "cause" before her. The gay movement scared her, and she feared what they could do if Chase provoked them.

She said simply, "Well, I do admire your courage, Chase. You're an unusual person. But please. Please don't get too mixed up with rednecks and fundamentalists. OK?"

"I'm my own man, Neeley. I won't let anybody or anything dictate what I do or say."

She breathed a relieved sigh. Smiling, she leaned over and kissed his cheek.

Chase kissed her back. But it was obvious that his mind was on their conversation.

9

Swallowing his antipathy, Branch Trumbull sat back in his favorite family room chair and watched the Dignity Channel again. Despite himself, he found Garden Monnoye's address to the Campaign for Human Rights convention fascinating.

Percival Garden Monnoye was incredibly impressive, he thought. Impeccably groomed and dressed, confident, nothing at all like the bizarre stereotype most Americans associated with leaders of the homosexual movement. Its leadership, Branch saw, had undergone a profound change in the past five years.

"It is truly going to be a New Age," Monnoye intoned. "The old order is in the final throes of extinction. You can see it every day, writhing and gasping for breath like a beached whale. A new order is supplanting the old, gradually but inexorably.

"And dominion by white males, heterosexuals, and assorted religious bigots, with their so-called Judeo-Christian ethos, will soon be a relic of a hateful past. Diversity will soon be realized, bringing dominion by feminists, lesbians, gays, and all the oppressed people who've been denied their rightful place in the sun."

There was a hearty round of applause. Monnoye flashed a bright smile, touched with just the right amount of humility, and continued.

"Law, government, education, and culture are going to foster a new openness to human potential and all life's possibilities. And at last humankind will begin to achieve freedom from poverty and strife. Freedom from bigotry. Freedom from the loathsome narrowness of old religions.

"People did not evolve to their present state in order to serve some archaic desert god or to follow myths out of an inconsequential old book. The godhead is in each of us. By our own intelligent efforts, we can achieve our full potential and realize the immanence of the god within us. We can—we *will*—usher in the New Age."

Cheers and louder applause greeted this statement.

Monnoye looked around the hall and went on. "We don't need to be told, 'Thou shalt not.' We need to hear, 'Thou shalt.' We need to follow the imperative that the greatest good is whatever produces the greatest happiness for the most people. Only that will create a new enlightened politics and equitable government.

"And let me say that anyone who prefers to keep humankind bound in the chains of superstition and the darkness of outmoded, patriarchal religion is an enemy of human freedom and has to be dealt with accordingly."

Branch Trumbull switched off the remote. The lingering image of Garden Monnoye smiled benignly as the audience gave him a standing ovation.

Yes, freedom, Branch thought. He felt bitter sadness in the pit of his soul. *You would have absolute freedom. But you are breaking your yokes of wood and making for yourselves yokes of iron.*

The daily spectacle of a nation once under God and now rejecting Him was almost more than a man of faith who also loved his country could bear. But Branch Trumbull faced it, routinely, in the realm of law and government, where human reason went about uprooting millenniums of law, custom, tradition, belief, and practice grounded in biblical revelation.

Branch closed his eyes and let his mind range over what had happened to his country in a few short years. He understood, far better than most, that America was engaged in a great civil war —fought on cultural and political battlefields but essentially a religious war. The nation was divided along the great fault line: who is sovereign, man or God?

That fault line had created two Americas at war with each other—except that, in Branch's opinion, the traditionalists hardly knew they were at war. He also understood better than most that one dimension of this struggle was now geographic.

Wherever humanistic law predominated, death from rampant crime was on the increase. Violence from drug lords fighting over control of their turf—and random, unprovoked murder by jaded young men just out looking for kicks—was now commonplace in the cities. Across the land it was an everyday occurrence to read of children murdering parents, of stalkers and rapists killing unsuspecting victims from the shadows.

AIDS and related illnesses, including infections from a new immune deficiency virus undetectable by the standard blood test, continued to take a rising toll. The AIDS epidemic among heterosexuals had not reached the catastrophic proportions once predicted, but it continued to decimate the homosexual population. By 1998 an estimated 10 million individuals carried the HIV, many of whom had no detectable symptoms.

Government leaders at all levels had decided in the mid-1990s that the only way to fight AIDS was to give out free condoms and sterile needles to junkies. The results had been predictable— more sexually transmitted disease and more drug abuse. Washington, DC, not only remained the murder capital of the nation but by 1995 had also become the AIDS capital.

The DC government went so far as to give out condoms to its prison inmates, even though sex acts in prison were presumably illegal. By 1998 AIDS in prison populations had reached crisis levels, as high as 50 percent of the inmates in some states. Now there was even less protection than normal from gang rape, especially of new, young inmates.

Prison officials were indifferent. A prison sentence in a liberal, heavily urban state, therefore, had a 50 percent chance of becoming a death sentence. This had an appalling impact on civil disobedients who refused, for example, to hire gays in defiance of local human rights ordinances.

An overgrown, mammoth federal government struggled futilely with the vast array of problems its own actions had fostered. The 1990s thus had produced a form of government that political theorists said was impossible—anarchy and tyranny in a dreadful symbiosis. Under the anarcho-tyranny of 1998, government at all levels intruded clumsily and inefficiently into every area of life. Yet it failed to do the one thing for which it was properly constituted— safeguard lives, liberty, and property.

The authoritarian aspects of government had taken on an increasingly ugly tone. Courts in Wisconsin, Michigan, New York, Illinois, and Florida, Branch well knew, were steadily reversing long-standing positions on equal housing laws under pressure from activists.

Previously, a landlord who could document sincerely held religious beliefs against renting to unmarried couples had been exempted from state civil rights laws and equal housing codes. Gays, however, argued that such exemptions were wrongful intrusions of religion into public policy. Such bigoted beliefs excluded them from renting, they complained.

The courts began to agree. And in a celebrated case in Madison, a young woman advertising for someone to share her apartment was convicted, heavily fined, and financially ruined after she refused to accept a practicing lesbian as a roommate.

On the anarchy side of the equation, so many people had become dependent on the government for income that its ability to meet all its obligations was unraveling. By 1998 recipients of Medicare, Social Security, and other welfare payments and entitlements were being carried on the backs of fewer and fewer productive workers. Public debt was enormous. The country was actuarially bankrupt and in danger of major economic collapse.

Branch knew that the family crisis underlay most other social problems. The emotional deprivation prevalent in single-parent homes made homosexual recruitment far easier. But at the same time, increased recruitment made it far more difficult to contain the HIV.

Children fortunate enough to have stable families were victimized by the education establishment. New Age and humanistic dogma, extreme environmentalism, behavior modification, and attitude control had largely replaced traditional learning.

This had become especially hard on religious parents, who had the option of seeing their children drawn away from their moral teachings or of paying the enormous expense of private education. Christian schools and home schooling were rapidly expanding options, but even they had come under increased pressure and legal harassment in progressive states.

Christians found themselves shut out from virtually all public sector employment. To be a public school teacher, a municipal bureaucrat, a district attorney, it was not enough just to keep silent about one's faith. One had to actively support the secular dogmas.

As their local influence waned and the culture deteriorated, Christians and other conservatives simply migrated, mostly to rural areas and small towns in the South and West, where the social, cultural, and political climate was more hospitable. Sociologists and demographers were now beginning to call this phenomenon the Great Migration.

On the other hand, regardless of what was happening nationally, gay activists could console themselves that they had gotten entrenched all across America in relatively secure urban enclaves. Their concentrations often represented the election-decisive bloc of votes, especially in local elections and on ballot propositions. And in accordance with the dictum that "all politics is local," gays focused their attention on passage of local and state ordinances, on influencing policy, and on electing their own to local office.

Nevertheless the Great Migration had kept truth alive. There were still tremendous reserves of spiritual and moral vitality in America, though no longer evenly distributed geographically. The doomsayers who had predicted the country's total and early demise were wrong—at least with respect to the timetable.

Conservative churches and denominations were still growing, though paradoxically in such a manner as to have little impact on the national culture. There were far more believers than anyone was willing to credit, but their influence was mostly confined to the inside of church walls.

In the traditionalist cantons were now tens of thousands of people who felt they had secured their homes, families, and livelihoods sufficiently and were now ready to begin fighting back. They were dry tinder ready for the match, yearning for leadership and direction. And Branch Trumbull was ready to give it to them.

To counterattack against this leviathan that beset the nation on every side was an intimidating task. It was intimidating simply to look for a place to begin.

I need a plan of action and a viable leverage point. Otherwise my best efforts will amount to no more than gnat bites on the hide of a rhinoceros, he mused.

But trusting in God, he had to start somewhere. The consequences were God's. And having thrown down the gauntlet on national TV, Branch Trumbull knew he had to strike fast to keep and build credibility among his own allies.

* * *

Branch did not have to seek out the first move—it came to him.

A Georgia family who had seen him months earlier on "Washington Spotlight" called and asked for his help in dealing with the Walt Whitman Clinic outside Marietta.

The clinic was a leading center for the treatment of AIDS and other homosexual diseases. Run by gays for gays, it included a hospice for AIDS victims in the terminal stages of the plague, a place where they could die in relative peace and dignity.

No one was to leave the hospice except under controlled conditions—to go to a hospital for special treatment, for example. But one patient at least was able to come and go at will, finding that the hospice had no meaningful controls or accountability.

This patient was not only an AIDS sufferer; he was also a convicted pedophile. He slipped out nightly from the hospice to cruise the neighborhood for young boys, one of whom he found, sodomized, and infected with the deadly virus. The indignant, sorrowing father of the victim called Senator Trumbull and begged for legal help in stopping this shocking irresponsibility and in gaining redress from the clinic.

This was the right issue, at the right time, and in the right place. Branch sprang into action.

By the next day he had secured the services of two of the best lawyers available, one in Washington and one in Georgia. The Nehemiah Foundation's legal defense arm had already been set up and funded, and he wrote a substantial check to the two men on the same day.

His legal team filed suit against the Whitman Clinic within the week. The venue was chosen, as his Georgia attorney had hoped, in Rome, a conservative area where they could count on a fair hearing.

The pace of the legal action, as well as the power of the motions and briefs filed against it, left the clinic stunned and reeling. Its board of directors first tried to get the trial moved to an area where gay influence could be brought to bear on the media and the legal structure, but that failed. They tried threats, including that of a countersuit, but its grounds were so dubious that the idea was quickly discarded.

Finally, they offered to settle out of court. But by that time the Whitmans' panicked reaction had persuaded the family and Branch's team that an outright victory was possible, and they settled down to await trial.

In the meanwhile, the victim's community realized it had a champion in Branch Trumbull and the Nehemiah Foundation. Nearby residents began to demand that local law enforcement press criminal charges against the administrators of the hospice. In due course, the willing district attorney did file criminal charges and obtained a court injunction forbidding the admission of any criminal offenders into the hospice. The outcome of the suit seemed a foregone conclusion, and damages against the clinic were expected to be sizable.

This first counterattack, minuscule though it was in relation to the magnitude of the work to be done, had a major impact. The Nehemiah Foundation was abruptly in the news. Conservatives, traditionalists, and believers suddenly had a champion and an organization with means, around which they could mobilize.

Of course, the case sent shock waves through the homosexual community as well. Their rage against Trumbull and the Foundation was savage, and their rhetoric unrestrained. But the damage was done. Trumbull had pulled back the curtain on a respected mainstream gay operation ever so slightly, but the glimpse was enough to reveal the irresponsibility of gaydom as an institution, its potentially deadly blight on the community, and the extent to which it would go to protect its own interests.

★ ★ ★

Chase McKenzie followed the story with intense interest. He brought on his program the family of the boy who had been victimized. He followed this with a debate between the family's lawyers and a spokesman from the Lambda Legal Defense Guild. The result was a complete rout of the gay spokesman, and one of Chase's best shows ever.

He began to hold Senator Trumbull in even higher regard.

10

At the head of the table presided Percival Garden Monnoye, handsome, elegant, poised, a New Yorker descended from ancient Old World families. To his left sat Wynn Pritchett, earthy, bawdy, bluff, a Southerner. Across from Pritchett sat the morose May Berg, daughter of a wealthy Wall Street lawyer.

At the foot of the table, respectfully unobtrusive, sat Monnoye's chief factotum, Tristram Kramer, ready to take notes, handle calls and interruptions, signal for the next course of the meal, and perform other duties that might arise in the course of the dinner.

There was an empty place for Leon Pound, the shadowy character who handled Monnoye's most delicate and dangerous assignments. Sudden, unexpected business had called Leon back to Washington.

Upon reflection, Monnoye was just as glad Leon had left. It would be better to keep him separate from his colleagues. Still, Leon was a shrewd judge of character—far more so than Tris—and Monnoye always liked to get his assessment of the players and the action after a big planning meeting like this one.

Monnoye's table in Upperville glittered with opulence, but not beyond the bounds of good taste. He did not stint at providing the best of everything for his closest associates—on whom he no longer had to make an impression. They knew it and were quietly flattered.

A rank of fine crystal goblets, one for mineral water and one for each type of wine, stood at the head of every place setting. The ancient silver, lying wonderfully heavy in the hand, was engraved with the quartered arms of de Monnoye and de la Roche-Guyon in such exquisite detail that it almost took a magnifying glass to decipher.

The menu was sybaritic: pâté de campagne, a feuillantine of lobster in ginger sauce, a roularde of melt-in-your-mouth tenderloin with fresh grilled mushrooms, a mixed salad with artichoke hearts. Only Monnoye's wine cellar could have provided a Chateau Filhot sauterne, with the best Louis Jadot Montrachet, and a Chateau Virelade bordeaux, all at the same meal.

Wynn Pritchett, whose modest if not humble south Alabama origins had accustomed him to simpler fare, had begun to develop a taste for Monnoye's dinners. His lifestyle was beginning to show. He was as tall as Monnoye, but heavier, with unruly hair and a deeply florid complexion. His suit was as costly as Monnoye's elegant Italian design, yet did not fit him quite right.

Pritchett had risen from modest origins to become one of the nation's most powerful media magnates. He was neither redneck nor Bourbon aristocrat, but somewhere in between—a notch above "good ole boy."

Vain, ambitious, and "not quality," as Southerners traditionally put it, Pritchett was driven to surpass his "betters" by attaining wealth, with which he hoped to purchase the social status he coveted. Gregarious and clever, Wynn Pritchett reveled in the astonishing success of his broadcasting conglomerate, the Satellite Information Service, and the power and deference it brought with it.

Ironically, Pritchett had launched his career as a traditionalist and conservative. He had taken an active part in the "Reagan Revolution" of the 1980s. But when the conservative political tide began to ebb, Wynn sold his soul rather than be swept out with it. He threw in his lot with various Northeastern moneyed interests promoting the New World Order and an end to the traditional American polity.

And as his communications empire grew to global proportions, he put it at the disposal of P. Garden Monnoye, gave him his own public affairs program, and became Monnoye's most important ally and devotee. But he knew—and Monnoye knew—that he had embraced the gay rights issue and the New Age agenda not from conviction but simply from expedience.

Pritchett was, in fact, a heterosexual of the womanizing variety. He secretly held homosexuals in contempt. At least he thought his attitude was a secret.

But Garden Monnoye was a good appraiser of those around him. He knew that Pritchett's ostensible support of homosexuals was a matter of self-interest. And his contempt for Pritchett matched the other man's secret contempt for him. In Monnoye's view, Pritchett was not the type that deserved to enjoy such a huge fortune—that privilege should be reserved for genuine elites.

But at the moment their interests converged. Monnoye needed Pritchett's media empire. Pritchett needed Monnoye's political and financial connections—and May Berg's—as well as their entrée to the elevated social milieu that he could not attain on his own.

As for money, occasionally even Pritchett needed new infusions of cash, and Monnoye always seemed ready to invest some of his vast holdings in new initiatives at SIS.

From under hooded eyes, May Berg darted rapid glances from one man to the other. She listened to the banter between the two men with distaste. In fact she exuded suspicion and belligerence, as if coiled to strike back at the slightest provocation.

But the grim exterior concealed a quick and subtle mind. In fact, among all those present, she was the shrewdest, as well as the most militant and implacable in her antagonism toward the old order. And even though Monnoye, with his wealth, personal charm, and huge following had surpassed her to become the unchallenged leader of the homosexual community in America, he still deferred to her whenever possible, partly out of policy but partly out of a genuine respect.

Despite their seemingly vast differences, Monnoye, Pritchett, and Berg had something fundamental in common. They represented America's modern aristocracy of wealth and influence.

The dessert dishes were cleared away, and the servants brought silver urns of coffee and tea, then left the house as ordered. Kramer left his seat and checked through the house and outside, to make sure they were alone.

Then they got down to business.

★ ★ ★

"Well, my friends," Monnoye began, "I guess you'd all agree we have a problem. This Senator Trumbull is not a threat we can afford to take lightly."

May Berg scowled across the table at him. "He wouldn't be such a problem if it weren't for that loose cannon McKenzie giving him a national platform. Otherwise he'd just be another reactionary bigot in the Senate. His colleagues can't possibly take him seriously. And without McKenzie, he wouldn't be able to go national. But if he forges a permanent alliance with McKenzie . . ."

Pritchett nodded. "May's right. It's his access to the media that worries me. I saw some ratings on 'Pulse of the Nation' last month. The DBN promo really worked. More people watched that show than any other similar broadcast in the same week. Course, most of 'em were in the usual places. The South, the West, you know. But that Trumbull show was a hit. And now McKenzie has a much bigger national audience, and his share's goin' up every week. We got to do something about him."

"Yes." Thoughtful, Monnoye put his fingertips together. "We have to figure out a way to deprive Trumbull of a beachhead in the mass media, and that means separating the two of them somehow. Or getting McKenzie to part company of his own volition. Any ideas how to do that?"

"Make him an offer he can't refuse," May said suddenly.

Monnoye looked at her wide eyes blazing in that pinched face. "Could you be more precise?" he finally asked.

"It's simple, Perce. Why would he want to stay with a network like DBN when he could double his audience overnight on SIS? Wynn, make him an offer. Bring him on board *your* network. Give him his own show."

"Uh—yeah, May, but that would defeat the purpose. If he's a threat, why give him a better soapbox?" Pritchett asked reasonably.

May laughed, and a note of scorn crept into her voice. "You guys! You're supposed to know how to maneuver in this town. Pay him twice what he's making now, dummy. Let him get used to that fine salary. Give him all kinds of perks. Special assignments. Exotic travel. Executive lunches.

"Sure, he'll hurt us for a while maybe, but not enough to do any fatal damage. He won't be putting Branch Trumbull on the air anymore. And you can start in subtle ways to retool his image, tone him down. Then, when you've really got him hooked on the good life and the big bucks, you can start putting the squeeze on his message."

Monnoye smiled faintly. "It's known as co-opting. Right, May?"

"Sure. It's the oldest trick in the book. And it'll also have the benefit of disarming your critics, Wynn—the people who say SIS lacks political balance."

"I see," said Pritchett dryly. "If you can't lick 'em, pay 'em to join you."

"Pay anybody enough," May said, "and you've got them. And when he's been replaced at DBN—and you're sure there's no chance of him going back there or to some other network—which you, Wynn Pritchett, could surely arrange—then dump him."

Monnoye played idly, thoughtfully, with his knife. Finally he said, "Why don't you give it a try, Wynn?"

"Well, I will, Perce. But d'you really think we can buy off this jerk?"

Unlike his cynical colleagues, Monnoye believed some people in the enemy camp could not be bought. He suspected Branch Trumbull was one of them. But maybe this Chase McKenzie didn't have the same iron in his character as the senator.

Could the man be bought? Monnoye wasn't sure. That was preferable to the only other alternative, taking Trumbull out of the picture—and maybe McKenzie too—by more extreme measures. Trumbull was the primary threat, not McKenzie. But Trumbull was too powerful to be attacked directly—they had to try the indirect approach. And one indirect approach was through McKenzie.

"It's worth a try," Monnoye said.

"I guess if it doesn't work, we can always try somethin' else," Pritchett conceded.

Monnoye was accustomed to creating consensus rather than applying superior force, although his preeminent status in their circle was undisputed. Every now and then he had caught, out of the corner of his eye, Wynn Pritchett smirking at him. And though Wynn never challenged him directly, Monnoye feared someday he would. The man clearly bore watching. But in the meanwhile he had proved himself not merely useful; he was indispensable. And so far, when Monnoye offered a suggestion, Pritchett usually took it as a command.

"Yes, why don't you approach McKenzie then, Wynn? And, May, let's you and I stay out of it totally. He knows me, and I understand he doesn't hold you in the highest esteem."

"About as low as I hold him. And as far as I'm concerned, he's an insect. The kind I'd like to step on."

"OK, then. It's agreed. Good luck, Wynn. There's no one else who could arrange this better than you. And listen, if you have to make him too generous an offer to—uh—gain his cooperation as it were, then don't let that deter you. Maybe Pathfinder Corporation, or even one of Paragon's subsidiaries, could sponsor another program that would put some more money into SIS. That would offset any losses owing to McKenzie, wouldn't it?"

"Well, sure it would," Pritchett replied enthusiastically. The message had been clearly sent and clearly received.

"And just so we don't have all our eggs in the McKenzie basket, I've got some other ideas that might neutralize Trumbull."

May Berg was immediately inquisitive. "What kind of ideas?"

"The key to Branch Trumbull is religion. It's his primary strength. But as in judo, perhaps we can turn his strength to weakness and exploit it."

"Oh, nobody pays much attention to those Bible-thumpers anymore."

"True, except his own people do. And if he gets them stirred up . . ."

Monnoye did not underestimate the strength of the traditional, religious communities. Fortunately they had been in a purely defensive mode for nearly a decade and now had limited impact.

If the religious fanatics could be kept on the defensive and bottled up, they would simply wither away eventually. But a Branch Trumbull or a Chase McKenzie could lead them over onto the offensive. Such men would have to be stamped out—at all costs.

"So what's your plan?" May demanded.

"I can't honestly say it's a full-fledged plan yet, May. But I'm beginning to learn from you. If Trumbull wants to use his mangy religion against us, we'll just have to get some enlightened ministers and priests to denounce the bigotry and homophobia that hides behind the religion."

May wrinkled her nose. "I don't know, Perce. I'm not sure I want to get involved with religious people of *any* type."

"I'm not suggesting you have to convert," Garden replied stiffly. "But we have to fight fire with fire. You're the clever one in this group, May. I'm just taking a page out of your book." He turned to Pritchett. "What do you think, Wynn? Wouldn't that idea work?"

"Yeah, if you do it right. In fact, an attack on Trumbull from religious circles could hit him where it hurts the most. First, you might reach some religious people who aren't reactionaries and fundamentalists. If it's really done right, it'll even confuse a lot of the fundamentalists. And what's more, Trumbull won't expect to be hit from that direction."

"Well, go ahead, if you think it'll work," May said grudgingly. "But I still think we should rely on the usual proven means. Undermine him politically. Isolate him. Separate Trumbull and McKenzie. Embarrass them both. Destroy their credibility. Drive a wedge between Trumbull and his Senate colleagues.

She rattled on. "Isolate him from the White House if we can. That's a big part of Trumbull's power base, you know. He was Jim Darby's best friend when they were in the Senate together. Their wives are still best friends."

"You're right, May," Monnoye conceded. "We have to counterattack on a broad front. Hit him from several directions at the same time."

Just then the portable telephone, no bigger than a pack of cigarettes, buzzed on the thick glass tabletop next to Tristram Kramer's dessert plate. Kramer picked it up, answered in monosyllables, and nodded vigorously.

"Hold on a sec," he said into the mouthpiece, then brought the phone to Monnoye at the head of the table.

"Garden," he said, "it's the call you've been waiting for."

Monnoye put the phone to his ear. "Monnoye . . . You're sure it's him? . . The Boston shuttle? . . Well, he could be going anywhere in New England. But I'm willing to bet it means he's heading for P'town. Is there time to get a team in place to follow him from the airport? . . That's great. Good work, Leon. Very good."

He listened to Leon Pound for a moment longer. "Right. I'm leaving tonight for Europe for the July Fourth holiday. I'll arrive in Merano about midafternoon on the third, and I'll be there a week. Report to me there when you hear from your team. When you're sure."

He replaced the phone on the table and grinned triumphantly.

"What is it?" May Berg and Pritchett demanded in unison.

Monnoye smiled. "A sighting. Someone that just might help put some teeth in these ideas we've been floating. Anyway, it certainly raises interesting possibilities. I'll tell you when things become clearer."

Monnoye's tone was pleasant but firm. It was a favorite technique to reassert himself at the end of a meeting, repairing any loss of control he might have incurred by appearing too conciliatory. Now he was clearly back in command, and the strategy session was at an end.

"Well, wish me bon voyage," he said cheerfully. "I'll check with you when I get back and see how it went with McKenzie. That's your mission, Wynn. I'll handle this other matter myself."

★ ★ ★

Two good looking men in their late twenties, dressed in jeans and sports shirts, lounged at the entrance to Logan International Airport's passenger terminal next to a gray Mercedes 200SL. A third man, the team leader, was inside, standing expectantly by the shuttle's arrival gate and holding a copy of the *Boston Globe*.

The Mercedes was fully equipped with an array of state-of-the-art communications gear, and Leon Pound had just transmitted to the car's fax machine a photograph of the man who had embarked on the shuttle at Washington National Airport.

Passengers began to stream through the arrival gate, and Leon's agent scanned the faces of the male travelers. Periodically he glanced down to compare them to the grainy but still legible picture concealed in the folded newspaper.

Soon the subject appeared, dressed in a blue blazer and polo shirt and carrying a folding suit bag. There could be no mistake about his identity—long dark hair, a lock falling across his high forehead, a long nose dominating an equally elongated face.

Hanging back a few yards, Leon's man followed him through the concourse to the rental car counter. By this time the agent was close enough to overhear the name in which he had reserved the car. The name did not match the name Leon had given the surveillance team, but that did not matter. The use of an alias only confirmed the team leader's suspicions.

He rushed out to the waiting Mercedes.

"Quick," he ordered. "He's getting a rental car. Pull around to the Hertz exit."

They watched the visitor emerge from the rental car lot in a red Buick. Pulling into traffic a discreet distance behind him, they followed as he drove through the Sumner tunnel into Boston. Then, as they had anticipated, he took the throughway south, heading along the bay through dreary South Boston and Roxbury. Once past the 128 cut-off, he turned onto the Southeast Expressway and went toward Cape Cod or possibly Martha's Vineyard.

At Buzzard's Bay they slowed to see if he would turn south toward Falmouth and the ferry to Martha's Vineyard or Nantucket Island. But he continued on Route 3, following the main road as it gradually looped east, then up the curving peninsula on the Mid-Cape Highway north toward Cape Cod. By now there was no doubt—he had to be going to Provincetown, next to Fire Island the most popular gay destination on the East Coast.

Cape Cod jutted eastward into the Atlantic from the shoulder of southern Massachusetts like a flexed arm. The forearm encompassed Cape Cod proper, with its scenic seashore, culminating in the fist at Provincetown—land's end—on the tip of the peninsula.

Soon P'town came into view. A strand of pearls, quaint clapboard houses bleached white by years of wind and sun, strung across the level sands against a rich blue backdrop of sea and sky.

The subject checked into the Watermark Inn. Shortly after, he went out for a drink at the Boatslip Beach Club, arriving just as the tea dance began, a favorite event of the gay and lesbian crowd that flocked to P'town in season and out. The young men shadowing him blended in with the others, casually dressed, trim, fit, and obviously well-to-do.

Their quarry had changed into a short-sleeved shirt of flowing dark blue silk, opened wide at the neck, a pair of very short, tight white shorts, and slip-on canvas deck shoes. An attractive man, he was lithe and tanned, with the casual yet studied elegant look popular among the up-scale Cape Cod gays. Yet there was nothing effeminate about him, nor any look or mannerism that openly declared him a homosexual.

Two hours later the subject emerged from the Beach Club in the company of another man. The surveillance team member on the passenger side of the Mercedes screwed on a 200mm telephoto lens and shot several frames of the two as they left.

Still at a discreet distance, the Mercedes tailed them down Commercial Street and back to the inn. Just before entering, Leon's men were able to record part of their conversation with a long-distance, highly sensitive directional microphone and overheard without surprise that the two subjects were going back to the visitor's room.

In the meanwhile, a third member of the team rushed the partially exposed roll of film to a one-hour developer. He then took the prints around to the Beach Club and paid the bartender $20 to identify the faces in the photos.

And then he reported back to the rooms the team had taken at the Watermark Inn.

"Did you find out who the pick-up is?" the leader asked him.

"Yeah, it was easy. His name is Wensley Ballard. He's pretty well known in town. An artist."

"Gay?"

"Sure."

The next day, Leon's spies tracked the two men unobtrusively for hours, shooting more photos and recording snippets of conversation. The team watched as they walked out into the bay's expansive sand flats at low tide and observed them lunching intimately at Ciro & Sal's. While the two gallants were out wading among the periwinkles and sea grasses on the sand flats, one agent managed to slip into the subject's room and plant a bug. As it happened, their target was not just a homosexual but was into dominance and sadomasochism as well.

"Well, I think we have all we need," the team leader said at breakfast. "I'll report in to Leon, and then we'll head back."

★ ★ ★

There were plenty of places Monnoye could go to get away. He had property all over the world, some under the family corporation, some under the Foundation, and some simply privately owned residences.

His main headquarters were in New York City, where he owned a spacious rent-controlled apartment overlooking Central Park, close to the offices of Pathfinder Corporation. Pathfinder was the revolutionary computer software invented by his brilliant but reclusive father, and the source of his immense wealth.

The Paragon Foundation also had a New York office, a small walk-up on 51st Street. But New York had become virtually uninhabitable. The affluent areas of Manhattan were no longer safe from the crime that had steadily risen in the 1990s to engulf the city. Although one could not say the civil order had completely broken down, New Yorkers dreaded that they were coming close.

Monnoye spent most of his time shuttling between his villa in Hyeres on France's Côte d'Azur, his condos in Vail and San Francisco, and his Washington headquarters.

Garden Monnoye's good looks, wealth, and charm assured him access to the most select gay circles wherever he went. But promiscuity was rife in all those places, and his anxiety over exposure to HIV, even though he took every precaution, began to spoil the fun of his usual travels.

That left his favorite trysting place, the luxurious Hotel Schloss Freihof. Once a medieval castle, the Schloss was now a five star hotel, perched high on a picturesque peak overlooking the resort town of Merano in the Italian Tyrol, the lovely northern part of Italy that once belonged to Austria.

On his rare visits to the Schloss Freihof, Monnoye found peace, beauty, and serenity. He enjoyed the finest wines, the most epicurean meals, the most elegant decor and surroundings.

There he could withdraw to a mountain aerie, while the deadly AIDS plague was kept at bay in the valleys and hinterlands of the outside world. And there boys were available who were especially procured from Italy, Germany, or Austria, depending on his taste at the time.

After recruitment, HIV testing, selection, and partial payment for services to be rendered, his European procurer would segregate the boys in a special villa for a period of time equal to HIV's incubation period plus a week, then have them HIV tested again. Those making the final cut were supervised closely on the trip to Merano, then tested again on arrival. Only such diligence could relieve the gnawing fear in Monnoye's gut that the deadly virus would someday track him down.

On the other hand, his travels gave him the change of perspective that helped set his thoughts in motion and endow them with greater clarity. He always hatched his most ingenious schemes during these vacations in Merano, and good things always seemed to happen to him at the Schloss Freihof. He had met Tris Kramer here, next to Leon Pound his most loyal and competent lieutenant.

Now he had gotten the best news in a long time, a lengthy report from Leon Pound. If he handled the information intelligently, it would give him a powerful lever at the pinnacle of the US government—the nerve center of the White House itself. For the man his agent in Washington had spotted heading for Provincetown, the man whom Leon's team had followed, bugged, and photographed frolicking with Cape Cod's gay community, was none other than William P. Kerrigan, the president's chief counsel.

Well, Mr. White House Counsel—Monnoye smiled—*we have tapes and photos of your latest assignation. Very interesting material, especially to a president who loves to talk about traditional family values. You don't know it yet, Kerry, but you and I are about to become fast friends.*

NEWS ITEM,
the *Des Moines Tribune*

In a hotly debated, late-night session, the Iowa state Senate yesterday voted to approve the Human Rights Amendment to the US Constitution. The Iowa House approved the measure last week. The narrow 48-41 Senate vote makes Iowa the thirtieth state to accept the Amendment, which would grant full civil rights to gay and lesbian citizens. Thirty-four states are needed to ratify the Amendment and make it part of the Constitution.

11

Eddie Webb cursed silently as he pulled the big black van off the highway and into the rest center on I-20. During the long drive from Little Rock, his mind had been on other things, and he had forgotten to make the turn south at Jackson.

Consulting the road map, he concluded that it was just as quick to continue on now to Meridian and then head south on I-59. That would take him a bit out of the way, and he groused that there was nothing to see and nothing to do in this nothing state of Mississippi. But I-59 appeared to be the shortest route from where he was. It was a fast Interstate all the way to his destination.

He continued east on I-20 through boring, flat, sandy plains and scrubland. Scrupulously observing the speed limit meant that even the locals in their pickups passed him constantly, casting curious glances at the windowless, black van with the California tags. Eddie Webb was on the way to one of the country's prime gay meccas, New Orleans, where life held out new promise—new people and, above all, a new job.

It had been hard to leave California. But after the great earthquake, there really hadn't been much to stay for. The state's economy had been in steep decline for years before the quake. Skyrocketing taxes, strangling business and environmental regulation, social unrest and riots, unrestricted immigration that swamped the state's education system and social services—all these trends had conspired to throw the state into bankruptcy several times.

At least the film industry had survived, providing him an occasional gig—until the Big Quake in '97. Now even the movie industry was devastated. The big studios, or what was left of them, were scaling back and moving to Phoenix or Santa Fe or even farther afield, and nobody seemed to need a free-lance film editor. Nobody, that is, except the porn filmmakers. One of them, an old friend from California, had had the foresight years ago to move to New Orleans.

Recently Eddie had done some free-lance videotaping in Denver and had edited a short documentary in Little Rock. The income from those jobs would get him to New Orleans as well. There he had the promise of a job.

He would miss the freedom and openness of California. On the other hand, the heat was getting a little too close up and down the West Coast. He was confident he had always been extraordinarily careful. He always checked everything out, never behaved in any way that would excite suspicion. But sooner or later you could slip on that hidden banana peel. Maybe it was a good thing he was moving on to virgin territory.

Virgin territory. The very term stirred him. What could be more virgin territory than conservative, Bible-belt Mississippi? Here the people were simple, unsophisticated. They probably don't even lock their doors at night. And in that instant an idea was born.

Eddie turned off the Interstate in Hattiesburg and gassed up the van, taking the opportunity to study his map again. A secondary highway, US 11, crossed the Pascagoula River ten or twelve miles away, and there was sure to be a bridge. A bridge with a landing and access to the river. He had made his best hit in just such a setting.

Backtracking northward on 11, he came to the Pascagoula, and sure enough there was a bridge with a broad, flat, muddy parking area under it. He turned slowly off the highway, checking carefully in each direction for other cars—highway patrol—before he did so.

And yes—it was too good to be true—a boy, fifteen or sixteen, sat fishing off the bank. There were a few trucks with empty boat trailers parked, but no one else in sight and no outboard engine noise to herald the approach of a boat from the river.

Eddie parked sideways to make sure the boy could not see the California plates. He presumed that California's reputation in Mississippi was as bad as Mississippi's was in California.

He got out and sauntered over casually as if to inspect the riverbed and the concrete boat landing that extended into the water. Then, keeping his hands tucked in the pockets of his jeans, he turned to the boy.

"Hi, there, son." He put on a convincing Southern accent, one of the skills he had picked up from so many years in the movies. "How's the fishin'?"

"Not doin' much." The boy seemed neither suspicious nor overfriendly, neither sullen nor alert.

"Whatcha catch here mostly?"

"Oh, I'm bottom fishing for catfish. And we get a few bass now and then."

"What kind of bait? I'm here to do a little fishing myself. Taking a little vacation. Why work when you can be fishing, right?"

Eddie caught a glimmer of a smile.

The boy seemed relaxed enough. "Night crawlers," he said finally.

"Say, son, how about a Coke?"

The boy cast a hesitant glance toward the van, and Eddie now wished he had thought to paint it some other color. It looked ominous there in the shade of the huge willow trees.

"Well . . ."

"You sit tight," said Eddie. "I'll get them."

Eddie brought back two frosty cans. He gave the boy one, then sat quietly and sipped on his own drink.

The day was hot, and the boy seemed to welcome the refreshment. He drank greedily and soon finished.

Eddie laughed quietly, a polite chuckle. "Say, you were thirsty. How about another one?"

"No, thanks, that's OK."

"Come on. Got plenty in the truck."

"I really oughtn't—"

"Tell you what," Eddie said. "I won't give it to you then. I'll trade for some good information on fishing around here. Where the good spots are. What lures to use and so on. Deal?"

"OK," said the boy, after a thoughtful pause.

Eddie fetched another drink, and they sat and talked idly about fishing.

The boy told him about the best places along the river and the best techniques. He was obviously proud of his knowledge and his prowess as a fisherman.

"If Moselle Landing's such a good spot, why're you here? You don't seem to be catching much," Eddie observed.

"Well, that's too far to go on my bike."

"I see. Where do you live. Hattiesburg?"

"No, sir. Eastabuchie."

"East of where?"

The boy grinned. "No, sir. The town's called Eastabuchie. It's about three miles."

"Oh, I see." Eddie laughed and noted the boy's relaxed smile. "Say, if you don't have to get home right away, and since you're not catching much here, why not let's drive up to that landing?"

Before he could finish the suggestion, the boy's brow furrowed. Whether from alarm or from weighing the offer, Eddie could not tell. But he backpedaled at once, fearing he had pressed the boy too quickly.

"No," Eddie said. "On second thought, maybe that's not a good idea without telling your folks. Shouldn't go off with strangers, right?" He smiled broadly.

He saw with relief that the boy was reassured. *Got to play this one carefully, reel him in slowly.*

"Yessir," the boy replied, as if embarrassed at having to honor the family guidance in the company of so affable and harmless a visitor.

"Parents pretty strict, are they?" asked Eddie sympatheticly.

"Well, my mom kinda is. My dad don't live with us."

"Divorced?"

"Yessir."

"Well, don't feel bad, son. That's pretty common these days. It don't mean a thing. By the way, what's your name?"

"Danny. Danny Hopkins."

"Well, whatya know. My name's Dan too. Dan Stilwell. How d'ya do, Danny." He extended his hand, and they shook warmly.

They sat close together now and gazed quietly at the hypnotic rippling surface of the brown river until young Danny broke the spell by rebaiting his hook.

"Your mom let you go out with girls?" Eddie asked suddenly.

"Some. But they ain't many girls around here I like."

"But you do like 'em, don't you?"

"Oh, yessir, I do like 'em."

"Ever kissed one, Dan?"

The boy blushed, then smiled, nodding. He seemed to like the adult version of his name and being treated almost like an equal by this likable man. Eddie guessed that the boy missed his father.

"Well, after all, Dan, you're nearly a grown man. Not too soon to be learnin' about these things, you know. "

He pulled a photo out of his shirt pocket, one of his best pieces, and handed it to Danny.

The effect on the boy was immediate and profound. Newly awakened adolescent desire warred against caution and guilt, and Eddie could ascertain the victor from the slightly glazed expression on the boy's face.

"Whaddya think, pardner?"

"Well, she's really somethin'. I've seen some like her in magazines at the drugstore in Hattiesburg."

"See, Dan, I'm a professional photographer. I took that one. Got plenty more. In fact, I make movies too. I got movies like you wouldn't believe. I bet you never saw a live skin flick before, have you?"

"N-no, sir. We don't have 'em here."

"Well, come on over to the truck. I got my gear right inside. VCR and tapes and everything. And you can stay right here at the landing and watch them."

"Well, I don't know . . ."

"Oh, come on. It won't hurt you any. A man's got to learn these things some time. You should be glad I happened along. I'm glad I did. You sure gave me some good tips on the fishing around here, and this is the least I can do to pay you back."

"I really shouldn't." Danny was still holding the photograph, his wide eyes drawn irresistibly to it.

"Well, Dan, it's up to you. But you already looked at the picture, and it hasn't hurt you any. I've got to tell you, though, there's a whole lot of difference in looking at a still picture and looking at them on film. I hate for you to miss this chance."

The boy glanced quickly around the landing, a slight look of fear showing through the curiosity on his face.

"Well, maybe just one," he agreed at last.

The boy stood and pulled in his line. He wrapped it around the cane pole and secured the hook, then picked up the bucket and tackle box at his feet and looked at Eddie expectantly.

"Come on then, Dan. And we can both have another Coke while we're at it."

They walked toward the waiting van, now darker than ever under the weeping willows in the failing afternoon sun.

★ ★ ★

Dixie Meggs, twelve, sitting silently behind the leafy curtain of the hanging willow branches, wanted to shout, *Don't go with him, Danny! Don't go!* But she was uncertain and confused, and the words stuck in her throat.

She had followed him down to the river on her bike hours ago. She had settled herself patiently under the canopy of willows, well back in the shadows, so she could watch him and daydream about him without being seen.

She had never loved anyone as she loved Danny Hopkins. But she had embarrassed him only day before yesterday, earning a tongue lashing. She had followed him to the ball field and stood watching him from behind the wire-mesh backstop, while he and other kids from school played a game of late afternoon baseball.

Two days before that she had tracked him down to the big cane patch south of town where he had gone to cut a new fishing pole. There they had been alone, and he had kissed her.

Don't go with him, Danny.

But Danny seemed to know the man. They had been talking and drinking Cokes ever since the man pulled up in his van. Maybe this was the uncle Danny was always talking about. But the uncle wasn't from California, was he? And this man didn't act like a family member. The way they shook hands . . .

Of course the man didn't look dangerous either. He was just a stranger, that was all. Yet Mama had always warned her. Never, never go anywhere with a stranger.

Anyway, she knew if she were to burst out of hiding, if she were to scream out to him, Danny would never, never forgive her. He would never speak to her again.

Please stay here, Danny. I love you. Please don't go with him. Please.

But Danny, smiling the strange smile she had never seen until that day in the cane patch, climbed into the back of the black van.

12

There's no other way to deal with this man."

Garden Monnoye gestured at the *Wall Street Trader* on his desk. As he read it that morning, a chill had settled in upon Monnoye's soul. *Trumbull understands. One of the few who does.* He looked directly at his agent. "You know what to do, Leon."

"Yeah. I've already got somebody in mind."

"From out of town?"

"Right. Just like you said. Has all the traits. And we've got the leverage."

"Toby?"

"Yeah, Toby."

"All right. Good. Go ahead with the planning."

"Right. Uh . . ." Leon paused expectantly. When Monnoye did not respond, he nodded. "OK, then. I'll leave right away, unless you have anything else."

Garden placed a friendly but not intimate hand on Leon's shoulder.

"No, I don't. Good night, Leon."

"Night, Perce."

"And, Leon."

"Yeah?"

"Thanks. You're doing a marvelous job."

Monnoye called Leon Pound his secret agent. That was the man's exact function—and his history. Pound was a former CIA agent—a field man, operations, not a policy-and-statistics analyst from Langley. He had served in the Middle East, then later in Eastern Europe in the late 1980s. He had been case officer for several high-ranking Communist apparatchiks in Poland and Hungary.

His field work eventually came to the attention of the KGB. In reviewing their file on him in Moscow Center, they discovered a weakness that Leon had frequently indulged in Cairo and Damascus, a weakness common in those cities. It was a simple matter for highly experienced KGB operatives to trap Leon in a homosexual operation. When they could not turn him, they compromised him to the Agency to get rid of him.

Monnoye had always thought it greatly to Leon's credit that he had preferred disgrace and dismissal rather than to betray the Agency and his country. The man could not be expected to deny his own sexuality. But he had shown integrity when caught up in the cruel intolerance of the straight world.

Later, when Leon was unemployed and down on his luck, Monnoye had learned about him and acquired his services, sexual as well as professional. Now he paid Leon handsomely and gave him meaningful work to do. Though he had ended their intimacy after a time, he trusted Leon completely.

If Toby Giton did turn out to be their man, Garden Monnoye wanted no personal contact with him. He could not afford to handle the negotiations for such a sensitive mission himself. But he needed more than a cut-out, as Leon called it—a connection breaker. He needed someone who could act on his behalf, yet be relied upon to carry out the mission with Monnoye's own attention to detail. That narrowed his choice to one person. Leon himself.

★ ★ ★

This is old hat, Leon said to himself. It was just like putting the squeeze on those hapless bureaucrats in Prague and Warsaw to recruit them as informers for the Agency.

Pound had asked Toby to meet him at the Paradiso Restaurant near Washington Square in New York's Greenwich Village. The restaurant had private dining rooms in the rear, and the gay proprietor was a reliable friend. Pound had no difficulty in arranging to be admitted discreetly through the kitchen entrance. Now he waited in a small reserved dining room for Toby's arrival.

He scrutinized the man carefully as Toby entered the semi-darkened room, trying to reassess his suitability for the mission from the first physical impression.

Toby Giton was not a tall man but was well-built and compact. Apparently he worked out regularly to stay in shape. Pound noticed that the disease had not yet begun to ravage his frame or features, and he carried himself with a certain grace, like a boxer or dancer.

Giton sauntered over to Pound's table, looking at him warily and scanning the empty room. He wore a cynical smile.

"Hi, Toby. Thanks for coming. I'm Leon Pound." Leon offered his hand.

Giton took the extended hand listlessly, then sat down.

"I've heard of you. Mind if I have some?" Toby Giton poured himself a glass of wine from the nearly full bottle on the table.

"Not at all. I thought what we have to discuss might go better with some lubrication. I'm told you're fond of it."

"Yeah, too fond. So what else have you been told? You seem to know who I am."

Aggressive type, thought Pound. "You're pretty well known around town."

"Yeah? What do you know?"

"For starters, that you're unemployed and nearly broke."

"Yeah," he said truculently. "Well, that's not unusual these days."

"I also know you're HIV positive," Leon said quietly.

Toby Giton did not respond, but Pound noticed his jaw clench.

Then Giton smiled his chilly smile again.

Pound continued, but in a suddenly severe tone. "I also know that you're still sleeping around, that you're deliberately giving it to people."

"I don't have AIDS. I'm just HIV positive. And I'm not sleeping with guys, not anymore," he protested. "Just women —whores. I swear."

"You must find that distasteful. I assume you have a reason for this commendable policy of discrimination."

Toby gripped his glass, staring into the dark liquid. Finally he answered. "It's just not fair for gay men to be dying by the hundreds every day. And the whole world blames us. But *we* didn't cause it. Somebody, or something, gave it to us."

"And so you're giving it back. Right?"

"I guess you could put it like that. Look, Mr. Pound—"

"Call me Leon."

"OK, Leon. It's just that—well, for years the government didn't give a hoot about AIDS and didn't do a blinking thing about it, just because it was killing queers. So I figured if enough other people had it too—I mean, if AIDS was killing off the straight world like it's killing us—then they wouldn't blame us for it. And the cruddy government might get moving and find a cure."

"The hookers pass it on to their straight johns, right?"

"Right."

"And so the virus continues to spread among straight people. And the more it spreads, the less it's a gay disease, right?"

"Right."

"Very ingenious, Toby. You're an idealist, a real crusader."

Leon Pound's sarcasm was all the more savage because of his own secret disappointment that Toby's scenario had not come to pass.

In the early years, public health officials predicted tens of millions of heterosexuals dead by the turn of the century, unless the taxpayers ponied up more money for AIDS research, education programs, and free condom distribution. The plague had grown exponentially, but the so-called mass breakout into the general population never materialized. AIDS was for the most part still a disease of gay men and drug abusers.

"Toby," Leon Pound said, "I don't think you give a flying rip about the gay community. You're just mad at the world because you're going to die from this plague, and you want to take as many people with you as possible. Am I right?"

"No, no! That's not it."

"Has it ever occurred to you, Toby, that if word got out about this, you'd do more harm to the gay community than a dozen Branch Trumbulls?"

"What d'you mean?

"The bigots and homophobes would love to have ammunition like this. They'd blame you, and they'd blame all the rest of us for what you're doing. No, Toby. You're not helping the cause. You're going to set us back a hundred years."

Toby Giton hung his head and stared at the inside of his wine glass.

"So you're going to stop sleeping around, aren't you, Toby?" Pound said in as menacing tone as he could muster.

"I—"

"Because if you don't, Toby, there're some powerful people in the city that'll see to it you get turned over to the public health authorities. Or the cops. And then you'll die in jail. Not even New York will tolerate what you've been doing."

Toby squirmed but did not look up.

Leon knew he had him. He began to take a more conciliatory approach. "On the other hand, if you really want to help the gay community, there's something you can do. And it would give some meaning to the rest of your life."

This time Giton gave him a puzzled look.

"Furthermore, if you accept the proposition I'm about to make and do a little job for my friends, we'll see you get the best medical treatment and long-term care in the best private facility in the country. Who knows? They might even find a cure by then."

"What is it you want me to do?"

"We want you to eliminate Public Enemy Number One."

"Eliminate. You mean kill?"

"Precisely."

"But why me? I'm no killer."

Pound snorted. "You are. By your own admission."

"But that's different."

"No, you're our man, Toby. You're just mad enough to do it. You want to avenge yourself on the world, and we're going to channel that desire into something useful. And you're a sick man, Toby. You look and feel OK now. But someday, maybe soon, you'll get sicker and sicker.

"And I don't have to tell you what lies down the road. You're going to waste away—in agony. But if you do this for us, we'll take care of you. You'll get every possible drug, including some new ones that slow down the symptoms. They're not approved yet by the FDA, so you can't get them anywhere else.

"We've also got access to the Army Medical Center at Walter Reed and the new vaccine they're working on. They say there may even be a true cure, Toby. If there is, you'll be among the first. And in the end, if you do have to check out, at least with our care it'll be relatively painless. And like I said, with us maybe you'll live until they find a cure."

Leon Pound saw the flicker of hope in Toby's eyes. The man was not wholly convinced, but he was on the way.

"But why d'you need me? Why not do it yourself? And who's the man?"

Leon ignored his last question. "My friends can't have any connection with it. So I suggested somebody with no ties and no record, so it'll look like the 'spontaneous outpouring of rage from a too-long victimized community.' We need someone who doesn't have much to lose," he went on, "and everything to gain. Somebody just like you, Toby."

Toby Giton said nothing, but Leon could tell he was close to a decision.

One more push.

"And one more reason," Leon added.

"Which is . . ?"

"Which is that you have killed before. You never got caught and have no record. But we know."

Toby said nothing, but his eyes widened.

"It's OK, Toby," Leon said soothingly. "We certainly don't hold it against you. It's a qualification, in fact. Proves you've got the stuff. It also proves that my principals have vast resources, including resources of information."

"Who is it, and how will I get away?" Toby asked after a long pause.

"We've planned the whole operation, including your escape, and we'll help. Money, equipment, resources are absolutely no problem." The man probably suspected a setup.

Toby scowled. "Well, if you can do all that," he demanded, "if you can guarantee the perp gets away, why *not* do it yourself?"

"Because there's some risk. Things like this don't always go according to plan. If it fails, or the perp gets caught, then better you, frankly, than my—uh—principals. Or me. But like I said, we'll do all we can to make sure you don't get caught."

"Well, I still don't know. I keep asking, who's the public enemy?"

"You can't guess?"

"No. I don't read the papers much."

"Senator Branch Trumbull."

"Oh, yeah, him," Toby said brightly, almost as if pleased. "It figures." But then his face darkened. "Well, after all, he is a US senator. I just don't know. I'd have the whole flippin' government after me. What if I decide not to do it?"

"Then we'll report you to the authorities and demand in the good name of the gay community that you be locked up. And if we demand it, it will happen. You'll die slowly, rotting in some stinking prison hospital ward. And all alone. Nobody'll care. And the gay community'll get credit for our public spiritedness in stopping a homosexual Typhoid Mary."

Toby Giton blanched. "I think you just convinced me, Leon."

"Good. I thought you'd see it our way." Leon reached into his inside suit pocket, pulled out a thick brown envelope, and handed it over.

Toby hefted it and looked at Leon with a question in his eyes.

"It's five thousand dollars. In cash. And an open plane ticket from New York to Denver. And it's all yours. I wouldn't bother reporting it to the IRS and giving Sam his share. They're all small bills and all clean."

A pleased look came over Toby's face. "And whadya want me to do with it?"

"Go have a good time. Take a vacation. Go to Key West. Fire Island. P'town. Eat, drink, be merry . . ." Leon did not finish the sentence. "Then call the number on the card in the envelope. Someone will meet you at the Denver airport. I want you there no later than the end of the month to start your training. And your regime with the new drugs."

Toby opened his mouth, then seemed to think better of it.

Leon read his mind. "Because five thousand is not enough, that's why," he said in a steely voice. "And because there's more where that came from. And finally, Toby, because of the drugs. Because you might be one of the first to get a real cure. So, will I see you on the thirtieth? Or will I have to send one of my goons down to South America or someplace to get our money back?"

"Oh, no," Toby said hastily. "I'll be there. I'll be there."

★ ★ ★

Irene Hopkins did not lose a moment in calling the county sheriff and the state police as soon as Dixie Meggs burst in, wild-eyed and crying.

Dear Lord, he's all I got. With shaking fingers, Irene dialed the battered old rotary phone in the kitchen. In a near hysterical voice she claimed for certain that Danny had been kidnapped, fearing that the slightest note of uncertainty on her part would result in a routine pursuit.

She hoped for the best. *Maybe he really hasn't been carried off. Maybe he'll turn up any minute now.* But in her heart she feared the worst.

Danny was a good boy. He seldom gave her trouble. But she knew he had a wild streak that had intensified without his father around to knock some sense into him from time to time.

But she could not imagine what possessed him to get into a van with a total stranger. *California!* She thought everybody knew what kind of folks came from out there. Where was Danny's mind! Thank God for Dixie. That was one smart girl. Came riding on her bike fast as she could. Thanks to her maybe the state troopers could catch him on the highway before he got away. *There can't be many black vans with California tags.*

Southern law enforcement had the reputation of being dilatory, unconcerned, even incompetent. It wasn't. The stereotype had been reinforced by decades of obese, drawling, tobacco-spitting sheriffs contemptuously portrayed in films and television. But local police agencies in the rural South were no more incompetent than any other institution in this age of pervasive irresponsibility.

When word came in to the highway patrol net that a local boy had been kidnapped and the subject was driving a black van with California tags, an all points bulletin went out immediately. All units on patrol sped to the search.

The arrest was unbelievably easy. A patrolman spotted the van only a few dozen miles south of Hattiesburg on I-59 near Poplarville. Hours had passed since the APB, which told the watch commander that the kidnapper—if indeed he was a kidnapper—had lingered quite a while in the Hattiesburg area. That was unusual behavior for an abduction.

By radio, state troopers quickly established a roadblock south of Poplarville, and two pursuing units were ordered to close in on the van from the north. Twenty minutes later the van stopped at the roadblock. The driver pulled off the road as directed, making no attempt to escape, and the patrolmen closed in around him in the grassy median.

An officer hauled the driver out and frisked him against the side of the van. The lieutenant in charge opened the back, hoping to free a relieved kidnapping victim. But there was no sign of Danny Hopkins. No clothing. No fishing tackle. No bloodstains. No other sign of foul play.

"What's this all about, officer?" demanded the driver plaintively.

The lieutenant saw the man was clearly shaken up by the arrest. But that was normal and certainly was no indication of guilt of any kind. And he seemed harmless enough.

"What's your name?"

"Edward L. Webb."

"Address?"

The man gave the address indicated on his driver's license. Santa Monica, California.

"I don't think I was speeding, was I, officer?"

The lieutenant said nothing, but doubts began to enter his mind. The report had been so emphatic, but this character, though appearing reasonably strong, didn't seem to be the violent type.

He peered into the van again, looking for a clue, a detail, anything that would connect the man to the alleged kidnapping.

The van had been customized. There were two plush chairs and a bunk, under which were cabinets containing electronic and video gear. Individual and banked flood lights with reflectors were stowed overhead. A television monitor and VCR stood in a stout wooden rack fitted into the heavily upholstered and carpeted interior. An unusually thick layer of insulation covered the walls and roof, something the patrolman had never seen before.

"Officer, can't you tell me what I'm charged with?" asked the driver, more insistently this time.

"What's all this insulation for?" the lieutenant countered.

"Well, officer, I'm a filmmaker," he replied in a friendly tone. To the policemen he had that common I'm-trying-to-be-helpful sound, with only a little stress in his voice. "I do documentaries and things, you know. Sometimes I have to do my editing and sound mixing right here in the van, and I have to keep the equipment cool, and I can't afford to let outside noise ruin the tape—"

He stopped abruptly.

The lieutenant looked at him doubtfully. Noise abatement could work in both directions. "Whatcha got here?" he asked, scrutinizing Webb as he pulled on a pair of supple kidskin driving gloves. If there was a crime, he wanted fresh prints from the scene, not his own.

"Oh, just video tapes. Movies, you know."

"How 'bout show me one."

"The whole thing?"

"No, just a sample."

The patrolman watched Edward L. Webb closely. The man had begun to sweat. But that could be from the heat and from the normal stress of being stopped by the law.

Webb put a tape into the VCR and turned it on, along with the TV set.

"Runs off the truck battery, does it?" the patrolman asked.

"Uh, not exactly. Sometimes I use an auxiliary generator. And I got extra batteries—" Again he stopped—as if fearing he had said the wrong thing?

The officer looked around the interior and the cab but did not see a likely place for an extra auto battery.

The movie was a steamy porn flick, highly erotic, though nothing worse than the lieutenant had seen as a young marine years ago in San Diego. But it gave him a funny feeling. True, there was no evidence at all of foul play, no body, no blood. But still . . .

"Pull up the floor," he ordered suddenly.

During the hours that had passed, the state troopers had gotten a search warrant, but this was just one of those inspired guesses springing seemingly out of nowhere that people call a hunch.

Edward L. Webb's smile turned ghastly, a sick grin that faded into fear.

Two troopers levered up the carpeted floor, exposing an eight-inch space underneath. There were the batteries to power the video system. There also were two handguns, loaded, and an assortment of knives and edged weapons.

The officers continued to remove portions of the false floor—easy to do, for it was made in sections and notched to fit around the chairs and other fixtures—moving toward the front of the van.

They uncovered a macabre, chamber-of-horrors assortment of chains, handcuffs, whips, and a knotted wire garrote. Some of the implements showed traces of dried blood. Then, in a stout wooden rack bolted to the true floor of the van, they saw another dozen video tapes.

Why here, and not with the porn flicks? The lieutenant picked one at random and thrust it into the VCR.

The other patrolmen were now gripping Edward Webb tight at the open back door of the van.

The lieutenant stared at the screen. Hardened as he was to the depravities of his fellow men, he found himself unbelieving as the video rolled.

"Get the techs here right away," he radioed. Then he motioned toward the squad car and stripped off his gloves. "OK—" he struggled to keep the rage out of his voice "—let's take the scumbag in."

13

Astride two fine Tennessee Thoroughbreds, Branch Trumbull and his son rode side by side along the towpath of the old C&O Canal. The track followed the canal all the way from Georgetown in the District of Columbia to Cumberland, Maryland, near the headwaters of the Potomac. For most of its length, the towpath ran within sight of the river, providing a well-maintained route for hikers, bikers, and horsemen through some of the most peaceful and lovely scenery in the nation.

The heat and humidity of August had given way to the cooling breezes of September. In Washington, the summer months were cruel, and those who could left for other climes until fall rolled around. But duty had held the Trumbulls prisoner in the area—the Senate was still in session. Now Branch IV—"Banks"— had surprised them by popping in for the weekend from Chattanooga, where he was a senior at the McGillie School. It was the first cool day of the season, and father and son had decided to get some fresh air and exercise.

The nickname was the boy's own doing. When learning to talk, that was the best pronunciation of "Branch" he had been able to manage, and the name had stuck. For a time his older sister, Elizabeth Christian—Libby—called him "Twig." But Banks hated the nickname devoutly. It was the only thing that could make him furious at his beloved sister, and she had wisely dropped the practice.

Branch could tell something was on the boy's mind.

"Dad, I've got to make a decision about my National Service Corps obligation," Banks said finally in a troubled voice.

"There's no decision," Trumbull said, trying not to sound too peremptory. "You're not going into the NSC, period. You're going to college."

"I know how you feel about the NSC, Dad." Banks obviously was trying hard to sound reasonable. "But it *is* an obligation. And a lot of my friends are telling me to go ahead and get it out of the way. I just don't want a year-long commitment hanging over me after I get out of college."

"Well then, take ROTC. Get a commission and go in the army."

"But Dad, I really don't *want* a military career. And even a Reserve commission would mean two years active duty, then four in the Guard or Reserve. Besides, the army's changed a lot since you were in. Even the Guard has changed."

Trumbull frowned. "I'm afraid you're right about that. In fact you don't know the half of it." He fell silent, recalling his own service in Operation Desert Storm, when the US military had been at the peak of its combat efficiency.

"Then you just won't do either," Trumbull continued. "But you're not going into the NSC."

"That's fine with me, Dad. I feel the same way about it you do. I just wanted to get it out on the table and hear you say it. 'Cause you know there's a penalty if you don't fulfill the obligation."

"Well, the penalty's mostly financial. In fact it's not really a penalty. You just can't get government benefits and so on if you don't 'volunteer.' But Banks, most so-called government benefits are anything but that anyway. And fortunately, we don't have to worry about money. It's those millions who depend on the government, like for National Health, that concern me. They don't have much choice."

The two rode on. The stillness was broken only by the sound of horses' hoofs, the occasional honk of a Canada goose overhead, or other people passing them on foot or bicycle.

What to do about the NSC obligation had become an wrenching dilemma for many families, especially Christians and others of like conscience. In 1996, citing the nation's growing unemployment, indiscriminate gang violence, crime, prostitution, and drug use among youth as its rationale, Congress had passed legislation establishing the National Service Corps.

Though NSC was supposedly a volunteer organization, a

year of national service was made mandatory for young people between eighteen and twenty-four, and optional for all others. One could volunteer at any age, and the program was already proving popular among retired people who still had much to offer but few outlets for their talents. Service in the military or the Peace Corps of course superseded the NSC obligation.

Volunteers—NSCVs—received a small stipend and living expenses if they decided not to live at home. Those who joined before attending college received partial tuition payment (only at approved state institutions), or they were allowed to write off part of their existing college loan indebtedness by performing two years of national service after college. Also, those completing national service after college received a special payment for job hunting and placement assistance.

Though the legislation authorized $250 million for the NSC's first two years of operation, everyone, friend as well as foe, knew it was an open-ended obligation and would eventually end up costing billions.

The concept was popular with the nation's academic and media elite, though, and was enacted with a solid majority in Congress. Consequently, the newly elected president, having just barely squeaked into office, had reluctantly signed the bill into law.

Only Senator Trumbull and a half dozen of his colleagues had effectively argued against opening another chapter in the federal government's long history of substituting itself for the family, the church, and local self-help organizations.

Gay groups had lobbied Congress tirelessly during committee and floor action on the bill. The gay lobby's handiwork was evident in many of the bill's provisions. Benefits to NSCVs could be paid only in connection with nondiscriminatory institutions. This had the effect of delegitimizing many religious charities and organizations that did not condone homosexuality. A major venue of national service was working with AIDS patients in hospices and clinics. That meant the NSC added enormously to the gay movement's national clout by putting literally thousands of homosexuals on the national payroll overnight.

Christians of all denominations quietly took advantage of the opportunities the NSC offered them. Unobtrusively, hundreds of men and women of faith, mostly retired, joined the NSC and went back to the cities to work in the hospices with dying AIDS patients.

But in short order, roadblocks were designed to stop religiously motivated volunteers, and soon conservatives learned that they need not waste their time applying to the NSC. Fundamentalists and evangelicals, traditional Catholics, conservative Jews, and many Mormons were effectively disenfranchised.

This had a profound economic impact on thousands, since those who didn't volunteer for the NSC, meet the obligation in some other service, or get an exemption were blocked from receiving government benefits. It hurt considerably when families were denied student aid for college, and above all, when put at the bottom of the list for National Health Care.

Abruptly the light went on in Branch's brain as he and Banks walked their horses along the sandy trail.

"Banks, you've given me an idea."

"What, Dad?"

"The NSC is one of the worst things the federal government has ever come up with, and that's really saying something. I think it's time we did something about it."

★ ★ ★

As the last openly evangelical member in the Senate, Branch Trumbull was on excellent terms with key pastors around the country, presidents of Christian colleges, with editors and writers at numerous Christian publications, and with Christian broadcasters, on whose programs he appeared regularly. Those contacts and relationships were beginning to pay off.

As soon as the Senate recessed at the end of September, Trumbull did a fast-paced two-week tour. He made dozens of speeches, broadcasts, and Sunday church appearances. At the end of his itinerary, the Nehemiah Foundation's legal team had the names of hundreds of Christians who had volunteered for the National Service Corps and had been turned down.

Branch's team screened the names to eliminate those who really should have been rejected and still came up with a pool of several hundred who had been turned away for their beliefs alone.

A week later his lawyers filed a class action suit against the NSC in the Federal District Court in Roanoke. The suit asked for civil damages from the NSC and its administrators on the unique grounds that the plaintiffs had been subjected to an unconstitutional religious test for office. Furthermore, they had been denied due process in the resulting loss of college loans and grants and assignment of low priority for National Health.

Soon the Nehemiah Foundation received notice of a special audit from the Internal Revenue Service.

Branch, however, had anticipated this kind of counterattack. His taxes and paperwork were in excellent order, and he had four of the best tax lawyers in the area available on call. All were volunteers, which defeated one purpose of the harassment—to eat up the Foundation's operating funds.

In gaining passage of the NSC bill, its supporters had made a strategic blunder. By making the Corps a quasi-independent government corporation to free it from political influence (except their own), they had also made the NSC vulnerable to the kind of action now mounted by Branch Trumbull. Normally he would have found it impossible to sue the federal government. Now it was not only possible, but he also found allies within the government itself.

He called the president and asked him to instruct the Justice Department to enter the case on the Foundation's behalf with an *amicus curia* brief. President Darby was extremely uncomfortable with this kind of messy social issue, but he agreed to help his old friend.

While the suit was proceeding in Roanoke, he moved again, this time with a stinging critique of National Health Care in a *Wall Street Trader* guest editorial. On the same night he appeared again with Chase McKenzie on "Pulse of the Nation" to discuss the problems of National Health.

Private health insurance had been in bad shape since the early '90s. The escalating cost of AIDS was a major cause—AIDS payouts simply could not be matched by individual premiums. The weakness in the economy hurt the industry, and there was the simple matter of corruption and mismanagement. These converging factors seemed to presage the collapse of private health insurance.

Having helped create the crisis, the federal government felt compelled to step in and solve the problem with National Health. In 1995 the dream of the humanists and collectivists had finally come true—socialized medicine. It was not called that. It was named the National Health Care Program, and it extended "free" medical care to every American.

Now, hardly four years old, the National Health Care Program was in deep financial trouble. Even the most pessimistic cost projections had proved to be too low. The skyrocketing costs of AIDS patient care was overwhelming the system. The government's automatic response was to raise taxes.

With his *Trader* editorial and reappearance on "Pulse," Branch Trumbull once again made himself heard. Traditionalists across the country—lawyers, health experts, medical researchers, computer experts, public affairs experts, teachers, and specialists of all kinds—volunteered their time and talents. The Nehemiah Foundation was gaining enthusiastic support.

14

Chase once had a wide circle of friends and reliable contacts in the White House. But during the two years of the Darby administration, the number willing to talk to a conservative broadcaster had steadily shrunk. Of those who were left, his best contact was Barbara Dunhill, Director of Presidential Personnel, whose office handled all political appointments in the administration.

Barbara knew virtually everything that was going on in the administration. Her position was not considered a policy-making post, but she understood better than most that you could influence, if not actually determine, the government's direction by appointing the right people.

And since most of those lucky enough to get political jobs wanted to keep in her good graces, they stayed in touch and kept her informed on what was happening in their respective departments. Over time, Barbara had shrewdly turned her function as personnel gatekeeper into an informal political intelligence network.

Barbara Dunhill was highly principled, tough, and brainy, with high professional standards to match. She used her information sparingly, judiciously, when she thought it would help advance the things she believed in. But she kept a low profile. The few conservatives left in the White House had to, for simple survival, since Langdon Smith, the chief-of-staff, distrusted anyone who "had an agenda."

Barbara would not talk to reporters while at her office in the West Wing. She was not one of those who fed tidbits to the press in order to undermine a rival or wage a vendetta. But she would direct information to the media if it would help sabotage executive policies she thought were harmful to the president and to the country.

Chase had her personal unlisted number. He knew generally

when to reach her at home in Alexandria. But to his surprise, one night she called him at eleven o'clock, a worried tone in her voice.

"Barbara, glad to hear from you," he said with genuine warmth. "What's on your mind?"

"The usual rules, Chase?"

He believed she trusted him, and he had never betrayed her trust. But as a matter of principle as well as habit she always got his commitment for nonattribution in advance.

"Yes." He recited the litany. "This'll be just for my use, so I'll know how to shape the story, and where to look. It's not for broadcast, but for background only. No attribution, and no identification as a White House source."

"OK, good. Well, today I heard some very disturbing news. The president's not going to sign off on Justice's recommendation to take the Bar Association out of the clearance role for federal judges."

"What do you mean, he's not going to sign off on it? I thought it was a done deal." Chase was genuinely surprised.

"It was—as far as the attorney general was concerned. But somebody got to the president, Chase. You know how he is. He means well, but his own convictions aren't very deep, so the last person who gets to him wins the debate."

"What somebody?"

There was a long pause on the other end, and Chase's journalistic sixth sense told him a major story was about to unfold. He could also tell that Barbara knew far more than she wanted to say. Or perhaps she was putting herself at risk and was searching carefully for the right words.

"The answer to that question is really why I called. It's more significant than the ABA decision itself." She took a deep breath. "It was engineered by Kerry Kerrigan."

The president's chief counsel.

Chase knew the man only by name. Kerrigan had acquired little in the way of reputation, good or bad, and had seemed typical of the gray men who inhabited the White House.

As far as Chase could tell, Kerrigan's main concerns had always been to draw his fine salary, enjoy the White House perks, stay out of trouble, and wait for a chance in a big law office somewhere. Kerrigan was a lawyer after all. Derailing the Bar Association decision was an easy way to earn credits with the bar that he might cash in at a later date.

"Yeah, him," said Barbara glumly.

"Do you know why?" There had to be a good reason to countermand a decision of this magnitude and antagonize the attorney general in the process. "Is he just making sure he has his golden parachute when he leaves the White House?"

"No, I don't think so, and that's why I'm troubled. This caught everybody over here by surprise, especially since the president likes the attorney general, and this is a definite poke in the AG's eye by Kerrigan."

"But nobody knows, Chase, except that he's suddenly behaving way out of character. All of a sudden he's taking a hard line against Justice, and he's lobbying hard inside the White House to jettison 'all this traditional values crap,' as he was overheard calling it today."

Chase mulled that over. "Why can't the AG get to the president and talk him back into the idea?"

"Kerrigan obviously thought of that. He's fixed it so the decision was put into motion before the AG could intervene. I think he's got the chief-of-staff on his side. And I've got to tell you, Martin is hopping mad at being blind-sided. I think he may even resign."

"Don't let him do that, Barbara. That's just what they want. He's the only guy with any guts left in the administration."

Martin Bell, the AG, was one of those frequently criticized in the liberal media, and thus in the White House, for "having an agenda."

"That's exactly what I told him. I think it settled him down a bit. But I also had to tell him to watch his back. Kerrigan's giving the impression of a man with all the zeal of a new convert—"

"Convert to what?"

"I don't know, Chase. But suddenly Kerrigan's a man with a mission. And as I was about to say, indications are he won't be content just to block the Bar Association coup. He really seems to want Martin out of the administration all of a sudden. If that keeps up, then I'm afraid Martin's position is going to deteriorate inside the White House."

Chase frowned. *This isn't just your usual contest between rivals over who gets the corner office.* "Is there anything you can do?"

"I'm not sure. To tell you the truth, I'm probably in trouble myself. Most people over here know I'm close to Martin, and I wouldn't be surprised if Kerrigan's been maligning me to Langdon Smith."

"What can I do? Would it help to put Bell on my show?"

"I'm not the best judge of that. It might actually hurt him more than it would help."

Chase thanked her for the information and hung up, puzzled. He was not totally surprised. He knew the cowardice and compromise that characterized the highest levels of the White House. But this was odd.

It has the earmarks of a gay activist's operation. Maybe it's time for a little investigative reporting.

But Barbara was the only one he knew in the White House. Who could provide the next link in the chain?

Well, at least he could invite Martin Bell on the program and let him talk about the Bar Association. It would be Bell's call, of course. But the broadcast could be structured to keep him out of trouble in the White House, yet still help shore up his base among traditionalists and conservatives. Cabinet officers appeared on talk shows every week. There was no reason the AG shouldn't do the same to defend a position taken publicly by the president.

The next morning he placed the call to Bell's office. The AG was not in, and the executive assistant promised to have him return the call quickly. In ten minutes Chase's phone rang.

It was not Martin Bell on the other end of the line, however. To his astonishment a Southern voice drawled, "Well, great, Chase, I've found you. This is Wynn Pritchett."

* * *

Toby Giton felt absolutely marvelous, refreshed if not altogether rested, after two weeks in Florida at Leon Pound's expense. He had spent a week sampling Miami's delectable night life, where he especially enjoyed its Latin flavor, a new experience. Then it was on to Key West, where he had enjoyed the sun, sea, and despite his medical condition, even a little sex.

But now it was time to go to work. As he deplaned at Denver International airport, he began to experience a queasy, anxious sensation that wasn't just the unaccustomed Colorado altitude.

A trim and fit, smiling young man in tight jeans, calling himself Rudy, met him. The youth took his luggage, and they shuttled to the satellite parking lot, where Rudy threw the bags in the backseat of a new Range Rover Clansman.

"Ni-i-i-ce car."

"Yeah, it's a beauty," the young man replied. "And you ought to see it off road. Goes straight up the bleeping mountain. And it's great on the highway too. So make yourself comfortable. We've got a long ride."

"Where are we going exactly?"

"You'll see. You'll see. Here—" he retrieved a pillow from the backseat "—get some rest. You look a little tired. And there's beer in the cooler, if you get thirsty."

Toby gratefully snuggled down against the leather seat, and soon the motion and steady hum of the road lulled him to sleep.

He awoke hours later to the rocking motion of the vehicle navigating a plateau between two high hills. They had left the pavement and were riding over a well-traveled, rutted dirt road.

Eventually they arrived at what looked like an old ranch, and Toby scanned the scene curiously to assess his temporary new home. He saw a rustic but spacious two-story log house. Barns. A bunkhouse. Other outbuildings. Nearby was a corral holding a half dozen horses. A pickup truck and Jeep stood by the barn. The ranch seemed to have everything but cattle.

"Welcome to Big Sky Ranch," said Rudy, pulling up in front of the main house.

Toby followed his escort into the ranch house, through an open well-lit great room decorated in typical Western motif, and upstairs to a comfortable pine-paneled bedroom.

"Bathroom's through there. We'll eat in one hour downstairs," Rudy said and left Toby alone to survey his new surroundings.

Dinner was simple but delicious and filling. At the table, in addition to the young man who drove him to the ranch, was another one just like him, down to the neatly trimmed mustache and tight jeans, and a much older man, tanned and weathered, iron gray hair clipped short. They introduced themselves only by their first names.

The older man spoke first, in a heavy Western drawl. "Evening, Toby, and welcome to Big Sky Ranch. Call me Jack. This is Rudy, who you've already met, and that's Nick. If you need or want anything, ask one of them. Now, I guess you're wondering why Leon had you brought all the way up here."

"Yeah, I was."

"Well, first, he wanted you to be comfortable. And second, he wanted you to get the best trainin' available anywhere. Course, the kind of training I do is best done away from pryin' eyes, so he sent us all up here for a couple of weeks."

Toby nodded to show he understood.

"I'm going to make you the best marksman with handgun, assault rifle, and shotgun in three states. And, if we got time, maybe teach you a little 'bout demolitions as well. So take it easy, relax, and get a good night's sleep. We'll start first thing tomorrow."

Toby had expected he was at some sort of boot camp, where he would run around in camouflage fatigues, shout cadence songs, and generally feel foolish. On the contrary, the training was relaxed, sedate, almost academic.

Jack was an excellent teacher. He made the entire experience interesting, even fun. He mixed practical training with pithy lectures on the theory and nature of firearms. He covered the mechanical function of the weapons, the various types of ammunition, and how to handle stoppages and misfires. Then the physiology of shooting and the basics of gun handling and safety. They spent long days on a professional shooting range in a pasture near the ranch house, and Rudy or Nick brought out cool drinks and excellent picnic lunches.

First came the handguns, a heavy Colt .45, then a Beretta 9 millimeter, and then a much lighter Glock 9 millimeter.

"The frame's made of a high tensile plastic—space age stuff," Jack explained when Toby remarked at how light the Glock was.

"Remember," Jack coached him over and over, *"squeeze* the trigger. Squeeze it, don't jerk it."

Toby fired at human silhouettes and bulls-eye targets for hours every day until he could reliably put ten rounds into a three-inch circle or into the kill zone of the silhouette. Then they started with the long guns. They fired two types of automatic rifle, a Heckler and Koch, and a Colt AR-18 carbine.

After the rifles came the shotgun. Toby spent hours on clay targets, learning to keep both eyes open, swing through the target, shoot, and follow through. *Just like golf or tennis,* he thought.

Then Jack put a piece of cardboard in the center of an old tire and sent it rolling across the firing range. Toby learned to hit this moving target with the assault rifles and another shotgun customized for combat.

At night the four men enjoyed the excellent meals prepared by Rudy or Nick. They were also Toby's medical orderlies and checked him thoroughly every day, giving him doses of the promised pills morning and night.

For relaxation they played cards, watched movies, took walks, or went horseback riding. Occasionally they took a Jeep ride up into the rugged hills behind the ranch where to Toby's amazement Jack popped off a startled, speeding jackrabbit at forty yards with the Beretta.

His housemates were friendly, if a little distant. Jack was professional and superficially friendly but never talked about Toby's mission. *I wonder if he even knows,* thought Toby.

As the second week of intensive training and coaching opened, they went back to the handguns, as if to repeat the cycle. Toby was a fair shot by now, and Jack began to lay on the finer points. He had Toby hold out the weapon until his arm began to wobble, then showed him how to squeeze off a round as the circular motion brought the muzzle across the target.

Toby absorbed the lessons, fired hundreds of rounds, and then one day could no longer contain his curiosity.

"Jack, do you know what I'm training for?"

"No, I don't. And I don't want to know. I get well paid for turnin' you into a marksman, and that's all."

Toby remained quiet for a while, then asked, "Jack, have you ever killed a man?"

Jack squinted at him hard, tight-lipped. Finally he said,

"Yeah, lots of times." His tone and his expression warned Toby not to pursue the subject, and Toby looked away.

"Look, if you're worried whether you can do it when the time comes—well, that's natural. But don't worry. By the end of my trainin' you'll be so good it'll be second nature. Just another target. All you have to do is get within range and let your trainin' take over, OK?"

"OK," said Toby.

"Good. End of conversation," growled Jack and handed Toby another full magazine for the Glock.

To Toby it was an extended vacation. He enjoyed the shooting and began to take pride in his new skills. He had everything he could possibly desire—except sex. Jack was clearly straight. Rudy and Nick were gay but obviously had been warned. When they knew you had It, he reflected, there was no such thing as safe sex.

But that would all change when he got back to New York. He had met a man in Miami, a networker for Friends Indeed, the new matching and dating service exclusively for HIV positives.

Suspicion and fear of AIDS had cast a pall over the whole gay community. People were always checking each other out, showing or demanding test results—which could easily be faked or be out of date. You just couldn't fall into bed with someone as in the old days.

But then some genius had come up with a brilliant idea. Once infected with the virus, there was no reason not to have sex with others who also had HIV. And for a fee of $500, Friends Indeed would match HIV positives in complete confidence. The only stipulation was that no full-blown AIDS patients were accepted.

Toby still showed no signs of the disease, although he had noticed a slight loss of energy. And thanks to Leon and his principals, Toby now had some wonderful drugs to keep AIDS at bay, and plenty of money. If he could just get Leon's job over with, he might find he still had something of a future.

After two intensive weeks Toby felt he was as good a shot as he was ever going to be. He said so to Jack, who agreed. He had crossed the threshold to instinctive shooting, and it was time to get out of here.

The isolation was beginning to tell on him. A ranch in Nowhere, Colorado, was fine for a while, but now he needed some night life, some action, some company. He began to long to return to Fire Island, where he would call on the man from Friends Indeed. There he could shake off his dread of the call from Leon, which he knew would be coming, and enjoy himself until they were ready for him.

Late that afternoon Jack came into Toby's room.

"I believe you're ready," he said gruffly. "As ready as I can make you, anyway. Here."

He flung a black nylon bag on the bed, unzipped it, and lay the two halves open. On one side was the Glock pistol and the Colt AR-18 carbine. The carbine was broken down and stowed in Velcro holders. On the other was the Remington shotgun with the black combat stock, its barrel also removed for stowage and travel.

"This is yours," he said. "You got the three weapons and a basic load of ammo." He paused, fingering the rough checkering on the shotgun's stock. "I thought the Glock would be best." There was an unusually solicitous tone in his voice.

Well, thunderation, Toby thought, *I think he's actually proud of me.* "Yeah," he agreed. "I like the Glock."

"Course, you realize this is not a carry-on bag." It was the closest thing Toby had seen to a smile on Jack's face in more than two weeks.

"Yeah, I guess not." Toby smiled back. "But even if it's checked through, how'll I get it out of the terminal? New York's got the toughest gun laws in the country. They inspect incoming bags for stuff like this, even on domestic flights. Just like Customs."

"You're not going to New York," Jack said evenly, his trace of a smile fading. "Leon wants you in Washington."

★ ★ ★

It was the first time in years that Chase had chosen not to return to the McKenzie farm for Thanksgiving. He felt slightly guilty. His mother was old and getting frail, and he feared in a few years she would follow his father, who had died in 1996. His older brother and sister would be there, along with their passel of children. And he knew the entire family would give him grief about getting "saved."

The question of religion had alienated him from his super-devout mother and siblings, and he rationalized that he would not be missed anyway. He would see them all at Christmas. That would be enough.

But on reflection he faced up to the true reason for his reluctance to go—his blossoming relationship with Neeley Durant. He was proud of her—or at least of his conquest. She was the kind of woman any man would be proud to display in the drawing rooms of Georgetown and Washington and at cocktail parties in Alexandria and McLean. But he was not so sure he would be as proud to display her at home.

His parents had nagged him for years to get married and settle down. Of course, he had been having too much fun as a Washington media star and political street brawler to think seriously about settling down. And his mother was always urging him to marry a "good Christian girl," whatever that meant. He supposed it meant some insipid little choirgirl from the Valley. And that he could not accept.

He was certain that taking Neeley home without some prior warning or explanation would throw the whole family into turmoil and subject him and Neeley both to a barrage of embarrassing questions. And though he was a grown man, Chase was still not ready to hurt his mother in this way—nor, frankly, to submit himself to the whole family's puritanical disapproval by parading before them the obvious fact that he was "living in sin."

Then an unexpected invitation came, making it even easier to excuse his absence from the traditional family gathering. Clare Trumbull dropped him a gracious note inviting him to take Thanksgiving dinner at the Trumbull home in Potomac.

He called back to RSVP and for the first time heard Clare Trumbull's charming, slightly husky voice. He could almost visualize her soft beauty through the telephone lines. He liked her immediately.

"Hello, Mrs. Trumbull, this is Chase McKenzie. It's kind of you to invite me for Thanksgiving. I'd be delighted to come."

"Oh, Chase, call me Clare. We're delighted too. Branch has told me so much about you, and we thought this would be a wonderful chance to relax and visit—away from the pressures of Washington and the Hill. And you can meet the children."

"The children?"

"Yes, our son, Branch the Fourth—Banks, we call him—and our daughter, Libby. And Jimmy Tolliver will be here with his wife, Janet. You know Jimmy, of course."

"Yes. But I haven't met his wife."

"Branch didn't say—you're not married, are you?"

"No, not married."

There was an inflection in his voice that Clare Trumbull obviously caught. "Is there perhaps a future Mrs. McKenzie? Or anyone you'd like to bring?"

Chase hesitated a moment, then replied, "Yes, as a matter of fact. If you don't mind, I'd like to bring my friend Neeley Durant. She works at the RNC. I believe the senator knows her."

"That's fine. We'll be delighted to have her too."

★ ★ ★

That night Chase dropped by Neeley's apartment, which occupied the third floor of a stately old townhouse close to Capitol Hill. He had a key, although he was careful not to intrude on her too much, or too soon. She seemed glad of his company. And she had once remarked casually that he ought to move in with her—for security reasons, she said.

Personal security had become the nightmare of everyone living on or near the Hill. Nightly muggings, rapes, and murders were common. Few people felt safe, despite the vastly increased police patrols demanded by an irate and frightened Congress.

But Neeley refused to move. Her fine old apartment was too comfortable and too convenient to her office at the Republican National Committee, just two blocks from the Capitol.

Chase was sipping her best Scotch when she arrived. She slipped out of her coat, kissed him, and began to putter around in the kitchen for a quick supper.

"Neeley, we've been invited out for Thanksgiving dinner."

"Oh, who?"

"Branch Trumbull. They live in Potomac," he added brightly, assuming she would be pleased to spend the day with a prominent Republican senator.

140

But Neeley did not appear pleased. She did not answer, except with a furrowed brow.

"What's wrong? Don't you want to go?"

She clattered a pan. "I was rather hoping you and I could spend the day together—alone. Maybe take a trip, a picnic, or something."

"Well, that would be fun. But we do that a lot already. It never occurred to me for Thanksgiving too. I mean, Thanksgiving's a time for a big, traditional meal with lots of friends or family. Don't you think so?"

"No, not necessarily. Anyway, I'm not sure I want to spend it with the Trumbulls."

Chase decided to confess. "To tell the truth, Neel, I've already accepted. For both of us. Come on and go with me."

She seemed suddenly to make up her mind. "No, Chase. I think it's a big mistake to get too tight with Branch Trumbull."

He did not want to quarrel or let his disappointment show, fearing that would cede too much power to her. He said finally, "Well, I think I'll go. I already told Mrs. Trumbull I would."

Neeley did not reply, but he noticed she slammed the cabinet doors harder than normal, and the noise level of the clattering pots and pans increased. The rest of the evening was shot. He knew that.

He went into the kitchen and put both hands on her shoulders as she stood with her back to him, facing the stove. Kissing her in brotherly fashion on the cheek, he said gently, "I'm going to shove off. I've got a lot to do. Night, Neel."

She turned in surprise. He thought she seemed a little sorry to see him go, but it was best that he did. Neeley was a strong force. At all costs he had to be the one to control the relationship in order to safeguard his self-respect—by which he meant his pride. On the other hand, he did not want to appear angry. *Studied indifference. That's the best way.*

He smiled at her from the door. "G'night, Neeley."

"Good night, Chase," she said in a tight voice.

15

He had seldom had such a wonderful Thanksgiving dinner or a more enjoyable visit. The Trumbulls possessed the gift of hospitality and made him feel at ease from the moment he arrived.

Banks was there, a serious but likable teenager, with his roommate from the McGillie School. Jimmy Tolliver was there with his wife, Janet, a plain-looking but vivacious brunette. And there was Libby, the Trumbull's daughter, just arrived that morning from Bristol, where she worked as director of public affairs for Crown College.

Chase had a tendency to compare every woman he met to Neeley. Few women could surpass her, and that always boosted his ego. Libby Trumbull, twenty-six, was as different from Neeley as night from day. First, she was younger, though she had a grave, sensible maturity about her that belied her years. Neeley was closer to him in age and experience, and he attached considerable weight to the fact.

But Libby, he decided, was quite pretty. She was blonde and fairer, with a softer, less dramatic beauty than Neeley's. Neeley was tall, statuesque, voluptuous. Libby was shorter and lithe. Though Neeley's hair was a light brown, her skin was dark. She had dark flashing eyes and pulsed with animal energy. He sensed spirit and fire in Libby too, but her fires were banked, and, instead of feral wariness, in her eyes resided kindness and sparkling good humor.

He listened to her conversation at dinner, on the rare occasions when she spoke. *She's witty, bright,* he noted, *and on the whole . . . well, joyful.*

In fact, there was something about both Trumbull women that gave him an unexpected sense of well-being. He found he liked being with them as much as he was stimulated by Branch

Trumbull's company. Clare Trumbull had a deep and mature beauty but, above all, kindness, warmth, peace, and harmony in her nature. Libby, he concluded, was a lot like her mother.

Branch was obviously much in love with Clare after all their years of marriage. Proud of her too, but not exactly in the same way Chase was proud of Neeley. What was the difference? he wondered. Whatever it was, it was elusive but fine, and a sudden doubt crept in that he and Neeley would ever experience it.

The day was bright and crisp, perfect for outdoor activity. After the meal, Banks, his roommate, Janet Tolliver, and Libby decided to go out for a game of tennis. Chase was tempted to join them, but the roommate completed the foursome. Chase's tennis was just mediocre anyway.

Besides, this was an opportunity to get to know the rest of the Trumbull circle better. Chase followed the Trumbulls and Jimmy into the spacious den, where they all subsided into leather-covered armchairs before a cheerful fire. Letting their dinner settle, they sipped coffee.

Chase picked up the thread of dinner conversation and said with a chuckle, "Senator, you know, you really have the queers on the run. What's the latest bombshell from your foundation?"

There was awkward silence. His hosts looked down at their hands.

Chase sensed that he had committed some sort of faux pas. "I'm sorry. Did I say something wrong?"

Branch Trumbull smiled indulgently. "Chase, you're not only an honored guest, you're a friend, and for the world I wouldn't make you feel uncomfortable. But we just don't use the word *queer*."

"Oh, I see," said Chase, still a little mystified. "I wasn't aware it was such an epithet. After all, they use it themselves, you know."

"I know they do. But it's still an attack word when *we* use it."

"Well, I apologize. I certainly didn't mean to offend anyone. It's just that since we're all fighting this battle together, I thought . . ."

Trumbull continued to smile his exculpatory smile. "I know you didn't mean to offend. And it's true—we *are* in this fight to-

143

gether. And you have no idea how glad I am you're on our side. But it's important to understand what we're fighting. For my part, I'm not interested in attacking homosexuals as individuals—only their agenda."

"I don't quite follow you, Senator."

Clare broke in. "What we mean, Chase, is that we have to distinguish between the person and the act. We want to treat all individuals with respect. But we can do that and still preserve our freedom to condemn immoral behavior."

"I see." Chase tried to be humble but couldn't restrain a touch of sarcasm. "As my mother says, 'Hate the sin, but love the sinner'?"

"That's it exactly," Clare said, in her low, mellow voice. "Every individual has innate worth. But not all *actions* are worthy. One goal of the humanist revolution is to obscure that distinction."

"So that you're considered a homophobe if you don't endorse what they do," volunteered Jimmy Tolliver.

Chase hesitated, then decided to dive in. "Well, that's all very lofty, but I'm telling you, I've dealt with these people. I *know* what they're like as individuals—a lot of 'em, anyway. They're vile, and I personally can't stand them." He paused for breath. "You should see our news tapes of the latest Gay-Lesbian Day Parade in San Francisco. It's bizarre beyond your wildest imagination. Naked and half-naked men, women, and some you can't tell the difference, dancing and copulating on top of their floats. All of them shouting the big 'F' word. You just can't believe this is happening in the USA. And it makes me mad. I don't think you can fight this effectively unless you do get mad."

"Chase," Clare said gently, "I'm not minimizing how awful it is. But our concern is also for you. Are you sure there isn't more involved here than just righteous indignation?"

"Well, but—sure, I'm indignant."

Branch looked at him sympathetically. "We agree with you, Chase, except in one regard. You have every right to condemn that kind of behavior, but you've also got to get the personal hatred out of your system. Remember, you said it—we can hate the act, but not the person."

Chase could only raise his hands and shrug.

The senator went on. "I really don't mean to criticize you. I value your friendship more than you know. Your help's been priceless, and I want to continue working with you. But for that very reason it's important that you understand us. You may feel you have good reason for hating these people. But, you see, hatred is part of the root problem. We can't win by meeting their hatred with hatred of our own. This is a spiritual battle we're in, and our secret weapon is the love of Christ. In fact, it's our only weapon."

"Well, forgive my saying so, Senator—" Chase put up his hands again "—but that sounds naive. To me it's simpler than that. We're dealing with simple conspiracy here. And the conspirators are a small, influential group of people with a clear plan of action and no scruples about what they'll do to achieve it. It'll take a lot more than love to stop them."

"I know they have no scruples. But it's not exactly a conspiracy in the sense you mean, Chase. It's more of a mind-set we're fighting. With a conventional conspiracy, all you have to do is expose the plotters and their plans, and—poof—it's gone. But this kind of conspiracy is different. It's far more subtle and pervasive, and it doesn't depend upon a few plotters."

"I don't follow you."

"Like I said, it's a mind-set. A large number of people acting out the natural consequences of their beliefs, but acting in concert. Tell me, have you ever been scuba diving in the Florida Keys, say, or the Bahamas?"

Chase failed to see where the senator was headed. "Yes, several times."

"You remember the schools of fish? How they all swim along together in formation, in the same direction? Then, in one instant they turn simultaneously and swim in a different direction. You've seen that, haven't you?"

"Yes . . ."

"Now let me ask you. Do you think there's one head fish giving orders to the rest, saying, 'Now hear this, prepare to turn. Everybody turn!'? Of course not. But somehow they're all on the same wavelength. I think our opponents are the same. They school like fish, for mutual protection and advancement. They recognize each other, often instinctively. And they act together in concert. That makes it all the more difficult to combat."

"That may be," Chase agreed. "It's a good analogy, in fact. But you can't dismiss the importance of people like Garden Monnoye or May Berg. They are Big Fish. They need to be exposed."

"Sure, Chase, there're a few prominent individuals in any movement who provide money and leadership. But they're not the ultimate power in this case. Or the final threat. Take them out of the picture, and the movement would still operate pretty much the same way."

Clare added softly, "It's the same with the church. Take a few prominent leaders out of action, and you might set it back some. But the Spirit of God would raise up others to take their place. In fact, the church's been the strongest when it was actually being persecuted."

"You leave the Garden Monnoyes and May Bergs alone to operate with impunity, and you'll see persecution again for sure," Chase retorted.

"That's true," said Branch, "and we're not arguing that point. But to deal with the homosexual revolution effectively, you have to stop thinking of them as all villains. In one sense they're victims too."

"Victims?"

Jimmy Tolliver spoke up from his corner of the den. "Maybe I can explain that. First, not all gay people are alike, and they don't all come into the life the same way. Initially, what the vast majority of them want is just to be loved.

"But they can't get fulfillment—real love—the way they are, so they're driven to more extreme acts to satisfy a twisted longing that can't be satisfied. Then they begin to see themselves as victims —victims of a cruel, intolerant society that stands in the way of their gratification."

He hesitated and looked at Chase as though to ask, "Are you understanding this?" Then he went on. "They *are* victims—first of their own false view of man. Then they're victims of their lust. But all of us are potentially victims of the same things. Our lust and pride may show in more conventional ways, but we all suffer from destructive passions."

Chase didn't disagree. "You sound like you think they're victims of biology, though. You don't buy the theory that being gay is caused by a person's genetic makeup, do you?"

"No, I'd describe it as a deeply rooted inclination. And it's a problem that sometimes goes all the way back to childhood—usually in families where they didn't get any affection. So far back that it may seem to the gay person that he was born that way. That makes it hard for a son to sexually imprint or for a daughter to form the right sort of loving attachment with the first and most important male figure in her life—her father."

"But they still have a choice," Chase insisted doggedly.

"Oh, absolutely. Everybody chooses what to do with his inclinations, sexual or otherwise. You can't commit murder, for example, and then say, 'I had no choice—my urges made me do it,' and expect to get off."

Jimmy appeared to be just getting wound up. "Of course, as they get deeper into the lifestyle, their urge grows stronger. But gay men, and lesbians too, want and need love, contact, connection. They ache for release—or relief. They want to love, and to be loved. That's all. Just like any human being. Their tragedy is they can't find real love in the way they're seeking it. And so they lash out at the normal world, which they feel is somehow to blame."

Chase shook his head. He had come expecting to join in a satisfying afternoon of convivial vituperation against all queers, sodomites, and pederasts.

Branch may have sensed what was going through his mind. "Chase, the human condition we all share is that in our natural state we fight against the truth God's revealed to us. The essence of our problem is the rebellion against God that resides in every human heart. All of us. Not just homosexuals."

"Sorry, but I just don't see that what homosexuals do applies to all of us."

"Because God says, 'There is none righteous, no, not one.' Heterosexuals included."

Chase stiffened slightly and stared at the patterns in the carpet. Somehow he had no facile answer.

After another pause, Branch said, "You see, the issue for me is not the tragedy of homosexuals wrestling with their inner feelings. God calls their sin an abomination, but He loves them—and has the power to change them. So we have to make a distinction between the individual who's trapped in an abominable lifestyle and his actions."

So why was Chase thinking of his and Neeley's lifestyle? He groped for an answer that would shift the spotlight of the conversation away from where it was—on his own spiritual condition.

"What about Queer and Present Danger, then?" he demanded. "What about this new group of gay terrorists, Come Out Fighting? Or the gay lobby? Or people like Monnoye—using money and influence to promote the gay agenda. Do you really think you can reach them with Christian love?"

"I don't know if we can or not," said Branch wearily. "But it's up to us to have the right attitude toward them. The outcome is up to God, not us. And yes, we have to resist—before homosexuals succeed in imposing their immorality on the rest of us."

"Or getting a constitutional amendment that gives them and their behavior the status of a politically protected class. Legal and social endorsement of homosexuality is a death sentence for society, so we have to resist that with all our might. I think you'll agree that's what I've been doing. Thanks in part to your help."

"Of course we have to fight," said Clare. "We're witnessing the collapse of Christian civilization. But that's due primarily to the apathy of Christians. And if homosexuality comes to be protected as a constitutional right, it will make outlaws of Christians who stick to their faith and practice. But we can still show tolerance to human beings, knowing that we're all sinners."

"I guess I'd like to believe you," Chase finally admitted. "But it's just too hard, after what I've seen and been through with these creeps over the years, to feel *any* charity or tolerance."

"Have you ever read Oscar Wilde?" Clare asked then.

"Not much. I know he was a homosexual."

"Yes. Convicted of sodomy and sent to prison for two years. It ruined him. Shortly before he died, he wrote, 'Terrible as was what the world did to me, what I did to myself was far more terrible still.'"

"I guess it really is a far more miserable experience than I ever realized," Chase said soberly.

"Most of them are miserable, and their misery eventually turns to hatred," put in Jimmy. "They want to change, but today they're encouraged to believe the lie that they're made that way and can't change."

Chase thought hard for a moment. Then, casting about for a proper response, he said, "Jimmy, you seem to know an awful lot about these people."

Jimmy looked directly at him. "I was one."

Chase felt his face redden. After an embarrassed silence, he stammered, "I don't know what to say. Here I've been shooting off my mouth and—"

"Don't fret yourself, Chase. I said I *was* one—long ago. But I'm free of that now."

"Then it *is* possible to change."

"Not easy, but possible. In my case it took the power of God."

"Y'all have sort of ganged up on me, but I think I'm beginning to see some things," Chase said, chastened. "More than I ever understood when I was investigating their call boy rings in the White House. But you know, Senator, nothing makes the gay lobby madder than the suggestion that it's *possible* to change. Or that religion is the best way to bring about that change. They'll never forgive you if you start making that case publicly. I'm worried. They're going to come after you."

"Maybe they will. But Chase, it's you I'm worried about."

"Don't, Senator. I know how they operate. I got them once, and they couldn't hurt me then. I don't think they can hurt me now."

"Well, don't be naive. You're a prominent media figure, but that's not going to protect you completely. They're not going to sit still on the defensive. They'll hit back—hard. They've got the resources and the power to hurt us, and they're smart. If, as you suggest, they want to hurt me, they may strike at me through you."

Chase thought of the call from Wynn Pritchett. He did not flatter himself that the media mogul wanted his talents as a broadcaster. Pritchett's overture could only mean one thing. The "enemy," as he had come to think of them generically, were trying to co-opt him. His respect for the senator's prescience took another leap upward.

"Chase, I'm goin' to Pennsylvania next week," Trumbull announced suddenly. "I've been challenged to a debate by the pro-HRA group up there, and we've got strong allies in the western part of the state who're calling for help. Why don't you come along? Maybe you can get some material for your show."

Chase reflected for a moment. He was a little tired of being preached at by the Trumbulls, although they always did it with well-bred tact and grace. Yet Branch was right. He *did* suppress thoughts about his relationship to God every time they surfaced.

Well, he was no coward. He would face any idea, no matter how uncomfortable it might make him for the moment. He knew he was probably getting in too deep with these folks, but the simple fact was that he liked and admired them—with the possible exception of Jimmy Tolliver, whose revelation made him decidedly uncomfortable.

But Neeley's words called him back. On several occasions she had begged him not to get too mixed up with Trumbull and his ilk. And besides there was the show to prepare for. And then he had a date with Neeley next weekend. Even if he wanted to break the date, he could hardly do so on the grounds that he preferred to go to a meeting with Branch Trumbull.

"Uh—no, Senator. I don't think I can make it," he stammered. "I've got a previous engagement."

But Branch smiled genially. "Well, sure, I understand. It'll probably be a dull time anyway. But one of these days I want to get you out in the heartland where our allies really live."

16

"Gentlemen, welcome to Waverly Ford Farm." Garden Monnoye smiled effusively and extended his hand. "Thanks for coming."

A most unlikely looking pair descended from the Rolls Royce Silver Cloud that Monnoye had sent to fetch them from Washington. The first man, Jones Raclette, was tall, angular, pale, cadaverous. An enormous head balanced on his thin neck. The other, William Philpott, was short, rotund, jolly looking. A profuse shock of wavy white hair made his face seem redder than it was. Both wore black suits and white clerical collars.

"Good of you to have us," boomed Raclette, as they mounted the brick steps to the entrance. The rich basso profundo voice was totally incongruous coming from such a thin frame, and Monnoye suppressed a smile. He escorted them both by the elbow through the antique and art filled central hallway and drawing room and on to the rear terrace, where another of his legendary lunches was waiting.

The three men settled into their places, and a servant decanted the first bottle of wine, then discreetly disappeared, as trained, so that Monnoye could talk freely with his guests.

"Bon appetit," said Monnoye. "Hope you enjoy the lunch."

"Oh, I know we will." Philpott surveyed the sumptuous meal.

For a few minutes they made small talk about the flight to Washington and the drive out from the city. Monnoye inquired politely about life in their respective cities. Then he directed the conversation to the business at hand. "Gentlemen, I wouldn't have asked you to come so far if it weren't important. I need your help. To be more precise, the country needs your help."

"We're here to help." Philpott looked up from his beef tenderloin *en chemise Strasbourgeoise.*

Jones Raclette, however, was more guarded. "What kind of help?"

Monnoye explained with a worried air. "Well, I know you're deeply concerned, as I am, about the ugly, intolerant turn this country is taking once again in regards to the diversity that makes America unique. I'm really worried we're seeing another upsurge of prejudice against gays like we saw in the late '80s and early '90s.

"Fortunately that spate of bigotry was short-lived—but it still hurt a lot of people while it lasted. Now, when the nation needs unity more than ever, and just when it seems we're on the threshold of a breakthrough in curing AIDS, we simply can't afford to go back to the Dark Ages."

"I certainly agree," said Philpott. "But I'm not sure I see how we can help. We're just clergymen, after all."

"Hardly *just* that," protested Monnoye. "You, Reverend Philpott—"

"Please call me Bill."

"Bill, you're the Stated Clerk of the Presbyterian Church of North America, one of the leading churchmen in this country. You speak for five million Presbyterians. You helped found the Presbyterian 'More Light' movement. You set an example of openness by inviting June Allen Spears to be copastor of your church in Rochester, even though she's an avowed lesbian. As a leading voice in the ecumenical movement, you have influence as well on other denominations."

"Well, Mr. Monnoye—"

"Please call me Garden."

"Well, Garden, I suppose that's all true, except it's not quite five million anymore. I'm afraid our membership is dropping, as it is with most churches these days."

"That doesn't change a thing. And Jones, you're the Protestant chaplain at the leading institution of higher learning in the United States, if not the entire Western world." He did not need to add "And you're also the most prominent self-confessed gay clergyman in America."

Garden Monnoye's flattery did not seem flattery. It seemed rather an odd mixture of strength and supplication, with a strong dash of sincerity thrown in.

152

"You're very kind," replied Jones Raclette. "But I never thought of myself as having much influence one way or another, either on the Episcopal church or on the university."

"You're both too modest." Monnoye sensed he had established a cordial rapport and was pleased. "The problem as I see it," he continued, "is that once again bigotry and hatred are on the march in the name of religion. And that's where you come in. You're both highly respected religious leaders. The nation desperately needs some responsible men of the cloth to stand up in public and say to the American people that there's no place for this kind of hatred in today's church. Religion should foster tolerance, not divide us.

"And what's more," he continued, "you well know this new outbreak of hatred could result in a setback for the Human Rights Amendment— just when we're only a few states away from gaining ratification. That would be a tragedy."

"Garden, I couldn't agree with you more," replied Philpott. "But this is what Jones and I already preach, I believe. And we've both gone on record in support of the HRA. What more can we do?"

Raclette agreed. "And I'm sure you know, Garden, I'm a gay man myself, though I'm celibate at the moment. In a strange but profound way, I regard my sexual orientation as God's own special gift—it allows me to identify far better with the persecuted and the oppressed whom it's the church's mission to help. I know far better than most just why we need the Human Rights Amendment. So you see, I'm already engaged in what you're suggesting."

"Yes, I know that." Monnoye looked up from his tossed salad. "That's precisely the reason I invited you both here. You're active and involved. But it strikes me that you could accomplish so much more with some financial help."

Both clergymen sat up a little straighter.

"I've been thinking that the enlightened religious community needs to be more involved in this issue—especially in support of the HRA. Otherwise, those who use religion as a weapon of intolerance will end up speaking for the religious by default. On the other hand, I know church work is not the most lucrative calling. Naturally it occurred to me that I could perhaps make it financially possible for churchmen of goodwill like yourselves to be more actively involved—as I know you would be if the resources were available."

Neither guest spoke, but both continued to look and listen expectantly.

Monnoye picked up the large brown envelope at his elbow. "I have here an offer which I hope you'll be able to accept."

Drawing out a sheaf of bound paper, he explained. "These are the incorporation papers and draft by-laws for a new tax-free educational organization which I recently set up. This document records the name as Churchmen United, but if you accept the leadership, you can file to rename it if you like.

"And of course, an organization like this can't run without money. I have here a check made out to Churchmen United in the amount of $100,000. All we have to do is complete the bank cards with your signatures, and the check can be deposited."

"$100,000?" Philpott asked softly, his eyes widening.

"Yes. And here are keys to your office space in the Ecumenical Building on Capitol Hill. The Paragon Foundation, which I chair, has leased an ample suite of offices there for one year. They're not quite as nice as space in the Paragon Building, but, in the circumstances, I thought it better for you not to be in my building. Since this is a religious organization, the Ecumenical Building seemed far more appropriate. However, I will lend you some core staff from Paragon to get started. That'll help keep your overhead down." Monnoye paused, waiting.

The two men seemed stunned.

Monnoye read their thoughts. With staff and office space provided, there would be little overhead. Most of the $100,000 could then go to pay the officers—themselves.

"Of course, the $100,000 is just for the first year of operation," he said next. "I would hope to be able to contribute a like amount—or even more—next year, depending on how well things go."

Jones Raclette cleared his throat noisily and looked at Philpott, who wore a dazed expression. "Ah, well, uh . . ."

Monnoye put on an abashed expression. "Look, I know it may seem as if I've taken too many liberties. But time is short. A

154

new crisis is about to break over our heads, especially with Senator Trumbull and his new gang of rednecks on the march.

"Believe me, time is of the essence. I felt we couldn't afford to wait until after we found the right people to start setting up all the administration and infrastructure. So I launched the effort a while ago in the confidence we'd find the right people. And I do believe you're the right men for the job."

"Oh, Garden, you needn't apologize for taking liberties. I think Bill and I are just struck speechless, that's all. First at your generosity, and then at your foresight. I for one will be honored to take part. Of course, I'll have to get approval from the University, but that'll just be a formality. How about you, Bill? Any reason why you can't co-chair Churchmen United?"

"Ah—no—none at all," Philpott burbled, seemingly still incredulous. "I'm honored to be asked. Thank you, Garden, thank you very much indeed."

"Excellent. I'm the one who must thank *you*," said Monnoye with humility. "With men of your caliber and standing in charge of Churchmen United, I think Branch Trumbull and his rabble will soon find out who really speaks for religion in America."

With business concluded, Monnoye engaged in desultory small talk, turning the full force of his magnetic charm on his visitors. Conversation and laughter flowed as freely as the wine, and the meal ended with strawberry tort and freshly brewed Jamaican Blue Mountain coffee.

Monnoye showed his new allies through the mansion and around the estate. The tour was followed by a high tea and brandy in the late afternoon. Then it was time for them to go.

He saw them off in the Rolls with great relief. His contempt for the pair had grown as the afternoon wore on. It had become harder and harder to smile and joke. Their high-sounding platitudes cloaked an avarice and lust for power as great as any ward-heeling politician on Capitol Hill.

May Berg was right—up to a point. He could see why she despised these pompous priests and their smarmy idealism masquerading as religion. But Monnoye had grown up in the church. He had once loved its ritual, music, stained glass, vestments—and above all, its mystery—though that had all disappeared for him long ago.

He understood these men far better than most gay leaders, and he could never hate them quite as much as she did. But he still shared her distaste. The important thing was that Raclette and Philpott would serve a useful purpose, at least as long as he kept them liberally supplied with funds, understood their limitations, and did not expect too much backbone from them.

★ ★ ★

Jones Raclette and William Philpott wasted no time in launching Churchmen United. They secured permission from their boards to proceed, and both telephoned Tris Kramer at the Paragon Foundation, as instructed by Monnoye before they left his estate.

Kramer sent over the designated staffers to the Ecumenical Building to get the new offices organized. Then he began the extensive advance work for the press conference announcing the new organization.

Ten days later all was ready. Philpott and Raclette had recruited leading clergymen and theologians from mainstream denominations and seminaries. An array of ecclesiastical heavyweights stood behind the two men as they gave their statement to the newsmen in the first floor press center.

Tape recorders turned, note-pads opened, TV cameras rolled, flash-bulbs popped.

"Ladies and gentlemen of the news media," boomed Jones Raclette, "welcome to this inaugural news conference of Churchmen United. We are a new public policy organization, but one with a difference. Our purpose is to apply what the church teaches to the great and troubling policy questions of the day—namely, tolerance, unity, and goodwill. By doing so, we hope to salvage the good name of the church and religion from those who would tarnish it by using religion as a weapon to spawn hatred instead of fellowship, forgiveness, and unity."

He introduced himself and gave a brief personal history. Then he introduced William Philpott.

"If we in the church are truly to practice what we preach," Philpott began, "we must bring Americans of all faiths and viewpoints together to promote the common good. We have largely won the battle for civil rights for people of color. But one group of Americans still labors under the lash of bigotry and intolerance —gay Americans. Churchmen United will fight to see that gay Americans receive their civil rights."

Raclette smoothly took his cue. "Our first priority will be to secure passage of the Human Rights Amendment. We've identified ten key states where we can help gain support for the HRA. Now we're organizing chapters of Churchmen United in those states . . ."

The two men finished the joint reading of their prepared statement, then opened the floor for questions. Excitement in the packed conference room was high. Most of the reporters were sympathetic to the HRA and the gay rights cause.

But the primary motivation of the majority was not political. They flourished in the midst of controversy of any type. Loud and proionged battles sold papers, attracted viewers, and made journalistic reputations.

The media denizens were shrewd enough to see what lay behind Churchmen United. It was, plain and simple, a counterattack on Senator Branch Trumbull and his new Nehemiah Foundation. It was diabolically clever to enlist liberal churchmen to discredit the man, who appealed to his constituents unequivocally on grounds of traditional religious morality.

As if to accentuate what everyone was thinking, the first question dealt with Branch Trumbull. As expected, both Raclette and Philpott denounced him as a bigot and reactionary, but in such dulcet tones as to preserve their own reputations for tolerance.

Most of the questions from a sympathetic media were softballs, giving the two leaders plenty of opportunity to expand on their basic theme and produce ample sound bites. But even sympathizers grew a little bored with the love-in and hoped someone would shake up the proceedings.

A young black man in the rear obliged. After thirty minutes of trying but failing to get recognition, he was finally called on to ask his question.

"Thank you, Mr. Philpott," the young reporter said. "I'm Jay Blaisdell from the Norman, Oklahoma, *Independent*. Tell me, sir, do these names mean anything to you?" He read a list of a dozen masculine names.

Consternation came over Philpott's already red face, and he stepped back from the podium. Jones Raclette looked at him in alarm and grasped an elbow to steady him.

But Philpott recovered quickly. He stepped back to the microphone and in a loud, angry, unsteady voice said, "If you don't have a serious question, let somebody else have a turn!"

He scanned the audience for another upraised hand. But the jaded newsmen sensed drama in the making. Clearly the good reverend was trying to muzzle this obscure black reporter. Whoever he was, he was one of them, and they did not like seeing a colleague slighted. Moreover, the reverend's unexpected reaction had piqued everyone's curiosity. The few lifted hands slowly fell.

Jay Blaisdell spoke out again, louder this time. "Reverend Philpott, you've heard the names of twelve young men. They range in age from twenty to thirty-five. All are from the central Oklahoma area. I have sworn statements from all twelve attesting that they were sexually molested by you over the ten-year period from 1984 to 1994, when you were the chief pastor at Canadian River United Presbyterian Church, which they all attended. Would you care to comment on this, sir?"

Reporters who earlier had been amused by the redness of Philpott's complexion, now could not believe how white he became. He shrank back again from the podium. His words seemed to stick in his throat. His arms threshed wildly in the direction of the Oklahoma reporter. Finally he sank onto one of the metal chairs on the dais. The clerical brotherhood on the platform closed ranks protectively around him. Someone fetched him a glass of water.

Jones Raclette tried to put the best face on an irretrievable situation. "I don't know who you are, young man, but if you've been sent here—"

"I'm Jay Blaisdell from the *Norman Independent*, Doctor Raclette. And I *have* been sent here, just like all these other reporters, by my news organization. And I asked a legitimate question. Now if Reverend Philpott doesn't want to answer the question for me, I'm sure he'll get a chance to answer before the Oklahoma city police and DA. This morning a warrant was issued for his arrest. An extradition warrant too, in case he refuses to report voluntarily to the Oklahoma authorities."

"Well, we—I—obviously there's an explanation," sputtered Raclette. "It could well be a case of mistaken identity. Or, more likely, the actions of agents put up to this outrage by Branch Trumbull.

"In fact," —his voice resumed its confident sonorousness— "we were warned yesterday that he and his people might pull a stunt like this. But I didn't dream that even Senator Trumbull had the temerity to attack someone so highly regarded as my good friend and colleague Bill Philpott, a man of the highest probity and ecclesiastical reputation."

The lie was so transparent that not even the most credulous believed it. But it was a valiant effort to salvage something.

Certain reporters, especially from the gay media, duly reported the next day the discovery of another sinister plot by the Trumbull homo-haters. But the editors of the mainstream, self-avowed "respectable" news organs judged the entire episode best forgotten, and the few stories that were filed were quietly buried in the back pages—except in the *Norman Independent*, of course.

NEWS ITEM,
the *Nashville Statesman*

In Nashville today a coalition calling itself Tennesseans United launched a campaign to recall Branch Trumbull, the state's senior US senator. The coalition, composed of a broad cross-section of Tennessee clergymen, church officers, lay leaders, university faculty, and students is the state chapter of Churchmen United, a new national lobby launched in Washington last Tuesday to support the Human Rights Amendment to the US Constitution.

In June, Trumbull created a storm of controversy with his testimony before the Senate Judiciary Committee in favor of Supreme Court nominee Hastings Whitmore, whose bid to sit on the High Court was defeated by the Senate. At that time gay leaders denounced Trumbull for his attacks on the HRA and gay rights.

17

Leon Pound made several random turns in Middleburg. In Upperville, he doubled back on his route to make sure he was not being followed. Satisfied that no one was tailing him, he sped out of Upperville in the dark.

Now he approached the turn to Garden Monnoye's estate. He flicked off the headlights briefly and wheeled into the long avenue leading to the mansion. He knew these elaborate precautions were probably unnecessary. He also knew that laziness and complacency could eventually lead to exposure, and Garden Monnoye relied on him to keep their connection well hidden.

He entered the mansion's underground parking garage and joined Monnoye upstairs in his richly paneled drawing room.

Monnoye was dressed in pajamas and silk dressing gown. He sat in a plush armchair, thoughtful, gazing into the fire that crackled on the hearth. His long blond hair fell carelessly across his forehead, and he held a large snifter of brandy.

Leon sucked in a breath at the sight of him, thinking that he had never known a more attractive or magnetic man.

"Hello, Garden," Leon said.

Monnoye sat still and staring, as if he did not hear.

"Garden, it's me, Leon. What are you doing?"

"'I sit and look out upon all the sorrows of the world, and upon all oppression and shame . . .'" Monnoye's voice, quoting Walt Whitman, was low but angry. He got up, gave a tired smile to his friend, and held out his hand. "Sorry to bring you out here on such a dreadful night, Leon. But things are coming to a head, and I wanted to get an update from you in person."

"I don't mind coming out," Leon said. He was bound to Monnoye by more than loyalty—by cords of desire and memory —and he cherished the hope that, one of these lonely nights, Garden might turn to him again. "I don't mind at all. But you've got your cryptotelephone now. You ought to try it sometime."

"Yes, I will. But I'm worried. I want you to relieve me of my worries, and the best way to do that was face to face."

"Well, you needn't worry. Everything's going fine," Leon insisted.

"Toby's working out all right? Can we rely on him?"

"I'm sure we can. His marksmanship training went well. And then I've been teaching him a few things—police procedure, how to penetrate a security screen, and so forth. As far as that part of the operation goes, he's as qualified and ready as anyone could expect."

"Has Rudy been taking good care of him?"

"Yep. Gives him his daily dose and has him on a special diet. Toby's tests show a normal white cell count. He feels good and looks good. He gives us the credit for making him well—or almost well."

"And so he should," noted Monnoye wryly.

"Anyway, he thinks he's well enough to start having sex again, which is about the only thing on his mind. He even sent off to join Friends Indeed. So he can't wait to do the job and get back to New York." Leon suppressed a chuckle.

"I see. Well, I'll be sorry to disappoint him." A sad smile came over Monnoye's face, and he looked directly at Leon for a long moment.

Leon found himself averting his eyes. "It does seem like a dirty trick. But—fortunes of war, as we used to say in the Agency."

"And we are in a war, as you know. So we all have to make sacrifices," Monnoye added gently.

Leon said nothing but nodded as he too stared into the dancing flames. He could tell his mentor was too burdened or troubled for conversation. *Fear?* Leon wondered. The risks were high. Or was Garden just suffering pangs of conscience?

Still, they had gone over this time and again. The planning and organizing had begun only after weighing every pro and con. Now all he needed to get the operation under way was a clear signal from Garden. The time for reflection was past. So it seemed to Leon, who wanted an unequivocal yes or no.

"Garden, is it a go or not?" he finally asked, trying to contain his impatience.

Monnoye continued to stare at the flames. He had not wanted this operation, he had told Leon earlier. He had only agreed to the preparation in order to have a trump card in his hand.

"Yes, Leon, it's a go," he said softly.

"OK, then." Leon was relieved. He hated the thought of all his preparation being wasted. It was some of his finest work.

"When is the—uh—event going to occur?" Monnoye asked.

"Tomorrow night. In Newton, Pennsylvania."

"You'll let me know right away?"

"Sure, soon as I know. Assuming everything goes according to plan, I'll call you around 10:00 P.M."

"Call me whether it goes according to plan or not," Monnoye said a little curtly.

"Well, sure. That's what I meant."

"On the secure phone."

"Right. On the secure phone."

"You've done extremely well, Leon. We're all grateful. You really are our secret weapon."

Leon smiled.

Monnoye got up and walked to the double doors of the drawing room. "Well, I'm going to bed. Forgive me for not sitting up for a while with you, Leon, but I'm really tired. Things aren't going too well. Our Churchmen United event turned into a debacle, and I don't know if I can salvage anything from it."

"Yeah, I heard."

"And this Eddie Webb case down in Mississippi is starting to cause us a lot of trouble. I've lain awake nights trying to decide how to deal with it."

"Yeah, I heard a little about that too," Leon commiserated. "Anything I can do?"

"No, thanks. You're handling the main problem, and that takes a real load off my mind. Good night, Leon. Mark will show you to your room."

★ ★ ★

Newton, Pennsylvania. A high school auditorium. *Should be*

a piece of cake, thought Toby Giton. Security would probably be light. Or perhaps there would be no inside security at all. And Leon had taught him a few tricks of infiltration and evasion, what he called "tradecraft."

Toby was confident he could get in, do the job, and get out in the ensuing confusion. Try to do it at the end, Leon had told him, when there would be a large crowd milling around. A crowd, according to Leon, was the best cover of all for a close-in hit. Trumbull would be greeting well-wishers—or maybe still up on stage.

Yeah, it ought to be easy. Toby smiled grimly.

But upon arriving at the nondescript brick school building, Toby became alarmed over the inadequacy of his escape plan. He had checked the place out thoroughly that morning and had identified a likely place to hide his getaway car. But to his frustration that spot and all other likely avenues of quick escape were now blocked by the long line of cars and trucks arriving for the evening event.

The getaway car provided by Leon had been stolen in Washington the previous day and equipped with Pennsylvania plates —also stolen. Toby had been careful to leave no prints, and, on final reflection, he decided he would park anywhere he could, do the shoot, and leave the car behind. He could vanish in the nearby woods, ditch the weapons, and make it into town.

Then he reconsidered. No, that wasn't too good an idea. He was a stranger. He would be readily noticed in this small community, especially if the cops were on the lookout after a murder. Maybe he could steal a car, or hijack one from a passing motorist, since he did not know how to hot-wire an ignition.

The lack of a good escape plan made Toby increasingly tense and miserable. He began to wish he had never gotten involved in such a risky endeavor. But then he remembered how Leon Pound had cajoled and threatened him. He thought of Rudy's capsules and of how well he had been feeling lately. He thought of Friends Indeed and getting back to New York when this was all over.

They've got me treed, he thought miserably. *Forget an escape plan. I don't see any cops. I'll just play it as it goes.*

The night was cold and blustery, but he was grateful. It made his big, bulky trench coat inconspicuous. Inside the long skirts of the coat he carried the short-barreled AR-18 carbine. The Glock pistol was secured in the webbed shoulder holster, also well hidden by the voluminous raincoat. The assault rifle would be a backup for the shoot in case he could not get close enough to use the pistol. But its main purpose was to frighten off any would-be pursuers.

These western Pennsylvania mill hands and oil workers were a mean lot, he was told, meaner than Southern hillbillies, and he wanted a more intimidating weapon than the handgun. A few bursts in the air with the carbine would get everybody out of the way, and he could walk out clean. And if anyone was foolhardy enough to chase him after that, well . . .

A huge crowd of men and women but no children—all strangely silent, thought Toby—streamed into the low, single-story structure, then filed down the long drab corridors and through the rear doors of the auditorium.

Toby had tried the stage entrances earlier but found them all locked. So there was no chance of getting in behind the target. The side doors down in front of the stage were open, yet he could only approach Trumbull through part of the crowd.

Of course, Trumbull would probably come out the back when the meeting was over. Then maybe he could get off a shot. His training had not included lock picking or breaking and entering. What did they expect? Clearly Leon and his principals were not bothering to make a James Bond of him, Toby reflected. And a chronic, underlying uneasiness bubbled back to the surface of his thoughts.

★ ★ ★

Western Pennsylvania was one of those traditionalist enclaves Branch Trumbull realized was the key to his hopes of successfully turning back the humanist tide of affairs. When he got the call for help from his old friend T. C. Moreland, he agreed to go without hesitation.

T. C. Moreland came from a working-class family in Johnstown, site of the famous flood. As a young man he had kicked around the country in a variety of jobs. Then he discovered his natural gifts as a raconteur, comedian, and musician and was in show business by the time he was twenty-one. But in California he had fallen in with a group of traveling evangelists. To his considerable astonishment—and that of his family when they later found out—he became a devout Christian, invested his earnings in college, and then went to seminary.

He was a captivating, stem-winding pulpit speaker, but he was more than entertaining. He had a quick mind, a thorough knowledge of Scripture, and a deep understanding of his times. Early in his career, he experienced firsthand the animosity toward the church of a gay-dominated legal system. More recently, he narrowly escaped a prison term for a failed attempt to counsel a young homosexual who later committed suicide.

That scarring episode led him into activism parallel to Branch Trumbull's efforts through the Nehemiah Foundation. He returned to western Pennsylvania to organize the Christian and traditionalist enclaves there. He hoped simply to stir up his people sufficiently to keep destructive trends at bay in their region.

But now the enemy had attacked through the public schools. It was not the first time. Many of Moreland's people wanted to home school. But the worsening economy was robbing them of their wealth and thus of the extra time they could devote to home schooling. Most wives had been forced to enter the work force to keep their homes and pay the skyrocketing tax for National Health Care. Few families could afford a nonworking parent at home to supervise or teach their children.

Many in fact worked at two or three jobs just to stay above water financially. Few could afford private schools. And Christian schools were under ever increasing harassment by the IRS and state human rights agencies.

Trumbull and Moreland knew it was a lost cause to try to reclaim the public schools. But perhaps the schools' very excesses would get people mobilized to do anything but silently and sullenly withdraw from the field. Once they were engaged and active, then maybe they could find new, creative solutions to the problem of educating their children according to their religious convictions.

Now Moreland had organized a rally to share with his supporters the latest outrage of the state's sex educators. The event was at Newton High School. Branch Trumbull had agreed to speak.

T. C. was gratified to see the huge attendance. At eight o'clock he took the podium in the school auditorium. Passionately he gave voice to the indignation of a conservative working-class population bewildered and deceived by the schools their tax money paid for. These people were more deeply devoted to their families and children than anything else in their temporal lives, and it grieved him to see them victimized by a school system that violated their most cherished beliefs and their parental prerogatives.

"Ladies and gentlemen," he began, "remember how indignant we were a few years ago when the sex educators came into our schools and tried to impose their views of sexual behavior—including an endorsement of homosexuality—on our children? Remember the books our kids were made to read in class? Remember when homosexual activists were invited into your kids' classes as guest speakers?

"Yes, we got worked up for a while. We wrote letters. We marched on the capitol in Harrisburg. And we scared the daylights out of the politicians and school officials. When they got a taste of our outrage, they quietly shelved a lot of their programs. So we went back to our routine of trying to make a living, didn't we?" He surveyed the sea of troubled faces.

"That was four years ago, and now it appears we won nothing. What the schools put on the shelf has been replaced by something infinitely more harmful. And, what's worse, this time we didn't even know about it. The only lesson the school politicians learned from our outrage last time was the need for secrecy. They bided their time, all the while developing a curriculum that's . . . well, I don't have words to describe it, but we're going to show you some of it in a moment.

"We wouldn't have known about this latest outrage but for the good offices of Senator Branch Trumbull here. Thanks to his resources, he was able to obtain the teacher's guide and other materials of a new program they're calling 'The Future Is Now.' Senator, would you like to say a few words?"

Branch stood at the podium and smiled. "Thanks, T. C., and good evening, friends. As Doctor Moreland said, a member of

166

my staff was able to get his hands on the 'Future Is Now' material. Here's what the introduction to the teacher's manual says: 'The instructional material in this curriculum must not be shown outside of the context of the program itself, nor to individuals not properly trained in its use, nor sensitized to the full complexity of the human development issues it raises.'

"Now obviously what that means, ladies and gentlemen, is 'Don't let the parents see this, whatever you do. If the parents do see it, then they'll tar and feather us as we deserve.' It makes us all mad, and it certainly makes us ask, 'Who's really imposing their values on whom?'"

Moreland returned to the podium then and commented on what they were about to see. "I have mixed feelings about showing this film. Frankly, it's nothing but the kind of filth you see in porn theaters. But they're showing this sleaze to our children under the guise of sex education and values clarification."

"It *will* offend you," Branch Trumbull interjected. "Even bestiality is treated sympathetically in the written material."

"So I'm warning you now," Moreland said. "If you want to go out in the lobby—especially you ladies—we'll call you back when the business part of the meeting begins. But I felt you really needed to see this to understand what we're up against. I want you to get mad. But I ask your forgiveness in advance for any offense. Remember, I'm not showing this to you because I approve of it, but because—"

"Excuse me! Excuse me!" a loud voice called from the back of the room, and a dark-haired, well-dressed woman, hand raised, strode down the center aisle. "I'm afraid you can't show that!"

"May I ask who you are?" T. C. Moreland demanded. "You're interrupting a meeting here."

"I'm Doctor Annunziata. I'm the principal of this school."

"Well, good evening, Doctor Annunziata," Moreland said brightly as she approached. "Thanks for coming out. Perhaps you can answer some questions about this curriculum when we're through showing the—"

"You're not going to show that!" She pointed a threatening index finger at him, then turned toward the stairs to the stage as if she intended to confiscate the film.

Moreland was not one to be intimidated. "Hold it right there, ma'am. We have permission to be here, and we're—"

"I'm revoking your permission. Right now!" she shouted, but she did stop at the foot of the stairs.

"On what grounds?"

The woman seemed flustered by Moreland's unflappable resistance. "You didn't stipulate in your request what the meeting was about. You didn't indicate you were going to be screening—uh—privileged material."

"Oh, yes, ma'am," he retorted with elaborate courtesy. "We did indicate the purpose of the meeting. It was to discuss proposed changes in the school curriculum and how we as parents might better support the education of our children. And that's exactly what we're doing. In any case, this is public property, paid for by the people in this room. We have a right to assemble here lawfully for any reason."

"You still can't show that tape. That's privileged material. It can only be used by certified teachers," she insisted, but more lamely this time.

By now the audience was becoming restive. "Sit down!" "Shut up!" "Show the film!" was heard across the hall, and a palpably menacing atmosphere was brewing.

Dr. Annunziata stood below the stage, indecision showing on her face.

"No need for you to come up here, Doctor. We're not leaving, and you're not going to get this film. Unless you're prepared to fight me for it." Moreland grinned, as if he would like nothing better. "And these parents are going to see it. After all, if it's fit for you to show in secrecy to our teenagers, certainly it's fit for parents to see. Don't you agree?"

At that the audience burst into a deafening round of applause, cheers, and whistles.

The principal scowled at Moreland, glanced over her shoulder at the sea of hostile faces, and began to retreat. "I'm calling the police!" she threatened as she scuttled back up the aisle.

"Call them!" Moreland shouted at her retreating back.

"Yeah, call 'em!" yelled dozens in the audience.

Pelted with hoots and catcalls, Dr. Annunziata fled the auditorium.

Moreland turned back to his audience. "Well, friends, I think what just happened tells you more about the state of our schools than a dozen speeches by me. So I guess we'd better go ahead and show the tape before the police get here. They might arrest me for violating pornography laws."

The lights went down, and Moreland threw a switch behind the stage, bringing down the screen. An assistant put the videotape into the rear-screen VCR projector, and the program began.

As pointed as Moreland had tried to be, his warning had not truly prepared these parents for what came on the screen. The tape went into graphic, explicit detail, depicting oral and anal sex. It told the viewer that all sexual practices were good as long as they brought pleasure and not harm, that the traditional family was an outmoded concept, and that parents' ideas of sexual propriety, of right and wrong in general, were not binding.

Discard the old values imposed by your parents, went the message. Develop your own personal view of the world and a code of behavior that's right for you. Talk to your school-based counselors, get your condoms, your sex ed, and be free now.

The tape was twenty minutes long. When the lights went back up, there was stunned silence in the hall.

Moreland wisely allowed the parents a few moments to absorb the shock and gain some control over their emotions.

But before he could take the floor and begin the business meeting, by which he meant formulating a plan of concerted action, a commotion broke out in the lobby. There was the sudden sound of scuffling and chanting. Then the double doors to the hall burst open with a crash.

Moreland glanced over at Branch Trumbull. Surely it was too soon for the police to have arrived. And if it was the police, why the shouting and scuffling?

Then a swarm of young men, yelling and brandishing billy clubs and sticks, rushed down the three aisles that ran the length of the auditorium. Some carried baseball bats. They wore dark clothing—some blue denim, some black, some leather. All had their heads close-cropped.

Skinheads! T. C. thought, surprised.

But they were not skinheads. In addition to the close haircut, he could see as they pressed closer that all wore pink triangles and the Greek letter *lambda* emblazoned in the center. And he recognized the group that until now he had only heard about. Come Out Fighting.

A jumble of thoughts flashed through T. C.'s mind. How did they get here? They must have heard about the meeting and come over from Pittsburgh. Or Philadelphia? Philly was hours away, but it had a large, militant gay population.

The men in the audience, mostly blue collar workers, were not to be trifled with in the best of circumstances. But after what they had just seen—and to have their peaceful meeting broken up by this violent, bizarre gang—seemed more than they could bear. Though unarmed, they outnumbered the invaders four to one.

The tumult was mind-numbing. Women shrieked and scrambled to get out of the way. The gay militants shouted obscenities and struggled to reach the stage. Tough, burly men from the audience yelled back. Ignoring the clubs, they counterattacked with fists and feet, pummeling the militants to the floor and knocking them down among the folding seats.

In seconds the hall was a seething mass of struggling, screaming, intertwined bodies. One group of workers moved quickly to the front. Some of these, displaying immense strength as well as rage, ripped off the armrests from the seats to use as weapons. They waited in a tense cordon around the stage, daring the attackers to come within reach.

But the Come Out Fighting brigade never made it that far. Before they reached the stage they were either knocked senseless or pinioned by powerful hands. Some attempted to bite their captors, who, fearing HIV infection, proceeded to beat them unconscious. Others retreated through the rear doors when they realized the attack was being repulsed.

The defenders had their casualties too. More than a dozen men and a few women had been injured. Some lay in the aisles, some among the seats. A few sat moaning and crying while their neighbors attempted to render aid.

There would be no business meeting.

170

No sooner had the militants been subdued or ejected than the police arrived, sirens blaring. At the doors, eight officers suddenly and unexpectedly encountered the broken, retreating files of Come Out Fighting. Entering the auditorium, they came upon the chaotic aftermath of a mass melee where, presumably, they had expected to find only a group of recalcitrant trespassers.

★ ★ ★

Tony Giton crouched at the back of the auditorium between two of the rear doors. He had positioned himself as well as he could to intercept Trumbull if he should exit that way. Then the irate woman principal had left, promising to call the police.

Toby's emotions alternated between extreme disappointment and relief. He had not liked this setup from the first. If the police arrived, no one, not even Leon, could blame him for that, and all bets would be off.

He lingered just the same. Maybe the woman was throwing out an idle threat. But then Come Out Fighting had burst in, and the battle began. Shrinking against the brick wall, Toby had been as totally surprised as everyone else, certain that opportunity was slipping through his fingers. And sure enough, soon more than a half-dozen uniformed officers were in the auditorium.

In the distance he heard the faint, shrill sounds of more sirens. *More cops—or ambulances*, he thought. In any case, this was no longer a viable opportunity for a hit. And the longer he stayed, the better his chances were of getting arrested. *And me with two automatic weapons. Branch Trumbull and Leon and his bleeping principals will just have to wait.*

Tony Giton hurried out quickly into the cold night.

18

Chase had been reluctant to accept Wynn Pritchett's invitation. He harbored no illusions about the pressure the media millionaire could bring to bear on him. But he was confident of his powers to resist—and above all, he was curious.

For several years now the swift rise of the Pritchett communications empire and the fabled success of its unlikely monarch had dominated the communications industry. Pritchett's face had appeared on the cover of every major news magazine. His business exploits, as well as his outrageous social conduct, made him a colorful character as well as a successful businessman who was always good material for a story.

Why, Chase wondered, would a man such as Pritchett become the ally of Garden Monnoye? Why join the ranks of people he would normally be expected, by virtue of his background, to despise? There was not even a hint that Pritchett was homosexual. He had too prominent a reputation for relentless womanizing. And he seemed too hard-headed a businessman to fall for those flighty New Age dogmas. That left only one other motivation—money.

Pritchett's Satellite Information Service was not significantly better than competing networks. In an era of rapid and broad advances in electronic media, the public had become accustomed to high technical quality in its TV viewing. Digital compression had boosted the number of available cable channels to 300, and that spawned a vastly increased variety in the public's television menu. Pritchett retained a slight advantage over his competition thanks to his constellation of Prometheus satellites that gave him instant access to breaking stories all over the world.

But in 1995 Pritchett had gotten into financial straits. He severely strained his corporate resources in trying to buy Heliotrope Studios and its successful movies-for-television subsidiary.

The Brahmins of the established networks laughed at the spectacle of the jumped-up Alabama redneck getting the comeuppance his brashness deserved.

But Pritchett had the last laugh. Someone—no one seemed to know exactly who—had bailed him out of his difficulties. He had managed to cling to SIS, acquire Heliotrope, and ride out the storm of a corporate counterattack. And the gamble had paid off. He was now the third highest money-maker in the communications business.

Many observers also noted that Pritchett's conversion from Southern traditionalist to globalist dated to that approximate time. Now he was a progressive and a New Age acolyte. More than that, he was a man who had played at the high stakes table and won. The winnings included an immense fortune and a degree of personal power that was used to having its way in all things.

Chase found it revealing that Pritchett had invited him not for lunch in an up-scale Washington restaurant, or to SIS's local offices, but for a weekend duck hunt at his waterfowl reserve on a marshy tributary of the Choptank River on Maryland's Eastern Shore.

He's been researching me, Chase mused. *He knows I like to hunt and thought he'd get me in the best circumstances.*

Chase had researched Pritchett as well. He knew the man lacked one thing that all his wealth and power could not purchase. In the Valley they called it "breeding." Pritchett had never quite been able to escape his origins. But he had tried, and Chase knew intuitively that he was going to Pritchett's lodge because *gentlemen* hunted waterfowl on the Eastern Shore.

SIS sent a car to pick him up in Alexandria. The black chauffeur silently deposited his gun case and duffel in the trunk of the limo and just as silently drove the long tedious way to the hunting lodge.

Chase was glad for the silence. He used the two hours to review all that he had learned about Wynn Pritchett and rehearsed for the verbal jousts they would soon have.

The rambling, two-story hunting lodge was an odd combination of rustic and modern and gave the appearance of genteel age. But Chase could tell it was of recent construction. The country exterior was just a pose, like the owner himself, who affected the mannerisms of a Southern good ol' boy to conceal a shrewd, calculating mind.

Chase arrived to find a hearty meal on the stove, nothing elegant or fancy, just good country fare—steamed crabs, beef stew, rice, and vegetables, along with plenty of cold beer.

Pritchett wore a pair of weathered old canvas hunting trousers and a faded green chamois shirt. He was a large man, slightly red-faced, exuding the hearty confidence of a self-made millionaire.

Chase found himself the only guest—as he had expected. A grave and silent elderly black man in a black suit and black tie served the meal. Chase and Pritchett ate and drank in an atmosphere of forced bonhomie, each warily assessing the other before committing to a first move. And as they talked, Chase thought he glimpsed in the man something far more profound and ancient than mere social difference.

Pritchett blustered, by now clearly trying to impress him, and Chase realized what a sheltered life he had lived. Most of the people he had known in his youth were reasonably good and decent. It been hard for him to absorb the reality that there really was such a thing as a genuinely bad person. And now, he sensed he was face to face with evil personified—with a man who had willingly renounced the beliefs of his upbringing, the code of his region, and simple human decency. It was an unexpected revelation that left Chase shaken.

Pritchett looked over at him knowingly. "If I were you," he said, "I wouldn't get too close to Branch Trumbull. You're hitchin' your wagon to a fallen star—or one that's about to fall anyway. And when it does, you'll go down with him." He was matter-of-fact, as if Trumbull's demise were a foregone conclusion.

A chill went through Chase. *What does he mean?* The thought raced through his brain that they were going to kill Trumbull. But they wouldn't go that far. This was only politics, after all.

He said evenly, "Wynn, I imagine most people would think twice about harming a US senator. There may be a lot of people in the government who hate him, but—"

"Oh, I didn't necessarily mean physical harm," Pritchett interrupted. "There's other means. Like a motion of censure in the

Senate. A public disgrace and repudiation. The big papers are all after him. Remember, no one man can stand against the power of an aroused citizenry."

Chase did not reply. Despite Pritchett's disavowal, the sudden conviction that the murder of his friend was a possibility wouldn't leave him.

His glimpse into the abyss told him this face-off was about far more than politics. It was about power—world-shaking, mountain-moving, history-making power. Branch Trumbull stood squarely in the pathway to that power. And Pritchett and his allies could not get around him. They had to stop him or get him out of the way.

Across the table, Pritchett continued. "I just hate to see you get hurt is all. You're a first-rate journalist."

Here it comes, Chase said to himself.

"Why don't you come work for me?" Pritchett said finally. "The money's sure good."

★ ★ ★

The Washington studios of the Direct Broadcast Network, Chase's employer, had become the target of a permanent picketing campaign by the city's gay activists. So far, no serious violence had occurred. DBN laid on extra security, and the dramatically rising audience share of "Pulse of the Nation" more than paid for the added expense.

"Pulse" was rapidly on its way to becoming one of the most widely watched and heatedly discussed public affairs talk shows. Chase McKenzie had become a household name in conservative homes—and a curse word in others.

But Hugh Mahan, his friend and producer, was the nervous type. He knew his resolute, irrepressible star had a burr under his saddle. It was Chase McKenzie who had coined the term *The Pink Decade* back in 1992, while still a young reporter for the *Washington Standard*.

Mahan worried that Chase was beating the drum against gay rights too loudly and too often.

"Chase," he pointedly suggested one morning, "you think maybe Senator Trumbull has perhaps worn out his welcome on the show?"

Chase bristled a little, but then gave in.

You didn't say anything about T. C. Moreland, he thought. *T. C., I'm going to make you a star.*

★ ★ ★

Moreland was an entertaining speaker and lively personality —a classic TV presence if ever there was one. And with the engaging exterior came an important message. Chase was glad to have another persona to broaden his show's repertoire.

His broadcast featuring Moreland was as dramatic as any show he had ever done with Branch Trumbull. He closed it with a bit of commentary of his own, designed to provoke his adversaries in the big networks. He liked playing David to their Goliath. And he had learned that whenever the establishment media condescended to advise conservatives on what not to say, then saying it was sure to be a winning issue with his viewers.

"The liberal news media," Chase ventured, "evidently thinks it's fine for militant gays to lobby, to riot, to do virtually anything to express 'their unarticulated rage at centuries of bigotry, intolerance, and oppression' —as Richard Colman wrote today in the *Washington News*. It's fine for liberal politicians to pander to them, promise them anything. But the Fourth Estate is always quick to instruct conservatives such as me that we must not—under any circumstances—make an issue of gay rights."

The telephones rang off the hook, and he was gratified that he could give a voice and a forum to a widespread set of beliefs that never saw the light of day on the mainstream networks.

The Moreland show, he later learned, had a nationwide effect, but its impact in Pennsylvania was profound. T. C. returned a hero to conservatives in general all over the state. Overnight he became Pennsylvania's primary spokesman for "traditional values." Shortly afterward he organized a rally in Harrisburg twenty times larger than the one broken up by Come Out Fighting.

Soon he was leading daily marches on the state capitol during the week the legislature was considering the Human Rights Amendment. And there on December 10, 1998, as thousands demonstrated outside, the Pennsylvania legislature refused to approve the HRA.

Though the Amendment was only four states shy of the required thirty-four for ratification, this was the first rejection it had suffered in more than two years. Informed political analysts began to wonder if this was a potentially fatal loss of forward momentum for the national gay political agenda.

Gay leaders must have wondered the same. They were poised on the threshold of victory and knew they had to proceed carefully. The movement could not afford any more dramatic defeats. A major misstep or another spate of bad publicity might derail their cause permanently.

★ ★ ★

Toby Giton still quaked inside when he remembered the tongue-lashing Leon Pound had given him for the failure in Pennsylvania. Despite all his explanations about the riot—the arrival of the police, the surging crowd, the confusion—none of it had satisfied Leon, who cared only about results. He threatened to cut Toby off from the steady flow of cash and, more ominously, from his daily dosage.

So far, according to Rudy, who clearly knew more about medicine than just dispensing pills, Toby's CD4 count was normal. Rudy even hinted that his HIV infection might be reversible. Still, Toby had to accept the possibility that he would die eventually of AIDS unless the capsules and diet kept him healthy long enough for the medical world to find a cure.

But if that did not happen and he had to die, he was determined to at least enjoy life a little before he went, to taste some of the heady gay life he had once enjoyed. And if the price of fulfilling his deepest urges was to kill that homophobic, rabble-rousing creep Branch Trumbull, then he would do it without hesitation.

This time, instead of driving for hours in an unfamiliar place such as rural Pennsylvania, Toby had to go only a few dozen blocks. Trumbull was to speak that evening to a large group at the Washington International Hotel. Located near the corner of Calvert and Connecticut, it was ideally situated for quick escape. It stood hard by Rock Creek Park, a rugged, tree-covered strip that bordered Rock Creek from near where the stream joined the Potomac River and ran all the way up through the northwest quadrant of the District.

The plan was as foolproof as human ingenuity and malice aforethought could make it. A four-lane, high-speed road ran the length of the park. Toby would hide a getaway car down the hill from the hotel, among the trees lining the parkway. After the shoot, he could slip out the kitchen complex under cover of the ensuing chaos, vault the low chain-link fence at the back of the hotel property, and disappear into the thick woods of Rock Creek Park in a matter of minutes. Another three or four minutes to reach his waiting car, and he would be far away from the scene before an effective search could be mounted.

Now all he had to do was get a temporary job as a waiter or food handler at the hotel. That would be easy enough. Leon had contacts in the catering and food service industry, which was heavily populated by gay men. And hotels typically laid on large drafts of extra help for big banquets like the one Trumbull would be addressing. Leon had assured Toby it would be simple to gain access to the banquet hall as a legitimately employed waiter or busboy.

★ ★ ★

The annual convention of the National Religious Communications Association was one of the biggest events in American Christendom. The church in modern America had taken full advantage of the revolution in mass communications. It had launched hundreds of radio programs, television networks, electronic churches, video and audio tape ministries, book publishing houses, and an incredible variety of newsletters and magazines.

Every year the people who made up this vast communications conglomerate assembled in Washington to buy and sell their products or services, promote their ministries, trade concepts or develop new ideas, and make new contacts.

For despite the contempt or outright hostility with which the secular world treated conservative religious groups, there were still some 40 million conservative Christians who read books, listened to the radio, and watched television and films. There was little for them in the secular market, and religious communications had become a big business.

The Awards Banquet was the highlight of the convention. It usually featured as keynote speaker a Christian or political leader prominent in the news of the day. Branch Trumbull was both, and was certainly prominent in the news of the day.

Many on the planning committee were embarrassed that the senator had generated such controversy inside as well as outside the church over gay rights. Others feared a backlash from the secular media or the gay militants. But two prominent members of the committee had campaigned hard to secure his invitation: the NRCA president, David Marks—an outstanding pastor who also had impressive credentials in marketing and broadcasting from the University of Illinois—and John Grice, a leading Indianapolis attorney and noted expert in broadcast law.

The committee finally relented, and on the final evening of the convention the vast majority of NRCA members girded their loins and settled in for what they knew would be a night to remember.

The banquet took place in the grand ballroom of the International Hotel, a beautifully draped and chandeliered cavernous space filled with enough tables to seat more than a thousand guests. The stage and bandstand area had been converted into a platform accommodating the head table and the speakers' podium.

The atmosphere was charged with suppressed excitement as the banquet program proceeded toward its culmination in the keynote address.

Trumbull was a natural speaker. He had a relaxed, conversational, but direct way of reaching out to an audience. He was confident but not arrogant. He spoke with sincerity, conviction, and authority, and without overly polished histrionics.

But tonight, as Chase watched Branch from his place beside Libby Trumbull at the head table, he sensed the senator was troubled about something. The man was subdued, picking at his food, and not his normal, voluble self. He seemed unusually attentive to Clare as she ate and conversed animatedly with the dignitaries at the head table. And once again Chase felt that odd stirring in his heart at witnessing such a profoundly loving relationship. No two people could be better matched. *I wonder if it'll ever be like that with Neeley and me.*

Libby had come in from Bristol for the event, and Chase was glad to accompany her. Leaning close, he whispered, "Your dad doesn't seem himself tonight. What's he worried about?"

She whispered back, "I guess he's worried about his speech. A lot of people objected to his doing the keynote. Some have even tried to paint him as a demagogue, or worse. A lot of people just don't realize what's at stake. They don't see the bigger picture beyond the homosexual issue."

Chase considered that for a moment. What could be bigger than queers taking over the government?

"Well, you know what Jimmy says," he remarked. "Even some conservative religious groups have compromised on gay rights. It's like they're ashamed that your dad has forced it into the national spotlight."

"Exactly. Now they've got to choose. Trouble is . . ." She stopped as T. C. Moreland, this year's banquet chairman, got up to introduce the keynote speaker, and shifted her chair around to better see the dais.

Chase studied her, admiring her freshness, her naturalness, her unaffected good looks. She was bright and well-informed too, which he liked in a woman.

Of course, no one could displace Neeley Durant in his affections. He knew that. But if he had to sit here for a long evening of speechifying, how much better to sit with an interesting, attractive girl than next to some boring evangelist who would doubtless ask him sooner or later if he were "saved."

19

When Branch Trumbull stepped to the podium, his tall, lanky build almost dwarfed it. Chase sensed the senator's commanding presence, his intelligence, a personality full of goodwill. And something more, an elusive quality that Chase could never identify—a mixture of kindness and authority that had drawn him to the man from the beginning.

The senator took off his glasses, pressed his thinning gray hair back along his temples, replaced the glasses, then looked out over the sea of faces. He began in his rich, resonant Southern drawl to make the usual acknowledgments of guests and Association officers, followed by congratulations to the award winners and the obligatory jokes and pleasantries.

Then his voice took on a harder edge. "My friends, I know some of you think I came here to indulge in what my critics have called my favorite sport—gay bashing. You can rest easy. That's not my purpose.

"I want to talk about something more fundamental, a theme that transcends the homosexual issue. And I want to consider this theme in light of your special responsibilities as Christian communicators."

Chase thought he looked relaxed and positive.

"I start with the proposition that God loves people and wants them to be happy. He has endowed them with worth and wants them to enjoy dignity and freedom, to be slaves of no evil taskmaster.

"Contrary to what the homosexual lobby would have America believe, Christians don't hate homosexuals. We disapprove of what they do. But our revulsion toward homosexual behavior flows not from hatred of them but from our deepest held convictions about the proper, natural relationships between men and women.

These convictions are built foremost on God's Word.

"In our history there has existed a sort of unwritten social compact regarding homosexuals. Society has said to them tacitly, we know you exist and aren't likely to change, but we won't bother you as long as you're discreet and keep your activities behind closed doors. Call it the closet door, if you prefer.

"Neither I nor the Nehemiah Foundation advocates hunting down and persecuting homosexuals, despite what the liberal media would have you believe. Furthermore, I recognize the extraordinary talents and fine human qualities that many of them possess. They are creative, sensitive, energetic, and highly intelligent people. They have added immeasurable richness to the arts and literature. They are capable of great loyalty and devotion. They are not monsters."

★ ★ ★

An army of waiters finished clearing away the dinner dishes quietly and unobtrusively. Toby Giton listened with mounting surprise as he bussed the crockery back to food service. He was curious about Trumbull in spite of himself and in spite of Jack's stern warning not to identify personally with the "intended." Think of him only as a target.

But the target did not speak like the typical gay-basher. He was critical of gays yet was not at all what Toby had been led to expect. Still, he was the enemy. He stood in the way of Toby's feverish hopes of future pleasure.

Soon the dinner shift was complete. Now the kitchen staff was placing goblets of chocolate mousse on broad trays for delivery to the tables.

Toby ducked out of the action and into the employees' locker room near the kitchen. He glanced around quickly. The room was empty. He opened his locker and took out his gym bag containing the Glock automatic.

He had already loaded a full magazine into the weapon. Now he pulled back the slide, chambered a round, and shoved it securely in the webbed shoulder holster under his left armpit. Then he went back to help serve the final course.

From now on he had to be ready to move instantly. He

planned to make his way into the darkened stage area behind the dais as soon as dessert and coffee had been served. To disappear before that might arouse suspicion, and he would be missed if he skipped serving his table the final course. But he had to be ready, as soon as the opportunity presented itself, to get in close behind the head table and squeeze off a few well-aimed rounds.

Trumbull was vulnerable in a public place, and security tonight was light to nonexistent. Toby knew he would never have a better opportunity. Indeed, for him personally, this might well be the last chance.

He recalled Leon's threats.

* * *

At the podium, Trumbull drew toward the close of his address. "But it's the militant, organized homosexual movement, not the church or society at large, that has broken that unwritten social compact. The homosexual lobby now defines tolerance to mean far more than it ever meant before. Today it means approval, endorsement, active acceptance, even subsidies.

"The price of continued resistance? A tiny minority will use the administrative and legal machinery of our government in an attempt to to coerce us into submission.

"The price of no resistance? Our jobs, our property, our fundamental rights of free speech and religion, our right to raise our children as God commands us, eventually our physical freedom, and ultimately I believe, our lives. We are already more than halfway there, folks!

"Most of you here tonight are communicators. You understand the power of mass communication. What do you think it means when the secular mass media, film and television producers, actors, publishers—the so-called cultural elite—spew out their contempt for the church in every outlet and medium they have access to? What is the cumulative effect of a daily diet of words and images portraying Christians as small-minded, ignorant bigots, and superstitious rednecks?"

Chase glanced around the room. The dinner guests were squirming uncomfortably. A low rumble of conversation arose from the tables as people reacted.

"The gradual Nazi takeover of power well before World War Two was accompanied year after year by portrayals of Jews as corrupt, greedy, spiteful, deceitful, and lustful. When the time came to start rounding them up, the German people were already prepared, and there was little outcry. Years of hate propaganda had made the Nazi persecution of the Jews far easier than it might have been otherwise.

"It should come as no surprise that the founders of Queer and Present Danger and Come Out Fighting took their instruction in intimidation and tactics from Hitler's *Mein Kampf*.

"Barely a decade after the fall of Soviet Communism, I see unmistakable signs of creeping totalitarianism in our own country. It's characterized by the inculcation—especially in our young—of an entirely false worldview. It's characterized by a growing, official hostility to Christianity.

"Whether we like it or not, we are engaged in a new civil war, a cultural war, a religious war. Biblical Christianity and militant secular humanism—of which the homosexual movement is only one manifestation—are totally opposed and irreconcilable systems. So far this war hasn't fully become a shooting war, although every day we see more church burnings, mob violence, and assaults on Christians.

"There is no common ground, my friends. No shared worldview around which we can meet. Even our sense of fair play in public discourse and politics, our commitment to objective truth, they despise and use as weapons against us. For the time being we have withdrawn to our enclaves here and there. But when militant secular humanism has won total power, thanks to our apathy and inaction, it's a fool's delusion to think we will be left alone.

"Do you doubt this? Listen to what they're saying. They are saying we are the enemy, and that they're at war. They've been saying this for years. The church can no longer afford to dismiss the reality of this rhetoric. When somebody says he's at war with you—that he's coming to get you—you'd better take him seriously."

Chase listened, riveted. Maybe he had never properly considered the connection between religion and politics. Good things like freedom and prosperity he just took for granted. Maybe the freedom and prosperity America had enjoyed were actually rare in the history of man.

He had been playing absently with a teaspoon, trying to take in what Trumbull was saying. Before tonight, he knew, his own main focus was getting back at the gay militants, enjoying the rush of power he felt when doing battle with a group he despised, building Chase McKenzie's reputation.

But now he was reluctantly seeing something else. Without necessarily believing in it or fully understanding it, conservatism had appropriated the moral and ethical content Christianity had contributed to American politics, government, and society . Maybe there really was a higher dimension to the gay rights issue than he had imagined.

That was obviously what Libby had meant a few minutes ago. He had thought he understood her, and it was a little disconcerting to find she was so far ahead of him. But then, she was her father's daughter.

He focused back on Trumbull's conclusion, glancing around the huge hall as he did so. He saw the intent faces of hundreds of people also in the grip of Branch Trumbull's vision.

Something's happening here. Something good and powerful will come out of tonight, he thought, moved in spite of himself by a feeling he could not even name.

"I feel a deepening spiritual antagonism aimed at us at from every side," Branch said with sadness. "But the church's mission is to be the salt of the earth as well as light, and you know what that means. When the Scripture was written, salt was used as a preservative. And without the preserving influence of men and women daily living out the precepts of God's law and His love, society would spin off into utter depravity and chaos.

"But if the salt loses its preservative character, then it's good for nothing. By definition, when homosexuality is endorsed and given special status, we are not preserving our culture.

"What is the answer? You know the answer is spiritual. As David said to his own tribe of Judah, which had joined Absalom's rebellion, 'You are my brothers. Why are you the last to bring back the king?' Around the globe, where darkness once reigned, they are 'bringing back' the true king, Jesus Christ. In South America, in Africa, in the former colonies of the Soviet empire, in Asia and the Pacific rim, even in China, they are 'bringing back the King.'"

Trumbull paused, then his voice almost broke for the first time. "Shall America—once claiming to be a nation under God—be the last to 'bring back the King'?"

Chase glanced about the tables again. All eyes were riveted on the senator, and the wide ballroom was hushed. He returned his gaze to the dais and tried to concentrate on the senator's concluding words.

At first he ignored the suggestion of motion in the periphery of his vision. But something in his unconscious persisted in sounding an alarm. The backdrop curtains. No one was supposed to be back there. *No one was supposed to be back there!* Then the drapery parted slightly. Frozen, Chase glimpsed a pinched white face peering through. Then a black-clad arm appeared at the curtain break. An extended hand held a stout, solid looking object, and Chase in sudden horror knew what it was.

"Branch, look out!" T. C. Moreland leaped up from his chair, trying to throw his body in front of the gunman.

A fusillade of shots rang out—four—in steady succession. Trumbull had begun to turn reflexively at the sound of Moreland's shout. Now he pivoted, and the first bullet missed him but hit Moreland in his upraised left forearm. The force of the slug threw Moreland on the floor at Branch's feet. The second bullet struck the water glass on the podium, showering Trumbull with shards of glass and cutting his face.

By this time he had spun completely around. The next two rounds, intended for the center of his back, caught him squarely on either side of his lower chest, flinging him back against the heavy oak podium, where he slowly crumpled in a heap.

It was over in seconds. The deafening crack of the pistol in the enclosed area and the sight of two blood-spattered men on the floor momentarily stunned the crowd. Then pandemonium erupted.

Clare Trumbull was at her husband's side in an instant, Chase and Libby seconds later.

"A doctor!" Chase shouted. "Get a doctor!"

Libby frantically grabbed linen from the head table and thrust it at her mother. Clare pressed it against the wounds to slow the blood flow. Two doctors rushed up from the audience, one carrying his medical bag. The physician jabbed a syringe of what Chase assumed was adrenaline into Branch's thigh.

But he could tell the senator was failing fast, not just from blood loss but from probable massive internal damage, especially to his lungs.

Branch's right hand sought Clare's, and she grasped it, whispering his name over and over.

A shocked but solicitous crowd gathered around the two wounded men as shouts went up for someone to call an ambulance. Moreland seemed in great pain but directed all aid to Branch Trumbull, who lay cradled in his wife's arms.

He looked up at her sadly and said in short gasps, "I love you. And Libby. And Banks. I'm so sorry . . ."

He tried to say more, but the effort left him drained and breathless. He lay back and closed his eyes. Then, as if suddenly remembering something important, Branch Trumbull opened his eyes and scanned the faces of friends and loved ones around him —until he came to Chase.

He smiled weakly and looked searchingly into Chase's eyes. "Redeem the time, Chase," he whispered. "Redeem the time."

Then a peaceful, faraway gaze came into his eyes, as if he had just recognized a dear friend beckoning from far beyond. His eyes closed gently, and a faint smile came over the now relaxed lips.

Clare hugged the sagging frame closer, rocking him back and forth, weeping, softly calling his name. But he did not respond.

The doctor holding the stethoscope looked up at Clare and shook his head.

"And so he crossed over, and all the trumpets sounded on the other side."

20

Branch Trumbull was to be buried in the ancestral plot on Lookout Mountain near Chattanooga, and the funeral would be held in Old First Presbyterian, his home church. But first came a memorial service at Potomac Presbyterian for the Washington friends and relatives. It was the largest and grandest service Chase had ever attended. There was no casket, only massive banks of flowers and a crowd that overflowed the seating capacity of the sanctuary.

Clare had asked Chase to join the family in the front pew. He felt honored, though still slightly like an intruder. He sidled unobtrusively into the pew and sat by the aisle on the far end near the church wall, not wanting to displace Trumbull blood kin.

Libby, on the other end of the pew, saw him, though, and beckoned for him to sit next to her. Libby was on Clare's right, and then Banks, looking more than ever like his father. A few moments later, a somber Jimmy Tolliver and his wife, Janet, red-eyed from weeping, sat next to Chase.

He felt the inquiring stares on the back of his neck as he sat next to Libby and wondered if people in the rows behind thought he was a new or prospective member of the family.

He sensed the warmth of Libby's presence but felt no disloyalty at all to Neeley Durant. She had declined to come. She "just didn't like funerals."

Well, I don't like them either, especially when it's to say goodbye to a friend. And, if the truth were told, especially when the funeral was held in a church where the ministers, instead of limiting their comments to a fitting eulogy, included remarks that made him think uncomfortably about the hereafter and the state of his immortal soul.

This minister was no exception. But his encomiums to Branch Trumbull were eloquent and triumphant. Chase was mystified.

Listening, he got the impression the preacher felt that being shot down in cold blood—and probably by a homosexual terrorist—was somehow a victory.

Until now he had felt only shock, which had settled into a kind of numbness. But now, as he listened to the tributes to his friend, anger began to pulsate within him again. There was no moral victory to celebrate as far as he was concerned. *They*—he was sure he knew who "they" were—could not be allowed to get away with this murder.

He became impatient for the service to end. Anger left him in no mood to dwell on a message of love, redemption, and salvation. And dwelling on Trumbull's death, and on what had been lost, just stoked the fires of his personal bitterness toward the gay militants. Indeed, toward all gays.

He could see Jimmy Tolliver out of the corner of his eye, two places away from him. He knew it was irrational, but he even felt dislike for Jimmy, though the man had been the senator's closest associate.

After the service, Chase joined the large number of friends who dropped by the Trumbulls' home in Potomac for coffee and a final visit. There he met many church leaders and celebrities of Christian communications and was surprised to learn how diverse and vibrant a group they were. Most seemed perfectly normal—even interesting and well-informed—and not out of place in this affluent suburb of the nation's capital.

He was leaning against the front staircase, deep in conversation with two publishers, when someone tapped him lightly on the shoulder. Turning, he saw Clare Trumbull's face, pale and strangely aged in the past few days but still lovely in the half-light of the hallway.

"Chase, please don't rush off. I'd like to talk with you after the guests leave. Can you stay?"

"Certainly, if you like."

Eventually the callers began to trickle away. As Clare, Libby, and Banks said their good-byes and thank-yous in the front foyer, Chase helped the housemaid collect the coffee cups and soiled dishes. He needed something to occupy his mind.

Finally the last guest departed, and Clare walked slowly to the glassed-in back porch. Settling wearily into an armchair, she wrapped a knitted shawl around her shoulders. The solarium overlooked a broad meadow behind the house that sloped down to a creek and a deep, inviting stretch of woods.

She seemed to be studying the landscape intently, and Chase watched her with compassion from the adjacent kitchen as he prepared a tray of coffee. Libby and Banks had disappeared. Soon the housemaid left, and only he and Clare remained in the downstairs living area.

"How're you holding up?" he asked gently. He set down the coffee tray on the table next to her.

"Better than I thought I would," she said after a moment. "All these wonderful friends have helped. But I dread what's coming. Soon they'll soon be gone, and then I'll have to face being alone."

He wanted to praise her courage and composure but found the words locked up. It was impossible to say anything. Instead he poured her a steaming cup of coffee.

She accepted it gratefully. "And that's why I wanted to talk to you. Soon you'll be involved in the work, and perhaps we won't see as much of you."

"I won't be far away," he said. "And you know if you need me for anything, anything at all . . ." He did not finish the sentence but asked abruptly, "Clare, what do you mean by 'the work'?"

She looked at him over the rim of her cup. "I guess we've all been hoping—including Libby and Banks and Jimmy—that you'd carry on Branch's work. I'm sure he would have wanted you to take over the Foundation. Jimmy can run the day-to-day business, but it will need a national spokesman or the whole thing will collapse."

Chase got up and paced along the glass partition, his back to Clare, looking out over the landscape. He did not want her to see the dismay that had to be written on his face.

Take over the Foundation? Who am I to pick up Branch Trumbull's fallen flag anyway? Besides—his thoughts raced—there was Jimmy Tolliver. *How could I possibly work with Jimmy Tolliver? No doubt he's been "saved" and all that. And he's married to a fine girl. But he's still an ex-queer.*

But common courtesy if nothing else prevented him from criticizing her suggestion.

"Clare," he said thoughtfully, turning back to face her. "You know how much I looked up to the senator. I was honored to be able to help him. And even more honored to feel like I was a part of his family. But honestly, I'm not the one to lead this fight. And I'm certainly not qualified to head the Foundation."

She laughed softly. "You won't believe this, but Branch didn't think he was qualified to do it either."

"But he was a natural leader. And a United States senator. And y'all have means."

"Yes, that's all true. But even so, he was a reluctant warrior."

"I find that hard to understand." He leaned against the glass doors. "Tell me about him, Clare. I feel I could never be capable of carrying the burden that y'all are expecting. But if I ever could be, I'd need to know him better. What can you tell me?"

Chase was more than merely curious. He and Branch had much in common. They came from similar backgrounds—old families with strong Southern roots and close ties to the land. Both had been raised in a tradition of honor, duty, and the code of the gentleman. And both had obeyed the high calling of service to their country, though in widely differing ways. That should be sufficient to give him the same strength of character as Branch, he rationalized. But Branch Trumbull had something more.

"Branch always understood that life is a struggle," Clare said slowly. "He longed for peaceful things—riding his horses, spending time with his family, walking in the woods, reading, fishing. Yet he felt it was his mission to contend against evil until Christ comes again. Reluctant as he may have been, he saw himself essentially as a Christian warrior. I think that's the only reason he ran for the Senate—it was a strategic location for waging spiritual warfare."

"He was a warrior," agreed Chase, "in every sense of the word. He fought hard for his principles in the Senate. And I know he was in combat in the Persian Gulf War. Though he never told me much about it."

"No, he never talked much about his experience in the Gulf, except to me." A stricken look came across her face. She put down her coffee, dabbed at her eyes with a tissue, and quickly regained her composure.

"Something happened in the Gulf, didn't it?" Chase asked. Perhaps here lay a clue to the man's character, and Chase wanted more than ever to understand him. When Clare did not answer immediately, somehow he knew.

He stepped away from the glass partition and sat down next to her again. "Tell me about it."

"I will," she said without hesitating further. "It was a pivotal experience for him. You know, the war was such a lopsided victory and the casualties were so low that most Americans have forgotten that our side faced death too. After all, they went up against the fourth largest army in the world, as I recall—one with modern weapons and equipment. Our boys expected the worst. The experts had been predicting we'd lose thousands of men."

"We all expected to see a lot of our men killed."

"Anyway, Branch was in command of an artillery unit of the National Guard that was called up to support the regular army. He never felt his men were in much danger since they were well behind the lines. They would shoot and move, shoot and move.

"But one night, he said, they shot and moved right into an Iraqi mine field. They were deep into it when a truck suddenly blew up. Somehow the mine-clearing people had missed this one. Miraculously no one was killed."

"What did they do?"

"Well, they tried to go back the way they came, but then another vehicle hit a mine, and that time some men were hurt. So they had to stay put, call for help, then sit and wait for them to come clear a lane. And since they were stationary for longer than usual, the Iraqi artillery began to get close. Of course the Iraqis didn't have those—uh—spotters—what do you call them?"

"Forward observers?"

"Yes, forward observers who could tell their guns where to aim. But still their artillery fire was sort of sweeping over a wide area, coming closer and closer. And his men couldn't move out of the way because of the mines. So you know what he did?"

"I can guess." Chase smiled, remembering the night they faced the hostile crowd outside the DBN studio.

"Yes." Clare smiled too. "He called the officers and non-coms together and prayed for help. In a mine field. With enemy fire heading right for them." She paused, and again the sad, longing look crept into her face.

Chase said quietly, "And the enemy fire passed over them, didn't it?"

"Yes, it did. Not a man was hurt. Some shells landed on one side of them, and Branch said they all were lying down under what cover they had, waiting to be hit. But then the next salvo fell on the other side. From then on, he said, he never doubted God's power and faithfulness."

Chase did not reply but again recalled the genuine fearlessness with which Branch had faced the enraged mob outside the studio.

"Later there was a pause in the fighting. Branch was ordered to stop and resupply. So he called together another prayer meeting —to give thanks for getting out of the mine field and the Iraqi fire. Every man who wasn't on some work detail showed up. They had a wonderful chaplain who preached a little sermon from Psalm 91.

"It starts, 'He who dwells in the shelter of the Most High will abide in the shadow of the Almighty,'" she quoted. "Then it says the Lord 'is my refuge and and my fortress,' and, 'He shall cover you with his feathers. . . . You shall not be afraid for the terror by night, nor for the arrow that flies by day.' The chaplain invited the men to trust Christ, and nearly a hundred soldiers responded.

"So if you want to understand Branch Trumbull, Chase, that's the key. It's very simple, really. He trusted God and believed His Word."

Chase looked down at the floor. *Then why did God allow him to be killed?*

As if reading his thoughts, Clare said, "Knowing all this, Chase, are we supposed to believe that God was not with Branch at the NRCA convention? Or that the Iraqi artillery passed over them and the mines didn't kill anyone purely by coincidence?"

"N-no." Chase suddenly felt as if he was choking. Anger

now gave way to pent-up grief and a helpless sense of loss. "But then how *do* you explain it? If all that's true, why did God let him be murdered? Where were the sheltering wings?"

"I can't explain all that. But also I don't question God. His ways are not our ways. I miss Branch. More than you can possibly imagine. And his children miss him terribly. And I know the real pain is just beginning. But I trust God too, just like Branch did. All I can say is that his Commander-in-Chief has called him to some other duty."

She straightened and looked directly at him. "Chase, he believed that the Lord is calling you to the same duty. Branch has fallen on the battlefield, and the Lord is calling you to step into that gap in the ranks and resume the battle. As close as Branch and I were, his last words were to *you*, remember?"

"How could I ever forget? He told me to 'redeem the time.'"

"Yes, redeem the time. But Chase, you can't enter this battle until you first enlist in God's army. You have to know the King— in your heart, not just intellectually. You have to really trust in Him, become one of God's people."

Chase got up again and paced the room. He did not want to reveal that he was offended or to hurt Clare's feelings in any way. He was not even sure what "redeem the time" meant.

Suddenly, senselessly, he was angry at Branch Trumbull. The senator was pursuing him even from beyond the grave. Every time he turned around there was religion, stalking him, making its claims on him. He felt cornered.

And yet how could he turn his back on Branch's work? He saw himself as a warrior too, a political warrior, a soldier in the service of ideals. He was willing to fight. He knew he had the mental equipment and temperament for it.

He knew befuddled Americans now casually accepted things that would have been unthinkable five years ago. Because they were gradually forgetting their moral code, their heritage, they watched blithely while the process of destruction continued unchecked.

He understood too that the disintegration of any great culture was incremental, almost imperceptible. Yet because he remembered, he could perceive what was happening by comparing things as they were now to what they had been only scant years past. Perhaps his destiny was simply to call people back to remembrance.

But couldn't he do what he knew was right, carry on Branch Trumbull's battle against the enemy, without having to get so fanatically wrapped up in Christianity? Besides, didn't he believe the Bible? He didn't go around quoting it to everybody, but he believed it. He had even begun to see how his whole political system, his patriotism, and his civic philosophy were all built squarely on a biblical foundation.

And didn't he believe Jesus was the Son of God? Of course he did, although he didn't go around asking people if they were "saved." People needed to be free to follow God in their own way. That's the way he saw it. If anybody asked him if Jesus was the Son of God, he would say yes. And didn't that belief make him a Christian? Of course it did. Maybe not as good a Christian as Branch or Clare Trumbull. Or even Libby. But certainly better than most people he knew.

Chase was beginning to feel better about himself. He didn't cheat, steal, and murder. He didn't get drunk—well, maybe he was drinking a little too much these days to counter all the stress, but he didn't get drunk. He didn't use drugs. True, he was sleeping with Neeley—but he was young and he cared for her deeply. At least he wasn't gay. That had to be the worst, the bottom of the list.

Comparatively speaking, he decided, he wasn't so bad.

When his thoughts finally ceased tumbling over one another, he knew he would pick up Trumbull's fallen banner. But he would carry it in his own way and not as head of the Nehemiah Foundation.

During all of Chase's chaotic thinking, he was conscious of Clare, silent in her chair, gazing out the glass doors and across the sloping meadow. Still standing, he turned and faced her again.

"Next to my own father and grandfather, Clare, your husband was the finest man I ever met. He changed my life, and I'm going to continue his fight. But first I'm going to go after the people who killed him. They think they got rid of their number one problem. Well, they've not seen anything yet."

Clare hung her head for a moment, then said in a voice full of resignation, as if she knew she could not dissuade him, "Chase, there's no passion of the human heart that promises so much and rewards so little as revenge."

"I'm not talking about revenge. I'm talking about justice."

"Well, I want his killer brought to justice too. But let the God of justice bring it about. In the meantime, I don't want you to use Branch's death as an excuse to make this a purely personal vendetta."

Her shot struck home, and he turned away again, jaw muscles tensing.

"Whatever you do," she continued gently, "I believe God will guide your path, though maybe in ways none of us can see right now."

Chase nodded. *Guide your path.* The words echoed. He leaned wearily against the heavy glass partition, and a movement outside caught his eye.

Trotting up from the lower margins of the meadow toward the house were two handsome bay horses. Against the wooden fence that separated the backyard from the pasture stood a lone figure, bundled against the chill of the gray winter day but still slender and clearly feminine. It was Libby. She was holding out her hand to the horses.

Something called his attention back to Clare. "Guide your path," she had said. The phrase echoed with odd reassurance. He possessed an active visual imagination, and an image suddenly flashed into his mind—the well-worn path on the Powell Mountain overlook, snaking up to Draper's Leap from his cabin down in the hollow.

Suddenly Chase longed to go there, to find refuge from his grief, anger, dismay—and, above all, from his confusion that God, if He was God, had allowed Those People to kill Branch Trumbull.

I'll go there tonight, he decided.

He sat by Clare, taking her cold hand. "Clare, I'm trying to absorb all you've said. I really am. After I met Branch, so many things have happened to me, and many things are new to me. I'm rediscovering many things from my upbringing. And frankly, it's all left me a little confused. I believe I *am* following God's path, that I *am* part of God's army. But you've got to let me try and work things out in my own way." He was trying to be gentle, but clear.

"OK," she answered gently. "I've said what I wanted to say, and I won't press you anymore. I know you'll do the right thing." She patted his arm and smiled.

"Good-bye, Clare. I'll go say good-bye to Libby." He leaned over and hugged her tenderly, then went out through the glass-paneled doors of the solarium and down the back stair to where Libby stood with the Thoroughbreds.

She was stroking their smooth necks. Chase joined her wordlessly and began to run his hands over a velvety muzzle.

"It's always amazed me how such a large, powerful animal could have such soft skin," he remarked.

Libby smiled. "I've always felt the same way. It's as if the touch of God is everywhere. In the most unlikely places."

He admired her serenity and courage under such a load of grief. And somehow he felt he could open himself up to Libby in a way that he could not with anyone else.

"You're like your mother," he volunteered.

"I take that as a compliment," she answered, surprised. "But in what way?"

"Well, lots of ways. You both seem so strong and brave after this—this incredible tragedy. You seem to understand the why of it all. I just had a long talk with her, and *I* don't understand. But I feel like I can talk to you about it."

"I'm glad you feel that way. It helps to talk. Helps all of us who loved him." She stroked the horse's cheek.

That was the word. Love. *I learned so much from him,* Chase said silently. *I respected him. I admired him. But I never realized until just now that I loved him.*

"Yes." His thoughts suddenly turned into speech, but with a tone of surprise. "I did love him."

"I know," she said. Still resting her hand on the horse's muzzle, she lowered her head and began to weep silently. The animal, as if grasping her mood, dropped its head and stood quietly.

Chase felt a moment's awkwardness, then stepped close and put his arm around her. She felt small and childlike under the bulky sweater.

She let herself be comforted, turning to him and crying softly into his shoulder.

After a short while he pulled out a handkerchief and offered it to her.

"No, thanks, I came prepared." She laughed through her tears and produced a sodden hanky of her own.

You also have Clare's beauty and charm, he thought but did not say so aloud. That would have trespassed on the solemnity of the moment, interposing a feeling that had no business being there. And he would rather die than have her think he was trying to take advantage of her vulnerability. A romantic attachment was not at all what he was seeking.

Besides, she wasn't as beautiful as Neeley. At least not in the same way.

"What're you going to do now?" he asked finally.

"Do?"

"Yes. Are you going to stay here, or—or what?"

"No. I have a job. I happen to think it's more than a job—it's a calling. And life must go on. So I'll be going back to the college after the funeral in Chattanooga."

An unexpected twinge of regret thrust in among the welter of emotions he was feeling—tenderness, protectiveness, a sense of burgeoning friendship. Why should he have assumed that she would remain in Washington?

"Well then, take care. I've got to go, but I'll miss you. I hope I'll see you again before too long."

"You take care too, Chase." There was an ominous note in that routine phrase that suddenly chilled him.

As if she sensed his alarm, Libby stretched up on her toes and kissed him on the cheek. "I'll miss you too. Thank you for everything."

She turned back to the horses, and Chase trudged up the hill to his car.

21

This time they did not meet at Monnoye's Upperville estate. Wynn Pritchett had complained about the long trek out to the country—it made him feel increasingly like a hired hand. He was an important business executive. His time was as valuable as Monnoye's. This time he insisted on meeting in town.

Late at night Monnoye greeted Pritchett at his office in the Paragon Building, and they made desultory conversation while waiting for May Berg. She arrived twenty minutes late as usual—her way of asserting herself with her powerful colleagues.

Monnoye did not have much to say about Senator Trumbull's murder. But he opened a bottle of Veuve Cliquot champagne and, after a toast to his allies, turned to the business at hand.

"Well, my friends, things return upon themselves. Hatred begets hatred, and the fates have kindly taken Branch Trumbull out of our way. Now how did we do with Chase McKenzie?" He looked pleasantly at Wynn Pritchett.

"Well, Perce," Pritchett reported gloomily, "I'm afraid it didn't work."

"Tell us what happened," Monnoye insisted.

"I invited him over to the Eastern Shore. I've got this huntin' lodge over there, and I knew he liked to hunt. So we went duck huntin' . . ." His voice trailed off dispiritedly.

"Did you make a good offer?" May Berg was impatient.

"Course I did. But first I tried to soften him up a little. You know. We talked some and had a couple of drinks and a good dinner. Not a Garden Monnoye banquet, but a good country dinner. I was trying to build rapport with him."

"And then?" Monnoye probed gently. Pritchett knew Monnoye was as full of impatience as May Berg. But ever the diplomat, he contained it.

"Well, like I said, it didn't work," Pritchett continued, still exasperated. "He was civil and all that. But . . . well, he just didn't take the bait. I spent the whole evening tryin' to get close to him, but he kept his distance."

Pritchett did not add that McKenzie had been exquisitely polite and courteous. Ironically, McKenzie's good manners had only served to proclaim an attitude of social superiority. *Oh so proper*, Pritchett still fumed, *all the while barely hiding his dislike. Like he thought he was too good to work for me.*

The snub rankled as much as the failure of their grand design. Now for the first time his personal motives were engaged in the process. He would bring McKenzie down yet.

"And then what?" May Berg asked, smiling her superior smile, as if she already knew the answer.

"We were out in the duck blind. It was cold outside, but cozy and warm in the blind. I fixed it up real nice," he said proudly. "Got a propane heater, and a little bar . . ."

He saw their impatience begin to bubble over. "Anyway, it was a perfect mornin', and so while he was in a good mood I made him a fine offer. He gave me a kind of polite smile and said he was content where he was. I offered him money and all the perks, but he said he had enough money for his needs. And so I said, 'Just what *do* you want?' And he gave me that chilly smile again and said, 'I just want to bag a few ducks.' So I didn't push him, and we sort of got things back on track and had a good shoot.

"But then, back at the lodge, I put some pressure on him and at the same time told him what a great career opportunity he was passin' up. He just kept saying he was happy where he was."

Pritchett felt his face redden at having to relive the humiliation, something he had not experienced for many years. "Finally I got a little mad, and that's when he told me to go to blazes—politely, of course. And that was it. I went back inside, and he left."

"I knew it," May muttered contemptuously. "I knew you couldn't buy off the little creep."

"*You* knew!" Pritchett exploded. All his suppressed anger at Chase McKenzie found a target in May Berg. "*You!* Listen, three weeks ago I sat right here while *you* suggested we buy him off. I was the one who said it couldn't be done."

"Stop it right now, both of you!" interrupted Monnoye. "We can't afford to fall out among ourselves. And we needn't get so worked up about it anyway. I'm not worried about Chase McKenzie."

May studied him a moment and said, "You're really not, are you? But don't you think you *should* be? Look what his TV show did to the HRA effort in Pennsylvania."

Pritchett looked from to the other. May was making clear that she thought the number one gay leader was not sufficiently alert to threats against the movement.

"Trumbull was the heart and brain of the homo-hatred backlash," Monnoye explained patiently. "He worried me. He had convictions and a kind of power that made him a dangerous enemy. But now that he's out of the way, Chase McKenzie won't cause us any more trouble. McKenzie isn't another Branch Trumbull. He was riding Trumbull's coattails into the limelight. Now he's just another two-bit talking head on television."

"But, Perce, I hear he's launched an investigation into Trumbull's murder," Pritchett objected. "Got DBN to put up a reward. Who knows what he might turn up?"

Monnoye waved a hand. "McKenzie's just a fly buzzing around the carcass," he replied smoothly. "There's no need to worry about him—and no need for taking unnecessary risks in dealing with him."

"Sometimes," May complained, "I wonder if you're not trying to have it both ways. You want to be accepted by the straight world, and you want to lead the gay world."

"Precisely!" Monnye said without hesitation. "Now listen, May. I know you were part of the original gay revolution, and I respect that highly. If it hadn't been for the old fighters like you, we never would have come out as a community or begun fighting back for our rights—"

"You don't need to patronize me, Perce."

"I'm not patronizing you. I'm trying to make an important point. The old Stonewall Riot tactics have failed. They've actually been counterproductive. You yourself admitted that confrontation and exhibitionism no longer work. We can't win without acceptance—or at least strong allies—in the straight world."

Wynn Pritchett sat listening impassively.

Monnoye smiled in his direction, then turned back to May. "You agreed that the time has come for a more subtle approach— persuasion, use of the media to create a positive image of the gay community. You promised to try it my way, and you've been a valuable part of this team. We need you. But if you can't stay with the program, then perhaps it's time for you to bow out gracefully."

Pritchett saw the woman's deep-set black eyes widen. In alarm?

Lowering her head she replied quietly, "No, I'm not challenging your strategy. I did agree. But that doesn't mean that every decision you make is the right one. What if McKenzie does give us more grief? He's got the forum to do it. Of all people, we ought not to underestimate the power of television." Unable to stand up to Monnoye, May glowered at Wynn Pritchett.

He ignored her.

"Then we'll think of something else," said Monnoye soothingly. "Since we can't buy him off, we'll discredit him."

"Maybe somebody'll knock him off. Like they did Senator Trumbull," Wynn said. He looked directly at Monnoye, hoping to provoke a reaction.

Monnoye, however, gazed back at him with unwavering eyes. There was no guilty response of any kind, not even a flicker of his eyelids.

Now even May Berg was regarding Monnoye a little strangely, with something like respect, as if what Pritchett was suggesting had never occurred to her.

"Well, perhaps someone *will* eliminate him," Monnoye said evenly. "A lot of people are angry enough to do it. But that's not anything we can plan on. No, if and when the time comes to get rid of McKenzie, we'll use the means at our disposal—and they are considerable."

The undercurrent in his voice let Wynn Pritchett know this trail was not to be followed any further.

"In any case, Wynn, I know you did your best," Monnoye added with a placating smile. "We can get rid of McKenzie if need be—and without recourse to violence."

★ ★ ★

Monnoye relived Leon's call a few days after the shooting—what Leon called his "after action report."

Toby had gotten clean away. No one at the hotel had seen him clearly enough to give a good description, much less identify him to the police. The next day Leon had given him a small amount of cash, then briefed him on the hefty bank account in New York supposedly set up for him.

Toby, full of swagger at his exploit and clearly looking forward to a wildly libidinous future, had taken his routine medication from Rudy. But this time he quietly went into shock, then respiratory and cardiac arrest. He had expired before he could realize how completely he had been betrayed.

It was unfortunate to have to do that to Toby, but, in Leon's expressive phrase, it was required by the fortunes of war.

Yes, Monnoye thought with intense satisfaction, it had all been very neat and clean, thanks to Leon Pound and to Monnoye's own foresight in keeping Leon in his inner circle. All potential troublesome loose ends had been neatly tied up and the Trumbull problem disposed of, leaving nothing that could ever point back to Monnoye.

But the risk of mishap or exposure had been there, and Monnoye was a cautious man. Cautious in all his dealings. He would not do it again except in the direst need. This McKenzie character could be taken care of with more conventional methods.

★ ★ ★

Wynn Pritchett sat glumly for a while, watching Monnoye pondering something. Pritchett wondered, as he always did, what went on in that complex, creative, devious brain.

Then suddenly Monnoye laughed aloud. "Listen, why the long faces? This shouldn't be so hard to handle, should it? The three of us and one minor league broadcaster who probably isn't worth the trouble in the first place. But if it'll make you feel better —if you must occupy your talents with getting rid of him and having a little fun—then I have an idea."

"Let's hear it," May said.

"McKenzie's not married, is he? Hasn't got children?"

"No, he's not married," replied Pritchett.

"What are you thinking, Perce? What's the plan?" May demanded.

"May, he's thirty-five and unmarried. And what—or who—does he hate the most? Gays. Don't you feel a delicious attack of irony coming on?" He chuckled.

The light broke on May's face, and she smiled wickedly. "Oh, Perce, of course! Of course!"

Wynn Pritchett felt he was the straight man among them in more ways than one. *I can hardly follow the secret code among these homos,* he had thought more than once. Monnoye's secretiveness annoyed him to distraction—and the way he kept the details of a plan to himself so he could claim all the credit if it worked and avoid the blame if it failed. But Monnoye made the rules, and Pritchett knew he was in the game for keeps. Especially if it meant delivering his comeuppance to Chase McKenzie.

"D'you want to let me in on the secret?" he asked irritably.

"All in good time, Wynn, all in good time. But first, some assignments—that is, if you two are really set on disposing of him."

When Pritchett and May Berg both nodded, Monnoye went on. "OK, Wynn, I want you to find out all you can about the TV network McKenzie works for. Who owns it. Their financial condition. When their FCC renewal comes up again. Who the network executives are. Who produces and sponsors 'Pulse of the Nation.'"

"Glad to. That jerk hasn't heard the last of Wynn Pritchett, not by a long shot."

"And May, find out if he has a girlfriend or fiancée, and if so, check her out. I'll have a little chat with our friend Kerry Kerrigan in the White House. We'll meet again next week, if that's convenient."

Monnoye stood up. "Meantime, there are some other matters I'll take care of myself."

★ ★ ★

As Chase prepared for his upcoming broadcast, anger still roiled and rumbled inside him. Despite Clare's warning, the sharp taste of bitterness against his traditional enemies was pleasing in a dark, perverse way.

However, anger impelled him to do *something* but did not tell him *what* to do. How could he strike back? There was hardly a better forum than "Pulse of the Nation." But where was the story?

Two days later, amid the usual flood of letters the network mail clerk dumped in his "In" basket was a large, brown, padded mailer. It bore a Mississippi postmark but a Norman, Oklahoma, return address. Aside from that discrepancy, there was nothing unusual about it except for the numerous "urgent" stamps all over the outside.

The package had been scanned by the mass spectrometer to check for explosives, and Chase ripped it open. A single-page typed note, a bundle of typescript and newspaper clips, and several audio tapes tumbled out. Curious, he looked again at the name of the sender. Jay Blaisdell.

According to the note, Blaisdell was a newspaper reporter from Oklahoma who had been covering a sensational murder trial in Jackson, Mississippi. The typed notes and clippings spelled out the particulars of the trial of a man named Eddie Webb, who had just been convicted of killing a young Mississippi boy. Evidence found in Webb's van pointed to his being a serial killer, and Chase's horror mounted as he read of the extraordinary, macabre twist to the story—Webb had actually videotaped his victims in the throes of death.

The evidence was overwhelming and incontrovertible. There seemed to be no doubt about Webb's guilt. The defense alleged no improprieties in the arrest. The court had the accused examined by a team of psychiatrists and declared him mentally fit to stand trial.

Chase frowned. Well-connected as he was in the news business, he had heard nothing about Eddie Webb or his multiple murders until he got this package from Blaisdell. When he read further and saw the defense strategy outlined, he began to understand why.

The unusual circumstances had predictably and inexorably drawn the homosexual legal establishment into the case. Chase learned that the best lawyers from the Lambda Legal Defense Guild had rushed down to provide a pro bono defense for Eddie Webb with the ringing battle cry "Just because he's gay!" Their only defense had been to argue that a gay man could not get a fair trial in homophobic Mississippi.

But the indispensable ally of the homosexual bar was the national news media, also dominated by gays or their sympathizers. Evidently the media establishment feared that Harmon Lait, president of the Lambda Legal Defense Guild, had made a strategic blunder in putting the gay bar's credibility on the line by defending such a man. Fearing a backlash from a public incensed at rising crime, the national media had simply suppressed accounts of the murders and Webb's eventual conviction.

To be sure, the case was widely reported in Mississippi and in neighboring states through regional papers and local broadcast media. But despite the gruesomeness of the crimes and the unique and therefore newsworthy aspect of the killer's recording his own crimes, it never became a national story. The big news outlets simply ignored it.

Chase was well aware that if a news organization wanted to influence public opinion on an issue, suppressing a story was sometimes better than reporting it.

By and large the public had learned to filter out much of the bias in what passed these days as news reporting. But if an event was met with deliberate, concerted silence by the national media —if reporters simply chose not to cover it—then, as far as the average American knew, it simply never happened.

Scrapping his earlier plans for the broadcast, Chase got on the telephone and invited Blaisdell to appear on that weekend's program.

I'll blow the lid off this, he said to himself with grim joy, *and it'll embarrass the national media by exposing a deliberate news blackout to protect the gay crowd. It may even show the links between the news media establishment and gay action groups.*

He would put his own spin on the case: the nation's most prominent and respected news organizations were colluding to black out a major story in order to spare the national gay rights movement embarrassment. It was to be pitched as a story about the news media. By framing his broadcast primarily as a media story he could still get the facts of the case out before the people. That

206

would constitute a major hit on the homosexual activists without appearing to be another gay-bashing broadcast.

Jay Blaisdell, a handsome young black man with a confident manner, duly arrived in Washington. On the evening of the show, Chase allocated extra time to discuss the program with him in detail before air time. He found his guest to be extremely articulate and well-informed, and he made a mental note to keep in touch with him.

This is the kind of guy I want on my side, Chase said silently as they prepared to go live.

He introduced his guest, then launched immediately into the story.

"Jay, the file you sent me on this Eddie Webb murder case in Mississippi is—well—incredible. These killings are probably the most bizarre and shocking serial murders since the highly publicized Dahmer case back in 1991.

"You've been covering this story for several months, Jay. In your opinion how does it compare to the Dahmer case?"

"Well, Chase, I'd have to say it's nearly the equal in horror and brutality. Maybe worse. In the first place, it appears that Eddie Webb has killed nearly twice as many young men as Dahmer did. And while he didn't engage in anything so horrible as eating his victims, there is one aspect to his crimes that we've never encountered before."

"And that is—?"

"Webb was a video technician and film editor. He had what amounts to a complete mobile film lab in his van, and he traveled around the country in this van picking up young men and boys. Then he actually videotaped his victims while murdering them."

"You mean he made what they call 'snuff films.'"

"That's right. But with one big difference—he taped his own killings."

"That's incredible. Why would anyone do that? I mean, he produced the very evidence that convicted him."

"Yes, he did. The experts in criminal psychology say he wanted to be able to relive whatever high he got from these murders. And over time he became so sure he'd never be caught that he became careless. Of course some would say he had an unconscious compulsion to get caught."

"Have you seen the tapes?"

Blaisdell paused. The camera zoomed in to a dramatic tight shot as his Adam's apple bobbed in his throat. Finally he said, "Yes, I have. Not all, but several of them."

"I don't want to wallow in the gory details, but can you describe what you saw?"

"That's not easy to do. In fact there are times when I wish I'd never seen them."

"I understand," Chase said patiently. "But try. Just give us an idea."

"Well, he—uh— tortured his victims to death. And that's all I can say—tortured them, sexually tortured, that is. I really can't go into any more detail." Blaisdell pulled out a large silk handkerchief and mopped his grim face.

Chase let a moment's dramatic silence hang in the air, then shook his head in disbelief. "Jay, how did you happen to see these tapes? Were they shown in the trial? As evidence?"

"The tape of the Mississippi murder was the only one allowed into evidence, and the judge closed the court while it was shown to the jury. Newsmen had a chance to see selected portions afterwards. But some people in law enforcement down there are unhappy about the way the national news media have handled the story, so they gave me access to the whole set. I guess they thought I'd be more forthcoming."

"And how *have* the media handled it?

"Well, in my opinion, the story has been deliberately suppressed. The reporting of the case has been limited to only local or regional newspapers and local broadcasts. None of the big networks or national papers or newsmagazines have carried it."

"If you're saying there has been an almost total news blackout of the story," Chase observed, "I would have to agree. I'm a professional journalist, and I've seen nothing on the wire service tickers, in the big papers, or on any of the major networks on the Webb trial. Do you have any idea why the news media haven't reported such an important trial? After all, reporters thrive on stories like this. In the past they've been downright ghoulish in covering serial killings and mass murderers, down to the last macabre detail."

"Yes, that's true."

"Well then, is there something else about this case that off-sets its newsworthiness? I mean, something that would cause the national media to suppress it?"

"I can only speculate. But the defense attorney—"

"Excuse the interruption," Chase interjected, "but who was the defense attorney?"

"Attorneys, I should have said. There was a local criminal lawyer. They had to have a member of the Mississippi bar. But the real defense was the heavy artillery from out of state. Namely, the head of the Lambda Legal Defense Guild, Harmon Lait."

"The Lambda Legal Defense Guild? That's a gay and lesbian group."

"Yes. Harmon Lait came down and took charge and wouldn't let anyone on the defense team give any interviews. He demanded a press gag order, which the judge allowed while the first phase of the trial was under way. Not everybody obeyed it of course, and it was lifted after the conviction. Naturally the jury was sequestered during the trial and didn't see any of the local news reports.

"But what struck me was this," Blaisdell continued. "The defense hardly bothered to dispute the facts of the case. Harmon Lait tried at first to argue that the very nature of the defendant's acts—he would never say 'crimes'—proved that the man was mentally incompetent to stand trial. But when that didn't work, it was like the defense just wanted to get the presentation of evidence out of the way as quickly as possible so they could employ their real strategy."

"But they really didn't have a case," Chase noted.

"No, they didn't. So their strategy was to attack the legitimacy of the trial itself."

"Can you give me an example—and how that ties in with a national news blackout?"

"In effect, they argued that Webb couldn't get a fair trial in the state of Mississippi."

"So they put the state of Mississippi on trial. Why couldn't he get a fair trial down there, according to the Lambda folks?"

"'Just because he's gay!' That was their case in a nutshell," Blaisdell answered.

"I see. In other words, the crime didn't matter. What did matter was that the defendant was a homosexual."

"That was the practical effect of their defense. For one thing, they cited the governor's statement a few years back that 'America is a Christian nation.' They claimed that statement fed the fires of bigotry and was just right wing code for hatred and intolerance against gays. They argued that since the jury pool was drawn from a population that was subject to such inflammatory rhetoric, the jury couldn't possibly be impartial with a gay man in the dock."

"I see. What else?"

"They moved for a mistrial on the grounds that the Bible had been used in the proceedings."

"The Bible! How could use of the Bible invalidate the trial?"

"Well, witnesses for the state were sworn in by using the Bible, which the defense argued was a homophobic book full of antigay rhetoric. And in his summation, the prosecutor had invoked the Bible in demanding a conviction and capital punishment for the accused. The defense argued further that by allowing the prosecution to invoke the Bible's religious condemnation of homosexuality, the court improperly allowed the jury to be prejudiced against the defense. Therefore, a mistrial."

"Don't most courts swear witnesses on the Bible?"

"Chase, I'm afraid you're behind the times. These days most courts *don't* use the Bible. Though some still do in the so-called Bible belt. But even there a witness can opt not to swear on it."

"I see. I'm surprised to learn that. But I guess I ought not to be. What else can you tell us?"

"Well, the Lambda team attacked the trial judge because he was a Southern Baptist. They argued that this was a judicial lynching and called attention to Mississippi's well-known reputation for lynching."

"A judicial lynching just because Eddie Webb was gay?"

"Exactly." Blaisdell paused and sipped some water. "I forgot to mention—at the beginning of the trial the defense used their peremptory challenges to disqualify every prospective juror who had a conservative religious background. And when they ran out of peremptory challenges, Lait tried to challenge them for cause on the same grounds—that they were homo-haters if they were religious."

"So you're speculating that news organizations didn't want to get the so-called religious right all stirred up over this case."

"No, I'm not saying that. The religious right is already stirred up—ever since the end of the trial last week—through their own media. But as you know, they're considered merely a subculture. The big networks and newspapers don't feel the nation as a whole pays any attention to religious people, so the 'religious fanatics' can scream all they like behind the walls of the church and it won't slop over into the general culture.

"The national media only get worried when the religious fanatics *do* somehow reach the general public—which this case certainly has the potential of doing."

"Well, it's clear enough then," Chase suggested. "The news organizations didn't want to get the general public worked up against the gay legal rights crowd."

"That's my opinion," agreed Blaisdell.

"Protecting the gay movement from a possible backlash, in other words?"

"You could put it that way, yes."

"As a reporter yourself, would you agree that's a legitimate role for national news media?"

Blaisdell snorted. "I think that question answers itself. All I can say is this—whatever happened to the public's vaunted right to know?"

"Indeed. So what's next? Webb has been convicted, and you say he'll be sentenced next week. What's your prediction about the sentence?"

"Oh, I think he'll get the death penalty, all right," Blaisdell predicted. "But that doesn't mean anything. This case will go on appeal all the way up to the Supreme Court. I believe it'll become another landmark case. It's a classic conflict between the so-called rights of the accused and the role of religion in our national public life—including the law. It's the sort of thing the federal courts love to get their hands on. It allows them literally to make new law."

"New law in which religion is further evicted from the 'public square,'" Chase opined. "Obviously, whoever gets elected president next November could determine the outcome, because he'll have the chance to appoint at least two new Supreme Court justices in the next term."

"Possibly, yes. But even the present liberal Court could make the landmark decision on this case."

Chase speculated. "But theoretically, if Senator Hopkins wins the White House and appoints a homosexual Supreme Court justice, as he's promised, and if the Lambda Legal Defense Guild is able to stall long enough to bring this case before a more liberal Court—say in three or four years—then Eddie Webb is sure to go free."

"Well, not go free exactly," Blaisdell corrected him. "He'll still be charged in California or Oregon on the other murder counts. But the Mississippi conviction would almost certainly be overturned. So whatever happens to him ultimately would be up to the other states."

"Of course, California and Oregon no longer have capital punishment," Chase reminded him.

"No, they don't."

"So this guy could still get off."

"Only if you mean escape being executed," said Blaisdell. "My guess is he'll probably spend the rest of his life in prison. Or a mental institution. There's a greater likelihood he'd be judged insane in either of those other two states."

"Even though four different psychiatrists found him sane for the Mississippi trial?"

"That's correct."

"So the bottom line is that justice won't be done. He'll escape the punishment that such crimes deserve. The victims and their families will be forgotten. And all because the trial in Mississippi invoked the Bible and had fundamentalists on the jury. Justice will be thwarted, even though the sovereign state of Mississippi is willing and able to impose justice. In fact, their whole case against him may well be thrown out by a higher court."

"It'll take a while, but yes, that's what I expect."

On that note Chase concluded the interview portion of the show and opened up the telephone lines. All incoming lines had been full and holding long before the interview was over, and a torrent of calls now poured in from appalled and angry viewers. The Eddie Webb murder trial, for all practical purposes unknown to a national audience, was suddenly a cause célèbre.

On the broadcast Chase had said little directly about the Lambda Legal Defense Guild or any other homosexual action group. He had simply walked Jay Blaisdell through the facts, and the facts spoke for themselves. But his method had appropriated the outrage felt in those areas of the South where the Webb case had been reported.

Now millions of other Americans across the land felt the same indignation that such a crime should go unpunished just because the accused was a gay man tried in a conservative region.

Chase knew that he had stirred up a tidal wave of public outrage against the gay rights movement—and especially its handmaiden, the supposedly objective news media.

In the days that followed, congratulations flowed in. Clare Trumbull called to commend him. Jimmy Tolliver assured him he had scored a direct hit on the shadowy gay high command.

But that was not enough for Chase. He was still determined to lay before the American people convincing evidence that the gay movement had been behind Branch Trumbull's murder. So far, that evidence was elusive.

★ ★ ★

Chase settled in his favorite armchair in the apartment and turned on the TV remote to catch the late news from the National Broadcasting System. In his opinion, this network was the best of a bad lot. A few years ago NBS's "Exposé" program had aired a number of deliberately rigged reports, and the network had been forced to offer more balanced news programming to restore its damaged credibility.

He tuned in to the middle of a story that immediately caught his ear.

"Last night at about 9:00 P.M.," commentator Paul Povey was reporting, "gay and lesbian activists in New York City attacked the Shanks Club, a Manhattan-based counseling center which has reportedly counseled thousands of homosexual men in changing their sexual orientation over the years.

"Residents of the facility interviewed on the street as the building burned charged that the gay militants had thrown large quantities of blood on Father Tom Dutton, a Jesuit priest, who is director of the Shanks Club. But Queer and Present Danger spokespersons denied the charge.

"Local sources report it was the action of a new militant gay group called Come Out Fighting. Father Dutton is said to be at an undisclosed local hospital and cannot be reached for comment.

"We now go live to May Berg, head of Global Sisters, editor of *The New Feminist,* and a leading national spokesperson for gay and lesbian rights."

At this point the camera shifted to May Berg, dressed in her shapeless black.

"Ms. Berg, tell me, does the gay rights movement approve of this kind of activism?"

"No, Paul, of course not. We don't endorse violence of any kind—we leave that to the bigots and gay bashers who dominate the straight world. But you have to understand the extreme provocation which the Shanks Club has represented to gay people for years. Understandably, their rage does sometimes get out of hand. Frankly, we don't need any help in changing our sexual orientation! Maybe heterosexuals need help in changing *their* orientation."

"Thank you, May Berg. This is Paul Povey for NBS News, reporting live from the Shanks Club in Manhattan."

22

His heart always began to beat a little faster when he mounted the stairs to Neeley Durant's apartment. They had shared some exquisite moments, but there were still times when a sudden tremor of disbelief would seize him—did she really care for him? She seemed happy enough with him. He did his best to please her. And yet there was always an intriguing yet infuriating elusiveness about her.

Since the early part of his Saturday evenings were spent at the studio, Neeley usually stayed home, and he would come by afterwards. Tonight she had prepared a simple meal of spaghetti and salad. Finally, contented, he sat back in his chair, full of a good dinner and looking forward to the evening with her. He was still glowing from the indisputable success of the Eddie Webb exposé and was in an expansive mood.

"So what did you think of the show?"

She obviously was not in a similar mood. "If you wanted controversy, it appears you certainly got it."

"Yeah, well, I didn't just want controversy for its own sake. I wanted a full discussion of an issue that needed to be illuminated. You work with the press, Neel. Do you think it's right for the national media to black out a story this big?"

"No, but I know what you were really after. You just can't seem to resist gay bashing." She got up from the table and began to clear the dishes, carrying them into the tiny adjoining kitchen.

"Gay bashing!" But he was determined to be conciliatory. "Look, I hardly said a word about gays tonight."

"That's not what some people thought. Do you know friends at the RNC called after the show to ask *me* why you're such a homophobe?" She gave the dinner plates and cookware a hostile clatter.

Chase had come to hate the term *homophobe*. But he swallowed his annoyance, still trying to salvage the evening, which suddenly seemed to be going off the rails. He felt tension in the air, a vague, indefinable sense of trouble brewing.

He got up and walked into the kitchen. Putting his arms around her tenderly, he nuzzled her neck and said softly in her ear, "What's wrong, Neeley? Something's been bothering you for a couple of weeks."

She banged the pots loudly as she removed them from the dishwasher and stacked them in the cabinet.

He was tired of her sulks and criticism, but rather than counterattack he tried once more to dispel her disapproval—without giving away his principles. He tried a softer tone.

"Look, Neel, I know what gay bashing really is, and that's not what I do. Disagreeing with the militants' political agenda is not bashing. I'll tell you what bashing really is. It's—well, it's bashing. Physically assaulting somebody. Lurking outside gay bars, waylaying people and beating them up. I know that happens entirely too often. And I know gays get harassing phone calls and hate mail and death threats. I know that some gays actually get murdered, just because they're gay. That's not right. That's never right. They deserve the full protection of the law just like everybody else."

She kept her back to him but turned her head and said angrily, "They don't get it, do they?"

"Not always and not everywhere. But that's not necessarily because of homophobia. Crime is just out of control—you know that. *Nobody* gets protection these days. There just aren't enough police."

Still hovering over the sink with her back to him, she said, "Did you know that gays have formed their own mutual self-protection group? The Pink Posse. They patrol the streets for gay bashers, especially around Dupont Circle and Adams-Morgan. If you really believe everybody has the right to live free from being beaten up, why don't you do a show about them? Highlight the problem of attacks on gays. Get some balance on your program and show you're not just another homophobe."

"Neeley, we live in an age of politicized language," he said, fighting off a sudden feeling of futility. "This use of *homophobia* and *gay bashing* corrupts the meanings of words. Nowadays a person is a homophobe, a bigot, and a fascist if he doesn't believe in teaching first graders how to commit sodomy. Surely you don't believe that, do you?"

"No, but you're so dogmatic on this issue, it just embarrasses me to be with you sometimes."

He made an effort to contain his hurt pride, for something was surely troubling her, and he began to suspect it was not his stand on gay rights. He put his arms around her again.

"You know, there was a time maybe when I wasn't sensitive enough to hatred and abuse of gays," he said. "But now I don't like that any more than you do. I feel nothing but contempt for the skinheads and rednecks who feel they have to prove something by beating them up."

"But Chase,"—she was not at all mollified—"the sort of controversy you stirred up tonight just encourages the skinheads and rednecks. Don't you feel *some* responsibility?"

She pulled away from him irritably and began to load the dishwasher.

Chase shrugged, almost ready to give up on her. He went to the liquor cabinet for another bottle of wine.

"No, I don't feel responsible. And I'm not the moral equivalent of a skinhead just because I tell the truth as I see it." Now *he* was getting angry.

She did not answer, but she gave him a look of finality that signaled the end of the discussion as far as she was concerned.

Well, good, he said to himself. *Maybe now we can get to the heart of the problem.*

"What's *really* bothering you?"

"I don't know what you mean," she said sharply.

She was more truculent tonight than she had ever been, as well as evasive.

But he persisted. "Something else is going on here—it's not my TV show or my 'gay bashing' that's really bothering you, is it?"

When she did not answer, he insisted. "Neeley, we need to talk. We don't always have to agree, but we have to talk. I love you, but you make it awful hard. If our relationship is going to go anywhere, we've got to communicate. Here we are, both of us professional communicators, and we can't even communicate between ourselves."

Seated again, he uncorked the second bottle of wine and poured a full glass.

"You're still drinking?" she said sternly, walking back into the dining nook to fetch the rest of the dinner things. "You've been drinking entirely too much lately."

He wanted to say, "You drive me to drink," but refrained. Instead he tried charm. Flashing his most winning smile at her he quoted,

"Wine does more than Milton can
To justify God's ways to man."

She was not charmed and went back into the kitchen.

He followed her. "What's wrong, Neeley?"

She put down the wine glass she was drying. "Chase, I'm pregnant."

★ ★ ★

Trying to make sense of the harrowing episode with Neeley, Chase sprawled in the big leather armchair in his apartment and drank, slowly but without stopping, until all the wine and beer was gone. Drinking dulled some of the pain as he agonized over what he might have said or done to change the tragic denouement of their relationship.

He knew it wasn't fair to blame her entirely. He shared responsibility. And he conceded she wasn't to blame if the Nulliparo implant had failed. It was the latest contraceptive on the market, said to be totally effective and without unhealthy side effects. But like many claims in this era of incompetence and irresponsibility, it had proved unreliable. No, that was not her fault. But nothing excused what she did later.

Looking back on the past six months of their star-crossed love affair, he could not see clearly what else he could have done. He went back to their first meeting and came forward in his memory, searching for a clue to what he might have done before things came to such a pass.

218

Neeley had proved to be no easy conquest. At first he respected her old-fashioned virtue and even felt slightly ashamed that he did not possess it himself. But in retrospect he wondered if virtue, or even prudent health concerns, were the real reasons for her reticence.

The thought stole into his mind that, for Neeley, sex was not a means of expressing love and deepening intimacy. He began to suspect she used it as a form of manipulation, the trump card in the age-old competition between men and women. A weapon.

Neeley had intimated in passing only a few weeks before the jolting news of her pregnancy that she was proabortion but was not explicit on the subject. Then one evening the topic came up indirectly during one of their many debates, and suddenly he found her opinion—to the extent that she revealed it—deeply troubling.

But before he could probe deeper, she said that the gay rights issue was even more divisive than abortion and suggested to him that neither was suitable for polite discussion, much less for unseemly battles in the political arena. That spun the argument off in the usual direction, and he never came back to explore her attitude on abortion.

The night she hit him with the fateful news, he "did the right thing" as soon as he got over the shock. But she declined to marry him. Reluctantly she told him she had come to the conclusion that they were not truly compatible. Personally, professionally, and philosophically they were on diverging paths. With such major obstacles in the way, she said, her being pregnant was not a sufficient reason to get married.

Deeply hurt and confused, he left hurriedly, not thinking until later about the possibility of abortion. He had harbored the hope that somehow he could preserve their love. He could not bear the thought of giving her up or of provoking her to the point of severing the relationship.

Yes, he wanted Neeley as his wife, but he soon found he wanted his child too, or at least for the child to have a chance at life. If she would not marry him, and if she would not keep the child, then he would figure out a way to raise it himself. He knew it would mortify his puritanical family, but that was a far better choice than killing the baby in the womb.

The day after Neeley told him the news, he tried over and over again to telephone her and resolve the dilemma. But there was no answer either at home or work. Her RNC colleagues told him she had gone away unexpectedly for a few days.

For several more days he continued trying to reach her, and all the while his foreboding increased. But still he hoped. He was prepared to argue for the life of his unborn child, to muster every ounce of passion and persuasiveness at his command. But it finally hit him—on what basis could he appeal to her? Custom? Tradition? Natural law? Religion? He began to see that without belief in any of these, none of them constituted a final authority that would outweigh self-interest.

Finally she returned, and he went to her apartment. As soon as he saw her face he knew. She had put her beliefs into practice. Without informing him, much less asking his consent, she had killed his unborn child.

Now to his feeling of rejection was added betrayal, immense sorrow at the thought that she would abort the baby so willingly, and guilt at his own failure to confront her in time. He felt responsible for the baby's death, as if he himself had killed it.

Tormented, Chase spewed out all his rage, guilt, and anguish on Neeley. Their parting could hardly have been more bitter and stormy. She threw him out of the apartment, screaming that she never wanted to see him or hear from him again.

Now, huddled in his leather chair, his thoughts lubricated with wine, he saw that he had confused sex with love. And for the first time he saw Neeley as something other than a purveyor of pleasure. Having the abortion without consulting him, depriving him of the opportunity to appeal for his child's life, she now appeared a purveyor of death. The abortion had been a murder for convenience in which he was made an unwilling accomplice.

It was his evaporating career prospects that had alienated her. She told him that. She did not believe in what he was doing or in his eventual success. The realization made him doubt that Neeley had ever really loved him, and that hurt most of all. How could he ever trust a woman again?

Come on, Chase, snap out of it. Millions are waiting—you've got a show to do.

23

Garden Monnoye loved to don the traditional garb of the Tyrolean mountaineer and roam the heights above Merano with pack and staff. He rested for a day after arriving at the Schloss Freihof and the next morning put on a loden green woolen jacket, corduroy knickers, and a Tyrolean hat. With his blond hair, fair skin, and handsome Nordic features he could have graced a travel poster. The concierge bowed graciously to him as he left the castle.

Monnoye tramped upward into the hills, alpenstock in hand. On his back was a small rucksack containing a thermos of coffee, a succulent lunch specially prepared by the hotel's chef, and his dog-eared copy of Whitman. As always, the exertion of the climb, the steady tramp of his booted feet, and the glorious scenery of the Dolomite Alps stimulated his creativity. All distractions and extraneous thoughts fell away like chaff.

Chase McKenzie. He was on Monnoye's mind. McKenzie had nagged at him all the way on the flight from Washington to Munich and during the auto trip up through the Brenner Pass to Merano.

The "Eddie Webb Show," as many media commentators called it, had created a storm of unfavorable controversy. An uncomfortably large number of pundits had been compelled to demonstrate their even-handedness and heaped stinging criticism on the head of Harmon Lait and Lambda Legal.

The gay movement's reliable allies in the media kept the damage under control as best they could. But McKenzie's exposé had stirred up the mud from the bottom of a deep well of anxiety in the body politic. Now the public was throwing great indignant handfuls of that mud at the national press. Few of Monnoye's friends in the industry cared to make targets of themselves.

Monnoye himself had thought it an opportune time to beat a hasty retreat to the continent.

In his last meeting with Harmon Lait before the Webb trial, Monnoye had foreseen the possibility of the backlash. He had tried to dissuade Lait, but in vain. *The Lambda Legal fiasco wasn't my error*, Monnoye mused. He had done his best to prevent the outcome he had foreseen. But he knew that even his power had limits, and there would always be some clown in the gay cast of characters who insisted on rewriting the script in midscene.

But that McKenzie. Monnoye now realized how badly he had underestimated the creep. That *was* an error, a potentially fatal one. The movement could not afford any more disasters like the Eddie Webb publicity. But at least now McKenzie was revealed unequivocally as an enemy. No longer was there anything fuzzy about his personal convictions. *Branch Trumbull must have had more influence on him than we thought.*

Still, Monnoye did not fear McKenzie as he had feared Trumbull. He was certain their plan of operation now in motion would get rid of the would-be television star quietly and with style. The particular twist he had in mind would even make it fun and far more of an object lesson to the watching, wondering world than simply killing the jerk.

It was gratifying to conceive and execute such a plan. In his imagination he could already see the headlines. Too bad he couldn't be there to enjoy it in person. But it was better to keep his distance while the operation was in progress and let his surrogates dismantle the troublesome Mr. McKenzie piece by piece.

There was much more to be done. The best time to take another quantum leap forward would be in the aftermath of McKenzie's downfall, when the psychic energy of Monnoye's people would be at its zenith.

It was here at the Schloss Freihof more than eight years ago that he had conceived the most successful and significant operation in the history of the gay movement—overturning the Pentagon's exclusion of homosexuals from the armed services. Long ago he had come to understand how important the military was as a symbol of legitimacy and public virtue.

Starting in the early 1990s he had recruited the best looking, most normal appearing young gays in the services, men with out-standing records, articulate, masculine looking, and clean-cut. Promising them a secure livelihood if and when they were expelled, he induced them to reveal their homosexuality and to challenge the military's exclusion policy head-on. At the same time he lined up political and media support and allocated a large sum of Paragon Foundation money for their legal action.

The plan had succeeded brilliantly. And its success produced a serendipitous benefit—the military chaplaincy, long a stronghold of religious conservatives, was in effect disenfranchised. When the services, however reluctantly, legitimized homosexuality, the freedom of the chaplains to teach the Bible was suddenly circumscribed. Those conservatives who could not embrace the new policy either resigned voluntarily or were gradually weeded out.

The unexpected effect of disenfranchising conservative chaplains was the seed of a profound concept that had lain dormant in Monnoye's fertile brain for years. Now, as he tramped the chilly foothills of the Wildspitze, that seed suddenly began to sprout furiously.

Within the military, homosexual rights had been the means of subordinating religion to the civil, secular power. Why, Monnoye asked himself, couldn't the gay rights amendment to the Constitution do the same thing within society as a whole—and disenfranchise the church?

His thoughts on the significance of the gay victory over the service chaplains led to a sudden new realization—Harmon Lait's defense of Eddie Webb, however ill considered and poorly executed, was not a true disaster. After all, the people would get angry for a while and then quickly forget. They always did. But Harmon Lait and Lambda Legal gave him the key to the puzzle he had been seeking.

One thought followed another. What did theological reactionaries always appeal to as the final authority when confronted with the legitimate claims of homosexuals? The Bible. It was the Word of God, they claimed. True, most Americans didn't pay much attention to the Bible anymore. But there were still 50 to 60 million evangelical Protestants and traditional Roman Catholics who did believe it, at least as far as homosexuality was concerned.

And, Monnoye had to admit, if you were backward enough to take the Bible literally, you didn't have much choice but to condemn homosexuality.

The challenge was to get rid of the book. And in getting rid of the book, you would automatically neutralize the conservative church.

And then he had an insight so powerful that it brought him up short on the mountain trail and left him momentarily breathless. Surely no one had ever seen it before as clearly as he, neither his allies nor his enemies: The purpose of the Human Rights Amendment wasn't so that gays could have full civil rights. No, the purpose of the HRA was to criminalize their ancient enemy the Christian church—at least that part of the church that preached the Bible.

In his vision Monnoye saw the demise of the service chaplains writ large. And with that vision the elements of a master plan began to fall into orderly ranks in his mind.

Once the HRA had enshrined total civil rights for gays as the supreme law of the land, then his friends in Congress could strike the fatal blow—strip the church of its tax exempt status.

The first subsidiary campaign, he decided, would be a media effort equating the conservative churches with neo-Nazis, skinheads, and the entire class of proscribed gay bashers. Backlash violence against gays was a real and growing problem. For Garden Monnoye it was convenient that it existed.

The second media campaign would be child abuse. He would intensify the portrayal of the teaching of religion, sin, and sexual abstinence as a form of emotional child abuse. And of course the fundamentalists' well-known penchant for corporal punishment would also serve his purpose.

The plan was an old one. Back in the early 1990s a leading gay leader had said, "All laws banning homosexuality will be eliminated, and if the churches oppose us, they will be closed." No one outside the gay community had taken him seriously, but the dream had persisted. It would take a man of Garden Monnoye's vision, strategic acumen, subtlety, and power to bring it about.

Monnoye saw that taxing the church was the pivotal issue, however. If the government could tax the church, then the government was paramount. Taxing church property and taking a just share of its income would do far more than generate new revenue, however desperately that was needed to meet the funding shortfalls in National Health, for example. Taxing the church would establish a radical departure from the fundamental American concept that the church stood separate from and coequal with the state.

Yes, he thought with excitement, *the time is finally ripe to cut the church down to size.*

Monnoye stood still, surveying the wildly beautiful skyline, and assurance swept through him. He would not fail as Communism had failed. Communism had tried to take away the spiritual, giving men and women nothing to fill the void. But man had spiritual hungers. Monnoye would satisfy them. He would not advocate stamping out religion. The New Age would supply a religion that all people of goodwill and social consciousness could embrace.

That thought convinced Monnoye that his grand strategy would have to incorporate support for the Global Harmonic Convergence.

On January 1, 2000, at the appointed time, New Age believers, whatever their persuasion, would turn the collective power of their thoughts toward peace, harmony, and unity. They believed the concentrated positive vibrations they generated would produce a wave of energy that would sweep over the earth and literally change human behavior.

They also believed that the negative energy of any contrary thought would interfere with the harmonic effect. By their reasoning, the most common source of such negative thoughts were Christians. Thus the church was a concrete obstacle to their millennial goal.

Until now Monnoye had rejected the appeals of various New Age groups to form a closer alliance. He rejected most of their beliefs—their channelers, their crystal gazers, their pyramid therapists. But he was quick to see that it was in his interest to focus the animosity of the New Agers against conservative Christians who would spoil the Global Harmonic Convergence.

Yes, it would be gays, with Monnoye at their head, who would become the vanguard of a new consciousness and usher in the New Age.

Such was Monnoye's plan. When carried out, it would permit gay men and women everywhere to emerge proudly from the secrecy and constant fear that weighed many of them down. To be relieved of such an intolerable burden was to know true freedom, and any price or effort was worth it.

But they needed political power to safeguard that freedom from the right-wing, hate-mongering church. And for the master plan to succeed, gays would have to discard their displays of bizarre behavior—at least temporarily. They would have to persuade the American people that they were just like anyone else.

The only serious challenge to gay power was the church and their book. But his master plan would eliminate that challenge and put the seal on the most momentous, far-reaching social and political revolution in the Western world since the Renaissance.

He could see it in his mind's eye. Someday soon the Rainbow Flag, the international symbol of gay activism, would fly next to the Stars and Stripes from every public building in the nation.

24

After work came pleasure.

As soon as Monnoye's Italian agent delivered his newest Adonis that afternoon, Monnoye would have all he needed on the mountaintop. Let disease and pestilence soil the squalid world beyond his mountain fortress. They could not touch him on his pinnacle. Up here he was a prince, and he defied contagion. The external world could take care of itself, for here he had all the appurtenances of security and pleasure.

He knew he was fortunate. Unlike many gays, he had self-discipline. He insisted on a strict testing and screening regime for all his new acquisitions.

AIDS and related diseases of promiscuous sex were still being spread through multiple sexual contacts. There were even horrifying rumors of a new HIV IV virus that was not detectable by the standard Western Blot blood test. Yet despite all the warnings, despite the multiple millions spent on AIDS education, and despite the climbing death toll, gay men were at it.

How Monnoye had escaped those early days of fatal ignorance he could not imagine. But he had been spared, and he had learned his lesson. Now he could take his pleasure with peace of mind, for he regarded his precautions as fail-safe.

And this visit to the Schloss was to be a particular pleasure, for his agents had brought in some new talent, a Persian boy, especially trained. If one had money and influence, one could still find them.

* * *

The call came to Chase McKenzie at his DBN office. Giving a name Chase did not recognize, the caller complimented him on his extraordinary exposé of the Eddie Webb case and the subsequent news media blackout. Chase waited to see where this would go.

"Listen, Mr. McKenzie, I've got some information about SIS's coverage of the Webb trial. SIS had a man down there, you know. And he actually got an interview with Webb, but the network wouldn't air the tape."

Chase was immediately intrigued. "You mean they have an actual tape of an interview with Webb?"

It was hard to believe but possible, knowing Wynn Pritchett's links to the gay high command. Perhaps Pritchett had used that influence to persuade Harmon Lait to allow an interview. Lait and the legal team had decided on the news blackout, and SIS slavishly complied. That would make a follow-up segment of the Eddie Webb story even more dramatic and convincing—if he could get his hands on the evidence.

He decided to probe deeper. "How do you know this?"

"I work at SIS," the man answered, to Chase's immense surprise. "And let me tell you, I don't like the way the media protected that killer any more than you do."

Suddenly Chase saw an extraordinary possibility—an informant inside the Pritchett media empire. But he would have to proceed with discretion and not let his journalistic acquisitiveness frighten the man away.

"I'm glad to hear that," he said. "People have a right to know about these things."

"They do," the caller agreed.

"Have you—uh—seen the tape of the Webb interview?" Chase asked carefully.

"Yeah, I have. Well, not the whole thing, but enough."

"How did you happen to see it?"

"Well, I'm in maintenance. I do cleaning and repair work on the video equipment. I just happened to be in there one night and saw the cassette. It had 'Eddie Webb' written on it. And since I had seen your show, it naturally made me curious. Nobody was around, so I ran part of it."

"I see." Chase paused, not knowing whether to press the man. He certainly sounded truthful—and sympathetic. Chase could not be certain. He did not regard himself as a cloak-and-dagger expert. But he was a good investigative journalist, and that meant sometimes he had to take risks.

"Any chance I could get a copy?" he asked, holding his breath.

★ ★ ★

Gotcha! Leon Pound exulted silently. He made a credible show of reluctance, expressed a reasonable fear of being identified as a leaker, and explained the difficulties of purloining a copy of the tape. At the same time he managed to convey the impression of outraged indignation over the media's handling of the Webb case.

Leon knew his quarry well—and exactly the kind of trail to lay that would lead him into the trap.

Finally Leon arranged to meet McKenzie to hand over the tape. He agreed to make the drop in a public place to allay any suspicion that McKenzie was being set up for anything unpleasant. The meeting would take place that same afternoon in Dupont Circle, near the SIS studios, a major hangout and pick-up site for the city's homosexuals. They called it the "Meat Rack."

At the appointed time, McKenzie was to arrive by Metro and sit on the park bench nearest the walkway from Q Street. Leon had hired Maurice Forster, one of the city's most notorious gay men, to meet him, posing as the bogus defector from SIS.

Leon's surrogate would arrive, sit on the bench, turn to McKenzie, and nod in recognition. Then he would leave a package and walk rapidly away. The contact should take less than thirty seconds, but it would be long enough for Leon to get plenty of photos.

★ ★ ★

An excited Chase had no sooner arrived back at DBN to view his prize than the telephone rang. It was the mysterious caller again.

"Mr. McKenzie, I called to apologize. I'm afraid the tape's no good."

Chase's heart sank. But then he became suspicious. "What's wrong with it?" he asked guardedly.

"Well, I should have realized it at the time. The video machine has a scrambler on it. I didn't have the code, so it didn't copy. It just scrambled the image. Frankly, that's why it's on the machine—to prevent pirated copies. I should have known."

"I see," said Chase, his disappointment audible.

"But I think I can bypass it and make you a good copy," the man volunteered.

"That would be great. Would you try to do that and call me back if you can?"

The man agreed to try.

Chase was greatly relieved and expressed his gratitude. But he still harbored a whisper of doubt. He put the tape the man had dropped off into a VCR, and, sure enough, there were the violent wavy lines across the screen that suggested electronic scrambling.

The man called back. This time he had a good copy. This time, he said, they would have to meet in a different location. He was afraid of being seen in the same place with Chase on consecutive days.

The next day they met in the public parking lot just north of the Pentagon along the Boundary Channel, a small tributary of the Potomac.

An odd place to meet, Chase thought. It was nowhere near the SIS building. *Maybe he's just being extra cautious.* After all, he was risking his job.

Along the bank grew a thick profusion of mulberry and laurel bushes, providing an effective screen from observation.

As Chase approached, Maurice Forster rushed nervously out of the screen of high shrubs, thrust a package into his hands, and hurried off. Chase tried to call him back, but the man seemed frightened. In seconds he was gone. Chase was intensely disappointed.

He was even more disappointed—and deeply puzzled—to find on returning to the studio that this tape contained the same wild squiggles. There was no interview with Eddie Webb. And this time there was no call of explanation.

★ ★ ★

The Direct Broadcast Network was a network only in the broadest sense of the word. In practical terms, it operated only a single station, albeit a "super station," that had started out in 1993

230

as a profit-making local access cable channel in the District of Columbia. Its founders had seen the growth potential of the new fiber-optic cable technology and had chosen that system.

At first the station grew slowly, expanding to the Washington suburbs of Maryland and Virginia only as the fiber-optic net expanded. Eventually fiber optics, combined with microwave transmission, allowed the station to broadcast nationwide.

It was a logical step for newly emerging broadcasters across the nation to associate in a franchise arrangement with the up-and-coming Washington superstation that had pioneered in the technology and was also ideally located for providing the best public affairs coverage of the federal government.

Chase had joined the station in 1994. Hugh Mahan, DBN's Vice President for Programming and Chase's boss, had been the original station manager, and they had remained on friendly, if not intimate, terms for years. They often went shooting, hunting, or fishing together. So he saw nothing unusual in the note on his desk requesting him to see Mahan as soon as he arrived at the studio.

But the distress on his boss's face told him something was wrong the moment he entered Mahan's office.

"Chase, I hardly know how to begin or how to tell you this," Mahan began painfully as Chase sat down in the chair opposite.

"Tell me what, Hugh?"

"Your show has been successful, but we think the time has come to change the format and break out of the . . . uh . . . well, there are a huge number of public affairs talk shows and—"

"But you just said it, Hugh. 'Pulse of the Nation' has been very successful. Why would you want to tamper with success?"

"Frankly, Chase, the CEO and the board of directors have discussed the situation, and they feel your show has been successful only because you've been exploiting the gay issue. They feel that this issue is about to run its course. And unfortunately, 'Pulse of the Nation' has become identified as a gay bashing diatribe. It's starting to turn people off."

Chase came halfway out of his seat. "Who says so?" he demanded. "Is there any market survey data that bear this out?"

"Well . . ." Mahan looked down at his desk.

"I'd like to see it," Chase pressed the counterattack.

"It's not exactly survey data, Chase. But we've had literally thousands of calls and letters from irate viewers. Remember, I warned you about this."

"Yeah, you did," said Chase, quietly relieved there was no survey data. "But those callers are all queers or their sympathizers. You know that. Are we going to let them dictate the content of our programming?"

"No," Mahan said in a small voice. "But the show goes off the air anyway."

Chase was stunned into silence. For some time he had expected Hugh to rein in his antigay programming. But take the show off the air! He had to think fast. From Hugh's inflection, Chase sensed that a hidden agenda was at work.

He trusted his own journalistic instincts, and he knew that "Pulse" had a wide and loyal following. There had to be some other reason. If he could only discover it, he was confident he could talk the network out of this self-destructive decision.

He cleared his throat nervously, knowing he was suddenly fighting for his career. "Listen, Hugh, we've been friends for a long time. There's more going on here than concern about my show. Come on and level with me—you owe me that much."

"Yeah, I guess I do. But I'm telling you what the front office has instructed me to tell you. And no more. You know I've stuck up for you as long as I could. You remember how I stood by you when you wouldn't go on the air if we put the gay ads on in your time slot?"

"I remember."

"Well, do you also remember it was me—not you—that got hauled into court for violating the state's gay rights ordinance?"

"Yeah." Chase said quietly, feeling guilty for thinking his friend disloyal.

Hugh Mahan had defended him then staunchly. The network had still been forced by DC law to accept the gay ads. But at least the network won the right to air them when it chose—and not on "Pulse of the Nation," which had been the real target of the gay groups in the first place.

"Chase, now my job is on the line again. But this time I can't protect you."

"So this *is* about the gay ads."

"No, this time it's much bigger than that."

"Then why can't you tell me?"

"Because I'm following orders, that's why."

"Then I'll go see the CEO. I don't want to jeopardize *your* job, but I *will* fight to save mine."

"He won't see you," Mahan said wearily, obviously growing more and more uncomfortable with the duty of destroying an old friend.

"Hugh," Chase exploded, "what's going *on* here? You mean after all I've done for this crummy network, I'm going to be canceled and nobody will tell me why? And I can't even appeal to the head of the company?"

Mahan did not answer but looked down at his hands. He was clearly in a state of extreme distress.

"I guess that's about it. Look, please believe me, Chase, I fought for you. And if I didn't have two kids in college—"

"Spare me the details. But I still have a right to know why. And you're telling me I can't even know why I can't know why. Wouldn't you be mad as a hornet if you were me?"

"I guess I would," Mahan agreed. "Look, if I tell you, will you give me your word you won't go popping off? You'll understand when I explain. The front office was afraid if you knew the whole story, you'd do a number on the people responsible. And that would kill us."

"If you're taking me off the air, how can I do a number on anybody?"

Mahan threw out his hands in acknowledgment of that logic. "Chase, the FCC is refusing to renew our operating license."

Chase sat still, once again stunned into silence. Yet as the implications of what he had just heard sank in, his disbelief turned to outrage. He got out of the chair and strode in tight circles around Mahan's office.

"Then *this* needs to be aired!" He shook an accusatory finger. "The company needs to fight back! We've got the perfect leverage. Hugh, don't surrender without a fight!"

"Chase, can't you understand? The fight is already over. We *have* surrendered. It was a simple matter of survival, and the decision's already been made at corporate level. Even if we had a sympathetic member on the FCC—but we don't. The chairman and the whole Commission have lined up against us. I'm sorry, but you were the price we had to pay if we were to have any hope of getting renewed."

Chase tried to make sense of it all. "You're going to look awfully bad—canceling a show when its audience share is at peak and just because the queers couldn't stand for me to tell the truth. And everybody'll know you caved in to them."

"Probably. But at least we'll stay in business."

"And for what?"

"We're in business to be in business, that's for what!" Now Mahan exploded. "Not everybody's a crusader like you, Chase. What did you expect the company to do, commit suicide?"

"Well, I would have expected them to show some guts, to stand by their journalists. And to show some self-respect," he added.

"Perhaps in another time, another world. But not this one," Mahan replied with sad finality.

★ ★ ★

Chase left the studio in a daze. Things like this weren't supposed to happen in real life—it was the kind of thing he read about. *But then,* he thought, *why not? They got to the FCC. I know they killed Branch Trumbull. Why should I expect any less?* And he remembered Branch's warning.

For all his experience in covering the seamy underside of Washington's power elites and their duplicity, deceit, arrogance, and amorality, Chase was still an innocent. He had never personally felt the laserlike force of genuine enmity concentrated upon himself, never had his livelihood or well-being threatened.

He had some money put away. That relieved him of immediate worries about making a living. And he was reasonably confident of finding another position somewhere. But still, it was a humiliating blow to be suddenly knocked out of the ring by the people he despised most. And coming so soon on the heels of his bitter fight with Neeley made the blow doubly hard.

At the remembrance of Neeley, who was never long out of his thoughts, black depression returned and settled over him. Morbid imaginings about the child he would never see still plagued him. Had it been a girl or boy? Did it look like him? Would he ever have another child to preserve the long chain of family continuity?

The guilt and the shame were still overpowering, and like a wounded animal seeking its lair he turned toward his refuge on Massanutten Mountain.

First he had to get a few provisions. Some time had passed since he had been up to the cabin, and he could not remember exactly what food was left in the larder. There was plenty of canned goods—and maybe a few bottles of wine. But he needed some fresh meat and vegetables.

Above all he needed a good stock of beer, maybe even some hard stuff. He thought he might stay up on the Mountain for a week or so and try to figure out what to do, and he had found that a few drinks were essential in fighting off stress and lubricating his thought process.

He pushed the heavily laden shopping cart to the counter and made desultory conversation with the checkout girl as she scanned and totaled his purchases. She was a cute blonde, not at all like Neeley. In other circumstances he might have flirted. But there was too much else on his mind, and he paid her scant attention after the first appraisal.

The girl finished bagging his purchases, and the total came to $225. He never carried more than a few dollars in cash. The risk of losing it to Washington's rampant crime, plus the convenience and security of plastic, had almost made cash obsolete.

He pulled out his EDC and handed it to her absently, mentally licking his wounds from the fight with Neeley, from the loss of his program and his income—from, above all, loss of his pulpit.

A moment later he realized the girl was speaking to him, apologetically.

"Excuse me. What did you say?" he asked.

"I said I was sorry, sir, but the scanner won't take your card."

"I don't understand. What do you mean, it won't take my card? Is the scanner broken?" he said stupidly.

"Oh, no, sir. It's working fine. I'm just getting a noncredit message." The girl was clearly embarrassed for him.

"Noncredit? That's impossible," he said, befuddled. "Try one of the other machines."

"We're not supposed to do that. The scanner debits your account based on the amount of the purchase entered. It's all automatic—"

"I don't care," he objected. "Something's obviously wrong. I've got plenty of money in my account."

"I'm sure you do, sir—"

"Then run the card through another machine."

"OK. But do you mind making a small purchase to activate the system? Otherwise I'll have to get the manager to enter a special code."

"Sure, sure," he said, his frustration mounting. "I just want to check it."

He pulled a six-pack of beer out of the pile of groceries and went around to the adjacent checkout counter.

The checker met him, scanned the beer, and then passed the EDC over the glass window of the machine.

Feeling the curious stares of other shoppers, Chase was suddenly embarrassed. He could tell they were pretending not to notice his discomfiture but were obviously watching.

The girl's polite smile faded. "I really am sorry, sir, but I'm getting a noncredit message again. I'm afraid we can't accept your card. Do you have cash?"

"I don't have cash. I never carry cash anymore."

"Then I am sorry."

"I am too. I wish I knew what's wrong with my worthless card."

"It's probably just a bank error," she said hopefully, trying to allay his humiliation.

"Yeah, that has to be it. I'll go to the bank in the morning—no, tomorrow's Saturday. Are the banks open on Saturday?"

"Well, most of them are—in the morning," she said, still trying to be helpful. "I hope you can get it straightened out."

"Thanks. Sorry for the trouble," he replied, swallowing his anger, and turned toward the exit.

"Oh, that's all right. Have a nice night," she said brightly.

As he drove away from the market, Chase was incredulous to think he could not make a simple grocery purchase with his EDC. *It has to be those stupid store scanners,* he thought irately.

He knew his accounts contained ample funds. Without the expenses of a family, he was able to save a third of his generous income from DBN. Like most Americans, he had lost much of the savings he had invested in bonds because of the numerous municipal bankruptcies around the nation. But he still had money in the bank. And if his bank had failed—as many had these days—surely he would have heard some news about it.

In all his life he had never encountered money problems. And since the advent of third-generation electronic banking, his EDC card had never been refused. Yeah, something was wrong with the machines at that store, he concluded. He decided to stop at the liquor store near his apartment and try again.

The liquor store's night clerk, a balding middle-aged man, nodded at Chase from behind a bullet-proof plexiglas barrier as he entered.

Chase picked up two six-packs of beer, two bottles of wine, and a quart of vodka. Placing the items on the counter, he fished the EDC from his wallet. Without warning, a tremor of something oddly like fear ran through him. He actually felt cold as he handed the card to the clerk through the sliding tray.

The checkout man totaled his purchase and ran the card across the scanner.

Chase could see the flashing red light in the machine's window, and his cold, sinking feeling intensified as the clerk ran it by again. Then again.

The man held up the card and shrugged his shoulders apologetically. "Sorry, sir. Card's no good."

Chase did not argue. He took the useless card from the movable tray and shoved it back into his pants pocket.

"Be glad to take cash," the clerk said encouragingly.

Chase did not reply but shook his head and walked out, cursing silently.

25

"W hen troubles come, they come not in single spies but in battalions," Chase quoted to himself. He could not even buy a little liquor to fight off stress and find some temporary oblivion. *What more can happen?*

He decided to remain in Alexandria over the weekend instead of dashing off to the Valley and his refuge. Tomorrow, as soon as the banks opened, he would march in and find out just what was wrong with his no-good EDC.

He recalled with growing temper that the banks themselves had promoted universal reliance on "total electronic banking" and the "cashless society." Now a banking error had rendered his EDC useless, tied up his funds, and made it impossible even to buy food and drink. Somebody at the bank was about to get a good verbal hiding.

Everything in the economy was falling apart, he brooded. Incompetence, ignorance, and irresponsibility ruled supreme. It was a rare thing to get good service anymore. The banking industry was clearly no exception.

He drank the last two beers in his refrigerator and calmed down a bit. He wandered around the apartment. He switched the television on and off in disgust and attempted unsuccessfully to immerse himself in a novel.

When nothing else could divert his troubled mind, he put on his sweats and joggers and went for a few turns around the neighborhood.

While he was jogging, an idea struck him. *I've got to do something about this FCC thing,* he thought. *I'll give Barbara Dunhill a call.* Perhaps her political intelligence network could tell him who was behind the FCC decision. Hardly anything of serious magnitude went on in the administration without her knowledge.

Maybe she could even recommend a way to get the White House to countermand the FCC decision, though he knew that was unlikely. The feckless White House crowd—Barbara excluded—was known to friend and foe as "the mice." They rarely intervened in any controversy on behalf of friend or ally. But if all else failed, maybe Barbara could use her clout as Director of Presidential Personnel to find him a job in the administration. That was an improbable and distasteful prospect, but it might give him a platform from which to operate.

By the time he returned from running it was getting late, and since it was Friday, he expected to find his White House friend out for the evening. But she picked up the telephone after the first ring.

Chase found himself suddenly a little nervous. He had never asked any political friend for a personal favor.

"Barbara, it's me, Chase McKenzie," he said, mustering his courage. "I've got some bad news."

"What is it, Chase?"

"Well, in a word, I've been canned."

"You've been fired? From DBN? But your show's been hitting the top of the charts!"

"Believe it or not, that's the reason. It's been hitting the wrong people. The FCC threatened to refuse our license renewal. I had to go if the network was to stay in business."

"Oh, Chase, I just can't believe it."

"Well, believe it. I mean, they yanked me right off the program schedule. No final show, no farewells, no nothing."

"But it was one of the best shows on TV! Far better than 'Frontlines!'" She still sounded shocked.

"Barbara, I think the gay rights people are behind this. If you've seen my last few broadcasts—"

"Oh, I have," she interjected. "I watch the show religiously."

"Well then, you know how badly we've hurt the gay militants, especially over this Eddie Webb case down in Mississippi."

"Yes. That was the television equivalent of the atom bomb. Everybody in the White House is still talking about it. The attorney general and Kerry Kerrigan had a big row about it just yesterday."

"Well, you know how the homosexual network extends into

the government. And you know how they nest in the agencies and look out for each other. I believe they've penetrated the FCC—especially with all the new gay emphasis on going mainstream, adopting the tactics of persuasion, using the media effectively, and so forth."

"Well, it's certainly possible, though nobody like that immediately comes to mind at the FCC. Of course, I'd know if any of the politicals there were gay activists. But if they're covert, I wouldn't necessarily know about it. I mean, that's not something we're allowed to screen for in selecting political appointees."

"I see. Well, that's what I wanted to ask—if you had any idea who might be behind it. I hate to see them get away with this—and not just for my sake."

"So do I, Chase. So do I." She paused. "Tell you what, give me a few days, and I'll nose around a bit. Maybe I can learn something. But it won't be easy. And even if I do learn something, I have to ask you—what good will it do? I mean, will it help you get your show back?"

"I don't know. Probably not. But at least we'll have learned who's doing this—and maybe how to fight 'em. After all, if the gays can do this to me, they can do it to anybody. And if they're strong enough inside the FCC to pull our license, they can squeeze out any broadcaster that criticizes them."

"And that's a chilling thought. OK, I'll look into it and get back to you ASAP."

"Good. Thanks, Barbara. I really do appreciate it."

"You don't have to thank me. I owe you the thanks. There aren't many conservative talk shows on the air, much less one as good as yours. You've been one of our few friends in the media."

He went to bed immensely encouraged by Barbara Dunhill's warm praise. And he was glad he had stood on his dignity and not asked her for a job. He could always ask later if the FCC mess could not be sorted out.

* * *

As soon as his bank opened on Saturday morning, Chase was there. He marched in wearing a determined scowl and sat down at the desk of the customer service manager.

She was a middle-aged woman with a pleasant manner and disarming smile. As Chase irately complained about the bank's error that invalidated his electronic debit card, she nodded sympathetically, clucking gently as if to convey her own distress over the terrible lapse in good service.

But when she pulled up his account information on her terminal, her smile faded. Peering at the screen closely, she picked up the telephone and made a call, giving Chase's name and account number. She listened intently, nodded, and put down the receiver. The smile had been replaced with a troubled frown.

"Mr. McKenzie, I hate to have to tell you this. I thought maybe we had made an error in your accounts, though that seldom happens these days. All EDC accounts are double cross-checked daily by our mainframe."

By now Chase was thoroughly alarmed. "But can I get access to my funds or not?"

"No, sir, I'm afraid not."

"Why in thunderation not?" he demanded, stunned, but fighting to keep anger and confusion and disbelief under control.

"The IRS has placed a lien on your account—both your operating account and your money market fund."

"A lien?"

"Yes. And by law, only the IRS can release your funds. And that's assuming you satisfy whatever claims they have entered against you."

"Claims? But I don't *owe* any tax."

"Well, be that as it may, we don't have any choice in the matter. In effect, the IRS is now the legal account holder as far as the bank is concerned."

"This just can't be!" he exploded. "I don't *owe* any tax, and I've got over $15,000 in your bank. You're saying I can't touch *any* of it?"

"I'm terribly sorry, but that's the situation." She sounded truly sympathetic.

"There's got to be *something* I can do," he said, less to the woman than to himself. He had been around long enough to believe that, with a little luck and effort, you could find a way around most any obstacle.

But the IRS! The very name of the IRS was enough to strike terror in the hearts of most Americans, especially since the passage of the Revenue Enhancement Act in 1994, which gave the IRS sweeping new tax enforcement powers. Perhaps the IRS was the one obstacle that could not be outflanked with persistent cleverness or political pull.

"Would you like to see the bank manager?" the woman offered. "Perhaps he can suggest something."

"Yes, thank you, I would."

The manager sat in a walnut-paneled office full of Queen Anne furniture and imitation antiques. He was a pallid, balding yuppie in a well-cut suit of banker's gray. Strands of wispy blond hair were combed from one side of his head to the other. He looked at Chase skeptically through tortoise-shell glasses as Chase explained his problem.

"Listen, Mr. McKenzie," he began when Chase stopped, "I understand how you must feel. But you must understand our situation. The IRS has in effect seized your account. Your quarrel is with them, not the bank."

"Well, I'd at least like to know what the nature of their claim is and how long my money will be locked up."

"You'll have to ask the IRS," the manager said brusquely.

Chase found himself bristling at the man's air of self-importance and condescension. He had never before been treated with such suspicion and disdain, but he knew an outburst of temper would accomplish nothing. And his money was at stake.

"You can't even tell me what the IRS has charged me with?" he asked. "How am I supposed to confront them intelligently unless I have some facts?"

The banker shrugged. "I really don't know that. The IRS doesn't tell us. All we know is that we receive a Form 27 and Notice of Lien. This process is governed very stringently by the US Internal Revenue Code and the 1994 tax laws. It governs our operations at the bank just as it governs your payment of taxes. Frankly, since there's nothing we can do to help you, I really don't see the point in pursuing this conversation."

"Will you listen!" Chase lost his patience. "I've been a loyal customer here for ten years. I've deposited money regularly and never had a single problem with my accounts. And now all you can tell me is basically to get lost?"

"I'm very sorry if it sounded that way. My advice is to get a good tax lawyer. There's absolutely nothing more we can do."

Speechless with rage and embarrassment, Chase stormed out of the bank and drove back to his apartment. *I'm sorry. I'm sorry. Everybody's sorry. Hugh Mahan. The store clerks. This bank turkey. My job's gone, the confounded IRS has stolen my money. And everybody's sorry.*

He did not know a tax lawyer, but he had a competent accountant who filed his tax returns, kept his records in good shape, and generally gave him sound advice. Chase had always been cautious in his tax strategies, just because he feared someday something like this could happen, especially if he achieved a highly visible status in the conservative political movement.

He knew how relentless the IRS could be in pursuit of the last unpaid tax dollar. The government was in reality bankrupt, and the tax laws had become little more than a legal form of extortion. Chase had heard too many horror stories about the fate of recalcitrant tax rebels who had tried to keep more of their hard-earned cash than the IRS thought proper.

When in doubt, pay. That was his policy.

No, he didn't owe any tax. This had to be the handiwork of the gay cabal inside the government. It was too inexplicable, too sudden, too unjust—just like the FCC bombshell. But this mess had to be straightened out. His top priority had to be getting access to his funds.

The trip to the Mountain would now have to be postponed until Monday or Tuesday, until he could see his accountant and find a tax lawyer if necessary, as he feared it would be.

★ ★ ★

Chase's head pounded cruelly with every ring of the insistently jangling telephone. The evening before he had found some twenty-five-year-old cognac in the cupboard, a bottle he had been hoarding for a special occasion for so long he had forgotten it.

"Too much cognac, especially after those beers," he said groggily, reaching for the phone. Who could be calling at such an ungodly hour? With effort he opened and shut his eyes a few times to squeeze out the fog of sleep and squinted at the clock. To his surprise it was already 10:00 A.M.—10:00 on Sunday morning.

"Hello, Chase, is that you? This is Clare Trumbull."

"Clare?" he mumbled, still not yet fully awake and alert. "Clare, how are you?" He hoped nothing was wrong at the Trumbulls. Then he thought she perhaps had some news about the murder investigation.

"I'm fine. How are you?"

Was there a strange note in her voice? Surely she didn't call just to make small talk.

"I'm OK. A little sleepy. Had a bad night. Guess you heard about the show, huh?" he said groggily.

"No. Why didn't it air last night?"

"Cause I've been canned. It was the queers. Somehow they got the FCC to pull our license. It was me or the network, so guess who got jettisoned over the side?"

"Oh, Chase, I'm so sorry. You should have called. We want to help you in any way we can. We're your friends, you know. And we'll stand by you."

"Well, that's kind of you," he said dully.

The silence on the other end of the line was deafening.

What's on her mind? he wondered. By now he was in control of his faculties, and he waited for her to say why she had called.

Finally he heard a deep indrawn breath on the line.

"Have you seen this morning's paper?" she asked.

He felt that sinking sensation again, what he had felt at the liquor store when his EDC was rejected the final time.

"Uh—no. I was asleep until you called." Alarm took over. "What is it? What's in the paper? Something about the show being canceled?"

"I'm afraid it's worse than that." She spoke now in haste. "But I want you to know, none of us—me, Libby, or Jimmy—believes any of it. Jimmy says you've been set up."

"In the *News?*"

"Yes."

The sinking feeling changed to nausea. The abominable Sunday *News.* The Sunday *News* went everywhere. All of Washington and half the rest of the country had probably seen whatever it was Clare was talking about before he even knew it was there.

"I'll call you back," he said abruptly. He slammed down the receiver without waiting for an answer and vaulted out of bed in his BVDs. He did not bother with robe or slippers but ran to retrieve the bulky newspaper from the front stoop of the apartment building.

The Sunday edition of the *Washington News* was full of advertising inserts and magazine supplements. It comprised ten full sections from the front page with its national and international news to the mammoth want-ads. He hunted frantically through the mass of newsprint, not knowing exactly what he was looking for.

And then, to his horror, there it was on the front page of the "Metro" section. The glaring headline read "Controversial Anti-Gay TV Host Revealed as Closet Homosexual."

26

Jimmy Tolliver and Barbara Dunhill were not close friends, but he knew her as a fellow soldier in the political warfare that raged so fiercely beneath Washington's polished veneer of civility and decorum.

They met at Cellini's, a fashionable but quiet and secluded Italian restaurant off Pennsylvania Avenue, almost exactly halfway between Capitol Hill and the White House. Jimmy stood when the maitre d' showed Barbara to his table and shook her extended hand cordially as she was seated.

A slight, attractive woman in her late thirties, Barbara had her brown hair cut short and businesslike and was dressed impeccably in a dark conservative suit. As always, she wore a grave dignity about her like a cloak. But her otherwise severe expression was softened by a cheerful kindliness.

They ordered their meals and a bottle of mineral water. As Jimmy poured her a glass she said, "I can't tell you how sorry I was when Senator Trumbull was killed. Sad for myself, but even sadder for the country. Words fail me even now, but I wanted you to know that."

"Thanks. It's still hard for me to accept. He was so much a part of my life—of the lives of everyone who knew him. In a way, it's like he's not really gone. Sometimes when I'm considering an issue or wrestling with a problem, I feel like I hear him talkin' to me."

She smiled sympathetically, then said, "I was also sorry to hear about what happened afterward."

An old political enemy had been appointed to fill the unexpired portion of Branch's term, and the new senator had given Trumbull's staff only one day to clear out of the office. Jimmy had felt a deep responsibility to the staffers suddenly thrown out of their jobs. He had called Barbara to try to line up positions in the administration for as many as possible.

He managed a laugh. "Oh, don't fret about it. That's politics. I didn't really expect any better."

"What are your own plans?"

"Well, for the time being I'm going to manage the senator's foundation and try to keep it together until we can get someone to take it over. Of course, Branch was literally irreplaceable."

He paused, unsure how she had taken the news about Chase McKenzie, for Chase was the true object of his visit with her. "We were hoping Chase McKenzie might come aboard and at least be the national spokesman. He has a large, loyal following nationwide. Branch told me he had hopes of getting Chase involved more fully in the work some day—if he could ever figure out how to woo him away from the network."

"I see," she noted. "Well, somebody else must've had the same thought. They got him out of the network, all right. But it sure ruins him as a spokesman for the Foundation."

"Maybe not, if we can show it was all a setup. You know it was a setup, don't you?" When calling to arrange their lunch together, he had told Barbara about Chase's encounter with the FCC and the IRS. And she had seen the *News* story, even more obviously a setup.

"Oh, of course," she agreed readily. "Nobody could have that much bad luck all at once simply by accident. It's got all the classic earmarks of an inside operation."

"Then we've got to help him."

"I wish we could."

"We can."

"How? I mean, what can I do?"

"Barbara, I believe you can do what nobody else can do. But it'll involve some risk."

"Well—" she looked up from her plate and smiled a fleeting smile "—you know we conservatives have a reputation for leaving our wounded on the battlefield. But Chase McKenzie is well worth some risk. If I can help, I will. I'm not afraid of sticking my neck out for a good reason. What you want me to do?"

Jimmy decided to explain indirectly. "You know, because of

Senator Trumbull's interest in the gay lobby and its influence in the government, I've developed some contacts around town. Nothing as good as your intelligence network, but still I do get good information about their underground. Frankly, I've begun hearing some disturbing things about Kerry Kerrigan."

"Oh. I see."

Jimmy interpreted her look as meaning she understood.

Barbara sighed and glanced about her like a condemned woman on her ride to the gallows. "That explains things then," she said. "Lately he's been behaving very strange—like somebody got to him all of a sudden. And he's become very hostile towards me. I'm one of the few conservative holdouts in the White House, as you know."

Jimmy nodded gravely but withheld comment. He knew she was less concerned for her own security than for maintaining some conservative influence in the White House, especially in the vital personnel function. He also knew that he was tacitly suggesting she put that influence at risk to help one individual. Finally he asked gently, "Just how imminent is the threat?"

"Oh, I wouldn't say it's imminent, but I get the unmistakable feeling he'd like to see me out of the White House. And you know what determined haters those people can be."

Jimmy knew the political culture intimately. If the number one White House lawyer—especially one who had the ear of the president and the chief-of-staff—decided to get rid of a mid-level staffer, it was done. The only remaining questions were when and how.

Barbara enjoyed a high standing among conservatives in the administration and on the Hill. Removing her summarily would stir up a controversy that might lead to embarrassing questions about Kerrigan's role in her dismissal. Still, if she were to violate internal White House procedure—or get caught spying on the chief counsel—Kerrigan would have all the ammunition he needed.

"Well," he mused, "if you have to go, you might as well go out fighting. And maybe help rehabilitate Chase's reputation at the same time."

Barbara laughed with genuine mirth. "Go out fighting? Sounds like I'd be joining the other side."

Jimmy laughed too. *"Go* out fighting, not come out. Amazing how much difference can be contained in two little words."

"Yes. Well anyway, I suppose it might be possible to find out if Kerrigan was involved in the FCC action. Or the IRS."

"Or both."

"Or both."

"How would you go about finding out?"

"I'm not sure at the moment," she said. "I'll have to give it some thought. Maybe I can get a look at his White House phone logs. See if he placed any calls to the two agencies right about the time this all happened. I have my resources, just as he has his."

"That would be a good place to start. Anything I can do to help?"

"I'll let you know."

"I can't thank you enough. Meantime," Jimmy said, "I'll do a little checking on my own."

★ ★ ★

Chase McKenzie had discovered over the course of his years in broadcasting that he had outgrown the need for notoriety.

To find his name blazoned across the pages of the *Washington News* in any connection was unwelcome enough. But now, to be portrayed as a closet homosexual, as one of those he despised most, was beyond his worst imagining. Yet that was not the worst, for the stories "outing" Chase were executed with such diabolical cleverness that he was sure even his friends would accept them as true.

First there was the "news" story. Come Out Fighting revealed that it had been shadowing the well-known gay baiter Chase McKenzie for some time. They suspected that he was in reality a secret homosexual because of the venom with which he attacked the inoffensive gay community. Such antagonism was a common phenomenon, the article explained. Gay men who suffered extreme self-hatred often took out this hatred on other homosexuals with more animosity than the bigoted straight world.

And there was the proof—photos showing him twice in contact with a well-known gay man, Maurice Forster, in two of the favorite areas in the city for homosexual liaisons. Forster claimed that McKenzie had first approached him for sex in Dupont Circle's Meat Rack, then arranged for a second meeting at the Boundary Channel strip.

The story provided background that gave the charges additional plausibility. Chase was thirty-six and unmarried, the product of a strict Southern fundamentalist upbringing, an extreme social aberration according to the *News*. The reporter speculated that an intolerant home environment and the family's religious bigotry had caused McKenzie to repress his latent homosexuality.

And, the story added, Mr. McKenzie had refused to return the many calls the reporter had placed for a statement in his own defense, further implying the charge was true. Of course Chase had received no such calls.

Accompanying the article was an editorial. It managed to condemn Chase as a closet homosexual without implying criticism of homosexuality or suggesting that to be gay was anything other than normal and good.

There it was, an unbelievably well orchestrated character assassination, done with all the subtlety and skill the *News* was famous for. To a credulous world he was now an exposed closet homosexual and a hypocrite. Who could doubt it if the *Washington News* said so—and had photos to prove it?

As he looked again at the headlines and the photos, a sense of helplessness immobilized him. He was publicly controversial and discredited. All his friends in the political world, including Barbara Dunhill, would drop him like a hot rock, and no one in the conservative community or broadcasting would ever touch him again.

Consumed with shame and indignation, his thinking clouded by self-condemnation, he assumed that other friends had deserted him as well. He refused to return Clare Trumbull's telephone calls. He ignored several messages Jimmy Tolliver left on the answering machine.

But there was one person he might call, one possible if tenuous lifeline to regaining his shattered reputation—Neeley Durant. She could refute the malicious falsehoods, if only she would.

Choking down his pride, he placed several calls, but there was no answer, and she never returned his calls despite the urgent messages left on her answering machine. He finally went to her apartment, but she did not answer the door, and her car was gone.

When Monday morning rolled around, he drove straight to the RNC building and went upstairs to the office of communications. He left in shock.

Neeley had quit the RNC to accept a new job at the Pritchett Corporation. To gather her wits for this major new responsibility, she had taken a few days' vacation courtesy of her new employer—at an undisclosed location.

Chase returned home in disbelief, fully aware of the implications of Neeley's job change and of the timing. If he was to refute the slander successfully, he had to do it now—today. A few days from now would be too late. By then the allegations would be fixed as truth in the public imagination. But the one person who might possibly refute the lies was out of town.

Searching the Monday papers for the follow-on stories, he found a feature profiling the up-and-coming Neeley Durant, Washington woman executive extraordinaire and newly hired as vice president for corporate communications by media mogul Wynn Pritchett.

Chase knew Neeley was a competent media relations professional, but she had never mentioned the slightest interest in leaving RNC, nor intimated that Wynn Pritchett had ever noticed her, much less expressed interest in hiring her. Obviously "they" knew all about Neeley and just as obviously had bought her silence with this cushy new job.

And then Chase knew Wynn Pritchett had sent him a personal message, courtesy of the nation's second largest newspaper. He recalled for a sour moment how he had snubbed Pritchett that weekend at his hunting camp. There was no longer any need to try to find Neeley and ask her to refute the slander. She had been sealed off from helping him as effectively as if she had emigrated to Antarctica.

He toyed with the idea of calling the *Washington Standard* —or DBN, where he still had friends who might see that this nightmare was a well-orchestrated lie. He would dare them to track Neeley down and ask her if he was gay. But the more he thought about her possible role in the affair, the more he feared outright betrayal.

What if a reporter called and asked her to corroborate his claim to have had an old-fashioned heterosexual relationship with her and she refused? A "no comment" would be bad enough, but what if "they" had primed her to confirm the lie instead? Either one would do more damage than leaving her out of it altogether.

His frustration mounted. If he had been so wrong about Neeley and about love, then he could be wrong about other things as well. If there was no love as he had believed in it, what was there? The tragedy with Neeley called everything into question, and he was no longer confident that anything he believed or thought he had learned was true.

The telephone continued to intrude with its incessant ringing, and the answering machine beeped and whirred nonstop as the metallic voices of reporters from other news organizations called him for a statement.

With each ring of the phone his anxiety grew until it bordered on panic. He felt trapped, alone, frightened, and helpless. He had kept the telephone operating in the vain hope that Neeley might call and rescue him, but now that clearly was not going to happen. At last he unplugged both phone and answering machine. That give him momentary peace, but not from his own inner torment.

In addition, he had very little food in the apartment and no beer or wine to ease his troubles. He could not buy any with his useless debit card. And he had no intention of waiting until the inevitable gaggle of reporters started camping in front of the apartment, the remorseless scandal patrol that turned into a death watch over disintegrating careers and reputations. He would give no one that satisfaction. He had food and drink in the cabin on the Mountain, and he knew no one could find him there.

He slipped out, unobserved, and left for the Valley. But as he drove west, even his mountain cabin no longer held promise as a place of restoration. It was just a lair for a wounded beast to crawl away and hide—and preserve the few shreds of dignity he had left.

27

trange how little we know about the people around us, Jimmy Tol-liver mused. He rode the elevator to the top floor of the Chamber of Commerce Building, where the Direct Broadcast Network studio was located.

He had gone first to Chase's apartment, but there was no answer to his steady ringing and pounding on the door. No one had seen him for days. People there were neighbors only in the sense that they lived nearby. No one took much interest in the neighbors or knew much about their lives.

Having failed to find Chase in Alexandria, Jimmy now hoped that his former employers at DBN could help locate him. Clare Trumbull reported she had been trying to reach Chase ever since the "exposé" had appeared in the *News,* but he was never home, nor had he returned her calls. Worried, she enlisted Jimmy in the search. And now Jimmy shared her nagging sense of urgency. Something was clearly wrong.

The receptionist showed him to Hugh Mahan's office, and the network executive greeted him warmly. No, he had not seen Chase since their unfortunate parting more than a week ago. He did know that Chase had a second home somewhere in the western part of the state. In the Shenandoah, Mahan thought, though he could not say exactly where. Some place Chase cherished and visited frequently to escape the pressures of the broadcast industry.

Mahan had little other help to offer. But just as Jimmy was leaving, disappointed, Mahan remembered that Chase had been seeing a girl, someone he had been quite serious about, evidently. Her name was Neeley Durant, and she was the director of communications at the RNC.

Pleased at getting hold of the first link in the chain he hoped would lead to Chase, Jimmy jumped in a taxi and went straight to the Republican National Committee building on First Street below the Capitol. No, they told him there, Neeley no longer worked at the RNC. She had just accepted a job at the Pritchett Corporation. They gave Jimmy the address, and back across town to Massachusetts Avenue near Dupont Circle he went.

Neeley Durant had been away for a few days before starting at the Pritchett Corporation, and Jimmy found it difficult to see her on her first day in a new and demanding position. He identified himself as chief of staff to the late Senator Trumbull and noticed a frown steal over the receptionist's face when she relayed the information—Ms. Durant seemed none too eager to meet him.

But he was persistent. And after keeping him waiting for a respectable period, the receptionist ushered him into the boss's elegant office, full of antiques and Persian carpets and overlooking Massachusetts Avenue through a wall of tinted glass.

A tall woman, shapely and dramatic looking, with long, lovely, light-brown hair, came toward him and shook his hand. Chase had never talked about Neeley to him or, apparently, to Clare Trumbull. He had no idea what sort of relationship this striking woman had had with Chase, but he could guess.

"Hello," he said politely. "I'm Jimmy Tolliver."

"Yes, I know," Neeley Durant said civilly, but without warmth. "You worked for Senator Trumbull, didn't you?"

"I was his chief of staff."

"Please have a seat." She motioned him to a sofa covered in red Morocco leather and distanced herself behind an imposing desk.

"I was very sorry to hear about his death," she said. "It was a terrible tragedy."

Jimmy thought she sounded sincere, but there was a faint echo of . . . was it insincerity?

"What can I do for you?" she asked, obviously curious.

"Well, I'm a friend of Chase McKenzie."

Her polite and slightly puzzled expression turned into a momentary scowl, but her face quickly took on a mask of impassivity.

"I see."

"I—uh—understand he's a friend of yours too."

"No, not in the least," she said. "Well, not anymore, I should say."

"Oh." There was obviously more in this situation than he had anticipated. He suspected he would have to tread carefully. "I'm trying to find him. He seems to have disappeared."

"As well he should, after what the papers have said about him."

Surprised at the bitterness, Jimmy wondered suddenly if the *News* story was true. Maybe Chase had been deeply involved with this woman, and the report that he was a closet homosexual was the reason for her obvious anger. No, he thought again, and he dismissed the idea. Branch had better instincts.

And if the truth be told, so do I, Jimmy said to himself. *I can read 'em—I had enough practice. Chase isn't gay.*

He decided to speak boldly. If Chase had been romantically involved with her, surely there must be some residual sympathy in this tough but attractive woman.

"Ms. Durant, you know that story wasn't true. Chase McKenzie is no homosexual. The whole thing was a setup. He was led into a trap." He looked at her with frankness and mute appeal, trying to reach whatever humanity and sense of fair play she possessed.

Neeley Durant hung her head slightly, then got up and walked to the plate glass windows overlooking the busy avenue.

"Why would somebody do that?" she said finally.

"Come now, Ms. Durant. Surely you know the answer."

She turned to him briefly, and he saw a flash of something that looked like sympathy.

"Yes, I suppose you're right. I told him many times this preoccupation with gay-bashing would only get him in trouble. I'm sorry if he's been embarrassed."

"I'm afraid it's more than embarrassment. He's been totally discredited, and his career's been ruined. It sure would help if his friends could set the record straight," Jimmy said, taking a chance with her.

"Look, Mr. Tolliver," she replied severely, with an audible touch of nervousness. "It's neither here nor there as far as I'm concerned. Chase and I are—well . . . we aren't friends anymore. I tried to warn him. What he does, and the consequences of his actions, are none of my affair."

"I understand. But Ms. Durant, I think you should know that there's a lot more to this than just the false newspaper story."

"What do you mean?"

"His livelihood has been totally destroyed. DBN canceled his show—and that happened before the *News* story. On top of that, the IRS has frozen his bank accounts on the grounds of some unspecified tax violation. He can't even buy groceries or pay his rent."

Her eyes widened, and Jimmy guessed she had known nothing of the other two incidents.

"Chase a tax evader?" She snorted. "That's not very likely. He had a healthy fear of the IRS and was extremely careful about his taxes. He used to warn me all the time. He said anybody who was visible in public life, especially a Republican, ought not to take the slightest chance with the IRS."

"Well, there you are."

"As for the show—well, I haven't watched it lately, so this is news. Why did they cancel it?"

"Because the FCC threatened to pull the network's broadcast license unless Chase was dumped. It was a clear case of political blackmail."

"Blackmail? That's a little strong, isn't it?"

"Ms. Durant, you just said yourself that you warned Chase about taking on the gay establishment. You've been around. Surely you're not naive enough to think all these incidents are just coincidental."

"Can you prove the FCC or IRS took improper actions? I mean, you're talking about some kind of gay conspiracy at high levels."

She seemed agitated at the thought, and Jimmy wondered if she suddenly suspected Chase had been right all along.

"Maybe we'll be able to prove it one of these days," Jimmy said. "But right now that's not my main concern. I'm worried about finding Chase. I'm afraid he's in bad shape, and I want to help him. With the IRS lien on his bank account, he can't survive without help."

"Well, I'm sorry for him, of course. But I haven't seen him or even talked to him for weeks."

"Do you have any idea where he might be?"

Her mouth was set in a tight line, and she bit the inside of her lower lip. Obviously the woman was torn between wanting to help and not wanting to be drawn into Chase's predicament by provoking the same people he had evidently provoked.

Jimmy understood. "I promise not to mention your name or get you involved with this in any way. You have my word. I just want to find Chase and help him if I can."

Suddenly her face softened, as if an internal debate was resolved in his favor.

"He has a cabin over in the Shenandoah Valley. Well—it's not actually in the Valley—it's up at a place called Powell Mountain, near Woodstock. His mother still lives at the family farm below the mountain, right by the North Fork of the Shenandoah. I remember being able to see the house from a high cliff near his cabin. And there's an old bridge close by, but I can't remember the name. The cabin is where he always goes to be alone, to think—and frankly, to drink. He's been drinking a lot lately."

Jimmy wrote down the few details she could remember to help him find the cabin.

"Thanks, Ms. Durant. I really do appreciate it." Jimmy stood up to leave and offered his hand.

"Yes, well—if you see him, tell him . . ." The black cloud passed over her face again. She left the thought unfinished and walked Jimmy to the door.

"I hope you find him," she managed to say as Jimmy moved to go out into the reception area. Then she laid a hand lightly on his forearm as he reached the door. "I do hope he's OK."

Jimmy smiled briefly and nodded. "So do I."

★ ★ ★

Chase settled back wearily into the old worn armchair in front of a now cheerless hearth. The fire had long since gone out, and evening had laid a mantle of darkness gently across the Mountain.

He had fretted and brooded in the cabin for two days now, finding little comfort in his once beloved retreat. And all afternoon he had been sitting in the chair, thinking without coming to any useful conclusions.

He could see no way to repair the damage to his fortunes, certainly not now, and probably not ever. All he had left was shame and disgrace. And shame was more devastating to one raised in the traditional Southern culture than the loss of wealth and career.

In addition, he now acknowledged that he was a fornicator—one of those who, the Bible said, would never enter the kingdom of heaven. And because of his sexual libertinism, an innocent, unborn child had died—which also made him an accomplice to murder, if not a murderer outright.

No longer could he take any comfort in the knowledge that at least he wasn't a homosexual. In a perverse way, the *Washington News* account, though a lie, still condemned him justly. In absolute terms he was no better than the most promiscuous AIDS terrorist. In terms of his relationship with the Creator, he was no better off. He had never come to God through the redemptive work of Christ. Pride and self-will had always stood in the way. They still stood in the way.

Branch's murder had been a convenient excuse to reject the claims of the gospel on his life. If he could blame God and keep His quiet insistent calling at bay, then he would not have to surrender his autonomy. He would run his own life in his own way.

Well, he *had* run his own life in his own way and now had to admit he had made a mess of it.

He tilted up the last bottle of wine, but only a few drops trickled into the glass. Morosely, he felt its emptiness mocked the emptiness of his own life. For all his drinking, defeat still lay on his heart like a sheet of lead. He could not dissolve it with alcohol.

He let the empty bottle fall to the floor, where it rolled with a hollow thud against the chair leg. Mercifully, then, he fell into a long sleep.

Later—perhaps hours later—he knew dimly that he was having a bad dream, and he clawed his way back to consciousness. Dreams weren't to be feared, he thought. When things got too bad in a dream, you could always force yourself to wake up, like a swimmer straining to reach the surface and the life-giving air.

But life, and this unbearable misery and shame, were a dream from which he could not awake. From this waking nightmare perhaps the opposite course was necessary—to go to sleep forever, to seek oblivion. That would end the torment.

Chase struggled to his feet. He had no idea of the time, but it was fully dark, inside and out. Bumping into the table and chairs, he pushed his way uncertainly from the hearth toward the front door and went out.

On the front stoop of the cabin he cried out into the night air, "Neeley, I would have forgiven you!" *Despite what you did to our baby.*

But he knew she would never forgive *him.* No one and nothing would ever stand in the way of Neeley's getting what she wanted. She would have thrown him over eventually in any case. Only his lust and monumental self-delusion had kept him from seeing that. That realization was a further condemnation, and it steeled his resolve to do what he had decided to do.

After so many years of coming to the Mountain, he knew the route to Draper's Leap in his sleep. Now he set out for the overlook in the dark. Still half intoxicated, he weaved unsteadily uphill. There was barely enough light to reveal the occasional stretch of trail where the rocky surface glowed palely, but by habit his feet found the pathway in the looming darkness of the woods.

Finally, there it was, the yawning blacker blackness of Draper's Leap, where the void made a vague smudge upon the night.

It seemed simple—there was peace for pain, right there off the path a few steps in front of him and then just five hundred feet straight down onto the jagged boulders below. It would be over in an eyeblink.

He reeled up to the lip of the escarpment. *It'll be over in a few seconds. They'll think it was an accident,* he thought illogically, still wrestling with shame, not wanting to leave behind the legacy of a suicide.

Then something like a physical force pulled him back. The force was internal, though, confused and jumbled, made up of the urgent buzzing sibilance of a dozen voices from a hundred times and places. Familiar voices, echoes, as if calling out to him from the back rooms and forgotten passageways of childhood memory. The words of Branch and Clare and Libby, of his parents and grandparents and teachers and ministers. The words of Scripture, read to him long ago.

Chase listened to them all and was suddenly horrified at the finality of what he was about to do. He lurched back from the brink—lurched too far, throwing himself off balance. The grass at the edge of the cliff was slick with dew, and his feet shot out from under him toward yawning space. He went down heavily, helplessly, feet first, thighs striking sharply on the lip of the rock. Then the back of his head thumped painfully, and he slid over.

"Oh, God, help!" he screamed and hurtled down into the dark.

★ ★ ★

There was a roaring noise in his head, mixed with plangent ringing. *So this is what it's like to die?* He felt strangely detached despite the sharp pain in his lower legs and the throbbing in his skull. *Am I still falling?* It took a moment for the answer to penetrate. No, he was not falling.

It was peculiar. There had been no sensation of a long drop, no sensation of passing time. Yet the fall from Draper's Leap would take several seconds—time enough for a final pang of remorse before nothingness or whatever came after. But no such time had elapsed. And now he realized that he was alive. Confused, in pain, but alive.

Fighting to remain conscious, to understand what had happened and how he could still be alive, Chase tried to focus on his surroundings. But could see nothing through the darkness or feel anything through the pain, and the blow and the sensory deprivation left him dizzy. Soon even that limited awareness receded to a tiny point of light and then went out altogether, like a candle flame consuming the last tiny bit of wick.

He came to, sensing he had been unconscious for a long time. *Yes, I really am alive,* he thought wonderingly. And with the return of consciousness came pain again. He was wet with dew and chilled, and now he felt grass beneath him—grass instead of rock. With that realization came the certainty that he had not plunged downward the five hundred feet from Draper's Leap.

He now realized, too, that in his earlier state—angry, full of remorse and self-pity, half inebriated—he must have taken the wrong path and turned aside from the main trail. He had not gone over the high precipice at all but had fallen instead fifteen feet to the grassy ledge before the Leap—the site of countless family picnics and where he had picnicked with Neeley.

Lying in frigid darkness on the ledge, Chase trembled from shock and cold but above all from a profoundly awed sense of the presence of God. Tears began to stream down his face. God had saved him, though not in the way he had prayed in sudden panic before the fall.

It could not have been a happenstance, for he had walked the path to Draper's Leap a thousand times. Even in his befuddled condition and in the dark, how could he have erred on his own and turned aside to the ledge? But he had.

He tried to get up but then lay back, dizzy. His head still pounded, and his body ached all over. He could not tell how badly he was hurt but decided against trying to move for a while until the pain and dizziness subsided. He began drifting in and out of consciousness.

He seemed to hear voices . . . see faces . . . his parents . . . Branch Trumbull . . . Clare . . . Libby. Long ignored verses of Scripture came flooding back from the past.

He had always thought he was above reproach, in contrast to the homosexuals and radicals and other enemies he had battled for years—so much better than they that he didn't need redemption. But he had enthroned himself as sovereign of his life instead of the true Sovereign, the King who had laid aside His glory to die in his place.

He too needed the Lord Christ, the sacrificial Lamb, the King of kings and Lord of lords. The One who had turned him aside from the path of destruction to the path of life. The only One who could strip off his chains of pride and self-will.

This time Chase prayed not in despair but in repentance and joyful hope—and in words from his childhood, "Lord Jesus, be merciful to me, a sinner."

★ ★ ★

The darkness of night imperceptibly yielded way to the soft pearly light of dawn. Then it was light enough for Chase to see that he had indeed fallen on the grassy ledge. A well-worn stairway of rocky outcroppings led from the ledge to the escarpment above.

He tried to get to his feet and make his way back up. But hot, excruciating pain shot through both ankles, and he realized he had probably sprained them both. He tried to crawl up, painfully dragging his twisted and throbbing ankles behind him, but he could not surmount the natural rock stairs without some pushing power from his legs.

It was getting colder. The dew of the previous evening crusted on his body, and, as he shivered uncontrollably, fear suddenly overtook him that he might die of hypothermia unless he could get back to the cabin. In the same moment, he recalled the psalm that Clare Trumbull had cited when recounting Branch's experience in the desert mine field. What was it? . . . "Under his wings you will find refuge."

No, God wasn't going to let him die here on the Mountain, though if He did, that was all right. Chase knew he could enter His courts now, not as a condemned rebel, but as a redeemed son of God. Still, the words of the psalm, and the new sense of God's covering wings comforted him. Strangely, he soon felt a little warmer, and the involuntary shivering stopped.

28

Jimmy Tolliver spent the night in the modest Blue and Gray Motel in Woodstock. He prayed for Chase and asked God's guidance in locating him and in helping him once located. He knew that Chase was a proud man, and Jimmy had always been a little intimidated by him.

At first light, Jimmy crossed the bridge over the Shenandoah on the narrow secondary road from Woodstock. The first unimproved road to the right after the bridge led up to Powell Mountain Overlook, Neeley Durant had told him, and, yes, there was a weathered wooden sign—"McKenzie."

Jimmy downshifted and began the drive up the long, tortuous unpaved road to the top of the mountain. After ten minutes of bumping along uphill, he spotted the cabin in the hollow, then the long meadow sloping up behind it to fade into the trees that crowned the peak.

And there by the side of the cabin was Chase McKenzie's Jeep.

Jimmy's heart soared. He parked the car, ran up the wooden steps, and rapped vigorously on the door. But there was no answer. Pushing inside, he entered a darkened room that smelled like a brewery, and his feet collided with empty beer cans that rolled metallically along the hardwood floor.

"Chase?" he called loudly but again was met with silence.

Chase had to be around somewhere. Perhaps he had just gone for an early morning walk. Jimmy went outside and saw the pathway from the cabin up through the meadow to the top of the hill. He followed it.

"Helloooo! Anybody up here?" he called, when halfway to the top.

His calls echoed faintly down toward the hollow.

Then, from a distance, "Down here! Down here! Below the cliff!"

Jimmy reached the summit and cautiously approached the edge. "Oh, there you are," he said with genuine relief, then realized something was wrong. "Chase, you're hurt." He clambered down to the ledge.

"Not too bad," Chase answered. "I fell in the dark, and I think I sprained my ankles."

"And you've got a bad gash on the back of your head. The blood's all clotted, so I guess you'll live." Jimmy grinned at him. "But we better get you to a doctor."

"Jimmy, I can't climb up to the top with these ankles. Back in the cabin there's some rope . . ."

Jimmy found the rope and strung it from a tree down to the ledge. Then he climbed down again to where Chase lay. "I'll splint your ankles so you can stand and put a little weight on them."

"I never expected to see you of all people. What brought you here? How'd you find me?"

Jimmy told him of his search. "I had to do a little detective work, but your friends told me you'd be here."

"I still have friends?"

"Sure, lots of friends. But you didn't give them much credit, running off like this without a word of explanation or givin' anybody a chance to help," Jimmy said reproachfully.

"Jimmy . . . you know, I used to not think too much of you. In fact, I harbored a real bad attitude toward you, and I want to ask your forgiveness."

"Oh?" Jimmy raised his heavy eyebrows. "Well, you never showed it. You're always the perfect gentleman. But sure, I forgive you. Beside, there's enough in my own life to feel bad about."

"No worse than in mine," replied Chase.

"Then we have something in common."

Jimmy supported him as Chase struggled awkwardly up the line to the top of the cliff, where he sank into the grass and rested. Finally they made it to the cabin.

Chase pulled on dry clothes, then rested while Jimmy made him a sandwich and brewed a pot of coffee for them both.

"OK," Jimmy announced, "I'm taking you to the hospital.

Is there one in Front Royal or somewhere close?"

Chase thought for a moment. "No, not to the hospital. You know what happened to me at the IRS. The gay network is stronger in the National Health Service than any other agency of the government. I'm already on the low priority list."

"Maybe you're right," Jimmy replied. "But you need to have that head looked at. It needs stitches. And those ankles—"

"All right. But take me to Doctor Lacy in Woodstock. He's an old friend of the family. He practiced for a while with my father."

Jimmy knew there were still many holdouts from National Health, recalcitrant libertarians and religious people, among the medical profession. If you could find one of these willing holdouts, you could still see him privately and pay for his services. The NHS bureaucracy had tried to crack down on private practice, but with the growing problems in the system, it had proved impossible to stamp out altogether.

"Sounds good," he said.

"And afterward we'll stop and see my mother," Chase added. "I haven't seen her in a long time—my life had reached a point where I just couldn't share it with her anymore." Humbled pride could no longer restrain his joy as the words spilled out. "Jimmy, I've got something important to tell her. The most important news of my life."

"Yeah?"

"You know, all my life people have been asking me if I was 'saved,' and I always resented it. Even Branch and Clare, as much as I love 'em. Well, last night on the Mountain, I was. God's forgiven me."

Jimmy smiled broadly. "Praise the Lord! Then we're brothers, Chase. Brothers in Christ."

"We're brothers," Chase repeated, and he embraced Jimmy Tolliver with all the sincerity and warmth he could muster.

★ ★ ★

As Director of Presidential Personnel, Barbara Dunhill always looked for courage in candidates for jobs in the administration, but she did not think of herself as particularly courageous. Her idea of courage was to ask herself simply, 'Is it the right thing to do?' And if the answer was yes, or more yes than no—since things were usually ambiguous in politics—then she would try to do it.

Barbara knew that Langdon Smith, the president's chief of staff and her boss, would be extremely unhappy—first at her spying on Kerry Kerrigan and, second, over having to deal with what she had learned.

Smith cared little for issues or principles. His idea of public policy was to make the president—and himself, of course—look good. To him that meant slavish attention to the needs and whims of the big media personalities, avoidance of controversy, and acquiescence to criticism.

She called nervously and detected Smith's annoyance through his receptionist when Barbara refused to explain the meeting's agenda in advance. Instead she told him vaguely that it was an important personnel matter, which it was—by a stretch.

At the appointed hour she left her office on the second floor of the White House West Wing and walked down to the office of the chief of staff.

Langdon Smith kept her waiting only a few minutes. He motioned her to an upholstered settee as she entered, where a tray of coffee was sitting on the low mahogany table.

Smith was a portly, florid man in his early sixties, who had achieved success as an investment banker in Washington. He poured Barbara a cup of coffee, and his graciousness ended there. "Well, now, what's this personnel matter that wouldn't wait?"

Barbara determined to be calm and businesslike. "I've come across some very disturbing information about a member of the White House staff. It could embarrass the president and all of us if it became public." She knew exactly how to frame the issue to get Smith's cooperation.

"Well, go ahead," Smith said, resigned but still irritated.

This was not the first time Barbara had produced allegations of misconduct about presidential appointees. Most of the time he acknowledged that her inside knowledge had been quite helpful. Still, she sensed it bespoke an independence that had always troubled him.

"You know Chase McKenzie, host of 'Pulse of the Nation,'" she said.

"Yes, yes," he replied impatiently.

"Well, then you know how popular and successful the show was."

Smith wrinkled his nose ever so slightly.

She saw that he did not wholly approve of McKenzie or his program and feared she had made a tactical error.

"Of course, not everybody likes the show or McKenzie," she said, recovering. "But the point is that regardless of what we may think of him, he has a very large and very loyal nationwide following. And it happens that most of the people who watch him faithfully are also the president's most loyal supporters."

"I see. So what's your point?"

"Did you know his network has canceled the show under pressure from the FCC?"

"No, I didn't." Smith seemed genuinely surprised. "What kind of pressure?"

"They threatened to pull the network's broadcast license unless the network got rid of him. The FCC bureaucrats argued that the show was homophobic and violated the 'public air-waves' doctrine and so forth. But the action was clearly improper. I would even call it a case of political blackmail."

"Then why didn't the network fight it? Or complain to somebody here in the White House? Surely our appointees over there didn't go along with it?"

"I'm afraid the chairman did go along—willingly—and I'll explain why in a second. And the reason DBN didn't make it a public issue is that they're involved in a major capital expansion in advanced microwave equipment to go with their new high-definition TV system. They're dangerously leveraged financially, and if the news got out that the FCC was holding up their license—even temporarily—then their stock would take a nosedive.

"Evidently the FCC threat was not to kill the license renewal altogether. The agency knew it couldn't get away with that in court if DBN decided to fight it. But they threatened to slow-roll the renewal process long enough to jeopardize the company's stock, once rumors got out that DBN was in trouble. The threat against their financial position was all it took to make them knuckle under on McKenzie."

"But how could they really believe their license renewal could be held up?" Smith was clearly struggling for a reason to disbelieve.

"Langdon, forgive me for saying so, but you have to admit this administration has not held the line very successfully on regulation in the marketplace. The FCC has tremendous power to regulate the broadcast industry—more than it did even five years ago, especially under the 'public air waves doctrine.'"

"I guess you're right," he finally agreed. "So what do you propose? And by the way," he added petulantly, "how is this a personnel issue?"

"I'll explain that in a minute too. But there's more. At the same time McKenzie was losing his show and his livelihood, he also found the IRS had frozen all his liquid assets. The IRS has slapped a tax lien on all his bank accounts, and he can't use his EDC or get any cash out. He can't buy or sell."

"Is he one of those right-wing tax rebels?" Smith asked hopefully.

"Not at all. Everybody I've talked to who knows him says the charge is preposterous. McKenzie's said to be very scrupulous about his taxes. He knew that a controversial public figure had to be more careful than the average citizen. Right now he literally has nothing. The IRS is controlling all his bank accounts."

"Well, if he's not guilty of tax evasion, I'm sure his lawyer or accountants can get it straightened out. I don't see how it concerns me or the White House—or you, quite frankly."

"Here's how it concerns us all. Our very own Kerry Kerrigan has been in communication with the officials at the FCC and the IRS that initiated the two actions against McKenzie."

Smith looked startled, trapped, as the implications of her report set in.

"What are you saying exactly?" he blurted, his red face turning even redder.

"I'm saying that Kerry improperly used his influence as the president's counsel to pressure two executive agencies into committing acts that are at best unethical and at worst illegal. He did so to retaliate against McKenzie and silence his criticism of the gay rights movement. And I'm saying that if this were to become public, it would severely embarrass the White House."

"Are you suggesting that Kerry's gay?"

"He appears to be. But in any case, he's tied into the gay activist underground."

As always, Langdon Smith took refuge in details, not substance, when cornered by a dilemma. He demanded with some heat, "How do you know Kerry was involved in the FCC and IRS actions?"

"Simple. I got Security to check the phone logs. He was in contact many times with the relevant staff in the two weeks leading up to both actions. And once I knew where to look, I went to my sources in both agencies for confirmation. They told me that the actions against McKenzie were taken by people either identified as or suspected of being part of a homosexual network entrenched in the agencies. The principals involved were able to cite 'interest from the White House' as a cover for their actions."

Smith shook his head. "I find this hard to believe."

"It *is* hard to believe. But these are different times from the ones you and I came up in, Langdon," she observed, trying to invoke a common experience and system of values.

It did not work. She could see Smith inexorably slipping into his shoot-the-messenger mode.

"And just what do you want me to do?" Clearly he did not want to do anything except keep the matter quiet and hope that it would go away of its own accord.

"Well, it's not my prerogative to decide. I thought I was doing the president and the administration a service by bringing this to your attention. If it were up to me though, I guess the first thing I'd do would be to make things right with the agencies. Get McKenzie's bank account freed at least. About the FCC, I just don't know. McKenzie's network has already canceled his show. The license renewal is probably no longer held up now that the damage is done.

"And of course," she went on, "I'd get rid of the people in the agencies who had a hand in this. At least the political appointees. We can't fire the career civil servants, but we could transfer them and break up the nests of gay activists. And then I'd get rid of Kerry Kerrigan."

Smith was appalled. "Listen, we can't just go around firing and transferring people wholesale. Especially the White House counsel!

That would raise all kinds of questions, and then . . . and you know where that would lead."

"Well, maybe you could do it piecemeal," she suggested. "But these are dangerous and irresponsible people. They've had a taste of power, they have an agenda of their own, and I can promise you, unless some action is taken this won't be the last such episode."

"I'll have to think about it," he said at last.

"Will you let me know what you decide?" Barbara pulled her notes together and stood to leave.

"Yes, I'll let you know this afternoon," he said sullenly.

At 3:00 P.M., true to his word, Smith called Barbara back to his office. This time he remained behind the safe bulwark of his desk and directed her to sit on the other side.

"I called the IRS commissioner and read him the riot act about allowing his bureaucrats to politicize the tax system," he explained. "Of course he knew absolutely nothing about the whole affair, and I believe him. He said he would personally look into the McKenzie matter, and if there was no evidence to sustain the charge of tax violations he'd have the lien removed."

Her heart sank when she realized Smith was only going to do the minimum he thought he could get away with. "But, Langdon, what if they fabricated the evidence? I mean, that's the whole point! They wouldn't be likely to impose a tax lien on someone's entire assets without some bogus evidence."

"Uh—I hadn't thought of that." He was visibly annoyed. "I'll call back and add that proviso."

"And what about the FCC? And Kerrigan? And the employees who were involved in this outrage?" Now she was fighting to keep her temper under control.

"Well, since DBN will get their license renewal and the question of McKenzie's show is now moot, I didn't see any need to stir that particular pot. And Barbara, I can't go into the president's office and tell him to fire Kerry Kerrigan just because he's gay. This is 1999!"

"No, *not* because he's gay, Langdon. Because he's misused his office to carry out a personal agenda. Abused his authority. Betrayed the president's trust."

"Perhaps in time I might have to do that. But right now I've decided to proceed with caution on Kerrigan—and on the other personnel actions."

Barbara caught the odd inflection in his voice and noticed he was looking at her strangely.

"There's one personnel action I *have* decided on though," he continued.

She heard the ominous tone, saw the unpleasant glitter in his eyes, and knew what was coming. She had known it for days, since her lunch with Jimmy Tolliver, and she had prepared.

"Barbara, I'm afraid you've gone way, way beyond your authority in this matter. In fact, I couldn't put it any better than you just did. You've misused your office to carry out a personal agenda, not only in this matter but for a long time. You've abused your authority. And frankly, you've forfeited the trust the president and I have had in you."

Without a second's loss of composure she shot back, "Is this *your* view or the president's?"

"Both. I'm speaking for him." He tried to meet her direct gaze and could not.

She knew he was lying. "Very well," she said briskly. "Let me finish this for you. You want my resignation, effective immediately, right?"

"Yes," Smith replied, with a faint note of triumph.

She reached into the file folder she was carrying, pulled out a sheet of paper, and handed it to him.

With furrowed brow he read her resignation, effective at the close of business that day.

"Well, I see you anticipated me."

"Yes, I did, Langdon. And since I did, I also brought copies of some other letters here I'd like you to read as well." She passed over the papers and noted with satisfaction the consternation in his face as he read her detailed account of her findings in the McKenzie matter addressed to Attorney General Martin Bell. Additional copies were addressed to a journalist named Jay Blaisdell, recently hired as enterprise reporter by the *Washington Standard*.

"Barbara, you can't do this!" Smith spluttered.

"I don't want to, but I'll send them if I have to." She hoped she was not betraying her nervousness in this high level confrontation. After all, he *was* chief of staff to the president of the United States.

"And if I do," she pressed on, "the attorney general will have no choice but to open a formal investigation. What we have here, you see, are felonies in the federal code. Conspiracy and misprision of a felony to start with. The AG is duty-bound to look into an allegation of this magnitude once it's brought to his attention."

"So what is it you want? Your job back?"

She knew she had won—and knew just as well that she could never work here again. Even if she did salvage her position, it could only be a temporary reprieve. Life and work in the White House would gradually become intolerable after this.

"No, Langdon, you've convinced me," she said with scathing sarcasm. "You're right, I'm just not fit to work here. I'll go quietly. But Kerry Kerrigan goes too, along with these three individuals in the agencies I've identified. They're Schedule C's. They serve at the pleasure of the president, and they can be fired with nothing more than a phone call. And if anyone does probe into this scandal, you can always say you acted for cause. I know it'll be difficult to stand on principle for once, but look at the bright side. You'll be doing the right thing."

"Unless it's the gay media who do the probing," he said miserably.

"Ah, yes, Langdon. In that case you'll just have to make a choice. After all, that's what governing is all about, isn't it?"

Before returning to her office to pack up, she had one final task to perform—immediately, while Langdon Smith was still in shock and before he could intervene to block her access.

She walked down the first floor corridor to the reception area outside the Oval Office and spoke to the president's executive secretary, a woman with whom she had been on cordial terms.

Barbara did not trust Langdon Smith to carry out his side of the bargain, nor did she want the president to think she had left under a cloud. She gave the president's secretary a letter she had not shown the chief of staff.

"Suzie, I'm leaving the White House," she said to the woman, who gaped at her in utter surprise. "Now don't look at me like that. Something's happened, and it's better for the president if I go. Here's a letter that explains the whole thing in detail. I'd like you to take this in and see that he gets it. Will you?"

Satisfied that the letter would be delivered, Barbara went back upstairs and packed her photos, books, and other personal things, completing the chore without sadness. She had enjoyed a long run in the White House and took comfort in knowing she had rendered good service to the country. She had never confused her own identity and self-worth with the status that accompanied a White House job. It was just another combat post in the ongoing twilight struggle, and she was confident she would soon find herself on another battlefront somewhere. It was her nature.

NEWS ITEM,
the *Washington Star*

Denver, CO–The Colorado state senate today ratified the Human Rights Amendment (HRA) to the US Constitution in a lopsided 56-32 vote, making Colorado the thirty-first state to approve the amendment that would outlaw discrimination against homosexuals.

Three-fourths of the states must approve a constitutional amendment before it becomes the law of the land. With the Colorado decision, the approval of only three more states, or a total of thirty-four, is needed to make the Human Rights Amendment part of the US Constitution.

Some supporters are already referring to the HRA as the "Twenty-Seventh Amendment" in anticipation of its final ratification. However, other national gay leaders have privately begun to express concern that the time limit on ratification is running out. Instead of concentrating on winning the approval of three more states, the focus of gay legislative action may have to shift back to the Congress, which must extend the time limit for ratification.

Beginning with the proposed Eighteenth Amendment, Congress has historically included in the resolution of ratification a "reasonable" time limit by which the states must ratify the amendment. In 1939 the US Supreme Court held that the "reasonableness" of the time period for the required thirty-four states to act is a political question to be decided by Congress. This means Congress can simply vote to extend the ratification period.

Congress passed the HRA in January 1995 and stipulated in the resolution of ratification a five-year time limit. Unless Congress votes to extend it, the HRA's five-year clock will expire in January 2000.

29

Garden Monnoye lost no time in implementing the new master plan that had come to him in a flash of brilliance on the Alpine trail above Merano.

He was not deceived by the relative ineffectiveness of contemporary Christianity. There were still many right-wing bigots in the ranks of the religious, and it took only a few Luthers or Calvins or Billy Sundays to rekindle the mass psychosis of religious frenzy at any time.

And if that were to happen, it could also rekindle a new anti-gay conflagration. The movement had to forestall such a possibility, and that meant they had to first gain passage of the HRA.

But as he began to implement the plan, Monnoye saw that he had underestimated the amount of money it would consume. He would need huge amounts to make the necessary contributions to his allies. Now he was finding that even his immense financial resources had limits. And when he tried to tap other funding sources to help fuel his plan, he ran into a strategy competing for available funds—the frantic research effort to find the gene that causes homosexuality.

Monnoye's plan was fine—even brilliant—as far as it went, but he saw that it did not go far enough. With money now an issue, he realized that those whom he could not buy he must coerce. And the plan lacked that one vital element—force.

As the HRA Campaign continued to unfold, he had to anticipate the possibility of a nasty physical encounter with the radical right, especially the religious bigots. The religious right had lost most of its steam as a political force in the 1990s. Both parties had turned on them, and the news and opinion media, thanks in part to allies such as Wynn Pritchett, had engaged in a successful campaign to discredit them. But there were still some diehards out there, Protestants and conservative Catholics and Orthodox Jews, who refused to go quietly onto the political and cultural dung heap where they belonged.

The campaign for the HRA was reaching its most critical point, and Paragon's demographic researchers were now telling Monnoye that the movement was unlikely to win any more states before the five-year period expired in January. He was frustrated to note that part of the reason lay in the population shift, "the Great Migration."

He was vaguely aware that many conservatives had left states unfriendly to their intolerant lifestyle and had moved to regions where their bigotry could survive a little longer, mostly in the South, West, and Midwest. But now he learned that this migration had tipped the voting balance in those regions even more favorably into the hands of the religious right.

It would take a few more years of government action, judicial activism, and media vilification to dilute their voting control of the states where they were concentrated. It would take a few more years of indoctrination in the public schools to seal the next generation for the progressives. First they would have to outlaw this detestable home schooling that was mushrooming everywhere, and put a stop to private Christian schools.

Until the movement could bring that about, Monnoye's forces would need more time. So now the main battle had to focus on the all-important extension of the HRA time limit.

Monnoye knew the opposition might also realize that the time extension was critical and might mobilize to oppose it. In his mind that was the worst possible scenario. But he had to anticipate the religious right just might make some kind of move to oppose the time extension, and that pushed him close to panic.

It was unlikely, but if the religious right were to focus its efforts on blocking the HRA time extension, could they really jeopardize the reelection of enough members of Congress to gain leverage over a time extension vote? He shuddered at the thought.

The question answered itself—the religious bigots simply could not be permitted to organize a pressure campaign to block the time limit extension. Those who couldn't be deceived must be intimidated, and that required a more disciplined and cohesive force than anything the gay movement could field at the moment.

The movement had an abundant plenty of spokesmen, lawyers, political activists, writers, analysts, researchers, advocates, and talking heads. What gays lacked was someone to wield physical force when necessary.

Monnoye had a particular interest in the growth of the most shadowy of all the direct action groups, Come Out Fighting.

COF had its roots in the Stonewall Riot in New York City in 1969, which sparked the rise of the gay liberation movement. The AIDS crisis led to the formation of ACT-OUT, and the Reagan phenomenon in the 1980s gave impetus to left-wing gays who formed the Lavender Left and the Commie Queers. But in the late 1990s, the most militant members pulled out of their respective organizations to form Come Out Fighting.

COF's founding members explicitly rejected the moderate gay agenda with its emphasis on political and media action, improved public relations, and persuasion. COF unequivocally favored violent confrontation. In reality, COF was a behind-the-scenes operation of Garden Monnoye and his inner circle in the gay high command.

And now Monnoye began to see the need for COF's muscle. He saw how much more useful it could be converted from a loose, barely organized, and ill-disciplined mob of angry gays into a homosexual elite, a specially trained and committed corps, a fighting force, the defender of the gay movement.

Starting now, Monnoye decided, Come Out Fighting would recruit only gay men who were tough, mean, smart, and aggressive. They would train to master the martial arts and, in due time, firearms and other weapons. They would embark on a scientific study of revolutionary action.

In a short time he would remold COF into an order, a deadly serious parody of the monastic military orders of the Middle Ages, the Knights Templar and Knights Hospitalers. COF would have the most stringent entrance requirements of any gay direct action group. And the best among the movement would clamor to get in.

Above all, the refurbished COF would be utterly loyal to him and dependent upon him for its resources and for its elite standing. It would take time to hone Come Out Fighting to a true fighting edge, and when he looked at the calendar, January 2000 loomed close.

There was no time to lose.

30

A concussion, six stitches in the back of his head, a compressed disc, one severely sprained ankle, one ankle badly twisted but not sprained, assorted bruises, scrapes, and contusions—not much damage, Chase thought, considering the alternative and especially considering what he deserved.

With the excitement of the new convert he marveled at God's mercy and at how Providence and only a few yards of pathway had saved him.

Old Doc Lacy in Woodstock had sternly ordered him to take at least six weeks to recuperate. The doctor was more concerned about the back injury than anything else, but he promised Chase that proper care and rest would make him as good as new.

As soon as Jimmy heard the prognosis and the order for care, he called Clare. Then he drove Chase home, not to his Alexandria apartment, but home to the Trumbulls' in Potomac.

They pulled into the circular driveway, and Jimmy gave the horn a few toots.

As Chase struggled out of the car with Jimmy's help and awkwardly got onto his crutches, Clare came out of the front door. Tears stood in her eyes and a broad smile of welcome lit up her normally serene face.

Chase smiled back triumphantly as he hobbled toward her. Then his heart skipped. On the porch, holding the door open and smiling as grandly as her mother, was Libby.

The two women fussed and hovered over him as he deposited his leg in its bulky cast on the king-size bed in the first floor guest room and rested his bruised back against a profusion of pillows.

Libby brought in tea, and the two women fluttered around him, chatting brightly, inquiring how he felt and what they could do to make him more comfortable.

There was little more they could do. Jimmy had already left for Chase's apartment to bring back clothes and books and some personal things. He was warm and comfortable, not too sore, and had never felt more secure or more welcome in a place since leaving home to report to VMI.

Above all, that yearning restless ache in his soul no longer vexed him, and he felt inner tranquillity for the first time. The war against God was now over, and to God's glory and Chase's benefit, Chase had lost.

He was content to stay with the Trumbulls for a few days. But old habits and customs reasserted themselves, and at the end of the first week he began protesting that he could not possibly impose on them for six weeks or more.

Clare and Libby dismissed his protests as they would the mewlings of a child. "Chase, just forget your courtly manners and your sense of propriety for a while," Clare told him. "We've been waiting a long time for this. You need to rest and get proper care, and we need somebody to care for. And Libby's taking a few weeks off from work, and she can help me."

That news sent an inexplicable surge of delight through Chase, a feeling for which he immediately felt guilty. *Why does that make me so happy? After Neeley, I'm through with women.*

"And besides"—Jimmy, who had stopped by, joined the argument—"you got banged up just enough to immobilize you for a while, without hurting you too much to function. God must have a reason for all this. You're not your own now. You're bought with a price—a very great price."

Clare added, "Don't hold cheaply what God's love has bought. Let us care for you for a while, so you can concentrate on making the most of whatever God's purpose is for you."

"OK. OK. You win," Chase relented. "Since all I can do is rest for six weeks, I may as well do it here, where y'all can teach me."

They had briefly discussed the future of the Nehemiah Foundation, and with some reservations Chase agreed to take over the role of national spokesman while Jimmy ran the day-to-day operation. But he still had two major concerns.

First was the rehabilitation of his good name. The false "outing" in the *Washington News* had shaken him deeply, and the memory of its shamefulness still burned. Though he committed the solution to that problem to God, his pride had not totally disappeared with his conversion.

And second, he was at an utter loss as to what the Foundation should *do*. He knew in broad terms what course to take but could not see clearly exactly even what the next step should be.

When he expressed his misgivings, Jimmy reassured him that they would know in due time what to do. In the meanwhile, he encouraged Chase to make the most of the enforced period of inactivity.

"Use the time to study and reflect."

Chase held up the worn leather-bound Bible in his lap.

"I'm studying. It was the senator's. He marked all the most important passages and made notes in the margins."

"Wonderful." Jimmy smiled. "He used to tell me all the time, 'There's no spiritual growth without knowledge.'"

Chase already possessed some knowledge of the Bible, long-suppressed but residing in his memory. Now the knowledge that he had acquired, lying dormant, began to make sense.

He began to assess his own life. Something profound and wonderful had happened. But how to translate what had happened into a practical course of action and way of living, how to master the new understanding that this Christian family seemed to have so abundantly—those were the problems he wrestled with.

He started to attend church regularly with Libby and Clare. After church, Libby would prepare lunch while Clare went off to Baltimore or Washington to work in one of her many ministries serving the inner-city poor. Chase began to look forward to this time alone with Libby.

One Sunday she sat beside him in the solarium. She had been reading aloud from the *Oxford Book of English Verse*, and Chase shared a discovery with her—his new awareness that the fullness of God could satisfy man's deepest longings for truth and meaning. Without involved explanation, she seemed to understand precisely what he meant.

From that day on, Libby began to crowd more and more into his thoughts. At first he reproached himself for thinking about her.

Still in the grip of spiritual renewal, he felt guilty, believing he should think only about "religious" things.

He felt guilty with respect to Libby as well, for he saw what a sorry business his relationship with Neeley Durant had been. He saw himself as soiled, "damaged goods," and not worthy of someone of such obvious inner as well as outer beauty.

She's good, he thought, *and true. Yet she's full of life and fire and intelligence and wit.*

Most of the time she was warm and friendly. Yet at times she could be strangely aloof. A growing fear began to gnaw at him— did she know about Neeley? Perplexed, he determined to resist anything more than a brotherly relationship with her. But self-discipline was hard where Libby was concerned, and he often found himself daydreaming about her despite himself.

She was still his superior in understanding and spiritual maturity. One afternoon, while she was dressing his head wound, he acknowledged that fact, trying to build rapport, and casually remarked that he wanted to learn all he could from her.

She smiled and did not seem at all flattered. "Be careful what you wish for. You just might get it."

He was taken aback. "Why do you say that?"

She did not answer as she snipped the dressing loose and looked at the stitches. "You're healing well." She applied a fresh bandage to his head, and her nearness was warm and fragrant.

"I think I could learn a lot from you." He winced as she worked deftly around the wound.

"Why don't you treat Jimmy Tolliver better, Chase?" she asked suddenly.

She figuratively rocked him back on his heels. "What does that have to do with anything?

"Why aren't you friendlier with him?"

"I didn't realize I *wasn't* friendly. He saved my life. Don't you think I'm grateful to him?"

"Grateful, yes. But you don't care for him as a human being. Tell me why," she insisted.

Suddenly he was ashamed. His eyes filled, and he said in a low voice, "I think—maybe it still bothers me that he was gay."

The instant he spoke the innermost truth she was all tenderness and solicitude. She patted his hand and looked at him kindly. Chase might have even said the look was affectionate.

"Yes," she said softly. *"Was* gay." She paused and then asked even more softly, "Haven't you ever done anything in the past *you* were ashamed of?"

His thoughts flew to Neeley in a jumbled kaleidoscope of images, and he looked down, speechless.

She took no verbal notice of his reaction. "Just so you'll know," she said after a moment, "after my father, Jimmy Tolliver is the finest man I've ever known. He's a new man, and he's a man's man. He deserves your respect and your friendship—and not just because he pulled you off the mountain."

"I believe you."

"Good," she continued. "Because when you begin the work he'll be a great help to you."

"What work?" he asked suspiciously.

"My father's work. The Foundation. Stopping the gay rights amendment, for a start."

He was slightly annoyed at the presumption. The Trumbulls still just assumed he would pick up Branch's fallen standard. Acting as national spokesman was one thing, but. . . . Was that why they were caring for him so attentively?

"I'm flattered."

She ignored his biting tone. "Chase, you're a lot like my father, and you'll do a fine job. To do a superlative job, you need Jimmy. You—and Dad—personify the confrontational aspect of the mission. You're a crusader. Because of his background, Jimmy personifies the compassion and understanding side. He's living proof of the Christian alternative. He knows what it really means to 'come out' —to come out of bondage and come to the Lord. Unless you balance the crusading side with the compassionate side, I don't think you can be fully successful in dealing with the gay issue."

"I'll think about it—seriously," he promised.

"Good." She smiled beatifically, gathered up her medical instruments and the soiled bandage, and stood to leave. She leaned over suddenly and kissed him lightly on top of the head. "You'll be OK," she said.

As she turned away he caught her hand. "Before you go, I have a question."

Her brow furrowed ever so slightly, and she stood waiting.

Chase looked her straight in the eyes and asked, "Have *you* ever done anything you were ashamed of?"

This time she smiled that sad, wistful smile he was beginning to know so well. "Most of my sins are sins of omission." Her fingers slipped gently out of his as she turned to leave the room. "But they're the worst kind."

★ ★ ★

Occasionally other callers and friends stopped in to distract Chase from the troubling digressions in his thought life. He was grateful for the interruptions, as well as for their solicitude.

T. C. Moreland dropped by to greet him, reminisce about Branch Trumbull, and pray for a quick recovery. Chase liked the man, and not merely because he had been a good friend to Branch. He thanked Moreland for his prayers and asked him what he should do.

"Chase," T. C. said, "it's not for me to say what you should do. That's up to the Master who's preparing you. But you can take comfort in knowing that He does have something in mind for you —something wonderful is my guess. You just have to be receptive to His guidance. I would encourage you to carry on the work you began with Branch, though."

"But God seems to have taken me out of that arena," Chase objected. "I've lost my platform—I've been discredited."

"Not at all." Moreland snorted. "I believe that what you've been through will only make you more effective. Now you have the spiritual weapons with which to wage a spiritual battle. And you're not alone. I was involved in this work with Branch too, you know."

"I know."

"You just let me know how I can help."

A few days later, during a visit from Jimmy, Barbara Dunhill called on the Trumbulls.

Chase greeted her with delight. He had been certain the gay underground had permanently discredited him in her eyes, and he said so.

Barbara shook her head with her usual air of seriousness. "How could you think that? You're not the first one to have a run-in with the gay movement. Anyway, don't stew about it. A lot of people are out there working to expose what they did to you. There's an investigation going on in the FCC. And Jimmy and that young reporter Jay Blaisdell are looking into a possible connection with Garden Monnoye's organization. Just be patient. You'll be rehabilitated in more ways than one." She smiled reassuringly and tapped his cast with her forefinger.

"Jimmy says I didn't give my friends enough credit. But when I saw the papers—and after what had already happened to me—it's just that the story was so believable."

"Well, *I* didn't believe it. Especially when I saw how they were trying to destroy your livelihood. It was all an obvious set-up." Barbara cleared her throat and said in a very businesslike voice, "You'll be glad to know that the 'Gay Deceiver' is now history."

"Who? Who's the 'Gay Deceiver'?"

"William P. 'Kerry' Kerrigan, former White House counsel."

"That *is* good news. The nickname your idea?"

"Oh, no." She laughed. "I found out that's what other gays call him. His code name, as it were. He's a Southerner, you know, and there's a line in 'Dixie' that says 'William was a gay deceiver.'"

"I see. Where'd he go?"

"Haven't heard yet. He's 'considering several options.'"

"Don't be surprised if he ends up on Garden Monnoye's payroll," said Jimmy.

"That's certainly possible," Barbara noted. "But anyway, he no longer has a base of operations in the White House. Which brings me to my next bit of news. Here's a copy of a letter to Langdon Smith from the commissioner of the IRS. It seems the IRS admits to a 'serious error' in levying the tax lien against you. In fact, the people responsible have either been dismissed or transferred."

"Well, a victory for once," Chase said with enthusiasm. "And I don't just mean getting my money back. I take it you were able to get the White House to break up this nest in the IRS."

"I think so. Temporarily at least. I'm sure we didn't get rid of them all, but they'll think twice before trying to use the tax system to punish their opposition."

"They did overreach, didn't they? But what about the FCC investigation you mentioned?" asked Jimmy.

"I'm afraid I couldn't get any satisfaction there." Barbara sighed. "I do think the White House inquiry put a scare into them. But Smith says that since DBN's license is no longer in jeopardy, it's a moot point. I could only push him so far."

After a while Barbara wished him a speedy recovery and got up to leave. Chase shook her hand warmly and thanked her, asking her to stop by again.

When Jimmy returned from showing her out, Chase remarked, "She really has been a good friend, far better than I deserve."

"You don't know the half of it."

"What do you mean?"

"Well, she made me swear not to tell you—at least not while she was here. But she lost her job over this."

"You mean, because she helped *me!*"

"Yep. She won't talk about it, though. In fact, she treats the whole thing like it was of little consequence. But what I hear through the conservative grapevine is that she went head-to-head with Langdon Smith and made him sack Kerrigan. And of course she made him get the IRS to remove the tax lien. But Smith was so mad he used the situation to force her out too. And when some of her friends on the Hill tried to intervene, she made 'em back off."

Chase said nothing, but her sacrifice on his behalf generated a deep feeling of obligation. Clearly God was directing him to a certain purpose, and the friendship of people such as Barbara and T. C. and the Tollivers and the Trumbulls demanded a corresponding sacrifice on his part. He knew he was being "called to active duty," as Clare Trumbull had once put it. But the battlefield and choice of weapons were still unclear.

31

Piece by piece the course of action Chase was seeking began to fall into place.

One evening he, the Tollivers, and Clare were in the Trumbulls' den. A cheerful fire sputtered and crackled on the hearth, and Beethoven's "Pastoral Symphony" played soothingly in the background on the CD player. They talked for a while, desultorily, sometimes animatedly, about a variety of things.

Then Clare said, "Branch and I used to sit here for hours and talk. He'd say it always frustrated him no end how the spirit of the times combined to make people *forget*. One night he jumped up from his chair while reading and said, 'Now I understand!'

"'Understand what? I asked him.'

"'George Orwell's *1984*, he said. 'The Memory Hole. I've read this book three or four times, and I never really understood the significance of the Memory Hole until now.'

"Branch felt that something about these times makes people forget everything they've learned and experienced. All the accumulated wisdom and lessons of the past just evaporate—just fall out of their brains.

"That's why he admired you so much, Chase," Clare continued. "Your upbringing, I guess, made you like a teacher on the air waves. You were a historian who wouldn't allow people to forget certain things."

Chase mused. Perhaps *that* was his calling. To teach. To remind people. Things were changing and disintegrating so rapidly, and people were accepting things today they wouldn't have dreamed of five or six years ago. Maybe it was his mission to remind Americans of their heritage. He had to use the skills God had given him . . . remembering . . . teaching . . . persuading . . . exhorting.

During the period of Chase's recuperation and study, Jimmy Tolliver was busy. He devoted the bulk of his time to fund-raising for the Foundation, organizing, and laying the groundwork for the confrontation of some sort that he sensed was coming, though he could not yet discern its pattern.

Jimmy was devoted to his wife, Janet, expecting their first child, and was careful not to neglect his family duties, but whenever he could, he spent time with Chase.

He explained the intricacies of the homosexual network, its penetration of the government and the news media, its ties to militant feminists, radical environmentalists, and New Agers. He wanted Chase to see that the movement was not a formal, centrally orchestrated conspiracy, but something more subtle, a mind-set, a shared tendency and set of behaviors—like schools of fish, as Branch Trumbull had once explained.

Chase was particularly concerned about the rising level of homosexual violence—violent rhetoric and violent behavior.

"Their violence should *diminish,* not increase," he complained one day. "These groups like Queer and Present Danger, and especially Come Out Fighting—don't they know violence only hurts their cause?"

"Not so," Jimmy replied. "The more successful they are, the more they'll use violent tactics."

"Explain *that* to me."

"You have to understand that the gay activists are following classic revolutionary theory—they're engaged in a revolution in which the use of provocation is critical. So violence actually helps the cause. It's a form of conditioning—of mass psychology. By behaving intolerably, they make the less extreme forms of behavior seem acceptable by comparison. So the limits keep getting pushed forward as we get used to radical acts."

"So now we accept things that earlier would have gotten us up in arms." Chase thought out loud. "Pedophilia, repealing age of consent laws, homosexual marriages and adoptions, and the rest."

"Right, but there's more to it. Remember that the gay movement is really a revolution, and you know what revolutions are ultimately all about."

"Power."

"Absolutely. And a shift in power of this magnitude is almost always accompanied by physical force from the revolutionaries. I'm afraid one of these days soon homosexual violence will be accepted as their natural 'right,' just like we've been conditioned to excuse riots and violence in the inner cities."

"As long as it's directed at us—the opposition," Chase added.

"Like in Colorado. During the fight over repealing Amendment Two and, later on, ratifying the HRA, the homes and churches of Christians were the targets of firebombings. Even cars with the fish symbol on them got shot at."

"Then whatever we're going to do with the Foundation, we'd better prepare for some real head-knocking violence. Is that what you're saying?"

"Maybe worse than head-knocking," Jimmy replied soberly. "Remember Branch."

Jimmy thought about that. He had heard rumors about the sudden rapid growth of Come Out Fighting, which seemed to be soaking up members from the more quiescent groups. But COF embodied a coldly disciplined violence, a controlled ferocity and centralized direction that were unique.

It reminded him uncannily of the Nazi Brownshirts, whose early leadership had in fact been militant homosexual revolutionaries. His contacts in the movement were not producing enough information on the aims and methods of COF, and Jimmy cast about in his mind for a way to find out more.

As if to confirm his apprehension, the following weeks saw renewed hostility in the media attacks on the Nehemiah Foundation.

★ ★ ★

NEWS REPORT, *SIS "Evening News"*

"The Washington-based Paragon Foundation, a leading public policy think tank with New Age overtones, will sponsor the Global

Harmonic Convergence planned in the capital city in early January to correspond with the opening session of Congress. Tens of thousands of New Age devotees are expected to assemble in Washington on January 7, the day the second session of the 105th Congress opens. Those gathering in Washington, in concert with New Age groups all over the world, will 'imagine' or 'visualize' global peace, harmony, and the unity of mankind.

"According to Tristram Kramer, spokesman for the Paragon Foundation, a special focus will be attaining unity through social justice in the United States. New Agers will be making a mass appeal to the Congress to extend the five-year time limit for ratification of the Human Rights Amendment, which expires next January."

★ ★ ★

Chase reached for the remote. "This Harmonic Convergence nonsense. How can anybody take it seriously?"

"Because," said Libby, sitting next to him in the den, "when men no longer believe in God, they don't then believe in nothing —they believe in *anything*."

He turned and looked at her intently. "My father used to say that all the time. I just now realized how much I miss him."

The same SIS evening news had featured an interview with Lane Bischoff, leader of the campaign to ratify the Human Rights Amendment in Colorado. The gay victory in Colorado was all the more significant in light of the state's history on the issue.

In 1992 Colorado had passed Amendment 2, which invalidated all state and local ordinances treating gays as a protected class, like blacks or Hispanics, or giving them preferential rights. Its repeal had long been a top priority for gay legislative action. Though a Colorado state judge delayed its implementation for several months after passage, it finally went into effect in 1993, and the full wrath of the movement and its allies in Hollywood and among the nation's ruling elite had been poured out on the state for exercising its political prerogative.

At first, the Hollywood and media-sponsored boycott proved ineffective. The homophilia of the Hollywood set was not as strong as their love of skiing at Aspen and Vail. But eventually the relentless barrage of vilification and propaganda wore down the traditionalists, and Coloradans repealed Amendment 2 in 1995 with the same narrow margin that passed it in 1992.

The homosexual agenda was steamrolling right along, Chase reflected. State after state had approved the HRA. Gay rights ordinances were being passed in hundreds of cities. Violence against gays was at an all time low, yet they seemed more militant than ever.

He switched to C-Span then and watched Bischoff, president of the Colorado Coalition for Human Rights, crow over his victory. "Now we must focus our efforts on getting a congressional extension of the HRA so that what we've gained can't be stolen from us by the artificial excuse of a time limit. There is no time limit on justice."

The last sentence resonated in Chase's brain. He turned it over and over, as though there was a hidden message in it.

The next evening SIS "News" profiled Peter Gaveston, new operations director of Come Out Fighting, and Chase, Jimmy, and the Trumbull women watched intently.

There's something different about this man, Chase found himself thinking. Gaveston was not in the least effeminate, but muscular and tough looking.

The interviewer, clearly sympathetic, asked the homosexual leader if he did not worry about frightening people.

Gaveston was rough and blunt. "America, you *should* be frightened! You've backed us into a corner, and now we're no longer afraid to come out fighting. We're going to make the government respond to our demands. We're mad, and our patience is exhausted. We're going to start fighting back, with violence if necessary, unless we get what we want. Depriving us of our constitutional rights justifies violence. Isn't that the American way?"

"And what is it you want?" the reporter asked him.

"Our civil rights! That means Congress *will* extend the HRA time limit and allow people in the remaining states to express their support for our rights—or else. We won't stop until we have achieved our freedom, our justice, our pursuit of happiness. We are among the most peace-loving of communities, but the straight world has forced us to defend ourselves with any means necessary. We are dying and have nothing to lose anymore.

"So a warning to the bigots out there—we are coming out in

ever increasing numbers! We are going to live our lives the way we want, and if you try to stop us, then . . ."

"Only the gay militants could talk that way." Chase said as the interview ended. "Whining and blustering at the same time." A tiny minority, yet demanding the right to dictate the nation's public policy. "Peace-loving," yet threatening violence.

"They're worried about something," he said to Jimmy.

"But what is it they're so scared of?" Libby asked. "They seem to be winning."

The men looked at each other with a simultaneous flash of illumination. It had been so obvious, yet remarkably Chase had not seen it until now.

"The time limit!" both shouted.

Chase had been struggling so intently with what, when, where, and how that he had almost missed the obvious: the realization that the HRA would fail without a time extension—a decision that Christians could influence.

He now knew what to do.

★　★　★

By now Chase's injuries were healing rapidly. He was able to hobble around the house and was full of unexpended energy and high spirits. Knowing he was on the mend added to his enthusiasm, and he threw himself into the planning with gusto.

The Nehemiah Foundation's quick survey of the states that had not approved the HRA showed it was unlikely that any of them would approve it in the short time remaining.

At Chase's request, Clare invited Jimmy and T. C. Moreland for dinner. Afterward, they sat around the table, first praying and then discussing how to go about derailing the time extension. In the course of their talk, Jimmy remarked on the connection between the lobbying effort for the HRA extension and the New Agers' Global Harmonic Convergence.

"And when is this so-called harmonic conveyance going to take place?" T. C. asked.

"Convergence. It'll be on January 7, the day the new session of Congress opens."

"And how many New Agers will be in Washington?"

"It's hard to say. You have to add in the gays, who usually can only turn out a few hundred thousand at the most for an event like this," Jimmy estimated

"So few?" said T. C.

"Remember the big flop in 1993," Jimmy pointed out. "They wanted a million; they got 300,000. Gay influence is grossly disproportionate to their numbers. We're talking about only one or two percent of the total population."

"They might really turn out for this though," Clare noted.

"And the news media will be sure to inflate the number present by at least a factor of two," Chase observed.

"All told, I'd say gay groups and New Agers combined can produce a quarter million or so," Jimmy speculated.

T. C. Moreland got up from the table and began to pace vigorously around the spacious dining room, a frown of intense concentration on his face. Then he stopped, his arms windmilling in the gesture he always displayed when excited. He shook a finger at his seated colleagues and said in a loud voice, "Elijah the Tishbite!"

"I beg your pardon." Chase was totally mystified.

T. C. grinned and repeated, "Elijah the Tishbite!"

The others looked at him as if he had lost his mind.

T. C. pulled out his pocket Bible. "Listen to this from First Kings. Elijah the Tishbite was God's prophet. Elijah called the Israelites together and in their presence challenged four hundred and fifty pagan priests to a contest on Mount Carmel to see who was really God."

He read the passage telling of Elijah's confrontation with the priests and his dramatic victory. "Let's do the same. Let us call the church together to confront these new pagans by prayer and confound the vote of the HRA."

"You know," Clare said enthusiastically, "T. C.'s right. We have to confront them just like Elijah, openly, as God's people —but by prayer, not by violence."

"Exactly." Moreland returned to his chair. "Such gatherings happened several times in the Old Testament when the nation was in danger."

"Then it's settled," Chase said. "The Foundation will sponsor our own convergence on January 7. We'll call God's people to oppose the Harmonic Convergence by prayer—in Washington and at home. We'll pray for the nation, and we'll ask for God's intervention in stopping the HRA time extension."

"Can we turn out enough people?" Libby wondered out loud. "I don't mean enough to pray. I mean enough to make a statement to Congress at the same time that we disapprove of any time extension."

"How many is enough?" T. C. asked.

Chase and Jimmy exchanged thoughtful looks. To have lasting impact would take a turnout so massive that only the Spirit of God moving supernaturally could bring it about.

Chase took a deep breath. "A million."

32

Chase began to experience doubts as soon as the initial glow of enthusiasm faded. The difficulties in mobilizing the church and in interesting a sufficient number of people to come to Washington in the dead of winter to pray were staggering. Were there enough left who would ignore the ridicule, the vilification, and the threats of violence?

The violence. Now in earnest they began to discuss the possibility of physical violence. Genuine risks would be involved. People should be warned of that. Branch Trumbull's death showed what the enemy was capable of. Memories of his murder, and the violent attack by Come Out Fighting on T. C.'s rally in Pennsylvania, were still painfully fresh.

T. C. asked of no one in particular, "Can it really be that we've come to this in the United States of America? It's going to take some inspired leadership to interest them and overcome their fear."

Jimmy and T. C. looked at Chase.

"But why *me?*" he asked. "Why not you, T. C.? You're a trained, ordained minister and a wonderful preacher. I'm just a journalist, a has-been media hack."

T. C. chuckled infectiously. "Not true. I'm small change compared to you. My base is localized. You—you're still a big time TV personality, a celebrity as far as our people are concerned. You had one of the top-rated shows on TV, and the most popular among conservatives. Tens of millions of people feel they know you as a personal friend. And I've never heard a more sincere, more convincing speaker. Myself included." He grinned.

"I've been discredited."

"Not at all," Jimmy objected. "Nobody who counts believes that lie, Chase."

"And besides," Libby argued softly and more passionately than the others, "nobody can lead the church today who hasn't suffered. Chase, it's because you've suffered at their hands that your appeal will have a power no one else can match."

Chase somehow knew this was his spiritual destiny. It was what God had spared him for that fateful night on the mountain. Still, he was plagued by lingering self-doubts. The pathway up this mountain was impossible without more faith than he had at the moment.

He looked at his friends helplessly and saw in their smiles and steady gazes the endorsement he needed.

Finally T. C. spoke up. "I know what you're going through. It's a mighty undertaking, but all the heroes of faith in the Bible experienced doubts. Even Elijah. Why, he was an ordinary man according to James 5:17, 'a man just like us.' Yet he appropriated God's power through prayer and stopped the rain for three years."

T. C. drew out the ubiquitous pocket Bible. As if he had written the passage himself, he intoned, "'And what more shall I say? For time would fail me to tell of Gideon, of Barak, of Samson, of David, and of Samuel and the prophets, who through faith subdued kingdoms, wrought righteousness, obtained promises, stopped the mouths of lions, quenched the violence of fire, escaped the edge of the sword, out of weakness were made strong, became valiant in battle, and turned the armies of the enemy to flight.'"

Chase was moved beyond words. He put his head in his hands and blinked back tears.

T. C. patted him gently on the shoulder and quickly left the room. Jimmy Tolliver followed him out, and then Clare.

But Libby came and sat on the floor next to him and laid her head wordlessly on his knee.

So many pressures, doubts, and uncertainties preyed on his mind, the foremost of which was Libby herself. He felt guilt again because he could not resist putting her before God's calling and the fate of the country.

"Libby, I can't explain how I feel about you, about everything. So much has happened to me . . ."

"I know. You don't have to explain."

"Yes, I do. I wasn't a very good person before I met the

294

Lord. No, I wasn't a homosexual or anything like the newspapers said. But still, I was—" He could not finish.

"Chase, please. You don't owe me any explanations. Can't you tell how I feel about you? Explanations aren't necessary. You have a new life."

"That's just it," he said brusquely. In the whirling upheaval of emotion—repressed love, guilty memory, confusion, and self-doubt—he spoke to her more harshly than he intended. "This just isn't right! We've got to put a stop to this right now. I'm not right for you, and if I get involved with you, how can I do what every-body expects of me? What God expects of me?"

He pushed her away and then abruptly turned away from the hurt in her eyes.

Slowly she got to her feet. "I understand," she said, not with anger but sadly. She leaned over and kissed him gently on the top of his head.

Her fragrant nearness was painful. He almost reached out and took her in his arms.

"I have to go back to the college in a few days anyway," she said softly. "I don't want to add to your burden. I just want to help you bear it. But that's for you to decide. I want you to know, if you decide to . . . well, I'll be there for you."

★ ★ ★

True to her word, Libby went back to her job at Crown College in Tennessee. She was gone less than an hour when Chase began to miss her terribly. But he vowed to stick to his resolve. First, he was not worthy of her. Second, she would only distract him from the awesome mission he was embarking on.

Libby's declaration left him confused and uncertain—uncertain about love, uncertain about all women, uncertain about any hopes for a personal life.

It was tempting to imagine that God had sent her to him. But then he reproached himself. He could not bear the thought of an-other mistake that might scar his heart forever against all loving.

He began to regret he had not at least told her he loved her—and rationalized that it was better to avoid cheapening the word by saying, "I love you." He had said it so often to Neeley without even knowing what it meant.

In the end Chase went to Clare. He respected her wisdom and would have consulted her sooner had she not been Libby's mother.

She was in the kitchen that evening, preparing dinner.

"Clare . . . " In great discomfort he told her the whole story. Of Neeley and the abortion, which still tore at his heart as he told it. Of his confused longing for Libby and of her intimation that she cared for him. Of his feelings of unworthiness, and fear that love would intrude upon the difficult tasks ahead.

Finally he stopped, half expecting she would discourage the relationship. Or call attention to the practical obstacles. After all, he was considerably older than Libby. Despite the Foundation, his career prospects were dim, and he had only his savings, which would not support a family for long. As he mentally cataloged the obstacles, he noticed Clare smiling.

"First let me say this," she began. "If you and Libby come to an understanding, and if you're both convinced this is God's will for your lives, then you have my blessing. I'd be pleased and proud to have you as a son-in-law. And I know Branch would heartily agree.

"Now, as to the rightness or wrongness of the relationship— well, naturally I can't speak for the Lord. But, Chase," she expostulated, "most of what you've said is nonsense! Hasn't it occurred to you that God may have brought you and Libby together? He knows the loneliness in both your hearts, and in His love He wants to fill it. He knows you need a companion, a helper, just as I was Branch's coworker. I didn't just stay home and bake cookies, you know."

Chase laughed in spite of himself. "No, I don't guess you did."

"I'm not saying Libby and you are meant for each other, but you owe it to yourselves to find out if you are. I know she has deep feelings for you."

"Did she tell you that?"

"Not in so many words. But a mother can tell." She paused and fixed him with a stern but loving look.

"I'm afraid I've been a considerable fool," he said in chagrin.

She gave him a reassuring smile. "I've heard it said that love is the folly of wise men, and the wisdom of fools. So why not let yourself love Libby if that's what God intends?"

"But how can I love her the way she deserves and do what's expected of me? This is no easy task I'm taking on."

"I know. But rather than being a hindrance to you, Libby may be just what you need. She'll complete you as a man—if this is God's will."

"I s'pose I wasn't thinking it through clearly." He paused, and then asked, "What should I do?"

"As soon as you're able to travel, go see her!"

After dinner, Chase went outside for the first time since coming home to the Trumbulls'. Only five of the six weeks Doc Lacy ordered had elapsed, but Chase tramped around on his leg with its bulky cast, testing the sprained ankle, and found it was only slightly sore.

Back inside, he ran a full tub and sat and soaked the cast for half an hour. Then with the sharp edge of his hunting knife, he carefully sawed the cast off. He experimented standing, and the ankle held his weight. With an elastic bandage to provide some additional support, he could manage.

He dressed and went to the solarium where Clare sat reading. "I'm ready to travel." He grinned as she looked up at him in surprise. "Tomorrow I'm going to Tennessee."

★ ★ ★

A smiling Clare packed a copious picnic basket and a cooler of soft drinks. Jimmy Tolliver stowed Chase's gear in his friend's Jeep, which he had fetched back from the Mountain. Jimmy, who had come over to confer on Foundation plans and to say good-bye, teased Chase roundly for all the gear and extensive wardrobe he was taking with him.

"Looks like you're migratin' permanently," Jimmy teased. He was obviously happy for his friend.

Chase laughed good-naturedly. "Yeah, I guess it does look like I plan to stay awhile. And I don't know why exactly. I just feel like something's going to happen on this trip, and I need to be prepared."

"Well, please don't run off and get married!" Clare said in mock alarm.

Chase smiled sheepishly. "Oh, no, I didn't mean that," he stammered. "I just had a feeling I might get a chance to do some speaking, maybe start putting out a call for the convocation of prayer if I get a chance. We *are* ready to start, aren't we?"

"Yep," said Jimmy. "Everything's falling into place. I have to tell you, this idea has really caught on in the minds of believers. And even plain old garden variety adherents. They're getting fired up about it, and several ministries and church groups have already signed on. Of course, T. C. has been marvelous. Right away people want to know what they can do to help. The only problem now is logistics. How we'll take care of a million people I simply have no idea."

"Ask T. C."

Jimmy laughed, shook hands warmly, wished him godspeed, and went inside.

Clare stood by the shiny black vehicle and smiled the wise, serene smile that always gave him a lump in his throat. Libby had the same smile, with some of Branch's confident strength as well.

"Well, time to go, I guess," he said awkwardly. *How do I thank her? And at the same time, how do I tell her I'm riding off to claim her only daughter?*

"Yes, it's time," she said gently.

"You know why I love Libby so much?" he asked her suddenly.

"Why, no," she said, her bright eyes going wide.

"Because she's so much like you."

Clare's eyes misted at once, and her mouth trembled slightly.

Chase stepped forward, gave her a massive hug, and kissed her on the cheek. "Thank you. Thank you for everything."

Soon he was on I-66 headed west toward I-81 and the Shenandoah Valley. *His* valley! He had never felt so wonderful, so free, and so full of hope. Even images of his beloved valley took on new luster when he thought about sharing it with Libby.

He felt delightfully giddy and began to sing a silly song from his childhood. "Froggie did acourtin' ride, uh-huh, uh-huh . . . sword and pistol by his side, uh-huh," he warbled.

Then the momentary bubble of giddiness burst, and he berated himself for behaving like this. *Don't get your hopes up. You're still a frog until she kisses you. And maybe she won't.*

Doubts began to creep back, spoiling the moment. Perhaps she wasn't ready for this. And how could you really know God's will in something as elusive and personal as love? *All I can do is offer myself,* he decided. *And let her know I'll love her with all the power I can muster.*

He came to the junction of I-66 and I-81 near Front Royal, turned south, and in fifteen minutes arrived in Woodstock, where he stopped and had a warm and satisfying visit with his mother.

He had seen her briefly the day Jimmy brought him down from the cabin, and he had written his brothers and sisters shortly after his encounter on the Mountain. But she rejoiced to see him again and have a long heart-to-heart talk. She blessed him, prayed for a safe journey and the success of his mission, and sent him on his way with the feeling that all family breaches had been healed.

From Woodstock it was a long 250 miles straight up the Valley to Bristol, through a landscape of placid but heart-stopping beauty.

Oh, God, how I love this land, he said silently. *Thank You, Lord, thank You for letting me be born and raised here. Help me to be worthy of it.*

Libby was director of public relations at Crown College. It was a private liberal arts school, small, five hundred students, but with a rich heritage, an excellent academic program, and a fine reputation. Founded in 1860, the college had helped lead the resurgence of Southern Presbyterians in the 1980s and had become a kind of Wheaton College of the South.

Chase thought he should perhaps have called first. But he really wanted to surprise her. He was sure that he could tell a lot about her true feelings from the unguarded expression on her face when she first saw him.

He drove through the sleepy town and onto the campus, with its handsome red-brick Georgian buildings standing in stately dignity amid the riotous colors of autumn. He asked directions from a friendly student, found Libby's building, parked, and walked apprehensively inside.

Heart thudding, he paused outside her office. "Elizabeth Christian Trumbull, Director of Public Affairs" announced the nameplate by the door. Forcing himself to breathe slow and deep, he pushed open the door.

As it happened, Libby was in the outer office, conferring with her secretary. When she saw him, her mouth dropped open, and her eyebrows shot upward.

But he was smiling happily—she should instantly know he had not come bearing bad news.

She glided to him with lithe grace. Her eyes were lit with the light of welcome and what he flattered himself was also love. He no longer had any doubts.

"I knew you'd come to your senses," she said, laying her head with great contentment on his chest.

He tilted her chin up and kissed her, gently but not passionately. That could come later. In private.

"It usually takes a woman to bring a man to his senses. I was a hard case. With me it took two."

33

By the end of 1999, opposition to the Christian worldview and practice had intensified more vigorously in education than anywhere else. The secular humanist elites were concentrating their energies on undermining the Christian education of rising generations.

As the decade closed, the nation's official higher education accrediting agencies were refusing to accredit Christian institutions unless they submitted to the full deconstructionist agenda, including the hiring and ordaining of homosexuals and the inclusion of "multicultural curricula." Institutions that refused to bow the knee could continue to operate, but the degrees they granted were no longer recognized by the mainstream.

Stripping the Christian schools hurt the career prospects of many students, foreclosing postgraduate or professional education to numbers of graduates who could not then compete in the upper echelons of the economy.

Yet most of the private colleges had remained true to their historic calling and the teaching of Scripture.

Chase knew none of this until he visited Libby at Crown College and got an eye-opening look at a robust segment of the Christian subculture. He was particularly impressed with the students. They were studious, cheerful, confident, and serious. Many were outstanding scholars who, under different circumstances, would have been accepted at any university in the nation. When Libby arranged for him to address the student body about his experiences in the gay rights struggle and urge them to participate in the prayer convocation, he agreed eagerly.

Chase's speech seemed to be a rousing success. He received a warm, enthusiastic ovation, and he stayed long after the prescribed hour answering questions. Many students volunteered to assist in organizing the "March on Washington," as some insisted on calling it. Many wanted to know the story behind the story of his "outing" in the *Washington News*. He was still sensitive about the subject but addressed it frankly and was gratified to see that almost everyone accepted his version of the episode.

That night at dinner, Libby praised his effort, which he had thought a little shaky and subject to improvement.

Suddenly she stopped in mid-sentence and asked him, "Chase, why don't you tour the Christian campuses? You saw the response you got today. It was extraordinary."

He immediately saw the potential inherent in a student-oriented movement. Students' idealism and enthusiasm made them natural candidates for activism, good or bad. Modern American history was full of examples of student-led or inspired movements, most of them unfortunately harmful.

Win their hearts and minds, he had always said, and the politics would follow. That was one reason he had gone into journalism. And now he lamented that Christianity had been relegated to a cultural backwater, with little representation in the broader world of journalism, television, films, the fine arts, or higher education. He could not get over his surprise at the lack of urgency in this regard.

He was aware of the partial contradiction in his own thinking. With all his emphasis on reclaiming the culture by prayer, he was still asking them to take part in an explicitly political action—preventing Congress from extending the time limit on the HRA. But this was a stop-gap measure, a matter of dire and urgent necessity.

After reflection, Chase enthusiastically agreed to a campus tour.

Libby got on the telephone the next morning and began to line up engagements. She booked him first at schools in Virginia, Tennessee, Kentucky, Indiana, and Illinois.

Chase took great pride and pleasure in watching her work. Libby knew everybody who was anybody in Christian publishing, broadcasting, key churches, nonchurch ministries, and colleges. In addition to the campus visits, she scheduled media interviews and speaking engagements. It was her job to know luminaries, but

Chase still marveled at the breadth of her contacts and her skill in booking appearances on such short notice.

He had his car. He had plenty of clothes. His EDC was working now, and he had taken the precaution of hoarding some cash. After calling Jimmy and Clare and advising them of his plans, he started off. He wished only that Libby had been able to go with him.

At every school Chase flung down the challenge, "Who will join me under God's standard in Washington on January 7?" And at each stop he became more confident.

After thousands of miles, dozens of appearances, two flat tires, and a duffle bag full of soiled laundry, he returned to Bristol, tired but excited, to see Libby and report on his tour.

Embracing in her office again, they both confessed they had missed each other terribly—one more day of separation would have been unendurable. And Chase remained for several days to rest and refit and get to know this remarkable woman better.

But time was marching inexorably toward the end of the old year. He had stirred up a tremendous response to the call for a prayer convocation, and thousands of believers—hundreds of thousands he hoped—were planning to be present in Washington. He and the Nehemiah Foundation were committed, for better or worse.

He knew his post was back in the capital, as much as he would have preferred to stay forever with Libby. She promised to join him soon, and he kissed her good-bye—this time a kiss full of passion as well as tenderness.

Chase climbed into the Jeep and headed toward Washington.

★ ★ ★

The news about Come Out Fighting had been nagging at Jimmy Tolliver ever since catching Peter Gaveston's harangue on SIS "News." He, Chase, T. C. Moreland, and the Trumbull ladies all agreed that the Foundation could be the catalyst to block a congressional extension of the HRA time limit. But the opposition appeared to be organizing a cohort of storm troopers, as if they had anticipated such a move.

Jimmy doubted the ability of a relative handful of Come Out Fighting activists to intimidate thousands or to break up the prayer convocation. But he had to find out more about their plans and capabilities, and his usual sources either knew nothing or had dried up. The only way to get the intelligence he needed was to uncover it himself. He would have to go back into the homosexual demimonde, meet and talk with active gays on the make, and find out firsthand what was going on.

It was distasteful to him to contemplate going back into the gay scene. He believed he was spiritually immunized against any of the old temptation, but it was still asking a lot of himself to go back. But he prayed and then made up his mind to go through with it.

He could not bring himself to tell Janet. She was sure he had renounced his former life. Their marriage was secure, a strong, loving relationship. But he had to wonder whether she ever questioned his irrevocable transformation into a normal heterosexual. And with her anxiety over the impending birth of their first baby, if he announced he was going to cruise the gay bars, however plausible and compelling his reasons, he knew that would only trouble her needlessly. He did not want to tell Chase for the same reasons.

But he had to tell someone, in the unlikely event that something happened. He told Clare.

Straight people seldom if ever went to the gay bars. They hardly knew where to go if they had wanted to. But he remembered. He started at the gay and lesbian bookstore on Dupont Circle. It was a focal point of the Community, and there one could usually find a wide variety of gay literature, newspapers, posters, and handbills.

The walls were lined with Mapplethorpe photos and other graphic depictions of gay sex acts. Plenty of posters advertised the Global Harmonic Convergence, encouraging gays to participate in freeing the world of antigay bigotry through mass, collective visualization. The message was clear, Jimmy saw—the homosexual network and the New Age movement were closely allied, and gays would probably be out in force on January 7. But oddly he saw no recruiting posters or anything specifically about Come Out Fighting.

He visited a few of the favorite gay bars in the area, sipped idly on a Coke, and listened. But little happened, and he soon began to wonder if he was wasting his time. Finally, in The Birdcage,

304

the most raucous gay hangout of them all, Jimmy made contact.

A "Big Bertha," a tall and heavyset young man, well-dressed in a black turtleneck sweater and gray tweed jacket, approached him at the bar and struck up a conversation.

Jimmy felt his skin crawl and fought hard to contain his unease. He worried that the man would pick up the negative emanations. Experience told him that gays could generally spot one another. There was something present, something subtle and unspoken but still communicable, in the homosexual's inner state.

The man showed no suspicion, though. He seemed eager to score and trotted out the usual array of pickup lines.

Jimmy responded in a friendly but not encouraging manner. His mission was simply to get information on the latest happenings in the gay world, not get picked up for an assignation.

"Lot of freaky types in here tonight, huh?" the man volunteered, seeming to sense Jimmy's reticence.

"Yeah," said Jimmy. "Too many freaks in the scene these days."

"Wall queens," the man said contemptuously. "But you're no freak," he added with an admiring look.

"You're not either," said Jimmy, revulsion threatening to cool the forced warmth in his voice.

"You—uh—attached?"

"No."

"Hungry?"

"No."

Finally the man dropped all his subtle maneuvering. "Say, ducky, you need some company. Come on, let's go back in the Glory Hole." The Glory Hole was a dark room in the back with cubicles where Birdcage patrons could pair off after meeting in the outer area.

"No, thanks," said Jimmy.

"Say, if you're worried about HIV, I've got my test results right here," the man volunteered eagerly. "I'm negative." He pulled out a paper and unfolded it. The National Institutes of Medicine seal was prominent at the top.

Jimmy read the testimonial that the man had tested negative

a few weeks ago. He knew it meant nothing—he could have easily contracted HIV since then.

"No, it's not that," Jimmy said. "Please don't be offended." He put on a mournful face. "You see, I just lost a friend."

"Hey, I'm sorry. Were you monogamous?"

"Yeah. We had a really wonderful love affair."

"What was it? AIDS?" the big man asked.

Jimmy thought fast. He knew better than to say AIDS—that might close the very doors he was trying to open.

"Uh—no. He was killed in a car crash. He'd been drinking pretty heavy for a while."

Next to sexually transmitted diseases, drunk driving accidents were a leading cause of death among gay men, so his story was plausible.

"Too bad," the man commiserated. "Well, listen. You look like you're a little bit at loose ends. Why don't you come to a meeting tomorrow night and do something meaningful to get over your loss? And help the Community at the same time."

"Oh? What kinda meeting?"

He handed Jimmy a business card, and Jimmy saw the pink triangle with a superimposed lambda symbol in the shape of a forearm and hand gripping an assault rifle.

"You heard of Come Out Fighting?"

"Sure," Jimmy said. "Haven't we all?"

"Good, then you ought to come."

"OK, thanks. I will." Jimmy pocketed the card.

The man gave him a nod and went off into the crowded, pulsating bar to find a more willing companion.

★ ★ ★

I believe they really love me, Garden Monnoye said to himself. He stretched his unaccountably sore limbs among the silk sheets covering the huge bed.

Just as he had awakened from a fitful sleep, an intern, checking his breakfast order, told him coyly that the staff was planning a surprise party to celebrate the end of Chase McKenzie and "Pulse of the Nation." The creep had not been seen or heard from for weeks. No one seemed to know where he had disappeared to.

It was a notable victory, next to offing Branch Trumbull the most successful operation he had ever run. Though no one would say openly, everyone in the industry knew why McKenzie had been forced off the air. Now the few scattered broadcasters who used to attack gays were pulling in their horns. Well worth a celebration. A "Garden Party." But here in his bedroom suite at the Paragon Building, not at the farm.

Surprise, indeed. Nothing went on in his empire that Monnoye did not know about. Enough of his vassals were vying for his attention so that one of them was bound to curry favor by spilling any news. The main thing was that the celebration was spontaneous, not requested or scheduled by him. That had to be a sign of love.

And it was good to have it here. Monnoye had been spending more time lately in Washington, planning the Harmonic Convergence, lobbying Congress to extend the HRA time limit, overseeing the training of Come Out Fighting, and, most of all, worrying about money.

He frowned. Time seemed to slip through his fingers these days. He noticed he was always tired. His sleep was full of troubling dreams, and activity seemed to tax him more and more. His energy level was lower than it had ever been, and he even noticed an occasional shortness of breath.

But soon the movement would cross its most important milestone. Once the HRA was put safely on another five-year clock —or even three years as some timid Senators were suggesting as a compromise—he could rest for a while. Then he would start delegating more duties to his lieutenants and take a long vacation in Deauville and Merano.

Ah, Merano. He thought back with satisfaction to his last trip. The sense of power as he tramped the Dolomites while the exalted thoughts, plans, and visions flowed godlike through his brain. The unexpected delights and pleasures of his specially trained Persian boy in the luxury of the mountain castle.

The Bible-thumpers say pleasure's a sin, he thought. *Well, they're wrong. Sin's a pleasure.*

While waiting for an intern to bring his breakfast, he dragged himself out of bed and into the bathroom. He splashed cold water onto his face, scrubbed vigorously with a towel, and blinked his eyes a few times before admiring himself in the mirror as he always did.

And there, in the middle of his left cheek, was a reddish oval, about the side of a half-dollar. He rubbed at it with the towel, but it took on a redder hue—and it was sore, a soreness deep under the skin.

Monnoye's heart skipped a beat, then began to race. Pulling back the collar of his watered silk dressing gown, he examined himself with growing panic. Frantically he scrutinized his neck, shoulders, and chest. He gasped. *Another one!* Another, larger, purplish-red blotch just where his neck joined his left shoulder.

"It can't be! It can't be!" he screamed. Just as the intern entered with the breakfast tray, Monnoye rushed headlong out of the bathroom. He collided with the young aide, and dishes, omelet, and pot of coffee went flying.

The intern was stunned.

"Get out! *Out!*" Monnoye yelled shrilly.

The shocked intern scurried out of the bedroom suite.

His boss, shaking violently, crossed to the telephone and dialed with trembling fingers, trying to hold down the nauseous fear that churned in his stomach.

When the party on the other end answered, he barked, "This is Garden Monnoye. Put Doctor Keppler on the line. Right now!"

34

Damon Keppler, head of Physicians for Human Rights, was Garden Monnoye's friend as well as his partner in the movement and personal doctor. He could hardly understand Monnoye at first—the man was incoherent and nearly hysterical. But when Keppler did understand, he left instantly and drove from his home in Bethesda to the Paragon Building.

Since the "Garden Party" was to have been a surprise, no one (except the intern) had wanted to alert Monnoye once they were sure he would remain in the building until late afternoon. Tris Kramer and Wynn Pritchett therefore were Monnoye's first visitors. When they arrived and went up to Monnoye's living quarters, it was Damon Keppler who greeted them at the door.

Keppler told them the news—though not the whole story at first—and they insisted on seeing Monnoye.

"No, Perce has gone into some kind of deep emotional shock," Keppler said. "He was awake when I came up but wouldn't speak or react. I've given him some heavy sedation, but when he wakes up—well, I don't know. You call me, Tris."

"OK. But we want to see him."

Reluctantly, Keppler admitted them to the bedroom where the boss was sleeping soundly. The doctor understood there was no point in denying the obvious—they could see the livid red blotch on his face—especially since these were two of Monnoye's closest associates. They had to know the situation in order to make wise choices, both for Garden Monnoye and for the Paragon Foundation and the movement.

Pritchett appeared amazed. "I knew how run-down and lethargic he seemed. But this skin cancer or whatever it is—it seems to have come on him all at once."

"Just how bad is it, Damon?" Kramer wanted to know.

"I won't know without a lot of tests, but it looks like the first stage of full-blown AIDS."

"But how . . ? I mean, he was so *careful*," Kramer wailed. "Haven't you been giving him his checkups? Didn't you—"

Keppler was in no mood to bear the blame. "Listen, Kramer. I've spent more time safeguarding Perce than I have with any dozen other patients combined. I designed his regime. I told him how to keep himself safe. And I know he wasn't promiscuous. But no system's foolproof."

Suddenly Keppler was overcome with despair. He had been on the front lines of the battle against AIDS since the first days of its discovery. A brilliant physician, he could have made millions in a more lucrative practice but had devoted his life to thankless combat against a deadly plague that still after fifteen years was decimating the gay population. The constant living with misery and lingering death had hardened him, but now a man he admired above all others was stricken, and he was sick and angry that there was so little he could do.

Keppler sank wearily onto the bed beside Monnoye and took his hand gently, automatically checking the pulse.

"The epidemic's bad enough as it is," Keppler said, "but now there seems to be a new virus—an HIV Four. That could be what we're facing here. It could be a mutation of an older HIV strain—or maybe a brand new virus—but it has the same destructive effect on the body's immune system. We just don't know exactly what it is. Frankly, we don't even know for sure whether HIV causes AIDS. And nobody's willing to talk about it for fear of creating another antigay backlash like we had in the eighties." He looked at the two men in mute appeal.

"But he had the *vaccine!*" protested Kramer.

"Yes," said Keppler. "But I told all of you when you insisted on having it—the vaccine's not foolproof. In fact, it's still in Phase II testing, and doesn't seem to be effective against this new strain. And it screws up the Western Blot test for the other HIV strains. It makes you show HIV positive, so when Perce got his usual test, the lab just assumed the CD4 count was low because of the vaccine. Of course, it was too late by then anyway. But we might've arrested some of the effects if we'd known sooner."

"What about this HIV Four? Where does it come from? Africa?" Pritchett asked.

"No one knows for sure," the doctor explained. "But they've seen a lot more of it in Europe than here in the States. And the epidemiologists there have traced it back to the Middle East. Some researchers say it's a mutation coming out of the Benny Houses in Damascus or Cairo. No one knows for sure."

"What's a 'Benny House?'" Pritchett asked.

Keppler glanced at Tris Kramer. *Isn't this guy one of us?* Then he took a deep breath and explained. "That's a slang term for a bordello where the—uh—occupants are young boys. It's an old practice in the Middle East. The boys are professionally trained."

"I see," said Pritchett.

Keppler checked the catatonic Monnoye one more time. He took his pulse. He listened to his chest with the stethoscope.

Kramer and Pritchett couldn't miss the other ugly purple patch on Monnoye's neck as the doctor opened his pajama top.

Keppler noticed the horror in their eyes and said, "Yes, it definitely looks like Kaposi sarcoma, except that it's redder than usual. And his lungs are congested. I hope it's pneumocystis carinii and not something else—we can treat that now. But we'll know more when the tests are done. Bring him in tomorrow morning, will you, Tris?"

Keppler packed up his medical bag and left the suite, shaking his head sadly.

★ ★ ★

Wynn Pritchett watched Keppler go. He was quick to see that, with Monnoye gone, his main source of largesse would end as well. Opportunist that he was, he mentally began to trim his sails and consider a different tack.

But there was more than opportunism at work. His secret contempt for Garden Monnoye and all these weird homosexuals began to percolate fiercely. He had chafed under Monnoye's arrogance for too long, and he had kept the peace with the execrable May Berg only because he needed Monnoye and his contacts and his money. But now the man suddenly appeared pathetically ridiculous.

Pritchett knew of Garden Monnoye's elaborate precautions to avoid the AIDS virus. And he had heard about Monnoye's revels in that castle in Europe. Pritchett had privately sneered at the man's assumption that power and wealth would protect him.

★ ★ ★

INTERVIEW, *WNCT TV (local) "Evening News"*

LEAD IN: Good evening. This is Beverly Bonner reporting. Tonight we have Tristram Kramer, executive director of the Paragon Foundation, in the studio to tell us about the Global Harmonic Convergence that has generated so much interest in Washington in the last few days. But first tell me, Tris—may I call you Tris?—tell me a little more about the Paragon Foundation.

TK: Well, Paragon was founded in 1992 by the noted philanthropist P. Garden Monnoye. It's a public policy research and education foundation.

BB: A think tank?

TK: Yes, you could call it that. Some people say we're New Age. That's a little simplistic. We're simply in the business of studying and promoting ways to ensure world peace, universal brotherhood, and social justice.

BB: Now, about this Harmonic Convergence in Washington . . .

TK: OK. Washington will be the focal point, since it is really the capital of the world—of the world's economic and military power, that is. But supporters of world peace and harmony will be participating all over the globe.

BB: And what will you do?

TK: Tomorrow at 12:00 noon our time, or 6:00 P.M. Greenwich mean time, we will gather en masse on the Ellipse below the White House and visualize world peace and harmony, just as others are simultaneously visualizing it worldwide.

BB: Now how's that supposed to work? I mean, how does your visualization bring about world peace?

TK: Well, it doesn't exactly. Hopefully it will create the preconditions for peace, harmony, and unity. You see, if thousands of visualized images are focused simultaneously on world peace, harmony, and unity, then the concentrated power of those images will converge and eliminate the negative energy in the human race that breeds suspicion, hatred, disunity, and conflict.

BB: That's very interesting. But do you really believe you can eliminate the negative energy, as you put it, by this kind of collective consciousness-raising?

TK: I believe we can at least reduce it.

BB: Tris, we're getting reports of large numbers of people—I mean in the thousands—coming into the city for the last couple of days. And thousands have been camping out in parks, across the river, and all around the city. A lot of these people are obviously not coming for the Harmonic Convergence. Many are talking about something called a prayer convocation. What can you tell us about that? Is that going to spoil the harmony or convergence of your visualization process?

TK: (chuckling) Well, there's no telling what these bizarre religious cults and right-wing fanatics will do. Frankly though, I don't imagine there'll be enough of them to upset our event.

BB: But what if there were?

TK: If there *is* a massive concentration of bigotry, intolerance, hatred, and disunity present here tomorrow, then yes, it will spoil the harmony. And you know, Beverly, that would just be a crying shame. It's regrettable but true—negative thoughts and vibrations are stronger than positive convections. That's why there's disunity and conflict in the world. And that's why we are going to assemble—in order to concentrate and harmonize the positive emanations.

But people who are full of hate, those who get everyone upset over the Human Rights Amendment, for example—you know, those religious-right people—they're actually obstacles to peace and goodwill. By blocking the paths of positive global energy and disturbing the convergence of harmonious vectoring, they really are making public enemies of themselves. The American people aren't going to stand for it forever, you know.

BB: One of their leaders says the Harmonic Convergence is of the devil (chuckling).

TK: To be fair, Beverly, somebody has got to stick up for the devil. After all, we usually only hear from the other side (laughing).

BB: And what about the former TV personality Chase McKenzie? I understand he's part of the convocation thing, and he's calling for right-wingers to lobby against the extension of the HRA.

TK: Well, you can just tell Mr. McKenzie for me, and for the millions that believe in social justice and civil rights for all Americans, that he'd just *better not!* We've had it with those people! He and his gang of Nazis and religious kooks had just better *not* come to this city with their bigotry and hate! They had better stay away if they don't want to get their—

BB: 'Scuse me, Tris, we've got to break away for a commercial message.

★ ★ ★

They did come, from every state in the Union, including a few brave busloads from Alaska and a planeload from Hawaii, though the vast majority came from east of the Mississippi. They arrived at first in trickles. Many were unemployed because of official anti-Christian bias. So many had the time to make the journey, if not the money. Most came in vans and cars, despite the high cost of gasoline and the difficulty in finding long-term parking. Many used public transportation. A surprising number sailed or motored up the Chesapeake and the Potomac and dropped anchor off Gravelly Point or the mouth of the Anacostia River. The poorest hitchhiked or bicycled. Or they employed the most ancient conveyance of all —they walked.

The trickles converged at churches or public campsites in Maryland and Virginia. Like the pilgrims and crusaders of old, they sometimes sang as the streams converged in the suburbs to form rivulets.

By this time it was the end of December. Many found lodging with the local volunteers who opened their homes to strangers in an effort organized by the Nehemiah Foundation. Thousands more slept on the floors and in the pews of surrounding churches, or they camped in their vans in church parking lots and used church kitchens and sanitary facilities.

Winter was unusually late in laying its icy grip on the city and suburbs. And since it was tolerable out of doors, many simply camped alongside their automobiles. At night, open fires began to twinkle along the Virginia side of the Potomac, in the well-kept park along the Boundary Channel, along the Mount Vernon Parkway, and in Rock Creek.

Soon the police reported to their superiors that something strange and unprecedented was afoot. Since it seemed to be a kind of spontaneous eruption from the heartland, no one knew how to get hold of the situation. They could not arrest everybody—all the jails in the area would not contain them. Besides, these people were peaceful.

There was a wonderful, even charming variety among them. Thousands of collegians were the forerunners. Bundled against the weather, trudging in with backpacks and sleeping bags, they inspired hundreds more students at colleges along the route to join them.

There were old people, married couples with children, and singles. Black . . . Hispanic . . . Asian . . . Caucasian . . . from every ethnic group. Conservative Protestants. Conservative Roman Catholics. Greek Orthodox. Greek Catholics. Independent groups too small and too numerous to name. All who in one fashion or another named the name of Christ. And some who did not. There was a large contingent of Conservative Jews in chartered buses.

Perhaps the most remarkable convocationers were the contingent of ex-homosexuals. More than anyone else these men and women understood the high stakes of the gathering. A humanist culture had tried to keep them in bondage, assuring them that they were born gay and had no reason to change. But they were an indisputable testimony that God's power was able to make a new creation of every man, regardless of his failings.

In such an unprecedented social phenomenon as this there were bound to be anomalies. Hundreds of political junkies and secular conservatives whose opposition to militant homosexuals was not necessarily biblical joined the throng. Washington-based activists and students of politics saw through the lens of practical experience that the triumph of gay rights would ultimately mean the triumph of totalitarian government and the end of their liberty as well.

There were important differences in doctrine and practice between them all, but this was not seen as a time for disputation over points of doctrine, however cherished and staunchly defended at other times.

The convocationers carried a striking assortment of flags and banners. Often just bedsheets strung on poles, the banners bore verses of Scripture or the logos of charities and church societies. State flags and Christian flags flew in tandem with countless American flags. The Stars and Stripes often flew upside down, a universally recognized distress signal.

They were not militant, or irreverent, or excessively solemn. They were coming to express their unity of convictions. And they were coming to unitedly raise a prayer of intercession and a cry for mercy. God had promised if His people would repent and pray, He would hear from heaven. They believed the promise and were joyous. They laughed and sang and joked. They made up amusing names for their contingents, traded names and addresses with future pen pals, and snapped countless photos to show that "I was there. I was there the day we stayed the hand of the Lord's judgment and brought healing back to the land."

35

In 1995, the District of Columbia had become the nation's fifty-first state, with the repeal of the Twenty-third Amendment to the Constitution.

The new state, amid much fanfare, sponsored a contest to select a nickname. New Columbia was its official name, but it needed a suitable cognomen such as the Volunteer State or the Empire State. Washington's gadfly newspaper, the *Standard*, sponsored a contest of its own, which inevitably produced sobriquets such as the Welfare State, the State of Confusion, and the Criminal State. However, with true bureaucratic panache, the official selection committee chose the inane Capital State.

They came to regret it later. The Capital State proved to be the capital of the nation in many respects. Washington had long been the Murder Capital of the nation. Now it was the AIDS Capital, beating out New York and San Francisco handily. It was also the Welfare Capital. More than a third of its citizens lived on public assistance. It had become the Abortion Capital, having more abortuaries for its population than any other US city. Its residents endured the highest local tax rate, which was in part responsible for the highest rate of new business failures and the fastest rate of old business departures to friendlier locales. That made Washington the Arson Capital as disenfranchised property owners torched their vacant buildings for the insurance.

New Columbia's treasury was practically empty, thanks to decades of financial mismanagement and utopian promises. In conjunction with the "domestic partners law," under which Washington assumed the medical risks of thousands of uninsurable gay men, the Universal Health Plan had virtually bankrupted the city until it was taken over by US National Health. The latter was now well on its way to bankrupting the rest of the nation.

Washington had also embarked upon an exorbitant pension plan for city employees, adding large numbers to the public payroll in the early 1990s to generate political power for the statehood effort. But that left the system with hundreds of millions of dollars in unfunded liabilities. It became vastly difficult to recruit the qualified public employees really needed—police and firemen. Washington's combat-zone dangers made the city unattractive to public safety professionals, especially if there was no reliable nest egg for the future.

The result was that, by the year 2000, there was little effective government behind the glitter of the Capital State. The police who did function had their hands full protecting the affluent neighborhoods, where the few sheep lived who remained in the city to be sheared.

The other police organizations in town—the US Park Police, the US Capitol Police, and the Federal Protective Service—were limited in jurisdiction to specific sites. The several National Guard battalions had not been called up since their shocking display of bad discipline and incompetence in the Dupont Circle and Adams-Morgan Riots of a few years earlier.

In short, there was little in the way of effective police power to harass the huge number of convocationers coming into Washington—even if the city-state government had been so inclined. And ironically, pilgrims who chose to camp in the city's public spaces discovered that the liberal local ordinances drafted to benefit the homeless benefited them as well. A series of city ordinances had been passed over the years protecting the homeless from harassment by police or passers-by and basically gave them free run of the city.

On the evening on January 6, a cold, crisp, but not unpleasant evening, people began to move into position to get the best seats at the west end of Washington's two-mile-long grassy esplanade extending from Capitol Hill to the Lincoln Memorial and known as the Mall.

* * *

On the night of January 6, Chase was in an acute state of nerves. He was certain only the warm and loving presence of Libby

318

kept him from flying apart in a dozen pieces. Male pride would not let him reveal to her how jittery he really was.

Chase, T. C., and a steering committee of pastors and lay leaders met in the Nehemiah Foundation office to pray together and to discuss final details. How would they move such a vast multitude in an orderly fashion to the assembly area at the Lincoln Memorial? Strangely, though, things seemed to be moving well enough of their own accord. Somehow people knew what to do and were doing it with minimal fuss.

The basic schedule of events had been explained to all, as well as its purpose and solemn spiritual significance. It was simple, really. They would assemble on the west end of the Mall at the Lincoln Memorial. At 11:30, Chase McKenzie would open the convocation with a few brief remarks. T. C. Moreland would begin the time of corporate prayer at 12:00 noon, timed to coincide with the Harmonic Convergence over on the Ellipse. Other pastors and leaders would then come forward to the public address system and lead the gathering in prayer.

All agreed it was important not to have a closing time. Let the people pray as long as they wished, T. C. had insisted. After that, individual contingent leaders would take charge, and people could go or stay as they wished. Then the next day, selected delegations would call on Congress and ask for a "no" vote on the resolution to extend the ratification period for the HRA. The debate and vote on the time extension were scheduled for later in the week.

To the convocation steering committee, this seemed the proper pattern—pray together, then act together. But the emphasis was on prayer. This was a spiritual battle, not a secular one. If the assembled Christian leaders had learned anything over the past decade, it was the abject uselessness of Christians' attempting to save a fallen world from itself by employing the world's own methods.

Thousands had already moved into position the night before, camping on the open Mall, ready to assemble at daylight. The logistical requirements had been vastly simplified by the declaration of a fast. People would consume whatever provisions each person brought the night before, and they would eat again at the end of the Big Day. As for other needs, there were ample watering stations, as many Porta-potties as the committee could lay hands on in three surrounding states, and plenty of volunteer nurses and doctors.

The US Senate, eager to get its most troublesome issue out of the way early, had decided weeks earlier to take up the resolution extending the HRA time limit on January 8. This date had determined Chase and Jimmy's choice of dates for the convocation. Both they and the New Agers wanted their respective events to influence the Senate's vote.

The House had not scheduled its own action on the HRA, but it was expected to be the first major item of business after convening.

"We have no chance to stop the time extension in the House," Jimmy had advised Chase, "but the Senate's another matter. If we can kill it in the Senate, the House might not even take it up."

Senator Quinn, Democrat of Massachusetts, was Senate Majority Leader. Weeks earlier he had reached a gentleman's agreement with Senator Lipscomb, the Minority Leader, to dispose of the HRA extension as quickly as possible. Having settled on January 8 for the debate and vote, the Majority Leader had gotten a Unanimous Consent agreement, the primary means of expediting legislative business in the Senate.

Jimmy checked with the Republican cloakroom and learned that the UC stipulated six hours of debate on the resolution to extend the time limit—to be equally divided between both sides of the issue, beginning at 10:00, right after Morning Business. Senator Forsythe, Republican of Mississippi, would manage the floor debate against the resolution. Branch Trumbull's old antagonist Norman Lockwood would manage for the other side.

If the debate began at 10:00 A.M., and if the Senate broke for the weekly luncheons, then according to Jimmy they could expect a roll-call vote sometime around 5:00 P.M.—unless unused debate time was yielded back, in which case the vote could occur earlier.

Chase and his fellow steering committee members put out an appeal for all who could to stay over an extra day to lobby members of both Houses on January 8 prior to the vote—especially the Senate, where Jimmy Tolliver believed they had a remote chance of winning.

Hoping to satisfy both sides of the gay rights issue, many members had taken the position that a vote in favor of the time

320

extension was merely a procedural vote and did not necessarily constitute an endorsement of the Amendment itself. The only way to pierce this sham was for citizens to personally call on as many swing votes as possible. They had to let those members know in unambiguous terms that a vote to extend the clock was indeed a vote for the Amendment and would be construed accordingly. Chase emphasized that there would be no demonstrations.

He surveyed the Mall. No one had any idea how many convocationers would show up, but he could see that the crowd was immense and growing. His greatest concern now was the absolute necessity of keeping order—and the proper response if gay militants should attack or try to break up the assembly.

They would have to keep clear of the Ellipse where the New Agers would converge harmonically. The Ellipse was not far from the end of the Mall where the prayer convocation would assemble, and everyone feared that the two large opposing crowds might get entangled, with possibly fatal results.

For some inexplicable reason, Jimmy Tolliver was not present at the final committee meeting in the Nehemiah Foundation office. He had called earlier, sounding mysterious, but saying only that something had come up. He would be late.

For the first time since that day on the Mountain, Chase found himself frustrated, then outright angry, at Jimmy. He needed him. Now. And Jimmy was nowhere to be found. Chase felt responsibility weighing on him heavily. What if the pink triangles did turn out in force and hurt or killed someone—or many someones! That was a terrible prospect, and he wished fervently that Jimmy were there to advise him.

The meeting had just closed with prayer asking God's blessings on the day to come, when the telephone rang. Chase picked it up and heard his friend Jay Blaisdell on the other end.

"Chase, by any chance have you been watching SIS news the past few nights?" he asked in a strange voice.

"Nope, can't say I have, Jay. We've been a little busy."

Blaisdell chuckled. "Yeah. I can imagine."

"So, has SIS been whipping up the usual hysteria about us?"

"Chase, it's the strangest thing—SIS has been doing a series for two nights on the two big extravaganzas, the prayer convocation versus the Harmonic Convergence. And it's incredible. As you'd expect, they're criticizing you guys for creating a public nuisance—although it's very mild criticism. But the stories have been even more critical of the New Age harmonizers."

"And this you won't believe, but I got it straight from a brother at the network. Tonight's segment's going to expose the connection between the New Agers and Come Out Fighting. Seems the New Age organizers have retained the services of the pink triangles for security."

"Just like the Nazi Brownshirts. That was their job—'security.'"

"Yeah, it's déjà vu all over again. Somebody's got to protect the peace-loving New Agers from all those warlike Christians. Anyway, the SIS editorial following the news segment will call for the city to deploy policemen down Independence Avenue to keep the groups apart."

Chase was stunned, then skeptical. "Are you sure this is Wynn Pritchett's network we're talking about?"

"Positively."

"I don't understand. It's a total about-face. He's been our worst enemy in the media."

"I know. But you just watch the evening news at 7:00."

Blaisdell rang off, and Chase came back to T. C. Moreland, Libby, and the others, still doubtful but suddenly hopeful. He relayed Blaisdell's message. He could not account for the apparent change in policy at SIS. But the more he contemplated the ways of the Almighty, the less he was inclined to doubt anything.

The committee members stayed to watch the SIS news, and it was just as Blaisdell has predicted. The broadcast was a reasonably even-handed look at both sides of tomorrow's confrontation. There was some smirking in the newscaster's voice as he explained such esoteric terms as "intercessory prayer." But he was even more critical of the New Agers and their relationship with Come Out Fighting, which he compared to the Nazis and fascists.

To the wonderment of all, the newsman concluded by saying, "It would be infinitely better for this embattled, overburdened city if none of these groups had decided to come in such huge numbers just to make a point—a point I might add that most Americans care little about. But I suppose that's the fate one must expect for being the capital city of a democracy.

"New Columbia police will be completely overextended trying to manage such large crowds. We at SIS can only hope—and urge—that the governor directs the primary efforts of the police at the true enemies of public order, those who wear the pink triangle and call themselves Come Out Fighting."

Still perplexed, but delighted at the remarkable change in attitude at Wynn Pritchett's empire, Chase could only shake his head.

"Maybe they got religion," someone ventured.

"Maybe they did," Chase said. "If it happened to me, it can happen to anybody. Anyway, I'll just settle for fairness and accuracy from them."

The committee broke up, and Libby and Chase were left alone in the office.

"You're troubled about something, sweetheart. Can I do anything?" she asked.

"No, thanks. Unless you can produce Jimmy Tolliver."

"Well, here I am." A disheveled but grinning Jimmy sprinted into the office from the corridor.

"Jimmy, where have you *been!*" Chase was relieved to see him but still annoyed.

"You won't believe it."

"That's the second time tonight I've heard that. Just tell me. I'll believe."

"I've been at a headquarters meeting of Come Out Fighting!" Jimmy said triumphantly.

"I don't believe it.

"And guess what? There won't be any organized COF action tomorrow."

"Are you sure? Why not?"

"One, SIS did a big exposé on them tonight, called them Nazis and everything. The police commissioner called Pete Gaveston and read him the riot act. Threatened to arrest anybody wearing a pink triangle caught on our side of Independence Avenue."

"That's wonderful news!" Chase exclaimed with relief. "But how do you know all this?"

"Tell you later. There's another reason for no COF action tomorrow." Jimmy was not smiling now.

"What?"

"They've lost their leadership and their money source. Garden Monnoye's had some kind of emotional breakdown. He's got AIDS."

★ ★ ★

No one knew exactly how many convocationers gathered on January 7, 2000. Police estimated the crowd at between one-half and three-quarters of a million. In fact, there was no reason to doubt Chase's claim that it was the largest gathering in Washington in recent memory. It certainly was the biggest prayer meeting in American history. People thronged all the way from the speakers' platform at the Lincoln Memorial to the Washington Monument.

At 11:30 A.M., under a bright, clear blue sky, the preliminaries began. Chase McKenzie, muffled in greatcoat, scarf, and gloves, mounted the six-foot-high wooden platform.

"My friends, we're here to pray, and we've already begun to see God's answer!" He gestured toward the sea of expectant faces before him. "However, our strength is not in our numbers. For, 'Not by might or by power, but by my Spirit, says the Lord!'

"We've assembled to ask God's blessing and mercy and to intercede with Him on behalf of an ungrateful nation, which has rejected Him.

"We're here to ask God for the Congress of the United States. We will pray for the Spirit of the Lord to come over them as they vote tomorrow on extending the time for the so-called Human Rights Amendment."

At this a deep-chested chant erupted rhythmically. "No more time! No more time! No more time!"

On the platform, the wind whipped Chase's scarf and hair. He waited, and when the crowd gradually fell silent, he continued.

"God has promised, 'If my people who are called by my name will humble themselves, and pray and seek My face, and turn from their wicked ways, then I will hear from heaven . . . and heal their land.' His people, He says, not unbelievers. It's up to us to act, and it's up to us to pray for the healing of the land."

Chase stepped down.

T. C. Moreland came to the microphone then and began to lead the prayer session. He prayed long and fervently as only he could. At length he was replaced by another pastor, and then another.

And Chase McKenzie, standing by the platform listening to it all, at some point realized something was happening within him. He found himself shedding the last vestiges of his longstanding contempt and personal antagonism toward gays.

After nearly two hours of prayer, Chase came back to the platform, eyes glistening. He struggled a moment to control his voice. "Brothers and sisters—let's now consider another matter for confession and prayer. We are not here to condemn homosexuals—only the practice of sodomy and its being sanctioned in the law of the land. But more important than this, we are here to share the news of Jesus Christ, the crucified and risen One who makes all things new.

"God's Word does *not* hold that homosexuality is an unpardonable sin. Without His grace and redemption, *all* of us are lost in our sins. These sins include homosexuality. But the rest of us—we who were once thieves, or liars, or slanderers, or swindlers, or drunkards, or adulterers, or whatever—we also were disinherited from the kingdom of God, just like the homosexual, until we accepted the atonement of Jesus Christ. Those who have called on Christ have been forgiven of these sins, and the same can be true of homosexuals."

A hush had fallen over the throng. Some wept, many prayed quietly. One, then another, of the leadership came to the microphone to pray for love and grace and wisdom to reach out to homosexuals, for whom also Christ had died. They asked God to cleanse them of their own sins and to make them a bridge of healing for those who needed the Savior. Individuals began praying softly all over the gathering.

Abruptly, the portable telephone in the pocket of Jimmy's overcoat beeped. He reached for it quickly and listened.

Chase, standing at the side of the platform with Libby and T. C., saw alarm cross Jimmy's face.

"But how did it *happen!*" Jimmy gasped into the device, staring wide-eyed at Chase.

"What's wrong?"

For a moment Jimmy couldn't speak. The color drained from his face, and he swayed.

Chase moved over and gripped his arm. "What is it, Jimmy? Libby, hand me that thermos, quick!"

Jimmy Tolliver, now looking nauseated, tried to sip the bracing hot coffee thrust into his hand and apparently to collect his wits.

Now the sibilant buzzing of those praying within earshot of the platform took on a new character. Instead of prayer there were murmurings of bewilderment. The convocationers nearby had witnessed what had happened.

Jimmy finally found his voice. "That was Senator Forsythe's office, Chase. They moved up the vote! The Senate is debating the HRA extension right now! They could start voting in two hours."

36

"hat's happening up there?" contingent leaders were now calling urgently to those close to the platform.

T. C. gave them a quieting gesture.

Jimmy Tolliver now said in a rush, "Senator Quinn and the pro-HRA senators got panicked at the size of our crowd. So this morning Quinn went on the floor while nobody was paying attention and got a new UC to move the debate on the time limit up a full day. Today! Right now!"

"Why didn't somebody object?" Chase was incredulous. He was no expert on Senate procedure, but he knew that a single senator could object to a Unanimous Consent agreement and block this method of streamlining Senate business.

"Our side was asleep at the switch," Jimmy said bitterly. "Legislatively, there's nothing we can do. Senator Forsythe wants his supporters to boycott the whole charade in protest, but that won't do any good. It'll still pass."

As the enormity of what had happened in the Senate chamber sank in, Chase was suddenly sick at heart with the near-nausea Jimmy had experienced. He looked at T. C. and Libby, stunned and crestfallen. Their historic assembly, which had begun on so promising a note, now seemed about to fizzle ignominiously.

The old Chase McKenzie came roaring back, and he paced the rear of the platform, thinking furiously and slapping a glove in his palm. In the corner of his vision he observed vacantly that some people had begun to drift away.

"It looks like people are starting to leave!" T. C. exclaimed.

Chase scanned the far limits of the crowd. Sure enough, the multitude was unraveling at its outer edge. Scores of convocationers were peeling off and walking back up the Mall. The event was starting to unravel.

Stop and think, a voice cried out inside. *No, stop and pray.*

He moved to the waiting microphone. "Father, You are the Lord God of Hosts," he prayed aloud. "You have brought us here. Tell us now what we should do."

T. C. Moreland stepped to his side, bowing his head and gripping Chase's arm tightly. He prayed, "Lord, we are Your people, and this is Your day. We know You didn't bring us here to be shamed and to see Your name ridiculed by unbelievers. Lead us now."

Chase took a deep breath. He had to act, but if things got out of hand, there was no telling what the consequences would be.

"Listen!" he shouted into the P.A. system, and his voice echoed across the Mall. "We've just heard that the Senate has moved up the vote! They're debating it now!"

Boos and angry shouts arose from the multitude.

"Wait—wait, this is no defeat. On the contrary, it's a dramatic answer to prayer. We're all here at the critical moment of the HRA vote."

"What should we do?" several voices called.

Chase's voice boomed over the speakers. "The Senate will be voting on the HRA in a matter of hours. What we need is prayer. Not violence. Not shouting. Not disturbance of any kind. What we must have is prayer!"

He stood looking out across the seething mass and saw people on the rear edges turn to face the Capitol. Then, singly or in pairs or in small groups, figures began slowly moving like ants up the Mall toward the Hill. Some convocationers seemed about to relocate there.

Those at the outer edges had already begun to move off. Now contingents in the center and front begin to trickle forward toward Capitol Hill. As he watched, the trickle became a silent, slowly rising tide.

Lord, keep this peaceful.

Chase grabbed his walkie-talkie and called his convocation marshals, guides, and spotters stationed at critical points on the outer perimeter of the Mall to keep watch on the New Agers and activists on the Ellipse. He had to be sure what Come Out Fighting was doing.

But the scratchy voices of his spotters assured him the enemy was quiet.

He marveled. The movement was spontaneous—thanks to the alertness of the Senate staffer who had passed the word to Jimmy—but this is what they had prayed for. Why should he always be surprised when God granted a request?

It took an hour for Chase, Libby, Jimmy, and T. C., now in the rear of the reverse-facing assembly, to cross the two miles of crowded Mall and reach Capitol Hill. Not an inch of empty space was visible on the West Front, where they finally stood.

The silent multitude covered virtually every square foot.

A small cordon of dazed and nervous Capitol Police stood on the steps and in the various entrances to the massive marble edifice. But they could no more turn away a crowd this size than King Canute could hold back the tide. The thin blue lines did the sensible thing and just stood, watching and waiting.

No one attempted to enter the Capitol, and only the murmur of prayer was heard.

Chase spoke into Jimmy's ear. "Can you get us inside?"

"Sure. This way." Jimmy took Chase, Libby, and T. C. in tow to the basement of the Rayburn House Office Building. Then they entered the Capitol from the House side through the underground tramway and went up to the second floor corridor outside the Senate elevators.

The Visitors' Gallery was closed, and Chase could no longer get into the Press area, but Jimmy Tolliver could. Friends, he said, might stash him in an unobtrusive vantage point where he could monitor the floor action.

He would try.

★ ★ ★

Within the Chamber, an aide whispered word to the Majority Leader of the silent gathering outside. Alarmed, he ordered the sergeant at arms to call for every available Capitol policeman, all the relief shifts, even those off duty, and to ask the governor to send National Guard MPs to protect the Capitol.

Within minutes Capitol Police reinforcements began to flow onto the grounds and into the building. The Majority Leader then directed the sergeant at arms to ask the police to clear the grounds. But the shaken, worried officers at the doors merely surveyed the throng that crowded the Hill and was now sitting stolidly.

The senior police captain sent details from one end of the Hill to another, however, shouting through bullhorns. The people could stay if they remained quiet. Otherwise, folks would get hurt as well as arrested. Given the size and uncertain temper of the multitude, it was an absurdly idle threat. But fortunately these were law-abiding people, people who still retained a residual respect for authority. Besides, the convocationers had somehow come to understand that shouting and marching would not sway this Senate. But prayer could.

The gathering returned to first principles. They began to pray more earnestly and contritely than before, and soon the Hill was wrapped in that strange sibilant buzzing heard earlier on the Mall.

★ ★ ★

Chase and Libby went out onto the grassy slope and found a spot to huddle, waiting for news. About them, groups stood, or sat, and prayed.

They waited—it seemed hours—praying together, full of discovering the wonder and depth of their love for each other, and full of joy at the day's astonishing events.

They had told Jimmy approximately where to look for them, and eventually he reappeared through the throng, tired and rumpled but obviously excited.

"Jimmy, what's going *on* in there? Any news yet?"

He sank down beside them on the grass. "Something unbelievable happened." His eyes shone.

"Jimmy!" Libby begged.

But Jimmy was not to be hurried. "I never saw anything like it, even when Branch was in the Senate."

"*Jimmy!*"

"Well," he began, "first Quinn stood up with a satisfied smirk on his face. Made a few remarks about protecting the integrity and inviolability of the democratic process—and how the Senate couldn't be intimidated by a mob, and so on."

Jimmy stopped and rubbed his face. "By then you could hear this rustling, buzzing noise outside. It was faint, but you could still hear it. At first they didn't know what it was, and everyone on the floor began to look at each other sort of strange. Then . . . something just happened. I don't know how to explain it. This . . . *feeling* just came over the Chamber."

Chase accepted the fact they weren't going to hurry him. "What kind of feeling?"

"I can't exactly say," Jimmy mused, looking off into the distance. "Arthur Peel had the floor and was trying to hold forth, and then all of a sudden he began to look around nervously. Then he began to kind of halt and stammer, then stopped speaking altogether and just stood there."

By this time other convocationers had gathered around them and were listening in rapt attention.

Seeing he had collected a larger audience, Jimmy smiled all around and went on. "At that point Senator Forsythe, who was down front managing the opposition, dropped to his knees by the desk and began to pray. That's never happened, I don't think—at least not in modern times. He didn't pray out loud, but you could tell he was praying. Then several other senators either sat at their desks and bowed their heads or knelt down. It was still as the grave in the Chamber, yet full of tension. Suddenly Peel sat down ashen-faced, and no one else sought recognition."

"Then what?" his listeners demanded.

"Well, you can't have dead time on the Senate floor in the middle of a debate, so the Leader asked for a quorum call—which is just a way of artificially filling up time. The clerk began to call the roll, and just about every senator left the floor and went into their respective cloakrooms. All except Forsythe. He kept on kneeling down there in front. A few minutes later the Majority Leader came back on the floor and dispensed with the quorum call. Senator Lipscomb followed Quinn to the front and tried to confer, but Quinn wouldn't speak to him.

"Then Quinn announced that no one was left on his side who wanted to speak in favor of the resolution, and he was prepared to yield back time and go to the vote. Then Lipscomb got real agitated, and this time the two Leaders huddled. The mikes were off, so I couldn't hear, but suddenly Quinn looked like he'd been stuck with a pitchfork. He jerked upright, then whispered furiously with Lipscomb, and then motioned to Lockwood and Peel who were peeking around the door of the cloakroom to see what was going on. It was the most bizarre scene I ever saw in ten years in the Senate."

"What did Lockwood and Peel do?" Chase asked.

"Scurried down to the two Leaders, and the four huddled for a minute. Then the three senators started arguing among themselves while the president tried to keep things on track and kept asking, 'Who yields time? Who yields time?' They ignored him, and the whole process just ground to a halt."

Jimmy glanced around. His crowd of listeners had swelled considerably.

"And was Senator Forsythe still praying?" Libby asked.

"No," said Jimmy. "At that point he got up and calmly watched the circus going on across the aisle as they tried to figure out what to do."

"I guess you could tell the tide had turned?" Chase suggested.

"By then the momentum was clearly building on our side, and the fence-sitters in both parties started to get worried. You could see 'em one by one falling off the fence onto our side as they went over and whispered in the ear of one Leader or the other. But, you know, it wasn't so much the crowd out here. I'm telling you, something miraculous happened in there. You could sense the power of God moving over the Senate.

"Anyway, it suddenly hit me that Quinn had lost a lot of votes. And sure enough, after arguing with Lockwood and Peel, he announced that fifteen senators had changed their minds and stated their intention to vote against the resolution. On top of the thirty-eight that were announced or leaning against it, that was a comfortable majority against the extension."

"What did that do to the pending vote?" asked Chase.

"Well, that's the point. Quinn went into this song and dance about how divisive this resolution had proven, inflaming passions, and so forth. He said he was willing to withdraw the resolution and not take up any more of the Senate's valuable time. He started to propound a UC to supersede the former agreement and put the resolution back on the Senate calendar—in back of the line, of course. That meant it could come up later if Quinn and company could bend some arms and change some votes back.

"But if they couldn't bring it before the Senate for action soon, then the time would run out, and it would just die. It was kind of a good compromise solution, typical of the Senate. And since Lipscomb seemed willing to go along, Quinn seemed to think he had salvaged the situation."

The crowd around them groaned.

Chase sat silent, stunned. This couldn't be. Was a shameful compromise all the convocation had accomplished?

Then why were Jimmy's eyes sparkling?

"Why did Lipscomb agree with Quinn's UC?" one of the bystanders asked.

"He didn't want it to come to a vote. He's a compromiser by nature," Jimmy said. "But then—I couldn't believe it—Senator Forsythe got recognition, and to everybody's shock objected to the UC. Wanted a roll call vote—a recorded vote." He grinned at the tense faces around him.

Beginning to understand, Chase grinned back. "He was taking some awful risk."

"Ordinarily that would be true," Jimmy agreed. "And I don't mind telling you, I thought so at the time. Here we had it won, or nearly so, I thought. The extension was about to get shuffled aside and might well die of asphyxiation, and here Forsythe up and demands a roll call vote. I mean, why take the risk?

"But he knew what he was doing. It was the most wonderful moment I ever witnessed. All debate time was yielded back, and then Forsythe moved to table the HRA resolution. The motion was seconded, and since that motion's not debatable, they went right to the vote. The clerk began to call the roll, and one by one the senators, most of them puzzled and some mad at having to be recorded on this issue when they thought it had gone away politely, came stumping down to the well to cast their votes."

Jimmy paused at the climax, the mark of a born storyteller, but the crowd was in no mood for histrionics.

"Jimmy!" Chase protested. "Enough is enough! What happened?"

"The resolution failed, sixty-seven to forty-three."

The crowd around Jimmy cheered.

"Why, that's exactly two-thirds!" Chase exclaimed.

"Right." Jimmy grinned. "The opposition somehow picked up far more than the fifteen shifts Quinn had announced earlier. How Forsythe knew that I can't imagine. Well, of course I can," he interjected. "God answered his prayer, right there on the Senate floor."

Chase said, "So the resolution's not just put back in the hopper. It's killed?"

"It's killed. A motion to take it off the table would require two-thirds, just the number we got, so the other side has no hope of sneaking it back for consideration."

"It looks like the senators from the Christian-dominated areas came through," Chase suggested.

"They did, especially Dirk Forsythe. A lot of 'em even used some of Branch Trumbull's old speeches," Jimmy said breathlessly, now trying to finish the story in a hurry. "Anyway, the Human Rights Amendment is dead and buried—at least for the foreseeable future."

"And they'll have to start all over?" a woman asked.

"Right."

"You can all go home now," Chase said, smiling. His eyes began to mist over.

"Until the next time," Jimmy muttered under his breath.

* * *

Huddled in their overcoats arm in arm for warmth against the late afternoon chill, Chase and Libby continued to sit on the grassy slope below the West Front. The Capitol shone with a gold luster in the setting sun.

Chase looked down the Mall, still full of convocationers drifting back to their homes or encampments or lodgings outside of Washington. It was almost impossible for him to take in all that had happened.

Libby snuggled close against him, silent, and every now and then, smiling tenderly, she wiped the cold tears off his cheek.

God had won a great battle, and he had learned a lasting lesson—earthly weapons alone were useless. Their numbers had struck fear into the hearts of the opposition, but action had to be accompanied by prayer in order to change hearts.

Chase was full of gratitude for the victory and overflowing with love and tenderness, all of which mixed inside him to stifle his normal articulateness.

"You've been awfully good to me," he began awkwardly, looking deep into Libby's eyes.

She twitted him just a trace. "Have I been good?"

"Yes . . . I mean . . . you've been a true friend," he stammered. "Even when I acted like a fool. You've helped me to . . . to get over my loneliness. And I hope that . . . well, I just want our friendship to continue, to—uh—deepen."

Libby retorted with that firm but indulgent impatience Clare often used with him. "Chase, when Adam was lonely, God didn't create a 'friend' for him. He gave him a wife." Scowling slightly, she gave his cheek another tender swipe with the handkerchief.

"Will you do that for me again?" he asked gently, smiling at her.

"Yes," she said, reaching with her hanky toward his already dried cheek.

"I don't mean now," he said, pulling her closer. "I mean forever."

"Yes. Forever."

"I love you," he brought himself to say finally.

Now it was her turn for tears. She laid her head on his shoulder. "If you knew how long I've waited for you to say that. I love you too."

Far down the Mall, the tall spindle of the Washington Monument stood silhouetted by the sinking sun. Beyond the low hills of Arlington and the Virginia skyline the sun began to set, and they watched its crimson fire flicker and fade out from the west.

God's holy fire, thought Chase, cleansing each day of its pain and sorrow and returning every morning with bright promise—until there would be a new heaven and a new earth and no need for that shining orb, for all creation would be filled with the light of His glory.

Epilogue

Chase put the Nehemiah Foundation to work helping the destitute travelers who had come for the convocation, and asked Clare Trumbull to head the effort. She had a warm heart for the poor and had acquired a cool administrative ability and grace under pressure from working with the desperately needy. The moral authority of the Nehemiah Foundation was high as a result of the astounding victory over the Human Rights Amendment, and the Foundation was able to raise funds and recruit capable help to get the rest of the convocationers started for home.

Jimmy Tolliver and Chase met almost daily in managing the Foundation, and Chase developed profound respect for his co-worker. The memory of Chase's earlier antipathy seemed only to strengthen their deepening friendship.

Jimmy was an amazing source of intelligence on the gay movement. He learned that a shadowy character named Leon Pound had been selected to take over the leadership of the Paragon Foundation, now that Garden Monnoye lay dying of AIDS. Pound was said to be an ex-CIA man with a vaguely sinister reputation.

Tris Kramer, Monnoye's executive assistant at Paragon, had vied for the leadership job but was considered something of a pansy, a soft fellow who lost his composure under stress. Paragon's board of directors had unanimously offered the post to Leon Pound.

Barbara Dunhill made a half-hearted attempt to land another job in the Darby administration—half-hearted because she suspected it was futile. Chase tried to offer her a position with the Foundation, but she laughed and declined, telling him, "No, thanks. That would only spoil our friendship. You'd find me entirely too obstreperous. I appreciate the thought, but this is just part of being in politics. Everybody knows conservatives abandon their wounded on the battlefield."

He later learned she had accepted a lucrative job as vice president for human resources with an international trade firm in Seattle. At least she would have a good livelihood, but it saddened him to think that the conservative movement—indeed, the country—had lost her matchless service, probably forever.

Stuart Chase McKenzie and Elizabeth Christian Trumbull were married in Potomac Presbyterian Church at 4:00 P.M. on Saturday, March 31, in the year of our Lord 2000, the first year of a new century, a new millennium, and a new life for them both.